Mrs. Thomson

Celebrated Friendships

Vol. I

Mrs. Thomson

Celebrated Friendships
Vol. I

Reprint of the original, first published in 1861.

1st Edition 2022 | ISBN: 978-3-37505-475-5

Verlag (Publisher): Salzwasser Verlag GmbH, Zeilweg 44, 60439 Frankfurt, Deutschland
Vertretungsberechtigt (Authorized to represent): E. Roepke, Zeilweg 44, 60439 Frankfurt, Deutschland
Druck (Print): Books on Demand GmbH, In de Tarpen 42, 22848 Norderstedt, Deutschland

CELEBRATED FRIENDSHIPS

VOL. I.

CELEBRATED FRIENDSHIPS

BY

MRS. THOMSON

AUTHOR OF "MEMOIRS OF THE DUCHESS OF MARLBOROUGH"
"LIFE OF GEORGE VILLIERS, DUKE OF BUCKINGHAM" ETC. ETC.

IN TWO VOLUMES

VOL. I.

LONDON: JAMES HOGG AND SONS
MDCCCLXI

PREFACE.

The plan usually adopted in writing biographies has, in this work, been materially altered. Particular aspects of character have been presented only; political events merely glanced at; literary productions mentioned, solely when closely connected with domestic life; for the history of "Celebrated Friendships" assumes no extended range, and pretends to comprise little more than the details of private affairs, and the analyses of the inmost feelings. Unshackled, therefore, by the necessity of narrating the graver events of our human condition, the writer of this book has been enabled to dwell minutely on the incidents which are generally considered to be beneath the "dignity of history." The scope of such a plan presents many advantages. It enables an author to place two characters in such a position as to show the influence of the one on the other. It deals with those small facts of which life is made up. Those who think that lives of eminent persons should be written with the precision of a biographical dictionary, will find the portraitures here given defective; those who like to look into the inner life of men, will have curiosity to a certain extent gratified.

But whilst the scope of this work may be limited, infinite care has been taken to render it accurate, and to perfect the outlines of every-day life which it contains, by all possible materials. In describing those characters belonging especially to the history of our country, one deviation has been made from the main design of the book: since their lives were public, recourse to public sources alone could be available. To the life of the Earl of Surrey, for instance, some few but important details are added from letters lately discovered in the Records in the Rolls. In one of these we find that Henry VIII., thirsting for Surrey's blood, absolutely corrected with *his own hand* the interrogations which formed the basis of Surrey's attainder. There are, in this work, first printed some fragments of Surrey's appeal to the Privy Council: and, broken as they are by erasures, enough is left to give us some notion of the fruitless efforts which he made in his prison. Hitherto all has been utter darkness between his last incarceration and his doom. A few curious letters of Sir Philip Sidney's, and one from his father Sir Henry, have been also obtained from the same unexplored source. Those introduced into the life of Sir Kenelm Digby are less interesting, but serve to connect the different periods of his life. With regard to the more modern characters introduced into this work, the facilities for collecting materials have been of late much increased by the practice of publishing diaries and correspondence under the auspices of sagacious editors. Private channels are, therefore, in respect to personages of more recent date, of less importance than they were even fifty years ago.

We fear the time is past for that close and careful correspondence which is of such inestimable value to a biographer; letters worth receiving (as descriptions or narratives) went out of date when franks were abolished, and Queen's heads introduced; diaries are gone by since railroads were brought into operation; we must, therefore, honour, as the last of their race, the shades of Lady Mary Wortley Montagu, Mrs. Piozzi, and of Mrs. Delany, for we shall see the like no more.

In offering this work to the public, the writer feels it incumbent on her to own that any merit it may be allowed to have is not wholly hers. For the execution, whether good or bad, she, and she alone, is responsible; the idea of the work was, however, suggested by a literary friend.

CONTENTS

OF

THE FIRST VOLUME.

JOHN EVELYN AND ROBERT BOYLE.

Evelyn's Baptism and Education. — His Description of Wotton. — Evelyn's Father. — A fine old English Gentleman. — Eventful Times. — Evelyn's Sister dies. — His Mother. — Evelyn at Oxford. — Robert Boyle. — His Lineage. — His Father's second Marriage. — Life of Richard, the great Earl of Cork. — Early Nurture and Education of Robert Boyle. — His "Seraphic Love." — Friendship with Evelyn. — Evelyn advocates Marriage. — Robert Boyle's supposed Preference. — Evelyn's Appeal. — Boyle's Appearance and Habits. — Evelyn entered in the Middle Temple. — Bad Times. — Death of Evelyn's Father. — Strange Meteoric Appearances. — Evelyn's Taste for Gardening. — He becomes a good Linguist. — Is attacked by Small-pox. — His domestic Life at Sayes Court. — The Plague at Deptford. — Sayes Court, with Pepys there. — Boyle's Aspirations. — His Peculiarities. — His Ill-health. — Evelyn's strong Constitution. — Boyle's Reverence for sacred Things. — Scene at Sir Harry Vane's. — Boyle's Speech. — Sir Harry's Reply. — Dreary State of public Affairs. — Jeremy Taylor. — His Character. — Death of Michael Evelyn. — The Invisible College. — Boyle invents the Air-pump. — Scene on the Pavement of Pall Mall. — Evelyn's Life and Pursuits. — Gaming at Whitehall. — Evelyn appointed a public Inspector. — His daughter Mary. — She dies of the Small-pox. — Death of Lady Ranelagh. — Death of Robert Boyle. — Boylean Lecture founded. — Evelyn, in old Age, at Wotton. — How the Czar comforts himself at Sayes Court. — Evelyn dies. — Jeremy Taylor's Opinion of his Essay on Friendship . . . . . Page 1

HENRY HOWARD, EARL OF SURREY,

AND

SIR THOMAS WYATT.

The Christmas of 1595. — Feat of Arms. — The Challengers, and their Names. — Wyatt's personal Beauty. — Old Customs: Placentia. — Wyatt's Lineage. — Born at Allington. — The old Mote-house. — Sir Henry Wyatt: his Portrait. — Lines on Allington. — Wyatt at St. John's College. — How Marriages were arranged in those Days. — Apology for Wyatt. — Wyatt and Anne Boleyn. — He is enraptured even with her Defects. — His Paraphrase of the Thirty-third Psalm. — Surrey and his Friends. — He is married to Lady Frances Vere. — Wyatt offends the King. — Surrey an Astrologer. — Wyatt's Opinion of Anne Boleyn. — His Lines in Prison. — Wyatt in a wretched Prison.— Defends himself and is set free. — His Verses on a Court. — His Difficulties. — His Letters to Secretary Cromwell. — Wyatt's Sayings. — Wyatt in advanced Life.— His Friendship with Surrey. — Geraldine and her Kindred. — Her extreme Youth when she first knows Surrey. — Surrey's Lines on his Lady Love. — Notions of the Day universal. — Surrey flies the Peril. — Geraldine's Marriage. — She attends the Coronation of Queen Mary. — Surrey becomes Ambitious. — Wyatt dies of Fever. — Wyatt's Letter to his Son. — Recommends the Fear of God to him. — His own Consciousness of Error and Sin. — Advises him to agree with his Wife. — Surrey's Epitaph on Wyatt. — Leland: the Old Mortality of the 16th Century. — Fate of Leland: his Epitaph on Wyatt.— Injustice done to Wyatt's Memory. — Surrey's Kindness to Wyatt's Son. — Poem to Clere: Anecdote of Clere. — Ceremony of cutting off the right Hand. — Surrey in the Fleet. — Letter to the Privy Council. — Surrey goes to Boulogne.— Is Governor there.— The Clock of Christchurch, Norwich. — Unworthy Conduct of the English Government. — Victim of a Cabal. — Surrey's touching Lines on Windsor. — Causes of Surrey's Ruin. — Letter from Garter King-at-Arms. — Draft altered in Henry's Handwriting. — Interrogations put to Surrey.—Surrey is summoned before the Privy Council. — Letter to the Council of State. — Testimony of the Duchess of Richmond. — He is indicted and condemned for Treason. — Anecdote of Surrey. — He is beheaded . . . . Page 53

WILLIAM COWPER AND MARY UNWIN.

Cowper's Family honourable. — His Mother. — Her Death. — Cowper's peculiar Temperament. — His School Days. — A startling Incident affects him. — Looks back to Westminster with Pleasure. — Falls in Love. — Gratitude for his Preservation. — Lady Hesketh. — The "Nonsense Club." — Colman and Thornton his Friends. — Country Cousins. — He writes in the "Connoisseur." — A Place in View. — Sad Effects of the Expectation. — Insanity. — Its Consequences. — His own Narrative. — His Remorse. — Placed with Dr. Cotton. — Opens a Bible. — His Recovery. — His Lines called "The Happy Change." — Mary Unwin. — Her Exterior and Deportment. — Huntingdon and its Castle Hill. — Cowper's Embarrassments. — His daily Pursuits. — His Life too Ascetic. — Mr. Unwin's Death produces a Difficulty. — Death of his Brother. — Cowper's Melancholy. — His Leverets. — Wishes to leave Olney. — Simple Pleasures. — Subjects for Poems. — Appearance of Lady Austen at Olney. — She settles there. — The Jealousy of Mrs. Unwin. — A Quarrel. — Lady Austen disapproved of. — She tells him the Story of John Gilpin. — Lady Austen's Opinion of Mrs. Unwin. — Introduction to Weston. — John Gilpin recited by Henderson. — Letter from Lady Hesketh. — Picture of himself. — Mr. Newton's Warning. — Worldly Contamination. — Theodora's Devotion to Cowper. — Mrs. Unwin's unselfish Friendship. — The Clerk of All Saints, Northampton. — Cowper's good Nature. — His Mother's Picture. — Hayley. — The Muse of Seventy. — Verses to "Mary." — Cowper's struggles against Insanity. — Lady Hesketh's Kindness. — Hannah, the Maid. — Mrs. Unwin's Death. — Death of Cowper. — Visit of Sir James Mackintosh and Basil Montagu . . . Page 119

MARIE ANTOINETTE AND THE PRINCESSE DE LAMBALLE.

Marie Antoinette's Arrival at Kehl. — Her Reception. — Her Lineage. — Court of Vienna. — Description of the young Queen. — Description of Madame de Noailles. — Her Situation at the French Court. — Anecdote of Madame du Barri. — Enemies of Marie Antoinette. — Madame de Genlis. — Her Attempts at an Introduction to the Queen. — Egalité, Duke of Orleans. — His Character and personal Appearance. — His Audacity. —

His Calumnies. — The Princesse de Lamballe. — Jean Jacques Rousseau. — His meeting the Queen at the Trianon. — Their Conversation. — The Count St. Germain. — His Origin doubtful. — Doubts about his Age. — His Servant, Roger. — Death of Louis XV. — Marie Antoinette becomes Popular. — Her Visits to the Little Trianon. — Simplicity of the Queen's Habits. — Birth of Louis her eldest Son. — Reflections by Madame Campan. — Friendship between the Queen and Princesse Lamballe. — It becomes the Fashion to have a Friend. — Louis XVI. at the Tuileries. — The Night before the famous Tenth of August. — A last Effort to save the Royal Family. — The Royal Family leave the Tuileries. — The Knights of the Poignard. — Before the Assembly. — The Convent des Feuillants. — They go to the Temple. — History of the Temple. — Miserable Rooms. — Hardships. — Princesse de Lamballe taken from the Temple. — The Employments of the royal Prisoners. — The Fate of Madame de Lamballe. — Her Head paraded through Paris. — Dreadful Scene before the Temple. — The Queen faints. — Her Son is separated from her. — Marie Antoinette parts from her Child. — Her Trial and Condemnation. — Her last Letter. — Injunctions to her Son. — She is taken to the Place of Execution. — Passes St. Roch. — The Insults heaped on her. — Louis XVII. — His Death and Burial. — Fate of the Temple . Page 177

JOSEPH ADDISON AND RICHARD STEELE.

Account of Addison's Family. — His Father, Lancelot Addison, leaves Oxford in Disgust. — Made Dean of Lichfield. — Addison born. — Gets a Demy-ship at Magdalen College. — His Friendship with Steele. — Friendship between the Families. — The different Characters of Steele and Addison. — Both at Oxford. — Addison dedicates a Poem to Dryden. — Steele's "Christian Hero." — Writes a Play. — Sacheverel the early Friend of Addison. — Steele's love suit to Mistress Scurlock. — His Letters. — Like those of Sir Charles Grandison. — Beautiful Letter to Mary Scurlock. — Mrs. Scurlock's Letter to her Mother. — Steele's Circumstances. — Letter to Mrs. Steele. — Her Verses. — Curious Life led by the Pair. — Steele's Affairs. — Furnishes a House. — Borrows Money on it. — Squabbles between Steele and Swift. — Steele resigns one of his Appointments. — Steele attacked in the House of Commons. — A Vote against him. — He is expelled the House. — Occupies himself in Authorship. — Speech of Lord Finch. — Steele's Difficulties, and Repentance. — Addison's Career is fortunate. —

Addison's Reserve. — Goes to Blois. — His Letter to Congreve. — Liveliness of the French. — Forms Acquaintance of Edward Wortley Montagu. — Proceeds on Journey with Edward Wortley Montagu. — Godolphin Wishes Addison to write on the War.—Addison receives Henry Boyle in his Garret. — Addison's Conversation. — He rose to Fame through the Pen. — Lends Steele Money. — Excuse in getting it back again. — The Society seen and described by Steele. — Superiority of the "Spectator." — Propriety of Queen Anne. — The "Spectator." — A Picture of domestic Manners. — Characteristics of the Day. — Addison purified Literature. — Steele's Notion of Love and Marriage. — Production of the Play of "Cato." — Steele packs an Audience. — He is knighted. — Makes a great Display on the King's Birthday. — Steele's Mode of getting Money. — Debt pursues him. — His Letters to "Prue." — Anecdote of Steele. — Steele's Letters. — How preserved. — Steele poor and unlucky. — His Sister. — Steele's natural Daughter. — Addison's Troubles. — His Letter to Lord Halifax. — Purchases a House at Bilston. — Addison attempts to improve young Lord Warwick. — He is married to Lady Warwick. — Holland House. — Quarrel with Steele. — The Friends part for ever. — Addison's Death-bed. — Steele's Children. — Their Fate . . . . Page 227

MAGDALEN HERBERT AND Dr. DONNE.

Quotation from Lord Herbert of Cherbury. — The Newports and Herberts. — Magdalen Herbert's Husband.—Montgomeryshire a fine School for a Swordsman. — Description of Lord Herbert of Cherbury. — Anecdote of him. — His Character.—Sources of Pride to Magdalen Herbert in her Sons.— George Herbert. — Magdalen, "The Autumnal Beauty." — Dr. Donne's History. — Izaak Walton and Fly-fishing. — What we owe to Walton.— Bishop Andrews. — His personal Character. — Lines by George Herbert. — Magdalen's second Marriage. — Donne called the "Pseudo-Martyr." — Made Dean of St. Paul's. — Donne's Letter to Magdalen Herbert. — George Herbert as a parish Priest.— Consoles his Mother.—Magdalen Herbert's Death. — Dr. Donne's Monument 295

SIR KENELM DIGBY AND SIR ANTHONY VAN DYCK.

Digby brought up as a Protestant. — Description of Sir Kenelm. — Sir Kenelm's Letter to James I. — He is knighted. — Venetia Stanley. — Her Connections. — The early Passages of their Lives. — Sir Everard's Fate described. — Lady Digby receives her Son home. — The course of true Love not smooth. — Venetia Bridesmaid to Elizabeth of Bohemia. — Dancing in Elizabeth's Time. — Venetia dancing. — Faustina's Intrigues. — Strange Story of Abduction. — Venetia escapes. — Artesia's Plans. — Venetia has a Rival. — Sir Kenelm goes to Italy. — Anthony Vandyck. — His Birth. — Anecdote of Rubens. — Van Dyck's Receptions. — Venetia supposed to be faithless. — Sir Kenelm invited to Spain. — His own Narrative of his Life. — Sees Venetia in a Vision. — His Mind obscured by Superstition. — Digby proceeds to Madrid. — Letter of Sir Kenelm Digby. — Sees Venetia in London. — Digby fights Mardontius. — Venetia's public Reputation. — The Sympathetic Powder. — Its Effect in healing Wounds. — Cures effected by Sympathy. — Sir Kenelm on Love. — Part taken by Sir Kenelm in Politics. — Digby's Letter to the Earl of Bristol. — Charles's Favour to the Earl. — Nicholas's Objections. — Sir Kenelm perseveres and succeeds. — Sir Kenelm at the Court of Charles I. — Henrietta Maria. — Van Dyck at Blackfriars. — Van Dyck's Receptions. — Van Dyck at Eltham. — A Letter of Van Dyck's. — Sir Kenelm changes his Faith. — Sir Kenelm converted to Romanism. — Charles interferes with the University. — Ben Jonson's "Eupheme." — Venetia's Death. — Digby's Grief. — Ben Jonson's Grief for Venetia. — His Verses. — Her Character beautifully drawn by him. — The Banqueting-house at Whitehall. — Death of Anthony Van Dyck. — His Tomb in Old St. Paul's. — Amount of Work done by him. — In what he excelled. — His "Throne" at Wilton. — Sir Kenelm imprisoned. — How he was released. — How to lengthen One's Days. — Writes to Sir Henry Benet. — Literary Society at his House. — His Death. — Digby's personal Demeanour. — His Descendants, and his Memoirs . . . . . Page 319

JOHN EVELYN AND ROBERT BOYLE.

JOHN EVELYN'S CHRISTENING. — HIS SPONSORS AND THEIR PRESENTS. — HIS EARLY EDUCATION. — DESCRIPTION OF WOTTON. — HE IS AFRAID OF THE DISCIPLINE OF ETON. — ROBERT BOYLE. — HIS BIRTH AND LINEAGE. — ANECDOTE OF HIS FATHER'S SECOND MARRIAGE. — LIFE OF RICHARD, GREAT EARL OF CORK; AT FIRST A SCHOOLMASTER AT MAIDSTONE. — IRELAND THE AUSTRALIA OF THOSE DAYS. — ROBERT BOYLE'S "SERAPHIC LOVE." — EVELYN'S ADVICE TO HIM. — THEIR FRIENDSHIP. — HENRY CARY, EARL OF MONMOUTH. — HIS CHARACTER. — BOYLE'S SUPPOSED ATTACHMENT TO HIS DAUGHTER. — EVELYN'S RENEWED ADVICE; ALL IN VAIN. — BOYLE REMAINS A BACHELOR. — BOYLE'S APPEARANCE AND HABITS. — BAD TIMES. — EVELYN'S FATHER DIES. — EVELYN TRAVELS ABROAD. — METEORIC APPEARANCE IN THE SKY. — EVELYN NO HERO. — DEVOTED TO GARDENING. — HIS DOMESTIC LIFE. — SAYES COURT. — THE CZAR PETER THERE. — PEPYS' VISITS. — BOYLE'S PECULIARITIES. — HIS REVERENCE FOR THE NAME OF GOD. — SCENE AT SIR HARRY VANE'S. — HIS SPEECH. — JEREMY TAYLOR. — SORROW VISITS SAYES COURT. — FOUNDATION OF THE "INVISIBLE," OR PHILOSOPHIC COLLEGE. — AIR-PUMP INVENTED. — BOYLE'S DEATH. — EVELYN'S OLD AGE AT WOTTON. — HIS VARIOUS BEREAVEMENTS. — HIS DEATH AND THAT OF HIS WIFE.

JOHN EVELYN AND ROBERT BOYLE.

It was in the year 1620, at that critical time when the Spanish alliance, as it was called, was first talked of, that a group of serious personages stood in the great dining-room of Wotton, in Surrey. It is a christening. Parson Higham, the incumbent of the parish, officiates. Richard Evelyn, the father of the babe whose life of eighty-six years was afterwards, to borrow the words of a modern author, "a course of inquiry, study, curiosity, instruction, and benevolence," stands by: he is a man of thirty; his hair, though light, is already tinged with grey, even at that age; his complexion is sanguine and (his son said) "inclined to choler;" his beard is brown, a little mingled with grey about his cheeks, and peaked below the chin; his face is clear and fresh-coloured, his eyes wondrously luminous and piercing: his ample forehead completes what his famous son called "a very well composed visage and manly aspect;" he is, nevertheless, low of stature, though strong.

Beside him appears, as we may conclude, Eleanor, his wife; "a proper personage," saith Sylva Evelyn; brown in complexion, with eyes and hair of a lovely black. Her face wears an expression of deep reverence, not unmixed with dejection and care; for she was, says her son, "inclined to religious melancholy, or pious sadness," and doubtless that disposition, contrasting strongly with the sanguine temperament of her husband, was betrayed, especially at that moment, by her countenance.

Near the font stands a neighbour's wife, with the infant who is about to be baptized in her arms. It was, even until the middle of the last century, the custom for persons of condition to put out their infants to nurse. Of a "good comely brown complexion," the foster-mother smilingly holds in her fat arms the future annalist of his times. The " susceptors," as they were styled, or sponsors, declare that to this babe the homely name of John, from his maternal grandfather, is assigned. A sister of Sir Thomas Evelyn, a branch of the family living at Long Ditton, is one of the lady sponsors, and a kinsman named Combe the other godfather.

Two very handsome pieces of curiously wrought and gilt plate are displayed, sponsorial gifts to the little scion of the Evelyns; and having been duly admired or duly pitied, for it seems probable that he was a sickly infant, from his baptism being in the house and not in the church, forthwith he is conveyed to the home of his foster-mother.

It was in a retreat near the Surrey Hills, and flanked with wood, and refreshed by delicious streams, that the infant, afterwards so distinguished, drew his first impressions of material objects; he ascribed to those around him then his love of solitude, and of nature, in after life. At four years of age we find John Evelyn learning to read in the church porch of Wotton, from a man named Frien. Promptly as his parents had parted from him after his birth, they kept him near them for some years after his return home. Meantime how delicious must have been his infancy in that exquisite region of wood, hill, dale, streamlet, meadow, flower garden, and park, which compose the almost unchanged domains of Wotton. Situated twenty-six miles only from London, yet as secluded as if it were three hundred; three miles from Dorking, six from Guildford, twelve from Kingston-on-Thames, Wotton is one of the favoured spots in the south of England. Within the last thirty years the deep seclusion of which its gifted owner speaks, lasted still. No sounds but such as the gentle Cowper would have rejoiced to hear, broke on the loiterer's day-dreams:

> "Not rural sights alone, but rural sounds,
> Delight mine ear."

The cooing of the ringdove, the first notes of the nightingale, the strange voice of the corn-crake, mingled with the *sough* or sighing of the winds in those dark woods, were all that could disturb reflection at Wotton.

> "Stillness, accompanied with sounds so soft,
> Charm more than silence."

Then, as the rambler emerged from the delicious shade into that kind of glen, intersected by a stream, which, behind the mansion of Wotton, presents a scene such as Ariosto pictures; the soft hum of the roving bee, or the current of the stream, or the occasional disturbance of the waters by the sportive fishes, were long all that could recall, to those who luxuriated in that spot, the infinity of life that teemed around, above, below, beneath even their very feet, crushing the busy ant at each foot-fall.

All is changed now: let us glance, therefore, at what we must at present live in, the past. Let John Evelyn, babe no longer, but in his mature reason, speak for himself about his loved, and our loved Wotton.

"I will say nothing," he writes[*], "of the air, because the pre-eminence is usually given to Surrey, the soil being dry and sandy; but I should speak much of the gardens, fountains, and groves that adorn it, were they not as generally known to be amongst the most natural and (till this later and universal luxury of the whole nation, since abounding in such expenses) the most magnificent that England afforded, and which indeed gave one of the first examples to that elegancy,

[*] Evelyn's Diary, vol. i. p. 3.

since so much in vogue and followed for the managing of their waters and other elegancies of that nature."

Then he adds that the contiguity of five or six manors, the patronage of the livings about it, and, what Themistocles considered not among the least advantages of a place, the good neighbourhood, conspired to render Wotton " an honourable and handsome royalty " for his " worthy brothers and noble lady, whose constant liberality gave them title both to the place, and to the affections of all who know them." And Wotton then must have exactly resembled, in some minor points of the description, Wotton in the present day. Like most old houses, it stands low ; yet, from Leith Hill, not far off, twelve or thirteen counties may, on a clear day, be seen, as well as the sea washing the shores of Sussex. A large and ancient house, ancient even in the days of Evelyn's father, formed then the main feature of the rising grounds; and it still establishes the accuracy of his delineation, that Wotton is " one of the most tempting and pleasant seats in the nation, and most tempting for a great person and a *wanton* purse to render it conspicuous."

Evelyn's father was a fine old English gentleman; " wise, acute, of solid discourse (no fool can come up to that character)," but affable, humble, " in nothing affected ; " neat in his habits, thriving in his plans ; methodical: silent, careful; yet nobly liberal, and a lover of hospitality; discreetly severe : nevertheless his son never saw him in a passion : well did he support the characters of patron, master, host, parent, husband, at a time when to support those characters well was looked upon as a part of a gentleman's necessary bearing. Yet he declined honours and titles, for he stood so well in his own county that they could have added nothing to his condition except burdens.

It is pleasant to read of such men, in these days of inordinate ostentation and unprecedented worldliness ; and to dwell in quiet admiration on their simplicity of manners. The son—not the heir, it is true, for there were two daughters and a son older—sitting in the church porch to receive instruction from some poor scholar.

Those were eventful times; and John Evelyn's boyish curiosity was piqued "by the stir and talk" about Gondemar and the Spanish match—about the Comet, too, of 1618, the effects of which he even believed were shown in the fearful revolutions in European affairs, especially those in Germany, at that time: then he recollected to the end of his life the muster for the Duke of Buckingham's expedition to Rhé; and he was awakened one morning out of his slumbers by the news that Felton had stabbed the "Great Duke" to the heart; and, whilst these impressions sank into his memory, he was picking up such knowledge as he could at the free school of Southover near Lewes, where he remained until sent to college.

But this was not his father's wish. Evelyn, whilst attending the free school, had lived with his grandmother, who had married again; he dreaded the severity of Eton, declined the advantage of going there proffered by his father, and all his life repented that he had done so and had been indulged in his wish; yet his father had enough to do, even with an ample fortune of 4000*l.* a year: he was sheriff for Surrey and Sussex, before those counties were disjoined: one hundred and ten servants, all in green satin doublets, formed his cortége; which was augmented by the attendance of divers friends and volunteers, who chose to assume the same livery, and to act as his servants; and gallant indeed must have been the show as the cavalcade turned out of the road down to Wotton, passed the mass of stables, and followed the high sheriff to his assize.

That great display was followed by sadder processions. Mistress Darcy—John Evelyn's elder sister—died in her twentieth year, "in virtue advanced beyond her years, or the merit of her husband," writes her brother, adding bitterly— "the worst of men." This was in 1634. During the next year, a malignant fever apparently carried off John Evelyn's mother; but her death was caused by grief. She had seen her young daughter laid in the tomb, after childbirth; the infant followed its mother to the grave, and Mrs. Evelyn's heart broke; too late, she strove, indeed, to reconcile herself to life; but the fiat had gone forth. Calling her children around her, she embraced and blessed them—giving to each a ring as a last token of love. Her latest request was that the money which she believed would be spent on her funeral rites should be given to the poor. A famous powder—one of the many specifics of those days of quackery—was tried in her case in vain. She expired in all sanctity, and was buried near the daughter whose death had cast a shadow over her last days.

Her son John, meantime, pursued the course usually then assigned to most men of condition. He graduated at Balliol College, Oxford, then remarked for its remissness of discipline, notwithstanding that William Laud, Archbishop of Canterbury, was Chancellor of the University, and very strict in all formalities. Those were pleasant days for the Church, and for everybody of the Laudian views. The Church of England was in her greatest splendour; all things were "decent," says Evelyn, "a blessed halcyon time in England." Stern, indeed, was the contrast of after days.

Whilst John Evelyn was beginning the actual career of life, a mind wonderfully congenial to his own, though of a different turn, was advancing with rapid strides in intellect and virtue. The very name of Robert Boyle inspires reverence, and calls up wonder at the various and great acquirements of one man. Illustrious in birth, superior to titles, and perhaps to praise, this great Christian philosopher was born at Lismore, in Ireland, in 1626–7, and was, therefore, six years older than Evelyn. Both these men, who do honour to their country, sprang from ancient lineage. Evelyn truly says, referring to his own descent, that "what the heralds say is often sorry, and mercenary enough;" he was able, nevertheless, he declared, to bring his own pedigree from one Evelyn, brother to Ambrogius, — who brought Julius Cæsar into Britain the second time? "Will you not," he adds, writing to William Wotton, "smile at this?" Most people would do so, undoubtedly. The Hattons, the Onslows, and the Evelyns came, he concluded, out of Shropshire into Surrey, about the same time, and during the wars of the Barons.

Robert Boyle, although born in the Emerald Isle, belongs, rightfully, by descent to Wales. He was the seventh son and the fourteenth child of Richard Boyle, the *great* Earl of Cork, whose family are said to have been settled in Herefordshire before the Conquest. Truth, however, compels the confession that the name of Boyle is said to be of Spanish origin: and a knight of Aragon, Sir Philip Boyle, having distinguished himself in a tournament before Henry V., the ancestry of this illustrious house has by some writers been derived from him.

"Sir Philip," however, says Budgell, who wrote the memoirs of the Boyle family, "was a kinsman, but no ancestor of theirs." Long before he called forth the unwilling praise usually given by the English to foreigners, the Boyles, then bearing the name of Bluvill, since corrupted into Boyle, were settled at Pixely Court, near Ledbury; in Queen Elizabeth's reign, however, Roger Boyle, the great Earl's father, married a Kentish maiden, Joan Naylor, and *his* son, the famous Richard, was born in Kent. Evelyn, indeed, states that Richard Boyle, first Earl of Cork, was a schoolmaster at Maidstone; he was, in fact, the penniless second son of a younger son; and it is very likely that after his education at Cambridge he turned his abilities to account in any way that was expedient at the moment.

An amusing anecdote is told by Evelyn of the great Earl's second marriage: —

"Coming to advise with Sir Geoffrey Fenton, an eminent Irish lawyer, and finding him engaged with another client, and seeing a pretty child in the nurse's arms, entertained himself with them, till Sir Geoffrey came to him, making his excuse for keeping him so long. Mr. Boyle pleasantly told him he had been courting a young lady for his wife: and so it fortuned, that sixteen years after it Mr. Boyle made his addresses in good earnest to her and married the young lady, from whom has sprung all this numerous family of lords and earls branching now into the noblest families of England." Of these Roger Boyle, whom his father sent young into England to be educated under the care of his relation, Evelyn's grandfather, at Deptford, was the eldest. There was then a famous school in that town. Such was the origin of the connection between the families of Evelyn and Boyle, and of the kindness that always existed between them. The Roger Boyle referred to, having died in the house of Sir Richard Browne at Sayes Court, was buried in the parish church of Deptford.

From this marriage sprang Robert Boyle. His name occurs low down in the list of seven sons and eight daughters; the sons, it may be certified, " with all their father's wit," the daughters, it may be presumed, " with all their mother's beauty;" for they became all the wives of peers or peers' sons, except Margaret, the youngest,—Margaret, Robert Boyle's only younger sister,—who died unmarried.

What Australia and New Zealand are to the present generation, Ireland was in those days to the speculative and enterprising. It was necessary to colonise that barbarous country in order to prevent the natives from tearing each other to pieces. The history of the Encumbered Estates Bill in our time, and its vast revolution in Ireland, is only a revived edition of the salutary but arbitrary acts of Elizabeth, of James I., and of Charles I. What has been done in the nineteenth century with consent of Parliament, was done in the sixteenth century without that process,—there is the sole difference. So Richard, the great Earl of Cork, marrying for his first wife an Irish heiress with 500*l*. a year in land, laid the foundation of an estate; added to it by grants from the crown, and more especially by purchasing the forfeited lands of Sir Walter Ralegh, consisting of 12,000 acres in Cork and Waterford. Let it not, however, be supposed that the lot of an Irish landholder was in those days any more like a bed of roses than in our own; for it had cost Sir Walter Ralegh 200*l*. a year to support his titles to the estate given him by the English Government.

The whole life of Richard the great Earl was a succession of prosperous events, until he came to the climax of his fortune, and became Earl of Cork, and the sturdy opponent of Strafford's oppressions. Singular indeed must have been the impression made at the trial of Strafford, the "Lord Deputy," when the Earl of Cork deposed, that on his prosecuting an action at law in a suit, considering himself aggrieved, Strafford had said to him, with unbounded arrogance: "Call in your writs, or if you will not, I will clap you up in your Castle; for, I tell you, I will not have my orders disputed by law or lawyers."

The Earl of Cork was the great upholder of the Protestant interest in Ireland. It was the former schoolmaster of Maidstone, as Evelyn has it, who exposed the imposition called St. Patrick's Purgatory, which he unmasked. His wise aim was to induce Protestants to settle in Ireland; and when the famous rebellion broke out in that country, he reaped the full benefit of his wisdom in the support given him by the English at the siege of Lismore.

The wisdom of this great man was shown in the education and rearing of his children. Like Evelyn, Robert Boyle was intrusted to the care of a countrywoman, whom the Earl charged to bring up the infant in as hardy a manner as possible. When he was three years old he lost his mother (the heroine of Evelyn's little history), and throughout life he regretted never having known her so as to remember her, especially as she was beloved and lamented by those of his family who had that privilege. It was not until he was seven years of age that his father sent for him home. He had then caught from some of his nurse's children a habit of stuttering, which he never entirely lost. At eight years old he was sent to Eton, and from that seat of learning he wrote a letter to his father, curious as showing the formal terms then existing between parent and child, and beginning, " My most honoured Lord Father ; " and this epistle, like most of those written by this great philosopher in after days, is composed with a degree of study, discretion, and stiffness, which plainly shows the character of the writer. For Boyle had not the facility, the circumstantiality, and the warmth which render Evelyn's letters so valuable both as memorials of himself and of his times.

Before Robert Boyle had attained his fourteenth year, his elder brother Francis was married to Elizabeth Killigrew. The espousals taking place at this early age, the boy bridegroom was ordered to travel with his younger brothers; and they set out on that *grande tour* which was thought an essential part of education. They stopped at Geneva; then proceeding to Florence, were at that city when Galileo died in an adjacent village. Returning, however, homewards, news of the rebellion of 1642 reached the young travellers at Marseilles, and they were obliged to pawn some jewels in order to bring them home. On arriving in England, Robert Boyle found his father dead, and every sort of property in utter depression. Stalsbridge, a seat in Dorsetshire, was indeed bequeathed to him by his father, as well as certain estates in Ireland; but no income, in the disturbed state of both countries during the great Rebellion, was to be derived from these properties. At length affairs, as far as Boyle was concerned, brightened, and in 1646 he took up his abode at Stalbridge with a mind prodigiously stored with knowledge of every description, and with a vastness of comprehension and a grasp of intellect rarely allotted to any human being.

He was now a young man of twenty years of age; yet, at a time of life when most men are pursuing their pleasures, he delighted in nothing so much as in doing good. And next to that almost heavenly gratification was his pleasure in seeking out eminent men, and in bringing them to his house.

His " Seraphic Love " was written before he had attained his twentieth year, and was the first of his productions. That he was ever in love, that the treatise had even any reference to actual feelings, is disputed by hard-headed philosophical writers, more especially by Boyle's biographer, Dr. Birch; Evelyn, however, himself a married man, was not so incredulous. Although, among all his experiments, Boyle "never," as Evelyn says, "made that of married life, yet I have been," he adds, "told he courted an ingenious and beautiful daughter of Carey, Earl of Monmouth;" and probably Evelyn, upon an acquaintance of forty years, knew more of Boyle's private affairs than any other man.

Gravely indeed does the editor of the " Biographia Britannica " oppose this idea, and remarks on it thus :—" To say the truth, he seems to have been persuaded that he was born for nobler purposes than the ordinary lot of man; at least, if he was not so persuaded, his actions were such as may persuade us."

Evelyn, however, does not appear to have held marriage in so low a scale as the learned writer just quoted; on the contrary, he availed himself of an intimate friendship to state his frank opinion on the subject of matrimony to Boyle.

The acquaintance between these two great men was begun by Boyle, who, drawn by similarity of characters and tastes, visited Evelyn at Sayes Court, near Deptford. Their intimacy grew, as Evelyn relates, " reciprocal and familiar;" civil letters, in the courteous and somewhat hyperbolical terms common in those times, passing at first between them; but " these compliments," as Evelyn, who survived his friend, stated, " lasted no longer than till we had become perfectly acquainted, and had discovered our inclination of cultivating the same studies and designs, especially in the search of natural and useful things."

In their benevolence, their philosophy, their love of nature, and their study of high art, Boyle and his friend resembled each other. But here the analogy ended. Evelyn was a busy, joyous, observant man of the world; Boyle, a devoted scholar, living in abstraction from all earthly ties, though not from earthly interests. In thanking him for his " Seraphic Love," Evelyn half playfully, half enthusiastically, in referring to his "incomparable" book which "is written (he says) with a pen snatched from the wing of a Seraphim," declares that Boyle has treated his subject and described it "to that perfection as if in the company of some celestial harbingers he had taken flight, and been ravished into the third heaven, where you have heard words unutterable, and whence you bring us such affections and such divine inclinations as are only competent to angels and to yourself; for so powerful is your eloquence, so metaphysical your discourse, and sublime your subject."

Then he goes on to say, "And though by all this, and your rare example, you civilly declaim against the mistakes we married persons usually make, yet I cannot but think it a paralogism or insidious reasoning which you manage with so much ingenuity, and pursue with so great judgment."

Nevertheless, Evelyn, happy in domestic life, puts in a plea for love and marriage. " Though you have said nothing of marriage, which is the result of love, yet you suppose it would be hard to become a servant without folly; and that there are ten thousand inquietudes espoused with a mistress; that the fruits of children are tears and weakness, whilst the productions of the spirits put their parents neither to charge nor trouble."

After admitting so much, he advocates eloquently that state which the world then regarded as holy; but which, if we are to judge by the shameless petitions for divorce, is now apt to be regarded merely as a conventional tie.

"The Scriptures," Evelyn continues, "are full of worthy examples, since it was from the effect of conjugal love that the Saviour of the world, and that great object of seraphic love, derived His incarnation, who was the son of David. Take away this love, and the whole world is but a desert; and though there were nothing more worthy eulogies than virginity, it is yet but the result of love, since those that shall people paradise, and fill heaven with saints, are such as have been subject to this passion, and were the products of it."
"By it the Church," added Evelyn, had "consecrated to God both virgins and martyrs, and confessors, these five thousand years." *

He wrote to one who he perhaps knew was impelled as much by disappointment as philosophy to the Seraphic state; and this, he seems to infer, was no disparagement to Boyle's intellect, no blemish to the objects of his glorious ambition. "Descartes," he observes, "was not so innocent."

Granting that the story of Robert Boyle's early attachment is true, it may be here stated that he must have made a judicious choice in the single passion of his life.

Amongst those of the nobility whom the death of Charles the First drove into retirement, none was more assiduous in gaining knowledge, none more modest in displaying it, than was Henry Cary, second Earl of Monmouth. Contemporary with the ill-fated Charles, and one of the Knights of the Bath who received that order with his young sovereign when Prince of Wales, Cary, best known as Lord Lepington, was a good specimen of the highly accomplished nobleman of the times. His fine thoughtful face and regular features, his flowing love locks, his broad Vandyck collar falling even over his shoulders, recall the costume which

* Vol. iii. p. 122.

formed a party emblem, and which the Cavaliers never abandoned. One would fain indulge the idea that Robert Boyle " loved and lost " the daughter of this nobleman rather than that he " never loved at all." She is said to have been as " ingenious" as her father, a man who filled seven folios, two octavos, and a duodecimo, when Earl of Monmouth, during his retirement, whilst many "others of the nobility," says Anthony à Wood, " were fain to truckle to their inferiors for company's sake." His brother, too, was a poet, and Sir John Suckling complimented the Earl of Monmouth by saying:

> " It is so rare a thing to see
> Aught that belongs to young nobility
> *In print* but their *owne clothes*, that we must praise
> You as we would do those first shewe the wayes
> To arts or to new worlds."

Gladly, therefore, would the admirers of Robert Boyle have seen him linked to a daughter of the house of Cary; and Evelyn did his utmost to show Cœlebs the error of his ways.

" But I cannot consent," he continues, " that such a person as Mr. Boyle be so indifferent, decline a virtuous love, or imagine that the best ideas are represented only in romances, where love begins, proceeds, and expires in the pretty tale, but leaves us no worthy impressions of its effects. We have nobler examples, and the wives of philosophers, studious and pious persons, shall furnish our instances. For such," he adds, " was Pudentilla, who held the lamp to her husband's lucubrations, and such a companion had the learned Budæus. In fine," he continues," they divert us when we are well, and tend us when we are sick; they grieve over us when we die; and some I have known that would not be comforted and survive."

Nothing, in fact, can be more natural, more earnest, or more true than the whole of the letter, from which we quote these various passages: —

"But, dear Sir," he proceeds to say, "mistake me not all this while, for I make not this recital as finding the least period in your most excellent discourse prejudicial to the conjugal state; or that I have the vanity to imagine my forces capable to make you a proselyte of Hymen's, who have already made the worthiest choice. I have never," he continues, "encountered anything extraordinary as dare lay claim to any of the virtues I have celebrated; but if I have the conversation capable of exalting and improving our affections, even to the highest of objects, and to contribute very much to human felicity, I cannot pronounce the love of the sex to be at all misapplied, or to the prejudice of the most seraphical."

In conclusion, Evelyn appeals to those affections which he knew are latent in almost every breast, and which he fondly hoped to arouse in the heart of the young philosopher.

"Dearest Sir, permit me to tell you that I extremely loved you before, but my heart is infinitely knit to you now; for what are we not to expect from so timely a consecration of your excellent abilities? The *primitiæ* sanctified the whole harvest, and you have at once, by this incomparable piece, taken off the reproach which lay upon piety, and the inquiries into nature; that the one was too early for young persons, and the other the ready way to atheism; than which, as nothing has been more impiously spoken, so not anything has been more fully refuted." *

All was in vain, and Robert Boyle's life presents no glimmering of those interests which make up the sum and constitute the very essence of domestic affections. Even the transient or unrequited attachment has left no visible trace, although it may have had a lasting influence on the character of the solitary and devoted philosopher.

Let him not, however, be regarded as a recluse, abjuring

---

* Corres. pp. 124, 225, to the end of the letter.

society, and degenerating into pedantry. Robert Boyle loved his fellow-creatures; "never," says Evelyn, "did his severest studies sour his conversation. A generous and free philosopher, not a dogmatic one;" "to draw a just character of him," says his friend, "one must run through all the virtues, as well as through all the sciences." In the following way his life was usually passed.

In the morning the young student (still enjoying the honorary pay of a company of horse, assigned to him by his father the great Earl of Cork), after his devotions, passed into his laboratory. His religion, be it remarked, was as replete with liberality and humility as with earnestness. It was without noise, dispute, or determining; owning no master but the Divine Author of it, no rule but Scripture, no law but right reason." Glasses and chemical and mathematical instruments so crowded his bed-chamber that there was room only for a few chairs. Like Descartes, he had a small library, learning more from men and from experiments than from books.

In the midst of this confusion appeared a tall, slender, emaciated man, a valetudinarian, whose tenement of clay seemed almost too o'er-informed to last out the usual span of man's life. Pale, gentle, as one of a sensitive nature usually is, refined, fragile, Evelyn, his friend, used nevertheless to compare him to a "Venice glass, which, though wrought never so thin and fine, being carefully set up, would outlast the hardier metals of daily use." It was true: this delicate frame did endure almost to threescore years, a good old age in those times; but in pain and weakness, such as to prove the holy resignation of that great heart to its utmost, did that frame live on. Often did Boyle's admiring friend find him struck down by palsy, so that he could neither move nor carry his hand to his mouth; and yet the enfeebled body was restored, and he lasted, as Evelyn relates, "though not to a great, yet to a competent age," and would, his loving eulogist thought, have lived longer, had it not been for a precious sister's death. The philosopher who had abjured the tender bonds of love, died heart-stricken from a bereavement.

His friend (unknown to him at that time), John Evelyn, was leading, meantime, the life of a young gentleman, whose means were ample, during what he termed that "blessed halcyon time in England." First we see him deriving benefit from the conversation of a Mr. Thicknesse, then a fellow of Balliol College; in those days, when foreign travelling was difficult, it must have been strange to see one Conopios out of Greece, sent from Cyril, the patriarch of Constantinople, to visit England. Balliol was then, owing to lax discipline, low in estimation. There, in 1637, did Evelyn first see coffee drunk, the great Oriental scholar, Conopios, taking it, to the astonishment of the dons, at Oxford. Nor was the use of coffee fully introduced into England until thirty years afterwards. Little did Evelyn, at the early age of seventeen, think of study, but more of being admitted to the vaulting and dancing schools, the art of vaulting being then reduced to printed rules. Soon we find all his enjoyment cut short by a quartan ague, and still more by the beginning of rebellion amongst the Scotch, "who madly began our confusion and their own destruction," as he writes in his Diary. Then he is anon entered into the Middle Temple, his father purchasing chambers for him and his brother, four pairs of stairs high, "which gave us," says the candid youth, "advantage of the fairer prospect, but did not much contribute to that impolished study" to which his father had destined him.

A stirring time must the young Templar have had of it, law thriving but little in his attic abode. From it he beheld Charles I., in all the peerless grace of his costume, surrounded by his court, coming from his northern expedtion, and riding through the streets amid the accclamations of his people, attended by a splendid cavalcade. It was a spectacle long remembered, for it was almost the ill-fated king's last appearance until he mounted the scaffold. He came to open what loyal Evelyn styles "that long, ungrateful, foolish, and fatal Parliament, the beginning of all our sorrows for twenty years after, and the period of the most happy monarch of the world."

A gloom was also gathering over the Manor House of Wotton. In the worst of times, "Richard Evelyn was taken from the evil to come." On the 2nd January 1640-1, his children, in the dead of night, followed his mourning-hearse to Wotton Church, where he was buried beside his wife. "Thus were we," writes Evelyn*, "bereft of both our parents in a period when we most of all stood in need of their counsel and assistance, especially myself, of a raw, vain, uncertain, and very unwary inclination; but it so pleased God to make trial of my conduct in a conjuncture of the greatest and most prodigious hazard that the youth of England saw; and if I did not, amidst all this, impeach my liberty nor my virtue with the rest who made shipwreck of both, it was more the infinite goodness and mercy of God than the least providence or discretion of mine own."

Poor Evelyn! He attended Strafford's trial, and his opinions thereon would not be fashionable in the present day; for he considered that those who witnessed that most touching scene, "were spectators and auditors of the greatest malice and the greatest innocency ever met before so illustrious an assembly."

He resolved, however, to leave his country; and having obtained permission to do so from Charles I., — a precaution similar to that of getting a passport in our days, — Evelyn hastened to the Continent.

His travels are delightfully described; and nothing escaped his observation, from the legs of a game cock to the School of Anatomy at Leyden. At the Hague, he kissed the hand of the Queen of Bohemia, who received him in a chamber hung with black velvet on account of her husband's death. He

* Life and Corres. vol. i. p. 15.

saw the brave and handsome Prince Maurice and the young Princesses. Then taking "waggon" for Dort, he attended the reception of Marie de Medicis, whose daughter, Henrietta of England, "tossed to and fro by the various fortunes of her life," was also there. He visited the then sad court of Brussels; and, returning to England, was elected one of the Comptrollers of the Middle Temple, and passed his time in London, " studying a little, but dancing and fooling more." Time passed on. Evelyn was now twenty-one years of age, full of curiosity, high spirits, and genius; an incipient man of the world, his mind, nevertheless, deeply imbued with superstition.

"I must not forget," he writes on the 12th of December 1642-3, "what amazed us exceedingly in the night before, viz. a shining cloud in the air, in shape resembling a sword, the point receding to the north; it was as bright as the moon, the rest of the sky being very serene. It began about eleven at night, and vanished out till above one, being seen by all the south of England. I made many journeys to and from England."

Evelyn, however, though devoted to the Royal cause, was no hero. He had been a volunteer in Goring's troop; he now retired, and kept that circumstance a secret; and retreating to Wotton, built, by the permission of his elder brother who had inherited the estate, a study, made a fish-pond, " and a garden, an island, and some other solitudes and retirements, which gave," he relates, " the first occasion of improving them to those water-works and gardens which afterwards succeeded them, and became at that time the most famous in England."

His taste for gardens was hereditary, and his very name was sylvan. Evelyn, written anciently Avelan or Evelin, means a filbert, or hazel: his grandfather, George Evelyn, who, in the reign of Elizabeth, had purchased the estate of Wotton, had been a great planter and preserver of timber. Wotton, corrupted from Wood-town, was a name given to it on account of the fine groves and plantations around it. The Evelyn family were famous for planting, and it was a relation of John Evelyn's that first planted Richmond Park and then sold it to Charles I. There was a mania, in those days, for introducing new species of plants and trees. To Lord Bacon we owe the plane-tree, which he first planted near Verulam. The introduction of the China orange into Europe was an event of the reign of Charles II. A certain Portuguese nobleman, when Prime Minister, received in a case a collection of plants of the China orange; only one had escaped being killed in the transit; from that one came all the China oranges in Europe.

When Evelyn passed a second time into France, we find that the gardens in or near Paris were his especial delight. That of the Tuileries, still even now grand and noble, but curtailed in extent, attracted his praise. It was, he thought, "rarely contrived for privacy, shade, or company;" he speaks of a plantation of tall elms and mulberries; of a labyrinth of cypresses; of hedges of pomegranates; of fountains, fish-ponds, and an aviary,— delights which have long since been swept away by time, or by fierce revolution; above all, "of the artificial echo, never without some fair nymph singing with grateful returns; — standing at one of the focuses, which is under a tree or little cabinet of hedges, the voice seems to descend from the clouds, — at another, as if it were underground."

Then there was an orangery which seemed a Paradise, and from a terrace was seen the *course*, now the *Champs Elysées*, a place of an English mile long, all planted with trees in four rows, with a stately arch up the entrance. "Here the gallants and fine ladies," says Evelyn, "take the air for pleasure." But there was another feature of the Tuileries Gardens: a building in which wild beasts were kept for the King's diversion.

Next he passes on to Rueil — Cardinal Richelieu's castellated villa—and doubted whether Italy had anything to exceed it in rarity or pleasure; but what most struck him, for the Sylva was ever in his thoughts, was "the garden nearest the pavilion, a parterre, having in the midst divers noble brass statues, perpetually spouting water into an ample basin, with other figures of the same metal; but what is most admirable, is the vast enclosure and variety of ground in the large garden, containing vineyards, corn-fields, meadows, groves (whereof one is of perennial greens), and walks of vast length, accurately kept and cultivated, that nothing can be more agreeable."

The study of horticulture in all its branches was not, however, sufficient for a grasp of mind such as that of Evelyn. In the spring of 1644, therefore, he made the tour of Europe, resolving to inquire carefully into the state of science wherever he went; he visited Rome in order to view not only the painting and sculpture there in their perfection, but to comprehend the state of the Romish Church. He travelled through Italy to perfect himself in a critical as well as practical knowledge of painting. As a key to all researches, he became a good linguist as far as French, Spanish, and Italian were concerned. (Few persons in that day attempted to master German.) He became almost an artist himself; but whilst he studied several minor accomplishments, "the works of the Creator and the minute labours of the creature were," says Horace Walpole, "all objects of his pursuit. He unfolded the perfection of the one, and assisted the imperfection of the other." The dignity of man, a subject on which Evelyn wrote a treatise, was well comprehended by this great and good man: happy indeed was his long and honoured life; that calm and favoured destiny has been summed up in a few expressive words. "He had one of the finest gardens in the kingdom, and was one of the best and happiest men in it. He lived to a good, but not to an useless old age, and long enjoyed the shade of those flourishing trees which himself had planted."

Before Evelyn's return to England he had accomplished

another object, — he had chosen a wife. The marriage which eventually proved so happy, was however prefaced by a severe trial — an attack of small-pox. That fearful disease, which Evelyn's friend, Robert Boyle, escaped all his life, was a scourge, the very thoughts of which cast a gloom over families. An act of selfishness, rare in the kindly Evelyn, was punished by the fearful visitation. Returning from his travels, he slept at a Swiss town. There was no vacant bed in the inn: Evelyn therefore requested that one of the hostess's daughters should be removed out of her bed, and that room made ready for him; heavy with sleep and fatigue, he would not stay to have the sheets changed, but got into the fatal bed whilst it was still warm. There was a suspicious smell of frankincense in the room, and the hostess admitted that her daughter had only recently recovered from the ague. The young traveller felt ill and heavy, but held up whilst crossing the Lake of Geneva, where, in spite of the conversation of Diodati, then resident at Geneva, who called on him, he could no "longer hold up his head," but felt as if "his eyes would have dropped out." A wearisome confinement of sixteen days, attended by a hideous Swiss matron with an immense *goître*, was followed by recovery; but convalescence had its perils. "By God's mercy, after five weeks keeping my chamber," Evelyn wrote, "I went abroad."

In the autumn of the year 1647, he arrived in Paris. Here he avows what many people might also do,—he passed the only time in his life that he ever spent idly; here and there "refreshing his dancing and other long-neglected exercises," and learning the lute. All this looks suspicious of love passages. Sir Richard Browne, then ambassador in France, had a fair daughter, whose fine regular features, luxuriant hair, and comely figure first attracted the youthful Evelyn; a marriage treaty was set on foot, and as Charles II., then Prince of Wales, was holding his court at St. Germains, his chaplain, Dr. Earle, performed the ceremony.

Henceforth we must regard Evelyn's life as one of a domestic character, in spite of the signal events which occurred during the whole course of his existence.

Charles I. was then a prisoner at Hampton Court, and Evelyn, on returning to England, hastened to kiss his Majesty's hand; "he being in the power of those execrable villains who not long after murdered him;" and, this duly done, the sturdy but prudent royalist repaired to Sayes Court, Deptford, to take possession, in right of his wife, of that old manor-house. With disgust one naturally turns in the present day from the very name of Deptford. Situated on the banks of the Ravensbourne, and anciently Depeforde, from the deep ford where the bridge now is, this large populous town, when Evelyn lived near it, had been until the reign of Henry VIII. a mere fishing village; under that monarch's rule the Royal Dock was established there; and it was still in the memory of man that Henry, Prince of Wales, his brother Charles, and the Duke of Buckingham had here often held council with Phineas Pett on maritime matters.

Long owned and inhabited by the Say family, the manor-house of Deptford had obtained the name of Sayes Court; it was held in copyhold from the Crown. Elizabeth, towards the latter part of her reign, granted it, with sixty acres of land, to Sir Richard Browne, for a term of years; and on Evelyn's marriage, it was given as a residence to him on account of his wife. For years this old place, on the site of which Deptford Workhouse now stands, was the abode of John Evelyn. Charles II. in 1663 granted him a new lease of it, at the nominal rent of twenty-two shillings and sixpence. Here Evelyn commenced his experiments, and worked out those ideas on gardening which he afterwards perfected at Wotton. From no place has a man's name so utterly perished, as that of Evelyn from Deptford. Trade, dirt, noise, and coarse language have long since superseded the quiet refinement of Sayes Court, that resting-place and gathering-place for letters and philosophy. Even in Evelyn's time there were local enemies to his peace. The frost of 1682 destroyed many of the trees of that garden, which the Lord Keeper Guilford declared to be "most *boscareque*," and an exemplification of its owner's work on forest trees. The plague, in 1695-6, carried off hundreds of Evelyn's neighbours in Deptford; but frost and plague were less injurious than the vulgar, dirty, clever Czar Peter, called the *great*. Evelyn, with the liberality of a true Briton, lent Sayes Court to Peter whilst he prosecuted his naval studies at Deptford Dockyard. One can easily imagine the result: Peter neither felt the delicacy of the compliment, nor respected the sylvan beauties of the place. Amongst one of Evelyn's sources of innocent pride was a holly hedge: he speaks of it in his Sylva. Now a holly hedge was the darling *chef-d'œuvre* of old-fashioned gardeners, and the boast of many a land-owner. That on which Evelyn prided himself was, as he says, "an impregnable hedge of holly, 400 feet in length, nine feet high, and five feet in diameter." Nothing, however, was impregnable to a low-minded barbarian who treated all men beneath him as slaves, and consequently one of the Czar's favourite diversions at Sayes Court was to drive through this hedge with a wheelbarrow. The rest of the gardens he utterly ruined; and so much injury was done altogether to the house and grounds, that Evelyn had 150*l.* a year allowed him in compensation.

In 1704, when Evelyn published a later edition of his Sylva, he says, with melancholy triumph:—

"I can still show in my now ruined garden at Sayes Court (thanks to the Czar of Muscovy), at any time of the year, glittering with its armed and varnished leaves, the taller standards, at orderly distances, blushing with their natural coral. It mocks the rudest assaults of the weather, beasts, or hedge-breakers."

Alas for the pleasant days of Sayes Court! days when the

clear Thames that laved Deptford, glided down and flowed pure and inodorous through the Royal Dock, bore on its pellucid bosom gaily decked barges, full of gay dames and cavaliers, or with a graver freight of philosophers, to visit Sylva Evelyn, as he was called. Alas for the days when, amid great and small, Samuel Pepys never "met with so merry a two hours in all his life," as there, on one occasion, with Sir J. Minnes and "Mr. Evelyn." "Among other humours Mr. Evelyn repeating of some verses made up of nothing but the various acceptations of *may* and *can*, and doing it so aptly" and so fast that he "did make us all die of laughing." Those were long, quiet, sunny afternoons when Evelyn used to show Pepys his gardens, "which, for variety of evergreens and hedge of holly," were the finest Pepys ever saw; and "thence in his coach to Greenwich, Evelyn all the way having fine discourse of trees and the nature of vegetables," until Pepys, leaving him, "renewed his promises of observing his vows as he used to do, and not let his mind go a wool-gathering," and his business be neglected: so far for the impressions made by good society and good example. Even whilst the plague raged, and people were frightening Pepys to death, by sending to him "for plaisters and fume," Evelyn's mind soared above all sublunary troubles; and, in the midst of a pestilence so near, his usual occupations cheered and interested him: — who can tell it so well as Pepys?

"By water to Deptford, and there made a visit to Mr. Evelyn, who, among other things, showed me a most excellent painting in little, in distemper, in Indian incke, water colours, gravening, and, above all, the whole secret of mezzo-tinto, and the manner of it, which is very pretty, and good things done with it. He read to me also much of his discourse he hath been many years, and now is, about gardenage; which will be a most noble and pleasant piece. He read me part of a play or two of his making, very good, but not as he conceits them to be."

At Sayes Court Evelyn lived as long and as serenely as the times would permit. Happy in the society of a wife of a congenial spirit to his own,— an accomplished companion, fond of etching and painting, yet neglecting none of the duties of the head of a family; of a wife, and a mother,— his felicity seems to have been as complete as any of which human nature is capable. It was perfected by friendships not founded on worldly motives, nor impaired by caprice, but engrafted on minds as holy, as pure, as generous as ever adorned what may, in one sense, be termed the "halcyon age of England." The vices that were so rife in the time of Charles II. had been checked in that of his father.

Evelyn doubtless regretted that, with all his gifts of nature and fortune, his friend Boyle could not enjoy the delights of a requited affection and the comforts of matrimony. But Boyle, in his works, exalted the power of reason far above the potency of love — which, notwithstanding the hint thrown out by Evelyn, he always declared he had never felt. It was not, however, that he undervalued the sanctity, or was ignorant of the blessings of marriage, which he considered to be a "legal exchange of hearts," but he advocated, on this and every point, the stern ascendency of reason over feeling. Thus he advanced a position that is heresy to the impassioned— namely, that "Reason is born the sovereign of the passions" —and possibly he found no difficulty in following out that axiom, for a life passed in abstract science is not favourable to sentiment. His books were his friends, his chemical apparatus his company, and the mind thus occupied had no space for love. One gentle sentiment, however, accompanied by a thousand traits of feeling and benevolence, softens this hard creed: at one time a report having been raised that Boyle was actually married, he wrote to his niece, Lady Barrymore, disclaiming the charge, and declaring that the supposed marriage had been celebrated by no priest but Fame, and made unknown to the supposed bridegroom.

"I shall therefore," he adds, "only tell you that I and the little gentleman are still at the old defiance." "But though this untamed heart be thus insensible to the thing itself called love, it is yet very sensible to things very near of kin to that passion; and esteem, friendship, respect, and even admiration, are things that their proper objects fail not proportionately to exact of one."

It was Evelyn's love of nature, that produced the friendship which had so much more of heavenly hope and Christian fervour in it than what worldly men call friendship. For that Boyle sought out Evelyn. They were in habits and constitution dissimilar. Boyle, in spite of his father's early attempts to fortify his temperament by the process of hardening, was always a fragile, sensitive valetudinarian; with such a feebleness of body, as Dr. Birch tell us, and such a "lowness of spirits and strength, that it was wonderful how he could read, experimentalise, and think as he did." Never did he quit the house without trying on "divers kind of cloaks," and, judging by his thermometer which to put on, according to the temperature of the weather. He never lost the habit of hesitating rather than of stammering, until warmed with conversation. Then he had a weakness in his eyes which made him fearful of blindness: still worse, at a very early age he became a martyr to a cruel disease, the sufferings of which were such as even to weigh down a mind like his, heroic in its Christian patience. This skeleton in the closet,—more terrific because the alleviations now in practice were not then even dreamed of; this mortal agony of agonies which prostrated even the stout-hearted Robert Hall to the very depths of despondency,—was the source of all Boyle's extreme care of his health. "As to life itself," he had, observes Dr. Birch, "that just indifference to it that became so true a Christian." But it is the will of our heavenly Father that certain trials should be the lot of the wisest and best of His creatures; and, generally, studious men of sedentary habits are the most frequent martyrs to that which haunted Robert Boyle's thoughts during his whole life. "He imagined also," says Dr. Birch, "that if sickness should confine him to his bed, it might raise the pains of the stone to a degree which might be above his strength to support it; so that he feared *lest* his *last moments* should prove too hard for him." Poor Boyle! that horrible dread vanished as his spirit neared death; and the shadow of death brought ease and peace; and the torment that he feared might rouse his expiring soul to murmur, was averted.

Hence, however, his simple diet, so guarded that for thirty years he never ate "nor drank to gratify the varieties of appetite, but only to support nature," was begun; nor did he ever transgress that rule.

Evelyn, on the other hand, was so blest by fate, that during forty years he never once kept his bed; and when, at eighty-six, he died, death seemed as a rest to exhausted nature.

In all the minor affairs of life, these two celebrated friends differed also. Boyle, in clothes, in furniture, in his house and equipage, was plain and unaffected; and his mode of life was consistent with his serious pursuits and grave character.

Evelyn, on the other hand, maintained state and show; his house at Sayes Court, though the rooms were low, was richly furnished; and Wotton was, as it still is, a stately and noble seat, which he greatly embellished; whilst Boyle lived chiefly, either with his sister, Lady Ranelagh, in Pall Mall, or in lodgings at Oxford, or in what he calls his poor "Cottage at Stalsbridge," the domain of which was large, but much encumbered, owing to the times, and the injury done during the Rebellion to all property. In other points they presented contrasts. Boyle was a man of the truest humility and candour. Evelyn, if we are to believe Pepys, was allowed to display a "little conceitedness." Boyle, in spite of a "choleric constitution," which he mastered, was never in his whole life known to have offended any one by his deportment. His manner of differing showed that he had the greatness to be open to conviction. In common with Evelyn he had large sympathies, and "had all the tenderness of good nature, as well as all the softness of friendship." If he had not the unwearied good spirits of Evelyn, he could break forth at times into a long vein of wit, in the flow of which Cowley and Davenant considered him unrivalled.

On one all-important point the hearts of these two men were in perfect unison. Both were devoted members of the Church of England: both stood aloof, therefore — for the spirit of our Church is that of toleration — as well from bigotry as from acquiescence in persecution, even if only of that sort which infringes on the liberty of society. Both were deeply reverent to Him whom we ought, as the Apostle says, "to sanctify in our hearts." Speaking of Robert Boyle, his biographer says*:—

"He had so profound a veneration for the Deity, that the very name of God was never mentioned by him without a pause and a visible stop in his discourse, in which Sir Peter Pett, who knew him for almost forty years, affirms that he was so exact, that he does not remember to have observed him once to fail in it. He was very constant and serious in his secret addresses to God; and it appears to those who conversed with him most in his inquiries into nature, that his main design in that, on which as he had his eye most constantly, so he took care to put others often in mind of it, was to raise in himself and others more elevated thoughts of the greatness and glory, and of the wisdom and goodness, of the Deity."

But, although charitable to all sects, Boyle deemed it unadvisable, if not wrong, to frequent the meetings of the Separatists; and on one occasion only did he swerve from that rule. He had once the curiosity to go to Sir Harry Vane's, and there

---

* Birch's Life of Boyle, p. 291.

to hear that singular man preach a long sermon to show that "many doctrines of religion that had long been dead and buried in the world, should, before the end of it, be awakened into life; and that many false doctrines being then likewise revived, should by the power of truth be *doomed to shame and everlasting contempt.*"

Boyle listened in deep disapproval; the text from which Vane had preached was taken from Daniel xii. 2: "And many of them that sleep in the dust of the earth shall awake, some to everlasting life, some to shame and everlasting contempt." Boyle looked around him, and saw in that assembly, chiefly, if not entirely, creatures whose very existence depended on Sir Harry Vane, of whom Bishop Burnet has said that "he had a head as darkened in its notions of religion as his mind was clouded with fear." Vane had set up a religion of his own; it consisted chiefly of an antipathy to all forms, and a hatred to the Anglican Church. Searching always after truth, yet encumbered with the gloomiest superstitions, Vane's disciples were called "*Seekers.*" Often did Sir Harry, in the midst of these dismal fanatics, preach and pray; yet, says Bishop Burnet, "with so peculiar adroitness, that though I have sometimes taken pains to see if I could find out his meaning in his words, yet I never could reach it." Some mysterious meaning was a key to the rest. With Origen, Vane leaned to the idea that even the devils and the damned should be saved, and he believed in the doctrine of pre-existence.

It must have startled the rapt, subservient "Seekers," when a tall form, that seemed as if it lingered on the very threshold of the grave, stood up, and, stretching forth an emaciated hand, in hesitating, nervous tones, claimed attention. The interruption was pardoned; for the wan, pensive, yet kindly face of Robert Boyle was turned on the congregation, and even then the fame of his youthful piety, of his learning, of his large charities and Christian forbearance, drew all respect towards him.

Then he spoke. He who could attack Sir Harry Vane was a bold champion for the faith; for Vane was noted for his pleasant wit, his quick conception, his great understanding, and his profound dissimulation.

It was the philosopher, fresh from his study, assailing the shrewd man of the world, covered with a shield of dissimulation; yet Boyle spoke: "I thought myself," he said, "bound to enter the lists with him, that the Scriptures should not be depraved." The argument that followed is thus stated * : —

Mr. Boyle said, that being informed that in these private meetings it was not unusual for any one of those present to state objections to any matters there uttered, he "thought himself obliged, for the honour of God's truth, to say that this place in Daniel, being the clearest one in all the Old Testament for the proof of the resurrection, we ought not to suffer the meaning of it to evaporate into allegory; and the rather, since that inference is made by our Saviour in the New Testament by way of asserting the resurrection from that place of Daniel in the Old. And that if it should be denied, that the plain and genuine meaning of those words in the prophet is to assert the resurrection of dead bodies, he was ready to prove it to be so, both out of the words of the text and context in the original language, and from the best expositors, both Christians and Jews. If, however," he added, "Sir Henry's observations on the resurrection were only by way of occasional meditation on these words of Daniel, and not to weaken the general sense, then he had nothing more to say."

On this Sir Henry rose and said, "His reflections were only in the way of occasional meditation, and that he agreed that the literal sense of the words was the resurrection of dead bodies." It was manifest that Sir Henry Vane inspired those

* Birch's Life of Boyle, p. 296.

around him with awe, owing to his great authority in the state. But Mr. Boyle thought it his duty to enter the lists with him, to prevent false interpretation.

Evelyn, meantime, was engaged in the more active cares of life, a preference to which he had advocated in his essay on Public Employment, in answer to Sir George Mackenzie's panegyric on Solitude. Still loyal to his sovereign, Charles II., he had, nevertheless, intimate friends among those who adhered to Cromwell; yet he wrote in favour of the royal party, and, after the Restoration, appeared often at court. It was in these serener times that he published his "French Gardeners," to which was added the English Vineyards Vindicated, by John Rose, gardener to Charles II., "with a tract of the making and ordering of French wine." Then amidst Evelyn's innumerable efforts for the improvement of social science, was a new instrument for ploughing, and sowing all sorts of grain, and harrowing at once, called the "Spanish Sembrador;" the description being a translation from the Spanish. Next came his "Pomona," or treatise on fruits, and after that his famous "Sylva," on forest trees; the one, it is said, having produced numberless orchards;— the other raised whole forests.

Evelyn, during the Commonwealth, passed, nevertheless, a dreary time. Christmas observances were forbidden under penalties, any offices of the Church being contrary to law on that day. Sometimes he was afflicted at seeing a preacher, who had been at the same time chaplain and lieutenant to Admiral Penn,—"using both swords,"— stand up in the pulpit whence the orthodox clergyman was driven. In private Evelyn received the Communion from some sequestrated divine, until, by the greatest possible good fortune, he was able to consider Jeremy Taylor henceforth as "his ghostly father." In visits to various noblemen's houses, chiefly with a view to the works of art contained in them; in visits to his "own sweet and native county;" in visits to Cambridge and Oxford, and in his almost endless variety of pursuits, a melancholy period, ended by perhaps one of disappointment, glided away. One incident marked the year 1655.

"I went to London," Evelyn writes, "where Dr. Wild preached the funeral sermon of Preaching, this being the last day; after which Cromwell's proclamation was to take place, that none of the Church of England should dare either to preach or administer sacraments, teach school, &c., on pain of imprisonment or exile. So this was the mournfullest day that in my life I had ever seen, or the Church of England herself, since the Reformation, to the great rejoicing of both Papists and Presbyters."* But there was good to come out of these evil times. Dr. Wilkins, afterwards Bishop of Chester, had married the sister of Cromwell. He took great pains to protect the Universities from the sacrilegious hands of Cromwell's soldiers; and he courted the society and friendship of those two illustrious friends, whose virtues then shone out so conspicuously.

Sayes Court became henceforth the centre of all that was graceful, good, enlightened, and pious. There the beautiful countenance of Jeremy Taylor might be seen, lighted up with a religious fervour (which had once well nigh settled into Romanism), as in secret and sorrow he read the prayers of the Church, or preached one of his incomparable sermons in the silence of the night, with closed doors and hushed voices breaking out in murmurs of praise that dared not express itself in hymns.

There Jeremy Taylor,— he who had the "good humour of a gentleman, the eloquence of an orator, the fancy of a poet, the acuteness of a schoolman, the profoundness of a philosopher, the wisdom of a chancellor, the sagacity of a prophet, the reason of an angel, the piety of a saint;"—there, in those low but ornamented rooms, in that choice library, he

* Diary, vol. 1. p. 311

found a welcome and balm to a wounded spirit. For not only had Taylor wept the doom of his royal master, Charles I., to whom he was chaplain, but he had witnessed the fall of the Church, and had sorrowed over the grave of his children. There he might find illustrations for his divine sermon, the Marriage Ring, as he looked at Evelyn and his faithful, congenial wife;—he, planning and executing numberless works: she, knowing the best way to a husband's heart, by joining in his pursuits,—illustrating some of these works by her etchings. There Robert Boyle admires, with Dr. Wilkins, Evelyn's rare burning glass; there, too, Dr. Taylor "falls to disputing in Latin with a young French proselyte to Protestantism, Le Fane," on Original Sin; that young Sorbonnist being afterwards ordained both deacon and priest by the Bishop of Meath, to whom Evelyn paid the fees, his lordship being, like most of his persecuted brethren, "very poor and in want."

How varied is the scene on a river's brink! One day, an infinite concourse of people is attracted to Sayes Court, to see a whale taken close to Evelyn's land; a creature fifty-eight feet long and sixteen high, yet the throat so narrow that it could not have admitted the least of fishes. Bishops, parsons, philosophers, and the host of Sayes Court, probably enjoyed the strange sight when the whale, after a long conflict, was killed with a harping iron.

But the sounds of sorrow are heard in that once peaceful home:—Evelyn's little son Michael, a prodigy "for beauty of body—a very angel," is the bereaved father's heart-stricken expression—"of incredible and rare hopes,"—he is taken. A quartan ague—who can wonder, at Deptford?—carries him off after six fits of that scourge which ravaged England before the word *sanitary* became practical. There was little hope for the child; for the peril of a too cultivated intellect made the sickness mortal. Not only could he, before he was five years old, exhibit a "strong passion for Greek," but once, "seeing a Plautus in one's hand, he asked what book it was, and being told it was comedy, and too difficult for him, wept with sorrow." "He declaimed against the vanities of the world before he had seen any," adds the sorrowing parent. The following touching account is related by that father of the last hours of his precocious child:—

"The day before he died, he called to me, and, in a more serious manner than usual, told me that, for all I loved him so dearly, I should give all my house, land, and all my fine things to his brother Jack, he should have none of them; and next morning, when he found himself ill, and that I persuaded him to keep his hands in bed, he demanded whether he might pray to God with his hands unjoined; and a little after, whilst in great agony, whether he should not offend God by using His holy name so often calling for Him."

"Here," exclaims the sorrowing Evelyn, "ends the joy of my life, and for which I go even mourning to the grave."

Yet he *did* recover the loss, and learned that there is scarcely any calamity that *cannot* be recovered. The next year we find him going to see the superb funeral of the Protector "Oliver, lying in effigy in royal robes, and crowned with a crown, sceptre, and globe like a king." In this style, the usurper was carried on a velvet bed in state from Somerset House to Westminster; drawn by six horses in velvet trappings, and followed by his guards, soldiers, and innumerable mourners. It was the "joyfullest" funeral Evelyn ever saw; "for there were not that cried save the dogs, which the soldiers hooted away with a barbarous noise, taking tobacco and drinking, as they marched through the streets."

A change on "the face of the public" is now observable. Richard the Protector is slighted; parties and pretenders strive for the government. "Lord have mercy on us!" was Evelyn's ejaculation. Fasts were kept in private by the Orthodox Churchmen for the good of the nation; and, during all this confusion, Monk, marching to Whitehall, "dissipates that nest of robbers," as he calls the pretenders to power, and convenes a Parliament — the Rump Parliament being dissolved. Whilst this crisis was at its height, the design of the Royal Society was first started.

"I communicated," Evelyn writes * (September 1st, 1659), "to Mr. Robert, son to the Earl of Cork, my proposal for erecting a philosophic and mathematical college."

In 1646–7 we find Robert Boyle writing to Mr. Francis Tallents, Fellow of Magdalen College, Cambridge,—from that "labyrinth, London," as he (even then) calls it — about the "*Invisible*" or Philosophic College. This society consisted of "learned and curious gentlemen," who, as Dr Birch relates, "after the breaking out of the civil wars, in order to divert themselves from those melancholy scenes, applied themselves to experimental inquiries."

The meetings were at first held in the house of Dr. Goddard, a physician; his abode being selected on account of his keeping an operator in his house for grinding glasses for telescopes and microscopes; sometimes in Gresham College; sometimes in Cheapside. All matters of theology and state-affairs were prohibited: a necessary precaution where Dr. Wilkins, Cromwell's brother-in-law, was one of the "corner stones." In the year 1648–9, some of the *Invisibles* went to Oxford, some remained in London. Boyle was then resident in Oxford, and the Society often met at his house; and often, also, at an apothecary's house, in which Dr. Petty, an eminent physician, then lodged, for the convenience "of inspecting drugs and the like." Oxford was, indeed, the only place where Boyle could prosecute his experiments in quiet, and with success. Fortunately there was a liberal spirit in Dr. Wilkins: there were several eminent professors and heads of houses, who "were certain," as Dr. Birch affirms, "that there was no certain way of arriving at any competent know-

* Evelyn's Diary, vol. i. p. 325.

ledge, unless they should make a variety of experiments upon natural bodies, in order to discover what phenomena they would produce."

Amongst the *corner-stones* was Christopher Wren, then a Fellow of All Souls.

It was during Boyle's residence at Oxford that he invented the air-pump. This admirable engine was perfected for him in 1658 or 1659 by Robert Hooke, a physician, who lived with Boyle. By the air-pump Boyle was able to form a just theory of the air, and to leave materials for future ages to build upon. Until the rise of the Royal Society, there had been no communion of interests among scientific men in Europe. What men had hitherto performed, they had worked out alone, rather by abstract reasoning than by experiments. The philosophy of Des Cartes, how fallacious soever it may be deemed, had infused a spirit of inquiry into the scientific world; and a disposition to think freely concerning natural objects, had spread from the Continent into England.

It is impossible, in this account of the friendship of two men eminently useful not only to their own generation but to ours, to enter adequately into their various works and discoveries. "The gentleman, the merchant, and the mechanic," writes one of Boyle's biographers, "are all obliged to him for several useful discoveries, which must render his memory dear to posterity." Yet Boyle, with the modesty inherent to a great mind, declared "that he had only drawn the outline of science, and charged posterity to consider all his writings as so many imperfect sketches."

Boyle's incessant labours were varied only by his occasional residence with his sister, Lady Ranelagh, in Pall Mall. It was on his return from his travels that he had first taken up his residence in the house of this sister; and to that circumstance he used thankfully to refer much of his happiness in life, much of his safety in those unsettled and corrupting times.

A strange medley of characters inhabited the "Pavement," as one side of the street of Pall Mall was then called. What had only been originally the place chosen in the time of Charles I. for the game of *Paille Maille,* was in the reign of his son the centre of fashion. Here dwelt two mistresses of Charles II., Madam Kingal, the singer, and Madam Elinor Gwyn; whose gardens behind, as well as those of the other residents, contained a mount, from which Nell could look into the King's garden, and hold converse with her royal paramour. Nevertheless, Lady Ranelagh, remarkable for her genius, her knowledge, and her piety, lived next door to this merry, lost creature; and Dr. Isaac Barrow, the divine, not far from her. Sydenham, the celebrated physician, had a house in the "Pavement:" he was the intimate friend and associate of Boyle. Certainly the moral sense was broken down in those days, even in the minds of the strictly virtuous, when Lady Ranelagh could endure to hear Charles II. holding a "very familiar discourse," as Evelyn terms it, with Nell Gwyn, before the very next door to her ladyship's well-ordered house; the virtuous Evelyn walking in the mean time with the King, whilst Nell looked out of her garden from the terrace near the wall, the King standing on the green walk beneath it. Evelyn a spectator of the whole, and then, "though heartily sorry at the scene," witnessing his Majesty's progress to the Duchess of Cleveland's, whom he, however, justly and indignantly terms "another lady of pleasure, and curse of our nation."

Boyle, meantime, was impervious to all attempts to withdraw him from his life of studious celibacy. In 1696, an overture was made to him respecting the Lady Mary Hastings, sister of the Earl of Huntingdon, a lady of admirable temper, of great understanding, and endowed with every quality desirable in a wife; but he refused the offer at once.

Evelyn, on the contrary, was passing his days in all that the gay and dilettante world could offer of amusement as well as instruction. Prince Rupert taught him mezzotint with his own hands: after his lessons forth goes the author of the Sylva "to take the air" in Hyde Park, where his Majesty and innumerable "gallants and rich cavaliers" paraded the ring. Then, one day, Mistress Evelyn presents to the King her copy of Peter Oliver's painting after Raphael of the Madonna, which she had "wrought with extraordinary pains and judgment:" next day, off goes her helpmate, that lover of plants, to see the famous Queen Pine, brought from Barbadoes, a present to his Majesty; remarking, at the same time, "that the first pines ever seen in England were those sent four years since to Cromwell."

Next, "to Mr. Palmer's in Gray's Inn," to hear tunes played on extraordinary clocks, that required winding up only once a quarter. Then Evelyn sails with his Majesty in one of his yachts, vessels only lately known amongst them; the King sometimes showing himself, sometimes talking to Evelyn about his book on the nuisance of smoke in London, which Evelyn had dedicated to him; his Majesty, the most charming of agreeable men, breaking off to deplore how rare the improvement of gardens was in England compared with other countries, or asking particulars of the bloody encounter at the Tower between the French and Spanish ambassadors in a contest for precedency. Then, again, at Whitehall, the King cannot let Evelyn go away one evening without calling him back into the royal closet, and showing him some ivory statues, and things Evelyn had not seen before. All these pleasant incidents were perpetually interspersed by inquiries from the King how the Philosophic Society got on, and talking about "the planet Saturn," &c., as he sat at supper "in the withdrawing-room to his bed-chamber." On the 18th September, 1661, the crowning point was put to the success of the heretofore "Invisible Society;" and a petition was read before the

King praying him to authorise it to meet as a corporation. What a melancholy contrast does the following scene present!

"This evening, according to custom," writes Evelyn, "his Majesty went to London, and opened the revels of that night by throwing the dice himself in the privy chambers, where was a table set on purpose, and lost his 100*l*. (the year before he won 1500*l*.) The ladies also played very deep. I came away when the Duke of Ormond had won about 1000*l*., and left them still at passage, cards, &c."

Not all the solemn fasts that were held so frequently in those days could wipe out or repair the injury done by such an example. The Duke of York visits Sayes Court, however, "my poor habitation and gardens," and looks over the great and curious collection: then off he and his host go to an East India vessel that lay at Blackwall; whence Evelyn returns to London with his Highness — but comes home "to be private a little, not at all affecting the life and hurry of a court."

Little touches of sadness are interposed between the annals of the busy, prosperous life of a flattered favourite of the court and public.

"This night," Evelyn relates, "was buried in Westminster Abbey the Queen of Bohemia, after all her sorrows and afflictions being come to die in the arms of her nephew, the King; also this night and the next day fell such a storm of hail, thunder, and lightning, as never was seen the like in any man's memory." Amid all the demoralisation of Whitehall, Evelyn appears never to have waived his higher duties for the sake of mere sublunary considerations, — never to have forgotten his responsibility as a Christian. It is difficult to imagine how he could reconcile the nicety of his principles to the impurity of what he saw and heard; but so it was. We know that some men do live in the world, without being *of* the world; and Evelyn may have felt that, to carry out schemes for the public benefit, court favour must be maintained. He seems, also, to have felt for the Stuarts that personal liking with which even the most reprehensible of that family inspired their followers. The visits to Whitehall were not so frequent as to interrupt the devotion which Evelyn paid to art, his love for which filled up the hours of his active existence. His first appointment to a public office was in 1662, when he was made commissioner for reforming "the buildings, ways, streets, and incumbrances," and regulating hackney coaches in London. No man could have been better suited to the task. He sat also on a commission of inquiry concerning the Gresham charities; on another, for regulating the Mint: but that which most engaged his attention and interested his feelings, was a commission for the care of the sick and wounded in the Dutch war.

His son, John Evelyn, who at fifteen years of age was honourably distinguished as the author of an elegant Greek poem prefixed to the Sylva, had been placed under the tuition of Edward Phillips, the nephew of Milton, who, though brought up by the great poet, was not, as Evelyn relates, "at all infected by his principles." This son grew up, and was imbued with all Evelyn's tastes and pursuits; but died in his father's lifetime. It was the son of this John Evelyn who built the beautiful library at Wotton for the reception of the books collected by his father, his grandfather, and himself; for the spirit of Sylva Evelyn was not extinct with his life, and his descendants were worthy of the name they bore. Evelyn had another trial still more poignant than the death of this son; for when *he* was taken Evelyn was so near the end of his pilgrimage as to render the separation less afflicting. His eldest daughter, Mary, died many years before her brother of the small-pox, at the age of nineteen. "The attack soon," writes her father, "left no hope of her recovery: a great affliction to me, but God's will be done!" This young creature, endowed with many natural gifts — beautiful, graceful, intellectual — resigned herself to death with the fortitude of a noble and purified spirit. Evelyn speaks with pride of her accomplishments, especially of her singing, which "charmed a large assembly at Lord Arundel's, of Wardour:"— of her knowledge of languages, even of her dancing; in which she excelled, " dancing with the greatest grace he ever saw,"—" and so said Monsieur Isaac, her master,"—of her talents for acting, and repeating poetry. With a deeper sentiment he speaks of her great piety, and solidity of mind : but there is one touch of pathos which must come home to every parent who has lost his child, the companion of his studious hours; who sees in fancy in the vacant chair the image that will never more meet his eye; who hears, in bitter remembrance, the voice or the footstep of one gone to another home; and who feels that vacant spot, that void and silent room, can never more be filled as it was wont; but that the void, the silence, will be not only to the eye and ear, but to the desolate, bereaved heart evermore.

"Nothing was so delightful to her as to go into my study, where she would willingly have spent whole days; for, as I said, she had read abundance of history, and all the best poets; even Terence, Plautus, Homer, Virgil, Horace, Ovid; all the best romances and modern poems. She could compose happily." *

" O dear, sweet, and desirable child," he thus breaks out, " how shall I part with all this goodness and virtue without the bitterness of sorrow and reluctancy of a tender parent? Thy affection, duty, and love to me was that of a friend as well as a child." †

Then, after the manner of parents, poor Evelyn goes into the circumstances which seem to have contributed to bring down on him this great sorrow.

Mary Evelyn had dreaded the small-pox, and that dread had exposed her to the greater peril, whilst staying with Lady Falkland and in all the full career of the gaieties of the court and capital. But in the midst of every earthly enjoyment

* Evelyn's Diary, vol. ii. p. 215.   † Ibid.

her heart was with God. Four gentlemen of quality, as her proud father relates, were in treaty for her hand in marriage, but she declined them. "Were I," she said to her parents, "assured of your and my father's life, never would I part from you." Well might Evelyn say, "Precious is the memorial of the just." "Never can I say enough, oh dear, my dear child, whose memory is so precious to me!" "Thus lived, and died, and was buried, the joy of my life and ornament of her sex, and of my poor family."

Mary Evelyn was buried at Deptford. Many great and good mourners listened, with tears, to the funeral sermon by Dr. Holden, in which her virtues were enumerated:—her parents not having the courage to be present. Her mother added to this heart-stricken account the simple words, "How to express the sorrow for parting with so dear a child is a difficult task." "The seventh day of her illness she discoursed to me in particular as calmly as in health; desired to confess, and to receive the Holy Sacrament, which she performed with great devotion; after which, though in her perfect senses to the last, she never signified the least concern for the world, prayed often, and resigned her soul. What shall I say? She was too great a blessing for me, who never deserved anything, still less such a jewel."

From such calamities Robert Boyle seemed exempt; but sorrows are the conditions of our lives, and his came in another form, and with a poignancy under which his strength succumbed.

It was ordained that Robert Boyle, though several years younger than Evelyn, should predecease him fourteen years. Towards the year 1691 the great philosopher and Christian benefactor of his time found it essential to put forth a sort of circular to his friends, warning them that his health no longer enabled him to receive casual visitors, to whom he had hitherto been accustomed to open his doors in the afternoons, even allowing them to come into his laboratory. Forty-six years previously he had complained to his sister, Lady Ranelagh, "of the busy idleness of receiving senseless visits," which, he thought, "might justify the retiredness of a hermit;" he now alleged also another reason for his retreat from daily interruption. Many of his papers, he stated, had been "corroded, here and there, or otherwise maimed;" so that he must, to make them intelligible, restore the lost passages. His age and sickness, he added, admonished him to put his writings into order, that they might not be quite useless; whilst his friend and physician, Sir Edward King, advised him not to talk daily with so many persons, as inducing him to sit too much, and therefore to add to his complaint in the kidneys. He therefore desired to be excused from receiving visits two days in the week, namely, on the forenoons of Tuesdays and Fridays, and on the afternoons of Wednesdays and Saturdays, that he "may have some time both to recruit his spirits, to range his papers, and to take some care of his affairs in Ireland." His health, however, continued to decline; he therefore determined upon making his last will, which he sealed and signed in July 1691.

He now suffered from a decay in his sight: when he looked at distant objects a thin mist seemed to be before them; "these apparitions," as he termed them, disturbed him greatly. On the 23rd of December that year, Lady Ranelagh died. She had lived longer on the public scene, and had been more conspicuous during all the revolutions of our country during the previous fifty years, than any woman of her time. She had twice, during the convulsions in Irish affairs, lost all she had; but she rose nobly above her own distresses, and was the general intercessor for all in want or sorrow. Her time, her interest, her property, were employed in doing good. No party considerations ever deterred her from extending her beneficence to any object, of any creed, of any politics. Her knowledge was vast, her affability, her humility still greater. She had the deepest sense of religion, and to God was her heart continually turned. "Such a sister became such a brother," said Bishop Burnet, in his funeral sermon on Robert Boyle; "and it was but suitable to both their characters that they should have improved the relation under which they were born, to the more exalted and endearing one of friend." Her brother survived her a week only. They lived together forty years in the bonds of an affection ennobled by a community of interests for the benefit of the world. He expired on the 30th of December, 1691, at three-quarters of an hour past twelve in the night; the brother and sister were buried in the same grave, and the chancel of St. Martin's-in-the-Fields holds their honoured dust. Boyle was in the sixty-fifth year of his age at his death. It was remarkable that Boyle was born the same year in which Bacon died.

Boerhaave, after declaring Boyle to be the father of experimental philosophy, adds these words: "Which of his writings shall I recommend? All of them. To him we owe the secrets of fire, air, water, animals, vegetables, fossils; so that from his works may be deduced the whole system of natural knowledge."

Destined, as it seemed, to succeed to the labours and inquiries of Lord Bacon, Boyle applied experimental philosophy to every branch of science. The world he regarded, not as a "rude heap of dull inactive matter," but, as Dr. Shaw tells us, "as a grand and noble machine, continually actuated, informed, and governed by a most wise and beneficent Being, who keeps all the parts thereof in motion, and makes them act one upon another, according to certain laws." "Too wise to set bounds to nature," this great man was never prone to say that everything strange must be impossible; he thought that all we have to do is "to keep our eyes open, and expect what nature and art will, upon due application, perform." [*] He possessed that noble faculty of suspending his judgment on any point until he had dispas-

---

[*] Birch's Life of Robert Boyle, p. 309.

sionately and fully considered any specified question, and gained the fullest information respecting it.

Candid, generous, accessible, it was his endeavour to render all things easy and familiar to others. "His soul," writes Dr. Shaw, "was as great and noble as his genius was comprehensive, or his invention fruitful."

Evelyn records Boyle's death as that of a pious, admirable Christian, excellent philosopher, and "his worthy friend." After repeating a few of the qualities upon which Bishop Burnet touched in his funeral sermon, he adds, "And truly all this was but his due, without any grain of flattery." Evelyn was made one of Boyle's trustees for his charitable bequests, which amounted to 8000$l.$; and upon consulting with the other trustees, Dr. Bentley, the great scholar and critic, and afterwards Master of Trinity College, Cambridge, was appointed to preach the first Boylean Lecture at St. Mary-le-Bow, against Atheists, Jews, Deists, and Socinians. The discourse was pronounced by Evelyn to be one of the most learned and convincing that he had ever heard.

Evelyn's life was prolonged until he had attained his eighty-sixth year. In 1697, we find him at Wotton, where he retired on the invitation of his brother, his circumstances rendering it, he says, desirable for him to accept that friendly proposal. His eldest son John was now ill of the malady under which he eventually succumbed; but Evelyn's interests seem to have been strongly attracted towards his grandson, for whom he was forming the library at Wotton. Sayes Court having been recently newly furnished by the King for Peter the Great, Wotton was made the deposit of many valuables.

"My grandson," he writes, "is so delighted in books, that he professes a library is to him the greatest recreation, and I give him free scope here, where I have near upon 22,000, with my brother's, and I would bring the rest had I any room, which I have not to my great regret, having here so little conversation with the learned, unless it be when Mr. Wotton (the learned gentleman before mentioned, the friend of Dr. Bentley) comes now and then to visit me, he being tutor to Mr. Finch's son at Albury."

His love for evergreens continued.

"For the rest," he adds, "I am planting an evergreen grove here to an old house ready to drop, the economy and hospitality of which my good old brother will not depart from; but — *more veterum* — kept a Christmas, in which we had not fewer than three hundred bumpkins every holy day."

Then he gives a cheerful picture of an intellectual and domestic old age, in the following sentences: —

" We have here a very convenient apartment of five rooms together, besides a pretty closet which we have furnished with the spoils of Sayes Court, and is the raree-show of the whole neighbourhood; and in truth we live easy as to all domestic cares. Wednesday and Saturday nights we call lecture nights, when my wife and myself take our turns to read the packets of all the news sent constantly from London, which serves us for discourse till fresh news comes."

In all his bereavements, in the death of several children, the marriage of his daughter Susanna proved a consolation. Resembling her mother in the direction of her hereditary talents, Susanna was an accomplished painter in oil. She was "discreet, ingenious, religious," and, according to her partial father, exquisitely shaped, and of an agreeable countenance. "This marriage proved," Evelyn adds, "in all respects to my daughter's and our hearts' desires." Her husband, Mr. Draper, proved a most deserving person, and they were among the happiest pairs in England; and she and her husband lived with her mother-in-law, " kept each their coach, and with as suitable an equipage as any in town."

Happy as he was at Wotton — soon to be his — Evelyn must have experienced some vexation when such accounts as these, of his former home reached him in a letter from his servant:—

"There is a house full of people, and right nasty. The Czar lies next your library, and dines in the parlour next your study. He dines at ten o'clock and six at night, is very seldom at home a whole day, very often in the King's Yard, or by water, dressed in several dresses. The King is expected here to-day. The best parlour is pretty clean for him to be entertained in. The King pays for all he has." *

On the 24th March 1699, Evelyn's only remaining son died about the age of forty-four, leaving only to the bereaved Evelyn family, to keep up the name and reputation of Wotton, a son then at Oxford, afterwards created a baronet, and long respected as Sir John Evelyn. In the October of the same year, Evelyn's elder brother George died, and Wotton became the property of the author of the "Sylva." The funeral of George Evelyn was conducted upon a scale of extraordinary magnificence, about two thousand persons attending it. On the 31st of October 1703, John Evelyn gratefully recorded his eighty-first birthday. "I find," he writes, "by many infirmities this year (especially nephritic pains), that I much decline, and yet, of God's infinite mercy, retain my intellects and senses in great measure above most of my age." †

He still went into the world, still delighted in gardens, carvings, pictures, statues, and even in jewellery. In his eighty-fourth year, he records how, visiting the Lord Treasurer Godolphin, he met the Duke of Marlborough, who took him by the hand with extraordinary "familiarity and civility," though Evelyn believed he might have forgotten him. "The great general had on a most rich George as a sardonyx, set with diamonds of very great value. For the rest, very plain."

On New Year's Day, 1705-6, we find the stout old man making up his accounts for the past year; though, on the

* Diary, vol. ii. p. 349.   † Ibid. p. 376.

twenty-seventh of the same month, his weak and trembling hand could still write one more record of his closing life:

"My indisposition increasing, I was exceeding ill all this whole week."

Next day he died.

His epitaph, engraved on white marble, covering a tomb shaped like a coffin in the dormitory at Wotton, truly declares that his "fame was perpetuated by far more lasting monuments than those of stone or brass."

Evelyn's name is perhaps dearer to England than that of any other of our countrymen who have been engaged in civil employments, if we except Shakspeare. He lived and died among his people, showing how erroneous is the idea that to be religious, or studious, or philosophic, it is necessary to be a recluse. By his social virtues he did as much good as by his works. He first introduced and ennobled the science of making English homes elegant as well as happy. Whilst Boyle soared into every branch of experimental philosophy, Evelyn adapted and enlarged all that was practical. They were well suited to live in the same age, the one to elevate and enlarge, the other to fertilise and humanise. In their friendship they were congenial, although dissimilar in character.

Boyle, it is said, taught the young nobility to value science, and to bring to its aid their influence and their fortunes. Evelyn was the very type and model of the true English country gentleman. To say thus much is but a fraction of their praise. Who can estimate the good they did in their lives? Who can state the result of their united efforts? Who can sufficiently reverence the piety that was so exalted in an age of infidelity, the sincerity that withstood so many variations in others, the purity of life that no evil example could ever shake, the simplicity of character that, in both these illustrious friends, remained alike unsullied to him whose hours were passed in the retreats of the university, and to him who lived not only in the world, but in its busier haunts?

Well might Jeremy Taylor write in one of his letters to Evelyn,—

"I perceive there is a friendship beyond what I have fancied, and a real, material worthiness beyond the heights of the most perfect ideas; and I know now where to make my book" (his Essay on Friendship) "perfect, and by an appendix to outdo the first essay; for when anything shall be observed to be wanting in my character, I can tell them where to see the substance, much more beauteous than the picture, and, by sending the readers of my book to be spectators of *your* life and worthiness, they shall see what I would fain have taught them, by what you really are."

Mrs. Evelyn survived her husband nearly three years. In her will, she desired to be buried in a stone coffin near to her "dear husband, whose love and friendship I was happy in fifty-eight years and nine months."

"His *care of her education*," she further records, "was such as might become a father, a lover, a friend, and husband, for instruction, for tenderness, affection, and fidelity to the last moment of his life."

The expression, "care of my education," is a striking one, but it is suggestive. A woman's education, as a responsible and immortal being, commences in its most extended sense at her marriage; and her career, for better or for worse, may be said to rest mainly on the character and influence of him who perfects the moral education of her soul.

HENRY HOWARD, EARL OF SURREY,
AND
SIR THOMAS WYATT.

THE CHRISTMAS OF 1595. — FEAT OF ARMS. — WYATT'S NAME AMONG THE CHALLENGERS. — HIS LINEAGE. — SIR HENRY WYATT. — LINES ON ALLINGTON CASTLE. — WYATT AT ST. JOHN'S COLLEGE. — HIS EARLY ACQUAINTANCE WITH ANNE BOLEYN. — SURREY AND HIS FRIENDS. — HE MARRIES LADY FRANCES VERE. — ANECDOTE OF WYATT AND ANNE BOLEYN. — VARIOUS INCIDENTS: ARRANGED MARRIAGES. — DR. NOTT'S OPINION OF WYATT. — WYATT THE GREATEST WIT OF HIS TIME. — HIS FRIENDSHIP WITH SURREY. — GERALDINE. — SURREY'S LINES ON HER. — HIS PASSION. — DEATH OF WYATT. — WYATT'S LETTER TO HIS SON. — SURREY'S EPITAPH ON WYATT. — LELAND THE OLD MORTALITY OF HIS TIME. — ATTACKS ON WYATT. — SURREY'S KINDNESS TO WYATT'S SON. — QUARREL AT COURT. — SURREY GOES TO BOULOGNE. — CABALS AGAINST HIM. — HIS LETTERS. — HIS TRIAL, AND DEATH.

HENRY HOWARD, EARL OF SURREY,

AND

SIR THOMAS WYATT.

It was at the feast of the Christmas in 1595 that a splendid feat of arms was performed before Henry VIII. and his queen, by the gentlemen of his "*Highness's* Bedchamber," for it was after that time that "Majesty" became the style. The court was at the ancient palace of Greenwich, then termed Placentia; and the Queen, Katharine of Arragon, in all her well-merited popularity, gave audience betimes to a herald from the King's servants, announcing the enterprise. Windsor Herald, or Chateau Blanche, as he was christened for the occasion, was dressed in a coat-of-arms of red silk, having a "goodly castle and four turrets of beaten silver worked thereon: in every turret sat a faire lady gorgeously apparelled." So says the chronicler Hall. The Queen received the compliment in her "great chamber," her consort Henry VIII. being present: then the sound of the trumpet echoed through the vaulted, spacious room, and Chateau Blanche delivered his message: "That, the King having given to four maidens of his court the Castle of Loyalty to dispose of at their pleasure, they had committed the custody thereof to a captain and fifteen gentlemen with him, which captain and gentlemen declared to the King and princes, and gentlemen of noble courage, that they would defend the castle against all comers, provided they were gentlemen of name and arms," reserving to themselves the privilege of choosing the weapons to be used, and of naming the ransom for all prisoners taken in that castle; which was, four yards of satin for every private man and fourteen for every captain, to be paid down, — satin being an article of great price and in constant demand. Then the names of the challengers were proclaimed, and amidst the Greys, the Cobhams, the Dudleys and Seymours, came the name of Wyatt; and Thomas Wyatt, commonly called the elder, appeared for the first time at court on this signal occasion. And that name was heard with pleasure; for the family of Wyatt had been favourites alike with the hard, sagacious Henry VII. and with his capricious son. There was a tradition in the family that Sir Henry Wyatt, the young courtier's father, who had been imprisoned by Richard III. in the Tower on account of his adherence to the House of Lancaster, had been saved from starvation by a cat which had daily brought some pigeons from a neighbouring dovecote to his chamber in that drear building. Be that as it may, there wanted no hereditary claim on the monarch's preference to establish Thomas Wyatt's favour. The young man was then in the very flower of his youth, and was distinguished by more than ordinary gifts. He was tall and strong and elegant, not moulded with the robust clumsiness of a ploughboy, but with the refined, though vigorous figure of a gentleman. Men are seldom enthusiastic in praise of the personal perfections even of their best friends; but Henry, Earl of Surrey, whom Leland calls "conscript enrolled heir," has thus described Sir Thomas Wyatt's bodily perfections: —

> "A valiant corpse, where force and beauty met,
> Happy, alas! too happy, but for foes,
> Lived, and ran the race that nature set,
> Of manhood's shape, where she the mould did lose."

With the perfection of form was united the perfection of feature, of contour of face, and of expression. Thus says, Lord Surrey: —

> "A visage stern and mild, where both did grow
> Vice to contemn, in virtue to rejoice;
> Amid great storms, whom grace assured so,
> To live upright, and smile at fortune's choice."

In these verses the moral qualities are commingled with personal attractions; but Leland, even though less partial, has told us that Wyatt's face was one of peculiar beauty. His features might have served as a model for a sculptor. His forehead was noble; his eyes were wonderfully brilliant and searching: there was something in his smile surpassingly sweet and winning. Let Surrey speak, since he felt all the influence of that beloved and beautiful countenance.

> "An eye, whose judgment no effect* could blind,
> Friends to allure, and foes to reconcile;
> Whose piercing look did represent a mind
> With virtue fraught, reposed, void of guile."

To this intellectual beauty were united immense activity and strength, and address in arms; so that in the encounter, that feat which Chateau Blanche announced as to be shortly performed, his dexterity was one of the great guarantees of its signal success.

Christmas in the olden time was festive indeed. Scarcely had the solemnities of the eve been ended, when large candles were lighted in every house, and a "yule-log" or "Christmas block" was brought into the hall, generally by the house or village carpenter, who had appropriated the root of some great tree to the purpose. As he deposited the log, each of the family, servants inclusive — for in those days servants were not kept at an inhuman distance — sat down in turn on the log, drank a merry Christmas to each person

---

* Passion.

present, and sang a song. This being over, the yule-log was laid on the great andirons of the ample chimney, and lighted with the last year's brand; fuel having been heaped up, it soon blazed; then the music struck up, and yule-dough and yule-cakes, on which was impressed the figure of the infant Saviour, were handed about with bowls of frumenty, made of wheat cakes or creed wheat, boiled in milk with spices; then tankards of spiced ale went round: and these customs, we are told, continued so late in the north of England as the 17th century.

> "Come, bring in with a noise,
> My merrie, merrie boyes,
> The Christmas log to the firing;
> While my good dame, she
> Bids you all be free,
> And drink to your hearts' desiring."

Placentia, no doubt, afforded the best specimen of Christmas festivities, and in its long since ruined tilt-yard sat Katharine of Arragon that Christmas, to view the Castle of Loyalty, of which the old chronicler Hall, delighting in such details, gives the following description:—"For this enterprise there was set up in the tilt-yard at Greenwich a castle, square every way twenty foot, and fifty feet in height, very strong, of great timber and well fastened with iron. When the strength of this castle was well beholden, many made dangerous to assault it, and some said it could not be won by sport but by earnest."

The King, he adds, "minded to have it assaulted," and even contrived engines for the attack: but the carpenters "were so dull that they understood not his intent, but wrought all things contrary; and so for that time the assault was prolonged, and all other points of the challenge held." And Henry, doubtless, was in a fierce temper at this obstacle to a will and pleasure that were felt by most men in that day, to be imperative, and by none, in time, more keenly than by Thomas Wyatt. But he was at that time in high favour. "To have been in Wyatt's closet" was a proverbial saying, indicating at once his influence, and the kindly disposition which led him to make use of it for the benefit and advancement of his brother courtiers.

We have seen Wyatt in one passage of his court life: let us trace him from an earlier period, and observe how that character, the nobleness of which has been undoubted, was nurtured and formed. Thomas Wyatt, "the improver of the English language, and restorer of modern English poetry,"[*] was descended from an ancient family originally of Southange in Yorkshire.[†] Happily for himself, his birth was only honourable, not noble, so that he escaped the jealousy which soon evinced itself in Henry VIII., as it had done to a fearful extent in his father, of any persons who could claim kindred with the old Plantagenet race, of whom, in that era of intermarriages, there were not a few in England. Surrey, who was one of the victims of that infernal jealousy, in the verses he addressed to his friend Wyatt, and headed "On the Golden Mean, and the Dangers of a too abject or a too elevated Station," thus refers to his friend's comparative mediocrity of birth and position:—

> "Of thy life, Thomas, this compass well mark:
> Not aye with full sails the high seas to bear;
> Ne by coward intent, in shunning storms dark,
> On shallow shores thy keel in peril frent.
>
> "The lofty pine the great wind often rives;
> With violenter sway fall turrets steep;
> Lightnings assault the high mountains and clives;
> A heart well stayed, in over thwartes deep."

---

[*] Nott's Life of Wyatt, vol. i. p. 1.
[†] The lineal descendant of Sir Thomas Wyatt—Thomas Wyatt, formerly of Long Ditton, Surrey—is now a prosperous landholder in Canada, near Hamilton, so that the illustrious name has been carried into that remote region.

Wyatt was born at Allington Castle,—a fortress on the Medway, said to have been built by the great Earl Warrenne. It was then inhabited occasionally by Sir Stephen de Penchester, and reverted afterwards to the Cobham family, but was given first to the Brentz, and from them alienated to Sir Henry Wyatt, the hero of the romance of the Cat and Pigeons. Allington, in the time of Sir Stephen de Penchester, who was constable of Dover Castle in the time of Edward I., had been a place of consideration, having a fair held there, and a weekly market. There is now little of its former importance, except the ruin in which he whom old Anthony à Wood calls the "delight of the Muses and of mankind," first saw the light. That decaying structure, still bearing the characteristics of a fortress, stands near the River Medway, hidden by trees: with a moat and the entrance gateway built by the Cobhams; and the still more ancient round tower, the work of Earl Warrenne. Henry VIII. visited the young poet during his time of precarious favour; but in the rebellion of the younger Wyatt, in the reign of Mary, the castle became escheated to the crown, and was given to Queen Elizabeth's Master of the Revels, Sir Thomas Astley, from whom it passed here to Earl Romney, to whose family the property was bequeathed by his relation, a lineal descendant of Sir Thomas Wyatt.*

Much of the poet's youth seems, however, to have been passed at the "Mote," anciently the possession of the Leybournes; then, after owning various proprietors,—for estates often changed hands before and during the wars of the Roses,—the Mote passed into the Widville or Woodville family, and Richard de Widville, the father of Elizabeth, the consort of Edward IV., became the lord of the castellated old mansion,—"a venerable, rambling building," we are told, standing, encompassed with a moat, in the lower end of the

* Beauties of England and Wales, vol. viii. p. 1237.

park, only a mile south-eastward from Maidstone. Richard Widville was massacred during a rising in Northamptonshire, and, his seven sons dying without issue, this domain became the property of Thomas Wyatt's grandfather, but was forfeited after the attainder of his son, Sir Thomas Wyatt the younger, in the reign of Mary. During her sombre rule, as if to triumph more completely over the family who had been so eminently Protestant, Cardinal Pole had a lease of the Mote. It passed eventually into the hands of the honoured family who have since, perhaps for valid reasons, taken down the old Mote-house, having previously erected one, in every way a contrast, on a finer site, with more beautiful views, doubtless better and larger apartments, but *not* the old Mote-house. The haunts of Wyatt can never be built up again except in fancy: so historic a fragment, so revered a monument of poetry and of virtue, it is not in the power of any proprietor either to replace, or to restore.

We may nevertheless form some notion by analogy of the interior life of the young poet. From a manuscript in the British Museum, quoted by Warton, we find that the following articles formed the furniture of a closet at Greenwich. A closet, in old parlance, corresponds either to a modern lady's boudoir, or to a young man's gun-room or smoking room. That of Wyatt probably resembled that occupied by the youths who hung about the court of Henry. — A clocke, a glass of steel, a map, a gun upon a stock wheeled, five paxes (or crucifixes) of glass and wood, a tablet of our Lady and Saint Anne, two or three pairs of hawkes' gloves lined with velvet, two combe cases furnished, a night-cap of black velvet embroidered, an ivory horn, a standing dial in a case of copper, a horn glass, eight cases of henchers, a folding table of images; these, with a hundred or more of common hawkes' hoods, with dogs' collars, riding rods for ladies, chessmen in a black satin bag, a table-cloth embroidered with a picture of St. George, some Araby birds stuffed, two long cases of black leather with pedigrees, a table with words "of Jhesus," a target and bows, composed the lumber of a young man's lounging room. Smoking, happily, was in those days unknown.

It is consoling, also, to find that the Earls of Romney, who were connected with the Wyatts by the marriage of Sir Thomas Marsham with Margaretta Wyatt, retain some traces of that relationship. In the present and spurious Mote-house, there is the picture of a grave and venerable man, with a gold chain round his neck. This is Sir Henry Wyatt, the father of the poet. We can fancy him just the man to perform a terrible piece of service to Henry VII. in conducting to the Tower the youthful Edmund de la Pole, Earl of Suffolk, whom the King of Castile had given up to the jealousy and cruelty of the English monarch. One can fancy him also sitting in the Star Chamber, and in Chancery,—soldier as he was, nevertheless, yet acting judicially; anon we trace him attending Henry VIII. to the plains of Ardres, to meet there the gallant Francis I.; and next we find him, in 1527, receiving Henry at Allington Castle, where the king awaited Cardinal Wolsey's return from France.

We can also conceive easily enough that Sir Henry Wyatt— looking at his portrait — should marry as he did, late in life. Not until he was forty-two years of age did the prudent courtier espouse Anne Skinner, of Reigate, in Surrey. By her he had three children: Margaret, married to Sir Henry Lee, ancestor to the Earls of Lichfield; Henry, who lived in Kent, a retired country gentleman; and Thomas, the elder son, and the poet. It is natural to ask how, with so sensible a father, composed of stern matter-of-fact and worldly wisdom, the youth's poetical genius and noble character of mind were fostered. No doubt, localities and early associations had their influence. Allington, where much of Wyatt's childhood was passed, though now a mass of ruins inhabited only by a farmer and a few labourers, retains the inalienable charms of situation. It stands on an angle formed by the Medway, and the verdant meadow on which the grim ruins are seated is opposite to a wooded bank, rising abruptly. Behind the castle the ground slopes, and groves and hop-grounds contrast with the dark grey and ruined edifice. In one of the towers, the old woman, guide to Allington, had still, some years since, the audacity to declare, was Sir Henry imprisoned: there the cat — and she pointed to the very dovecote — used to take the pigeons every day to the forgotten and starving captive. Nay, even one of Sir Henry's descendants recorded the merits of the cat in an inscription placed on his tomb at Boxley, in Kent.*

Surrounded by scenes so smiling, yet familiarised nevertheless; insensibly, with traditions of the past, Thomas Wyatt, as he grew up, displayed a luxuriant fancy, combined with a deep and reverent sense of the great and beautiful:— we call that romance; and romance, in a strong mind, is one of the safeguards of the young: and it brought Wyatt back to virtue even when drawn aside from her paths by the temptations of the court.

One word more about Allington ere we quit its precincts, and picture to ourselves its young inhabitant pressing forth to the business of life. Allington has not been forgotten by the Muses, although now it bears those two mournful attributes, a ruin and a show-place. In the "Censura Litteraria" we find these lines:—

> "Then let me fly to Medway's stream,
> Where flowing Wyatt used to dream
> His moral fancies! Ivied towers
> 'Neath which the silver naiad pours
> Her murmuring waves thro' verdant meads
> Where the rich herd luxuriant feeds,

---

* Nott's Life of Wyatt, p. 11.

> How often in your still recesses
> I've seen the muse with careless tresses
> Scatter her flowers as Wyatt bade
> In spring's enamelled colours clad."*

In regard to Wyatt's early education, in the accepted sense of the word, all, as far as his childhood is concerned, is obscure. At twelve years of age he went to Cambridge: was entered at St. John's College, and took his Bachelor's degree three years afterwards, in 1518, and his Master's in 1520. Anthony à Wood, eager on all occasions for the glory of Oxford, declares that Wyatt, after leaving Cambridge, went to Wolsey's College (Christ Church), which was founded in 1524, there to complete his studies. But in 1524 Wyatt was at court, and in 1525 tilting, as we have seen, at the Castle of Loyalty, thinking of something very different to the jargon of schoolmen in those days. From the same authority it has been alleged that Wyatt was sent, on quitting Oxford, to travel on the continent. But his silence on this point in his poems, and that of his eulogist Leland, and of his friend Surrey, disprove, in the opinion of Dr. Nott, this surmise. Wyatt did not visit Spain until a much later period; and besides, there was another circumstance that must have checked travelling, and somewhat lessened romance: Wyatt was at this time not only a married man, but the father of a son; Thomas Wyatt the younger having been born in 1523 or 1524,—indeed, according to some accounts, so early as 1521.

Of his wife and the mother of his children, little is known, except that she was the daughter of Brook, Lord Cobham, and that her name was Elizabeth. She may have had every attraction, all virtues, — but she was only second in the heart of her accomplished husband; for all his soul was centred in another object,— the beautiful, intellectual, ill-fated Anne Boleyn.

---

* Beauties of England and Wales, vol. viii. p. 1263. From "The Wizard."

As his passion for her, as well as his friendship for Surrey, forms one of the notable influences in Wyatt's life, let us take a view of the circumstances, the state of society, the known details, and the mournful issue of his blamable and ill-starred affection. Platonic attachments were, to a certain extent, authorised in those days, as far as the world was concerned, by the usages of society; and although they must always have been attended with risk in public, and with a consciousness of impropriety in private, they were allowed by moralists as excusable, tending, it was said, to humanise society; and they were adopted by poets as convenient for the imagination to rest upon some especial object of romantic interest and attraction.

The marriages of that period were like those, to the disgrace of France, still obtaining in that country, — mere monetary contracts in the first instance. A thousand motives, but the ruling one, money, prompted the hard bargain, in which all the skill of the lawyer, all the judgment of the parent, were called into requisition; no intimacy was allowed between the young couple even after the contract, which preceded the espousals forty days. The unhappy pair were thus bound together, and sent home to live for ever and a day, for richer for poorer, for better for worse (but it was too often for worse), as well as they could. The consequences were sometimes fearful. An enforced tie begot a sense of injury in the mind of a child, betrothed often at ten or eleven years of age and married at fifteen, towards a parent; and engendered hatred to the object of a bond which, in the secret heart, was detested. We blush at the revelations of the divorce courts; but they are pure as a sheet of white paper, compared with the old Star-Chamber examinations. In Roman Catholic times it was difficult for the married to get loose (in our own among Catholics, it is impossible): hence, in the middle ages, murders, poisonings, infidelities, horrors almost inconceivable, and mysteries almost unfathomable, and incomparably more dread and revolting than anything — and it is saying much — that can occur in our times, were the foundation of the *causes célèbres*. Such was the case among the wicked and desperate: among the refined, the virtuously disposed, a Platonic devotion was thought to be a safety-valve, and was the resource even of loyal-hearted and pious men, and among others, of Thomas Wyatt. It has been said that his passion was a feigned one, and, like that of Cowley, assumed in order that he might have an object for his verse. Dr. Nott (who, though holding at one time a fellowship at All Souls, retained still the romance that seems likely to be buried within those walls) thus writes on this point, at once candidly and with liberality : —

"But I should be insincere were I to offer such an apology. There are many passages in Wyatt's verses which convince me that he felt what he expressed. I rest his defence, where alone I think it ought to rest, on what has been said, in Surrey's instance, on the habits and the opinions of his time." *

It was from the Italian poets, as Warton in his "History of English Poetry" tells us, that Wyatt was taught to "torture the passion of love by prolix and intricate comparisons, and unnatural allusions." † In some of his sonnets he says that "all nature sympathises with his passion, the woods resound his elegies, the rivers stop their course to hear him complain, and the grass weeps in dew."

Such images incline one to a belief in a fantastic and poetic passion, rather than a real one; but there are passages in Wyatt's poems that show a deep and bitter conviction that "the shadow of a shade" on which he had fixed his hopes had been fatal to his peace. It was from a suffering heart that such lines as these came, in his Epistle to John Poines: —

* Life of Wyatt, p. lxxix.
† Hist. of English Poetry, vol. i. p. 33.

> "Make plaine thy harte that it be not knotted
> With hope or dread, and se thy will be bare
> From all affects whom vice has never spotted,
> Thyself content with that in thee assinde.
> And use it well that is to thee allotted.
> Then seke no more out of thyself to fynde
> The thing that thou hast sought so long before,
> For thou shalt feele it sticking in thy minde."

There exists no record of the earliest acquaintance between these two remarkable individuals; no clear annals of the passion too fondly cherished by Wyatt, except his own poetry. Anne Boleyn, being born in 1501, was two years older than her lover. When she was eleven years of age she lost her mother. Until that period of her life, she had lived at Blickling Hall, in Norfolk, where she was born; but after her mother's decease she resided at Hever Castle, in Kent, not very far from Tunbridge Wells. Here, until she entered her fourteenth year, Anne remained under the care of a French governess named Simonette, and it is not improbable that in the seclusion of Heven an intimacy with the Wyatt family, generally, may have subsisted. It is supposed, indeed, that Anne and Wyatt were playfellows, from the circumstance of Sir Henry Wyatt being coadjutor with Sir Thomas Boleyn in the government of Norwich Castle; but of this there is no proof, nor is it likely, from the precautions which would naturally encompass a young girl of condition, that Wyatt and Anne ever met intimately until they were both in the court of Henry VIII. and Katherine of Aragon.

When appointed maid of honour to the Queen of England, Anne had attained her twentieth year.

Wyatt has left his first impressions of her beauty in the following brief, but telling passage:—

"There was at that time presented to the eye of the court, the rare and admirable beauty of the fresh and fair and young Lady Anne Boleyn. In this noble imp, the graces of nature, adorned by gracious education, seemed at the very first to have promised bliss unto her in after times. She was taken at that time to have a beauty not so whitely as clear and fresh above all we may esteem, passing sweet and cheerful." He was even enraptured with Anne's defects, one of which was a double nail on the left hand, somewhat like an additional finger; "but that," he says, "which in others might have been regarded as a defect, was to her an occasion of additional grace, by the skilful manner in which she concealed it from observation."

Anne, indeed, introduced the graceful hanging sleeves, which were soon imitated by the ladies of the English court. But it was less the beauty of Anne than her intelligence, her grace and vivacity; the smile that played on her lips, the ready repartee to which her flexible and speaking face gave force, the perfect elegance of her movements:—these were the real attractions which not only riveted the fancy, but retained the heart once caught.

These two fascinating beings, Anne and Wyatt, met on equal grounds in the various revels of their sovereign's court. Wyatt was a gay, gallant, and even dissipated man, whose youth, a brief period of levity and extravagance, was judged by himself severely when the season of that intoxication had passed away. He was, however, as we have seen, deeply imbued with the Platonism which permitted to the truant heart a predilection, even when every tie of duty bound the Platonist to another. Anne had been the belle of the French court, and had encountered much detraction; both were versed in those delicate arts of flirtation, which are never intended to end in marriage.

Both were brought to a full sense of their imprudence by the hand of destiny; Wyatt, even in the stormy period of his passion, felt remorse. How beautifully he touches upon his escape from worse sins than those of *thought*, is expressed in his paraphrase of the 33rd Psalm.

"Oh! happy they that have forgiveness got
Of their offence, not by their penitence
As by merit, which recompenseth not,
(Although that get pardon hath none offence
Without the same), but by the goodness
Of Him that hath perfect intelligence
Of heart contrite . . . .
And happy they that have the wilfulness
Of lust restrained afore it went at large,
Whereby they have not on their backs the charge
Of others' fault to suffer the dolores,
For that their fault was never execute
In open sight, example of errour."

Meantime, whilst Wyatt, to adopt Dr. Nott's words, regarded Anne Boleyn "with the lively tenderness of an innocent but dangerous friendship," there was opening before him a nobler interest in his intimacy with Henry Lord Surrey, his truest friend, the companion of his pursuits, the object of his greatest admiration and respect.

The Howard family were devoted adherents of the House of York, and John Howard, first Duke of Norfolk, fell on the field of battle at Bosworth, fighting for Richard III. His son, Thomas, Earl of Surrey, was taken prisoner at the same time. When reproached by Henry VII. for fighting against him, he made this politic and specious reply: "Sir, he was my crowned king. Let the authority of parliament put the crown on that stake, and I will fight for it; so would I have fought for you, had the same authority put the crown on your head."

From henceforth the prosperity of the Howards was assured. Thomas, Earl of Surrey, becoming Duke of Norfolk, married the Lady Anne, the youngest daughter of Edward IV., but Henry Howard, Earl of Surrey, the poet, was not the offspring of that marriage. The Lady Anne died young, and, at the age of forty, the Duke of Norfolk made a second union, Lady Elizabeth Stafford, daughter of the Duke of

Buckingham, being his choice, and eventually the mother of Lord Surrey.

In the absence of parish registers, which did not begin till 1546, the place even of Surrey's birth is unknown. Conjecture points to Kenninghall, in Norfolk; by the same indefinite means, it has been supposed that the young poet spent much of his time at Windsor with the Duke of Richmond, the natural son of Henry VIII. Both ideas are equally well founded. One thing is certain, that the Howards were an intellectual, ambitious race, and that Surrey's early training was of the most careful description, it having long been a custom in their family to send the sons into the house of some learned prelate, in order there to be instructed in the literature of the age. His kinsmen, his associates, also were of cultivated minds. Among the most interesting and ill-fated young noblemen of the day was George Boleyn, Lord Rochford, the brother of Anne Boleyn, and the friend of Surrey and of Wyatt. The Duke of Richmond, Henry's natural son, was also devoted to learning, and a youth of great promise. These young noblemen began life at seventeen or eighteen. In compliance with the custom of the day, they were sent to school at four years old, to be taught languages and the first principles of manners; from ten to twelve, dancing, and "to speak of gentleness;" at fourteen they were initiated into the sports of the field, and were thus prepared for the exercise of arms (and in a good training for "muscular Christianity"); at sixteen, before which period of life, if they went to college, their academic career was usually ended, they learnt to joust, to fight at the barriers, to manage the war-horse, to assail fortresses, and began to wear armour and to contend in feats of arms: henceforth they were men, not boys. They lived no longer than men of the nineteenth century, but began life sooner; before the freshness and ardour of youth were over; and the system had this good effect, that it employed their energies at an age when men are either, active and industrious, or dissolute. There seems to be no medium: the wild animal must have scope, whether for good or for bad.

At seventeen these juvenile statesmen or warriors began their career.

Marriage was the next point, and at sixteen Lord Surrey was affianced to Lady Frances Vere, the daughter of John, Earl of Oxford; there were seventeen trustees to their marriage settlement, which is among the MSS. at Norfolk House. The Duke of Norfolk took charge of his son's clothes, the Earl of Oxford of those of his daughter, — articles of immense expense in that rank of life in those times; but it is supposed that the young couple did not, for some time, live together, on account of their extreme youth. Nor was it until the year 1535 that the nuptials were publicly solemnised, when Surrey was about seventeen years of age.*

Previous to his appearance at court, the romance of Anne Boleyn's mournful destiny had half passed away. Her youthful engagement to Lord Percy, the disappointment which ensued, the intimacy with Wyatt, were incidents which occurred before the year 1530; but the jealousy of Henry had already been excited towards Wyatt by the following incident.

One day, while Anne Boleyn was busy at her embroidery frame, and Wyatt was hovering near her, he snatched from her a jewelled tablet which hung by a chain out of her pocket, and thrusting it into his bosom swore that he would never restore it to her.

Wyatt, it is thought, would have been Anne's choice, after her disappointment with regard to Lord Percy, had he not been a married man: he perhaps thought so too, for he kept the stolen tablet, only now and then showing it to Anne, and then hiding it again in his cassock. In the long hours

* See Hardinge's Chronicle, quoted by Mr. Ellis in his preface, 1812.

of waiting when they were both in attendance on the Queen, the theft was the occasion of much raillery on the one hand, and of compliment on the other: but Anne was either too indifferent or too discreet to let the matter be made one of importance; so the tablet was forgotten, except by one jealous, watchful observer,—no less a person than the King. Anne, in fact, avoided Wyatt, for her heart was set on higher game.

One day, however, Henry, charmed with her prudence in regard to Wyatt, began to talk to her of marriage, and, in the earnestness of his admiration, snatched from her finger a ring.

A few days afterwards the King was playing at bowls with the Duke of Suffolk, Sir Francis Brian, and Sir Thomas Wyatt. Henry, who was in high good-humour, boasted that he had in a cast of the bowl surpassed Wyatt, who was his opponent.

"By his Highness's leave," said Sir Thomas, "it is not so."

The King, pointing to the bowl with the finger on which he wore Anne Boleyn's ring, replied,—

"Wyatt, I tell thee it is so."

Wyatt paused a moment. He knew that ring well, but, ever ready at an answer, he drew out of his bosom the tablet: it was well known to Henry.

"If it may like your Majesty to give me leave to measure the cast with *this*, I have good hopes that it may yet be mine."

He forgot his usual caution; a frown passed over the face of his sovereign.

"It may be so," he said, "but then I am deceived;" and he broke up the game hurriedly.*

Surrey was still a youthful bridegroom when Anne, whom, to use the words of Andrewes, the historian, "none but the most partial bigots have accused of more than childish levity," was tried, condemned, and beheaded.

---

* Wyatt MS. See Miss Strickland's "Life of Anne Boleyn," vol. iv. p. 193.

Surrey was then a father, his eldest son Thomas being born in March 1536. On this occasion he caused his child's nativity to be cast: the aspect of the stars was adverse; and not only was misfortune augured to his son, but an untimely death, so said the calculation, threatened to himself.

Whilst the heavens were thus clouded and portentous, Surrey, believing as he did in astrology, must have viewed life in sombre colours. On the 15th of May in that same year, his young cousin, Anne Boleyn, was brought to trial: his father was then Lord High Steward, and Surrey sat under him as Earl Marshal, sentence on the unhappy murdered Queen being pronounced by the Duke of Norfolk. It needed no astrologer to tell the world that an action such as this would, and must bring down retribution upon the remorseless uncle and his son; and it soon followed. Lord Thomas Howard, Surrey's uncle, having married the Lady Margaret Douglas without the King's permission, was committed to the Tower, where he died two years afterwards of a broken heart. The marriage had been one of mutual attachment. Lady Margaret, who became mother of the ill-fated Darnley, was released after her husband's death, but was forbidden to retain anything that had belonged to him, or to cherish his memory.

Wyatt, meantime, was suffering not the prospective, but the real trials of life. That he passionately loved Anne Boleyn seems to be admitted, even by the gravest and most sceptical historians. That all suspicions which pointed to any guilty connection between them were unjust, is also admitted on the same authority. Wyatt's was the sentiment of love, and Anne's participation in his pursuits, her love of poetry, her sweet, heroic, thoughtless nature, bound him to her in links never broken. Whilst in her prosperity she advanced his fortunes; in her prison his songs and sonnets were her mournful resource in the long hours of hopeless gloom. Perhaps, in the desertion of others,

Anne may have remembered the lines, "Of his love, called Anna," which Wyatt had written in happier days:—

> "What word is that, that changeth not,
>   Though it be turn'd, and made in twain?
> It is mine Anna, God it wot,
>   And eke the causer of my pain.
> (Who) love rewardeth with disdain;
>   Yet is it loved: what would ye more?
> It is my health, and eke my sore."

It must have been a consolation to her to know that one tried friend, who had seen her in her hours of confidence, and who had been long devoted to her, believed her innocent.

"For the evidence," Wyatt said, "I never could hear of any: small I believe it was. The accusers must have doubted whether their proofs would not prove their reproofs, when they durst not bring them to the light in an open place." And he did the poor Queen the justice to add, "It was reported without the doors that she had cleared herself in a most wise and noble speech."

He had the satisfaction, meantime, of knowing that a kinswoman of his own was near the beautiful captive. It was a Wyatt who accompanied Anne from Greenwich, went with her to the lodging she had had at her coronation, heard her hysterical bursts of crying and laughter wildly mingled, and listened with commiseration to her agonised and piteous question, "Wherefore am I here, Master Kingston?" It was a Wyatt — some say, Sir Thomas's sister, Margaret — who courageously attended her to the scaffold, and received, at the last farewell, a small book of devotions, bound in gold and enamelled black, which she had carried in her hand from the Tower. Anne's last words are said to have been a message to Wyatt, uttered in a low and earnest voice to the weeping, but undaunted Margaret.

Wyatt had not escaped imminent peril. The following lines, entitled "Wyatt being in prison, to Bryan," show how bitterly he felt the state of affairs, not only on his own account. It is uncertain, however, whether they were written at this time or later.

> "Sighs are my food, my drink they are my tears,
> Clinking of fetters such music would crave:
> Stink and close air away my life wears:
> Innocency is all the hope I have.
> Rain, wind or weather, I judge by mine ears.
> Malice assaults that righteousness should have.
> Sure I am, Bryan, this wound will heal again,
> But yet, alas! the scar shall still remain."*

And the "scar" did "remain." Wyatt became a humbled, penitent, and holy being; a man still mingling in the world, yet chastened and hating its vanities. Witness his stanzas on "The Courtier's Life:"—

> "In court to serve, decked with fresh array
> Of sugred meats, feeling the swete repast,
> The life in banquets and sundry kinds of play,
> Amid the press of lordly looks to waste,
> Hath with it joined sometimes such bitter taste,
> That whoso joys such kind of life to hold,
> In prison joys, fettered with chains of gold."†

Greatly as Wyatt was to be pitied, one must even more strongly commiserate Lord Surrey, who, at his very entrance into public life, had seen the fairest ornament of his family perish on the scaffold, and had assisted at her trial. From the moment of Anne Boleyn's death, Wyatt forswore love, "and vowed that its baited hooks should tangle him no more." Not so with Surrey: his hour of temptation was still to come. Let us, for a time, still consider him but as the friend of Wyatt; and let us trace the remaining years of the sorrow-stricken lover of Anne Boleyn, before commencing a scarcely less touching episode of history, the fanciful love of Surrey for the fair Geraldine, and his sad doom. There is more reality, more poetry, more tragic interest, in the story of Thomas Wyatt's deeply repented attachment, than in the

---
* Wyatt's Poems. Nott's Life, p. 71.   † Ibid. p. 74.

unreal poetic flame of Surrey. Henceforth, thus Wyatt thought, study should be his consolation. For a time his "travail," as he called it, was carried on in the seclusion of the Tower. Fresh causes of complaint and suspicion were raised against him; the year of his arrest is doubtful. He incurred the fearful enmity of Bishop Bonner: his former incarceration on account of Anne Boleyn had been transient and lenient; he was now plunged into an unwholesome dungeon, and so closely immured that he could only judge of the weather by the pattering of the rain upon the window of his prison, and the blowing of the wind.

The following minute from the Privy Council, dated March 15, 1541, announces his submission, and at the same time proclaims in vainglorious terms, worthy of the adulators who composed that body, the clemency of the King.

The document is indorsed : " *Mynute to my Lord Wilton Howard*," 26 *Martij at night.*

"His Highnes hathe nowe commanded us to make you participant, what hath been sithens doon, aswel in that matier, as touching Sir Thomas Wyat; to thende you may take your oportunyte to declare the same as of yourself, bothe to the French King and to such of his Counsail as youe shal thinke expedient," &c. &c.

"His Highnes having also most humble sutes and intercessions made unto him, both for him (Sir John Wallop) and for Wyat, by the Queenes Highnes," &c. &c.

"Nowe to Wyat; he confessed, uppon his examynation, all the thinges objected unto him, in a like lementable and pitiful sorte as Wallop did : whiche surely were grevous; delyvering his submission in writing, declaring thole history of his offences, but with a like protestation, that the same proceded from him in his rage and folishe vaynglorios fantazie, without spott of malice; yeilding himself only to his Majesties marcy, without the whiche he sawe he might and must nedes be justely condempned. At the contemplation of whiche submission, and at the greate and contynual sute of the Quenes Majestie, His Highnes, being of his oune most godly nature enclyned to pitie and mercy, hathe given him his pardon in as large and ample sorte as His grace gave thother to Sir John Wallop; whiche pardons be delyvered, and they sent for to come hither to his Highnes at Dover." (The King was in Dover on the 27th of March untill the 31st.) "Nowe that your Lordship knowethe this progresse, His grace wold you shuld utter it as befor proscribed." *

Wyatt was permitted to defend himself before the Privy Council, and was pardoned in the month of June 1541. The King, who had always favoured him, received him more into his confidence than ever, and gave him lands and places of trust. Yet "the scar remained." Wyatt was weary of public life; he had seen the vanity of the world, he had known the misery of strong excitements. To "deep himself" in study, as he termed it, to obtain a mastery over his passions, to employ his noble powers in a work of penitence and praise, became his aim henceforth.

He went to Allington, and became now a country gentleman, hunting and hawking, and shooting with the bow, yet still devoting much of his time to poetry. Witness the satire, addressed to his friend Poines, in which he speaks of his inability to flatter and deceive as a reason why he cannot lead a courtier's life, and why he preferred the independence of thought and action which could alone be met with far from the capital. His second satire, in fact, delineates as noble a character of an intelligent English gentleman as can possibly be conceived.

> "My Pointz, I cannot frame my tongue to feign;
> To cloke the truth for praise, without desart
> Of them that lust all vices to retain.
> . . . .

---

* From the State Papers (Domestic), No. 668, f. 544.

> I cannot crouch or kneel to such a wrong,
> To worship them as God on earth alone,
> That are like wolves these sely lambs among.
>
> . . . . . .
>
> I cannot, I, no, no! it will not be.
> This is the cause that I could never yet
> Hang on their sleeves, that weigh, as thou may'st see."
>
> . . . . . .

Then he goes on to say:

> "This maketh me at home to hunt and hawk,
> And in foul weather at my book to sit,
> In frost and snow; then with my bow to stalk;
> No man doth mark wherere I ride or go.
> In lusty leas at liberty I walk,
> And of these news I feel nor weal nor woe.
>
> . . . . . .
>
> I am not now in France to judge the wine,
> With savoury sauce the delicates to feel; —
>
> . . . . . .
>
> But here I am in Kent and Christendom,
> Among the Muses, where I read and rhyme,
> Where, if thou list, my Poynz, for to come,
> Thou shalt be judge how I do pass my time."*

Full of these impressions, Wyatt looked back with compassion on those who were still in the ways of error, yet who, nevertheless, loved and admired virtue.

> "None other paine pray I for them to be
> But when the rage doth leade them from the right,
> That, lokinge backwarde, virtue they may se,
> Even as she is, so goodly faire and bright!"†

His fortune had now considerably suffered in his public employments, and the following letter, dated from Brussels, and addressed "to Secretary Cromwell," shows his almost despair on this point:—

"I must beseech your lordship to move unto the King's Highness, for me, this one suit. Among my many other great

---

* Poems, Nott, vol. ii. p. 88. † Ibid. p. 90.

debts, I owe his grace 500 marks for my livery, which I could not get out till my last being in England; and I must pay it by 40*l.* yearly. I owe him beside 250 marks of old debt, which in all maketh 500*l.* If his grace will so much oblige my good lord as to let me take out all mine obligations and bonds, and take good surety in recognizance for the said 500*l.* after 50*l.* a year, truly to be paid, I would trust so a little and a little to creep out of debt, with the selling of little land more. If not, on my faith, I see no remedy. I owe my brother Lee as much, beside other infinite that make me weary to think on them. I have written to Sir Thomas Poynings to know your lordship's answer in this, and also most humbly to thank you for your goodness toward me, touching that he moved you for me of the lordship of Ditton, that is John Lee's. But surely I am not able to buy it, unless the King's great liberality be shewed unto me in this case; and yet the thing is so necessary for me, as that that lieth in the midst of my land, and within a mile of my house. I remit me wholly to your good lordship, in whom is my only trust next to the King's majesty. But above any of all these things I recommend unto your lordship the good remembrance when time shall be of my revocation; and I always your bond bedesman, as our Lord knoweth, who send you good life and long.—At Brussels, this Shrove Tuesday, 1540."[*]

His occupations were various; not only did Wyatt figure as an ambassador, but as a military commander, and also in the navy, which was not then considered a distinct profession. Few men accomplished so much; for in the intervals of leisure he instructed young Henry Lee, his nephew, a boy ten years of age, who lived with him at Allington. Meantime he exercised all the duties of a neighbour, and his hospitality was at once free and graceful. People went to dine with him, first, for his generous entertainment; secondly,

[*] Harleian MSS. No. 282; also given in Dr. Nott's Life of Wyatt.

for his free and knowing discourse of Spain and Germany; thirdly, "for his quickness in observing, his civility in entertaining, his dexterity in employing, and his readiness in encouraging every man's peculiar grace and inclinations; and lastly, the favour and notice with which he was honoured by the King."

Wyatt was considered the greatest wit of his time, yet, in an age of gross indelicacy, was never known to utter an improper jest or word. He had a horror of joking on serious subjects. "It does not," he observed, "become Christians to do so. If the Athenians would not permit a comedian to exhibit his farces on the scene where Euripides had acted his grave and solemn tragedies, much less ought we to suffer the levity of a joke to come, as it were, into the presence of things holy and religious." *

As he advanced to middle life, as a man after thirty was in those days considered to be, he respectfully declined entering into the amusements in which the court was necessarily engaged. On being urged by Henry to join in a midnight mask, he refused: the King asked his reason. "Sir," he said, "he who would be thought a wise man in the daytime, must not play the fool at night."

Wyatt was so great an admirer of Julius Cæsar that he used always a beautiful antique gem with Cæsar's head on it, hoping that, thus keeping up the memory of so great a man, he might himself be stimulated to generous actions, and do something worthy of record.

It was one of his common sayings, "Let my friend bring me into court, but let my merit and my service keep me there." He was also wont to say that in our jest we ought "never to play upon any man's unhappiness or deformity, for that is inhuman; nor on superiors, for that is saucy and undutiful; nor on holy matters, for that is irreligious."

* Wyatt's Life.

As he advanced in life he became bald, and wore a beard of remarkable length; the dignity of his person, the intellectual beauty of his face, were never diminished; his smile was sweet as ever: his habits were energetic, his frame vigorous, his nature enterprising, so that, had it been his lot to have been in the profession of arms exclusively, Wyatt would have become a distinguished commander. Frank, unsuspecting, generous — careless of money, but not personally profuse, — ready to forgive, fond of giving, he was the idol of his servants, the leading star of the social circle in which he moved.

But whilst naturally gay, full of spirits, and fond of society, Wyatt had a holy, heavenly frame of mind, combined with purity and elevation of thought. His paraphrase of the Penitential Psalms was the work of expiation for real or supposed sins. The character of David, the mental disquietudes, the poignant remorse, the hope, the faith of that erring, great-minded man, were singularly in unison with Wyatt's feelings.

> "Seeking to counterpose
> His song with sighs, and touching of the strings,
> With tender heart, lo! thus to God he sings!"

are lines as applicable to Wyatt as to David, to whom the poet applied them.

Possessed of numerous friends, Wyatt enjoyed the happiness of having three in whose affection he peculiarly confided. Poynings he liked for his generosity of character, Blage for his wit, and Mason for his learning.

Poyntz, to whom he addressed one of his satires, was also among his intimate associates; he was a courtier of no remarkable note. Sir Francis Brian, to whom Wyatt's third satire was addressed, was one of the most accomplished men of his time, a busy, restless courtier. Wyatt addressed a remonstrance to him on his perpetual activity.

> "To thee, therefore, that trots still up and down
> And never rests, but running day and night,
> From realm to realm, from city, street, and town.
> Why dost thou wear thy body to the bones?
> And mightst at home sleep in thy bed of down,
> And drink good ale so hoppy, for the nones." *

And to these friends Wyatt was never dictatorial; neither did he presume upon his own superiority of learning, which even Camden has praised as above that of most men. When Wyatt differed, it was deferentially, with "Under favour, sir;" and "It may be so," was his frequent answer to an argument which he might, with his powers of reasoning, have crushed at once.

The friendship between Surrey and Wyatt began, it is supposed, during their attendance on Anne Boleyn. Wyatt was considered the most elegant poet of the day; Surrey, therefore, sought his friendship, and addressed to him the first verses that he ever wrote. Their affection was based on congeniality of taste and respect, and it was sincere and lasting.

The verses beginning "Thomas, of thy life mark," were Surrey's early tribute to his friend. On the other hand it is believed that the following monitory lines, so appropriate in a man of maturer age to one young and inexperienced, were addressed by Wyatt to Surrey. They are styled

> "THE ARGUMENT.
>
> "Sometime the pride of my assured truth
> Contemned all help of God and eke of man;
> But when I saw how blindly man he goeth,
> In deeming hearts which none but God here can,
> And his dooms hid, whereby man's malice groweth,
> Mine Earl this doubt did tumble then,
> For errour so might murder innocence.
> Then sang I thus in God my confidence." †

---

* Nott's Life of Wyatt, p. lxxxviii.   † Ibid.

In refinement of taste, in elevation of thought, Surrey and Wyatt were peculiarly congenial; but another record proves that their domestic circumstances led, though at different periods, to similar results. Surrey, though married and apparently happily, loved, or affected to love, Lady Elizabeth Fitzgerald, to whom he assigned the more romantic name of "Geraldine." The example of Petrarch and the fashion of the times incited, if they did not excuse Surrey, in his passion for the far-famed Geraldine.

She was the daughter of Gerald Fitzgerald, ninth Earl of Kildare, whose ancestors are said to have been the Geraldi of Florence; her mother was the daughter of Thomas, Marquis of Dorset. Geraldine, as Surrey, discarding her prosaic name of Elizabeth, styled her, was born in the Castle of Maynooth in 1529, and was brought to England, while yet an infant, under most adverse circumstances. Her infancy and childhood were both marked by family misfortune. Lord Kildare, in 1534, died in the Tower, of grief on account of the rebellion of his son Thomas Fitzgerald. That restless Irish insurgent was eventually executed at Tyburn in 1535, five of his uncles suffering death at the same time and place. Gerald, the eldest son of this ill-starred family, became a fugitive when only ten years of age, and wandered about in peril and penury; and Lady Kildare was obliged to apply continually to Henry VIII. for assistance in her destitution. She appealed to him as a kinswoman, her father having been half-brother to Elizabeth of York, the King's mother; nor did she always appeal in vain.

"Men are not all evil;"

and though Henry was essentially cruel, he took compassion on the wretched Lady Kildare, and placed her daughter Geraldine in the household of his daughter Mary, to be supported and educated.

Poor Geraldine, when she attained her fourteenth year, was made one of the ladies of the Princess Mary's chamber; a sad sort of provision, for Mary was cold, solemn, bigoted, and unpopular. Geraldine was still a child, scarcely thirteen, when Surrey, in the autumn of 1541*, first saw her, attending on Mary at Hunsdon. Either the constitution of our nation, or our habits have produced a marvellous change in the chronology of life. A girl of thirteen, in the sixteenth century, was on the verge of maturity. It is true that Lord Surrey owned that Geraldine

"Wanted years to understand the grief that he did feel,"

when he first betrayed his passion to her; but it seems extraordinary that one who was scarcely removed from childhood should have inspired the romantic verse of Surrey. Yet so it was.

In the extreme youth of Geraldine there was a parallel in that of Laura, Petrarch's mistress, who was only thirteen years of age when the poet first conceived his famous passion "which twenty years of suffering," as Dr. Nott remarks, "could not diminish, and which continued unabated even when death itself had extinguished hope." If this be true certainly men must have been very different in those days to the lovers of the eighteenth and nineteenth centuries. Equally dissimilar must their fair mistresses have been; since they were considered to be fit objects for idolatry even at twelve years of age. Chaucer, a great painter of manners, dates the marriage of the Wife of Bath from her twelfth year:

"Lordings, since I twelve years was of age,
(Thanked be God that is eterne we live),
Husbands, at church door, have I had five."†

It appears, however, that Geraldine had attained the dis-

---

* See vol. i. p. 121, of Dr. Nott's Life of Surrey.
† Canterbury Tales.

creet age of thirteen when Lord Surrey began really to admire her, during one of the court revels at Hampton Court. The lovely and simple girl must have contrasted advantageously with the grave, gloomy Mary, her young mistress, and with the plump Katharine Howard, at that time Queen, with her *nez retroussé;* and Surrey made no attempt to conceal his impressions of the surpassing beauty of Geraldine. He soon proclaimed his passion in verses beginning,—

> "The sun hath twice brought forth the tender green,
> Twice clad the earth in lively lustiness;
> Once have the winds the trees despoiled clean,
> And once again begins their cruelness,
> Since I have hid under my breast the harm
> That never shall recover healthfulness.
> The winter's hurt recovers with the warm,
> The parched green restored is with shade:
> What warmth, alas! may serve for to disarm
> The frozen heart that mine inflame hath made?"*

Then, in another strain, he narrates her origin, in the following well-known lines : —

> "From Tuscany came my Lady's worthy race;
> Fair Florence was sometime her ancient seat.
> The western isle whose pleasant shore doth face
> Wild Comber's cliffs, first gave her lively heat.
> Fostered she was with milk of Irish breast,
> Her sire an earl, her dame of princes' blood.
> From tender years in Britain did she rest
> With a King's child, who tasteth ghostly food.
> Honsdon did first present her to mine eyen.
> Bright is her hue, and Geraldine she hight.
> Hampton me taught to wish her first for mine,
> And Windsor, alas! doth chase me from her sight.
> Her beauty of kind; her virtues from above:
> Happy is he that can obtain her love!"

---

* Surrey's Poems, vol. i. p. 3.

Such were the notions of those times, that even after Geraldine and her lover were both married, there seems, from Surrey's poems, to have been a decided understanding between them, since he writes of

> "Her strangeness when I sued her servant for to be;
> And what she said, and how she smiled, when that she pitied me."

So that what in the present day a woman from a married man would construe as an insult, was, in this instance, received as a mere matter of course. Surrey, in fact, seems to have been watchful over the conduct and reputation of his mistress, if we may take his own assurance for that fact, when he says,—

> "But mercy him thy friend that doth thee serve,
> Who seeks alway thine honour to preserve."

Geraldine, indeed, appears to have repelled his ardour, and whilst, perhaps, her young heart turned to the accomplished poet, she prudently endeavoured to hide herself from his observation. Surrey, in fact, addressed to her some beautiful lines on her always wearing a veil in his presence.

> "I never saw my lady lay apart
> Her cornet black in cold nor yet in heat,
> Sith first she knew my grief was grown so great,
> Which other fancies driveth from my heart,
> That to myself I do the thought reserve
> The which unawares did wound my woful breast;
> For on her face mine eyes might never rest,
> Since that she knew I did her love and serve.
> Her golden tress is always clad in black,
> Her smiling looks do hide thus evermore,
> And that restrain which I desire so sore."

His verses constitute the only history of the passion inspired by Geraldine. How beautiful is the following lament, written in spring!—

> "The sooté season, that bud and bloom forth brings,
> With green hath clad the hill and eke the vale;
> The nightingale with feathers new she sings,
> The turtle to her mate hath told her tale.
> Summer is come, for every spray now springs:
> The hart hath hung his old head on the pale,
> The buck in brake his winter coat he flings,
> The fishes fleet with new repaired scale;
> And thus I see among these pleasant things
> Each care decays, and yet my sorrow springs."

After many vicissitudes of feeling, and vain struggles with his passion, Surrey resolved to fly the peril that he could not conquer. He had found Geraldine fickle, pleased with admiration, and forgetful of his undying devotion. At length, at a ball, Geraldine publicly insulted him, and Surrey declared in these terms that he was undeceived:—

> "Too dearly had I bought my green and youthful years,
> If in my age I could not find when craft for love appears;
> And seldom though I come in court among the rest,
> Yet can I judge, in colours dim, as deep as can the best."

Jealousy, reproach, resentment, follow in the train of wounded and unjustifiable feelings; yet Surrey still loved the cold, vain, rather than retiring being, to whom the most passionate effusions of what can scarcely be termed Platonic love were thus poured out:—

> "The fire it cannot freeze,
> For it is not its kind:
> Nor true love cannot lese
> The constance of the mind."

Few are the annals of the love passages between him and Geraldine, except in his burning verses; they are closed by his reflections on visiting a scene which had once witnessed his happiness, a happiness the poet now believed transferred to another. Like all disappointed men, Surrey now perceived that happiness is not to be found in the strong and unhallowed excitements of passion; he writes therefore:—

> "But happy is that man
> That scaped hath the grief,
> That love well teach him can,
> By wanting his relief.
> A scourge to quiet minds
> It is, who taketh heed;
> A common plague that binds,
> A travail without meed.
> This gift it hath also:
> Whoso enjoys it most,
> A thousand troubles grow
> To vex his wearied ghost.
> And last it may not long
> The truest thing of all;
> And sure the greatest wrong,
> That is within this thrall."

Geraldine, it is evident, did not appreciate the poetic flame which could never add to her welfare, nor enhance her success in life. She soon consented to become the bride of Sir Anthony Browne; and Surrey retired to Boulogne, resolved to conquer his passion, to which, except as in regret for past pleasures, he makes no further reference in his poems.

It was, perhaps, a struggle in Surrey's mind, for Geraldine was supremely lovely at this time; and although, had it not been for Surrey's attachment, her name might never have reached posterity, there remain records of her charms, which were possibly intellectual as well as personal. She was very fair; her eyes were light, and her hair golden and flowing in rich tresses. Thus, in all the pride of almost girlish beauty, was she led to the altar by Sir Anthony Browne, a man of sixty.

This marriage has been deemed a proof of a mercenary spirit in Geraldine, but it was probably inevitable, for Henry VIII. regulated all the matches that were made by any one about the court, and the sacrifice of youth and beauty was most likely performed at his command. Besides, the family of her father was overwhelmed with misfortune. Lord Kildare, whom Holinshed styles " a wise, deep, and far-searching man, valiant without rashness, and politic without treachery," was long immured in the Tower, where he died; and " after he deceased," adds the chronicler, his lady " did ever not only live as a chaste and honourable widow, but also nightly before she went to bed she would resort to his picture, and there, with a solemn congé, she would bid her lord ' good night.' " *

Under these circumstances, poor Geraldine must not be too sternly condemned for obeying the mandate which consigned her to Sir Anthony Browne. She remained in Mary's court, and graced the coronation of that princess; on that occasion the lovely Geraldine was dressed in white satin, her horse's trappings being of the same material. When Mary expected her confinement, Lady Browne was made " Serjeant of the Pantry." When the Queen died, she followed her remains in the second mourning coach. Various presents attested Mary's favour for the portionless bride. After the death of Sir Anthony in 1549, Geraldine married Henry Clinton, Earl of Lincoln, whom she survived. She was the third wife of this nobleman, and possibly he was much older than herself.

Lord Lincoln left her most of his fortune, and Geraldine remained still in the great and gay world. In Queen Elizabeth's time, we are startled to hear her styled " old Lincoln." Happily for all the illusions of romance, Surrey had then long been in the tomb.

The poet Churchyard, speaking of the ladies attendant of Queen Elizabeth, thus refers to the once peerless Geraldine:—

> "Old Lincoln now, that stands on mighty mount,
> Yet low on earth the first foundation lies,
> He drew for that it was of great account,
> And lifted up in favour to the skies.

---

* Holinshed, p. 307.

> The best, we know, did love old Lincoln well:
> In former age her beauty did excell;
> In later times her credit was not small,
> For some do say old Lincoln passed them all."

Thus ended Lord Surrey's passion for Geraldine, which his excellent biographer, Dr. Nott, admits to have been real. If it was the one error of a life singularly virtuous, it was not without illustrious precedents that the young poet yielded to its influence, and thus followed the fashion of the day.

Bernardo Tasso, the father of the great Torquato Tasso, had then written his famous sonnet on Ginevra, which was in every one's mouth. Bernardo had been attached to a beautiful and accomplished woman, who had married a richer suitor; his devotion, and that of Petrarch to Laura, had broken down the line of distinction between the love *tout en honneur* and that against which a struggle should be made, and which *is* made by good men. Sir Philip Sydney, the very paragon of virtue, subsequently gave language to his hopeless love for Lady Rich. All we can say in excuse for Surrey's love-story is, that it was far less degrading and disgraceful than the low amours of many of his compeers.

He shook it off, however, and ambition took the place of love. Dr. Nott, a Doctor of Divinity as well as a Fellow of All Souls, believes that "a passion of this nature, however repugnant to the plain dictates of that pure religion which forbids the aberration even of thought," may not be "incompatible with virtue."[*] We scarcely dare affirm as much, yet it is certain that purer verse, nobler thoughts, holier reverence, never emanated from English poet than from Surrey. His spirituality, his romance free from sickliness, his earnest piety, and, above all, his almost passionate friendship, resemble, to our minds, the heart and intellect of Tennyson.

The death of the young Duke of Richmond, the natural son

---

[*] "Life of Surrey, by Dr. Nott, p. 112.

of Henry VIII. by the Lady Elizabeth Talboys, was the first blow to his heart that Surrey received from death. The next was when Wyatt ceased to exist. It was in the autumn of 1542 that Wyatt was despatched by royal command to Falmouth, to meet an ambassador from Spain who had arrived at that port. Henry, in thus deputing Wyatt, showed the judgment which characterised the Tudors in the choice of their ministers and envoys, and he was perhaps proud to show the very model of an English gentleman, the accomplished traveller, who spoke several foreign languages with fluency. Wyatt had never been intrusted with any public employment since his trial; he therefore rode hard, anxiously hoping to be in time to return, and to accompany the Imperial ambassador to London. The weather was unfavourable, and when Wyatt reached Sherborne he was stopped by an attack of fever. Happily for the sufferer, a friend named Horsey was living in the neighbourhood; he hastened to the bedside of the fever-stricken Wyatt, and, defying the contagion, nursed him to the last. The disease, however, soon manifested a malignant character, and Wyatt sank under the malady. Horsey never left him, but, according to Leland, closed his eyes, when, on the 11th of October, the admired, beloved poet expired.

His remains were not conveyed to Allington, on account of the infectious character of the fever, but were deposited in the family vault of the Horseys, in the great church of Sherborne.*

Thus, in his thirty-ninth year, died one of whom it was truly at that time said the world was not worthy. Religious without superstition, the influence of Wyatt over Henry might, had the poet been spared, have obviated many of the miseries which ensued. Wyatt seemed, indeed, a man raised

* The Horseys lived at that time at Clifton Manbank, about two miles from Sherborne.

up for high and holy purposes. The enthusiasm and poetry of his nature, which made him the hopeless lover of Anne Boleyn, directed to higher objects, rose into piety and benevolence. To his example, to his writings, is due the restoration of polite learning in this country. His writings remain; but his example, which might have humanised society, was closed by his premature death.

Amongst the most beautiful of his works is the celebrated letter to his son, written when Sir Thomas was in Spain, in the year 1538. The youth, whom he addressed in terms such as only a warm heart could dictate, was then fifteen years of age. His subsequent career, as Sir Thomas Wyatt the younger, in the reign of Queen Mary, is one of the most mournful episodes of history.

To the letter here quoted, and to its author, the celebrated Ascham refers in his discourse on the affairs of Germany. " A knight of England, of worthy memory for wit, learning, and experience, old Sir Thomas Wiat, wrote to his son ' that the greatest mischief among men, and least punished, was unkindness.' "* That observation occurs in this letter:—

" Inasmuch as now ye are come to some years of understanding, and that you should gather within yourself some frame of honesty, I thought that I should not lese my labour wholly if I now did something advertise you to take the sure foundations and established opinions that leadeth to honesty. And here I call not honesty that men commonly call honesty, as reputation for riches, for authority or some like thing, but that honesty that I dare well say your grandfather (whose soul God pardon) had rather left to me than all the lands he did leave me; that was, wisdom, gentleness, soberness, desire to do good, friendship to get the love of many, and truth above all the rest. A great part to have all these things, is to desire to have them; and although glory

---

* See Ascham's Works, 1761, p. 7, quoted by Dr. Nott.

and honest name are not the very ends wherefore these things are to be followed, yet surely they must needs follow them as light followeth fire, though it were kindled for warmth. Out of these things the chiefest and infallible ground is the dread and reverence of God, whereupon shall ensue the eschewing of the contraries of these said virtues; that is to say, ignorance, unkindness, rashness, desire of harm, unquiet enmity, hatred, many and crafty falsehood, the very root of all sham and dishonesty. I say the only dread and reverence of God that seeth all things, is the defence of the creeping in of all these mischiefs into you. And for my part, although I do well say there is no man that would his son better than I, yet, on my faith, I had rather have you lifeless than subject to these vices.

"Think and imagine always that you are in the presence of some honest man that you know, as Sir John Russel, your father-in-law, your uncle Parson, or some other such; and ye shall, if at any time you find a pleasure in naughty touches, remember what shame it were afore these men to do naughtily. And sure this imagination shall cause you to remember that the pleasure of a naughty deed is soon past, and the rebuke, shame, and the note thereof shall remain for ever. Then, if these things ye take for vain imaginations, yet remember that it is certain, and no imagination, that ye are always in the presence and the sight of God; and though you see Him not, so much is the reverence the more to be had for He that seeth and is not seen.

"Men punish with shame as greatest punishment on earth, yea, greater than death. But His punishment is, first the withdrawing of His favour and grace, and in leaving His hand to rule the stern, to let the ship run without guide to its own destruction; and suffereth so the man that He forsaketh to run headlong as subject to all mishaps, and at last with shamefull end to everlasting shame and death.

"You may see continual examples both of the one sort and

of the other; and the better if ye mark them well that yourself are come of, and consider well your good grandfather, what things there were in him, and his end. And they that knew him noted thus: first, and chiefly, to have a great reverence of God and good opinion of godly things; next, that there was no man more pitiful, no man more true of his word, no man faster to his friend, no man diligenter nor more circumspect, which thing both the kings his master noted him in greatly. And if these things, and specially the grace of God that the fear of God alway kept with him, had not been, the chances of this troublesome world that he was in had long ago overwhelmed him. This preserved him in prison from the hands of the tyrant that could find in heart to see him racked; from two years and more punishment in Scotland in irons and stocks; from the danger of sudden changes and commotion divers, till that, well-beloved of many, hated of none, in his fair age and good reputation, godly and christianly he went to *Him* that loved him, for that he had always Him in reverence.

"And of myself, I may be a near example unto you of my folly and unthriftiness, that hath, as I well deserved, brought me into a thousand dangers and hazards, enmities, hatreds, prisonments, despites, and indignations; but that God hath of His goodness chastised me, and not cast me clean out of His favour: which thing I can impute to nothing but the goodness of my father, that, I dare say, well purchased with continual request of God His grace towards me more than I regarded or considered myself; and a little to the small fear that I had of God in the most of my rage, and the little delight that I had in mischief. You therefore, if ye be sure, and have God in your sleeve to call you to His grace at last, venture hardily by mine example upon naughty unthriftiness, in trust of His goodness: and besides the shame, I dare lay ten to one ye shall perish in the adventure; for trust me, that my wish or desire of God for you shall not stand you in as much effect as I think my father's did for me. We are not all accepted of Him.

"Begin therefore betimes. Make God and goodness your foundations. Make your examples of wise and honest men: shoot at that mark; be no mocker; mocks follow them that delight therein. He shall be sure of shame that feeleth no grief in other men's shames. Have your friends in a reverence, and *think unkindness to be the greatest offence, and least punished amongst men:* but so much the more to be dread, for God is justiser upon that alone.

"Love well, and agree with your wife; for where is noise and debate in the house there is unquiet dwelling, and much more where it is in one bed. Frame well yourself to love and rule well and honestly your wife as your fellow, and she shall love and reverence you as her head. Such as you are unto her, such shall she be unto you. Obey and reverence your father-in-law, as you would me; and remember that long life followeth them that reverence their fathers and elders; and the blessing of God, for good agreement between the wife and the husband, is the fruit of many children.

"Read oft this my letter, and it shall be as though I had often written to you, and think that I have herein printed a fatherly affection to you. If I may see that I have not lost my pain, mine shall be the contentation, and yours the profit. And, upon condition that you follow my advertisements, I send you God's blessing and mine, and as well come to honesty as to increase of years."

The death of Wyatt was viewed differently by the two great parties of the day.

The Protestants mourned him sincerely, whilst the Roman Catholic party exulted that so able, so popular an advocate of the Reformation was taken away for ever. By Charles V., no ordinary judge, Wyatt, who had during his favour with the king been sent on an embassy to that potentate, was declared to be one of the "most accomplished gentlemen of his times, and a man of as great penetration as any he had ever conversed with." Wyatt, it is well known, had seen through the duplicity of the crafty emperor. Truly did Lord Surrey declare that Wyatt was

"Sent for our health, but not received so;"

and Surrey was the first to compose an epitaph to the memory of his honoured and beloved friend. The lines are so beautiful, that, although one or two verses have been already quoted, in reference to Wyatt's personal attributes, they are here given at length.*

AN EPITAPH ON SIR THOMAS WYATT THE ELDER.

"Wyatt rests here, that quick could never rest,
Whose heavenly gifts increased by disdain,
And virtue sank the deeper in his breast
Such profit he of envy could obtain.
A head where wisdom's mysteries did frame,
Whose hammers beat still in that lively brain
As on a stithy, where some work of fame
Was daily wrought, to turn to Britain's gain.
A visage stern and mild; where both did grow
Vice to contemn, in virtue to rejoice:
Amid great storms, whom grace assured so,
To live upright, and smile at fortune's choice.
A hand that taught what might be said in rhyme,
That reft Chaucer the glory of his wit,
A mark, the which (unperfected for time)
Some may approach, but none may ever hit." *

Other eminent writers composed epitaphs, or rather short biographies, upon the mournful though fruitful subject of Wyatt's virtues and death. Of his numerous admirers and friends, John Leland, the first and last Antiquary-royal of England, was the most learned and the most sincere. Henry VIII.

* It is to be regretted that popular editions of Surrey's and Wyatt's poems are still a desideratum.

made this accomplished scholar his chaplain, appointed him his library keeper, and added to the office that of Antiquary-royal. In 1536 Leland set out on his travels: and, journeying through England and Wales, spent six years in collecting materials for the history of national antiquities. Born, as it seemed, to be the Old Mortality, upon a large scale, of the sixteenth century, this indefatigable man penetrated into every remote country house, spied into charter-chests, and made out inscriptions upon windows. He was seen haunting old cathedrals, and monasteries: now in chapter-houses, then diving into vaults, and crypts; then deciphering old registers: sometimes, on the sea-coast, where there was neither a bay, creek, cape, haven, pier or river, that escaped his cognizance: he was to-day on a river, or lake,—anon, ascending a mountain, or traversing a valley,—anon, half lost in a forest or rough chace,—next by a fire-side in an hospitable old hall, or farm-house,—at length, retreating to a college (perhaps his own dear, conventual All Souls', at Oxford), resting awhile to compress and arrange his materials in the comfortable library of that ancient society. Such were his labours,—but stop, we have not done yet. Wherever there were forts or steps of Roman, Saxon or Danish depredators, and conquerors,—there Leland tracked them, often in great difficulty and even hardship. Tumuli, coins, inscriptions, were his game; and he lived but to discover and to chronicle the remains of antiquity.

In the course of his investigations he became acquainted with Wyatt; their tastes, in some respects, may have differed; but there is always a certain congeniality between cultivated minds, be the cherished pursuit what it may. We can conceive what their topics of conversation were: how, whilst rejoicing at the dissolution of monasteries, they grieved at the indifference of the English to the preservation of the old writings, and curious missals, and rare copies of the Scriptures, which were regarded by Thomas Cromwell (whose mind was as vulgar as that of the Protector in after times), as only so much waste paper. How Leland and Wyatt must have deplored the loss of monuments of learning, more especially when German students, hearing of the indifference of our countrymen, came over to glean all that was valuable from the churches and monasteries. Then, instigated, perhaps, by Wyatt, who had great influence with Lord Cromwell, Leland wrote to the Secretary of State, as Cromwell then was, begging his assistance to save many ancient authors buried then in the dust, and asking permission to place them in the king's library. And Henry rewarded Leland's zeal, to the king's credit be it said, with 'a' rich living, and a canonry. Leland did not forget his friend Wyatt: he wrote, what was then called, an epitaph on his memory, which he addressed to Lord Surrey, under the title of "Næniæ in Mortem Thomæ Viati incomparabilis," Johannæ Lelando, Antiquario, auctore. Londini. Anno, M.D.XIII.

Poor Leland! his fate was melancholy. It is true he survived Henry VIII., which is something to say in the days of that tyrant, and, in 1545, presented to his majesty "a newe yere's" gift, with a scheme of what he intended to do in future; but the future never came to Leland, or, rather, it came darkened by insanity. In 1550 he was consigned by letters patent of Edward VI. to the custody of his elder brother; and, two years afterwards, the mind that had been taxed too hardly by his own energy, wore out the exhausted frame. He died insane; no return of consciousness being permitted to the ardent and accomplished mind of John Leland. His very tomb was destroyed with the Church of St. Michael-le-Merne, in the great fire of London. Peace be to the spirit that had no rest here! Societies of learned men are doing now what John Leland, alone, plodding, solitary, passing through drear forests, or toiling over trackless hills, did unaided, except by royal safeguards, and, perhaps, funds: — great, therefore, was his merit, inestimable his services!

Such was Wyatt's panegyrist: and the praise of such a man

was no slight honour. In dedicating the epitaph to Surrey, Leland expressly stated that he did so on account of the affection that subsisted between the two great men.

Sir John Mason, Sir Anthony Saint Leger, Sir Thomas Challoner, and Parkhurst Bishop of Norwich, also composed elegies in his honour; yet no memorial of Wyatt remains in the great church of Sherborne, no stone marks his tomb, not even a tradition points to the spot where his dust was laid. It is, Dr. Nott declares, only from conjecture that we are led to believe that his remains are deposited in the vault of Horsey his friend.

It appears, however, that, either from party spirit or envy, the memory that Surrey venerated was attacked. Neither was he satisfied with the sorrow that he knew to be, in the case of his own noble mind, so genuine. His lines, headed "Of the feigned grief which some express at the death of Sir Thomas Wyatt, compared with Surrey's deep and reverent sorrow," will touch the heart of those who feel how cold, and how often ungrateful, are the worshippers of the honoured when alive, who, when in the darkness of the grave, can help and protect them no longer:

> "Divers thy death do diversely bemoan!
> Some, that in presence of thy livelihedd
> Lurked, whose breasts envy with hate has swoln
> Yield Cesar's tears upon Pompeius' head.
> Some that watched with the murderer's knife
> With eager thirst to drink thy guiltless blood,
> Whose practice break by happy end of life,
> Weep envious tears to hear thy fame so good.
> But I that knew what harboured in that head,
> What virtues rare were tempered in that breast,
> Honour the place that such a jewel bred,
> And kiss the ground whereon thy corpse doth rest.
> With vapoured eyes, from whence such stream availe,
> As Pyramus did on Thisbe's breast bewail." *

---

* Surrey's Poems, p. 46.

Surrey's friendship to his lamented friend was shown in a mode that attested his sincerity—by regard for his son. The young man who bore the honoured name of Thomas Wyatt, and who is generally called Thomas Wyatt the younger, was twenty-one at the time of his father's death. He is believed, even in his father's life-time, to have received the honour of knighthood; probably from the interest of the Norfolk family, the duke, Lord Surrey's father, being Thomas Wyatt's godfather.

This ill-fated man, with whose career the glory of the Wyatt family terminated, had little taste for letters, but showed a thirst for military distinction. Married, at sixteen years of age, to Jane, the daughter and co-heiress of Sir William Hawte, of Bourne, in Kent,—his restless disposition still pursued him to his ruin. Wyatt had trembled for the well-being of this only son: he had not feared in vain. Still Surrey clung to the younger Wyatt, striving to engage him in pursuits worthy of his name;—in the narrative of Surrey's life, Thomas Wyatt the younger figures conspicuously and frequently.

Surrey, at the time of Wyatt's death, stood high in the favour of his sovereign. An invasion of the English territory in France being apprehended, he had been sent, with Lord Russell and the Earl of Southampton, to see that everything was arranged for the defence of the frontier; on this occasion Surrey completely satisfied the expectations, and gained the approbation of Henry.

But the young impetuous earl was not fitted to pass peaceably through the world. Society was then in a state of bondage: and despotism had almost debased the English character: Surrey hated injustice. Amongst the attendants he most loved was Thomas Clere, a man of high birth, and Surrey's favourite knight companion, and attendant in arms. Witness the epitaph on Clere:—

> "Norfolk sprung thee, Lambeth holds thee dead;
> Clere, of the county of De Cleremont hight.
> Within the womb of Ormond's race thou'st bred,
> And saw'st thy cousin crowned in thy sight.
> Shelton for love, Surrey for lord thou chase (chose)
> (Aye me, while life did last that league was tender,
> Tracing whose steps, thou sawest Kelsal blaze,
> Landrecy burnt, and battered Boulogne render.
> Ah! Clere! if love had booted, cares, or cost,
> Heaven had not won, nor earth so timely lost!" *

It happened that Clere was struck by one Sir Edmund Knevett within the precincts of the court. This was a great offence in times when all men of a certain rank wore weapons: and was generally punished by branding, or the loss of a limb; at the same time, the honour of the subject was to be protected. Surrey, therefore, undismayed by the connections and position of Knevett, who was also a kinsman of his, brought the matter before the Privy Council, and Knevett was sentenced to lose his right hand. The scene must have been a singular one. Knevett and Clere had both been committed to custody, and were now brought out for judgment, and Knevett being found guilty, certain functionaries were called to put the sentence into execution. First came the serjeant-surgeon, who, in the words of Holinshed, appeared "with the instruments appertaining to his office;" then "the serjeant of the woodyard, with the mallet and the block whereupon the hand should lie; the master cook for the king, with the knife; the serjeant of the larder to set the knife right on the joint; the serjeant feuer, with the searing irons to sear the veins; the serjeant of the poultry with a cock, which cock should have his head smitten off upon the same block, with the same knife; the yeoman of the chandry, with sear cloths; the yeoman of the scullery with a pan of fire to heat the irons, a chaffle of water to cool the ends of the irons, and two forms for all officers to set their stuff on; the serjeant of the cellar, with wine, ale, and

* Surrey's Poems.

beer; the yeoman of the eurie in the serjeant's stead, who was absent, with bason, ewer, and towels."

In what agony must Knevett have witnessed these preparations; no more jousting, no more archery or shooting at the popinjay, no more glory in the wars, no more dancing at court. Who would dance with a maimed knight? with whom could he now shake hands in the brawle, or set to in the measure?

Then the whole affair implied such utter ruin. His lands were to be confiscated — such was a portion of his sentence; imprisonment also, during the king's pleasure, and how long *that* king's pleasure might last no one could say. Englishmen were as likely to be immured for life as for a month.

Knevett must have shuddered as he saw the towels, and the mallet, and the knife, and the block, and the searing-irons, and the cock, his fellow-sufferer in ignominy, whose head was doomed. But Knevett perhaps knew that kind words had been said to the "King's Grace" by Surrey. When all was ready, the poor delinquent had the presence of mind to say that he hoped the King's "benign Grace" would take his left hand instead of his right, for then might that right hand do the "King some service." This being favourably reported, Henry was pleased to remit the whole sentence, in consideration of Sir Edmund's "gentle heart,"—or, more likely, of his noble and influential connections.

We next find Surrey himself in durance, and that in the Fleet, where he was sent on account of his having challenged John à Leigh, who had pretended to the favour of the fair Geraldine. It appears from the following lines in Surrey's Poems, that he was jealous of this man, in spite of the inferiority of John à Leigh's condition to his own.

"I see her pleasant chere* in chiefest of thy suit;
  When thou art gone, I see him come that gathers up the fruit,
  And eke in thy respect, I see the base degree
  Of him to whom she gave the heart that promised was to thee."

---

* Countenance.

The punishment of the offence was severe, for the Fleet was the most pestilent of regions; and Surrey, humbled, soon petitioned for mercy. The second letter which he addressed to the Privy Council is preserved in the Harleian MSS. In it he pleads "the fury of reckless youth," for mitigation; he declares that the penalty he is paying, which he terms a "gentle warning," will teach him "to bridle his heady will." He begs of them to consider his previously "quiet life;" he urges that their grave heads should well consider that he was not "the first young man that governed by fury hath enterprized such things as he hath afterwards repented." He was released, and soon afterwards distinguished himself honourably in Scotland.

He was speedily, however, in prison again; two charges were alleged against him, and to both he pleaded guilty. One was,— strange as it seems, when England professed itself to be Reformed — that he had eaten flesh in Lent: the other, that he had walked through the streets of London at night, breaking windows with a crossbow.

Surrey, in regard to the first offence, pleaded a licence; to the second he replied in the following characteristic manner:

"My motive was a religious one, though I confess that it lies open to misconstruction. It grieved me, my Lords, to see the licentious manners of the citizens of London. They resembled the manners of Papal Rome in her corrupted state, and not those of a Christian communion. Was I to suffer these unhappy men to perish without warning? That common charity forbade. The remonstrances of their spiritual pastors had been urged, I knew, in vain. I therefore went at midnight through the streets, and shot from my crossbow at their windows, that the stone, passing noiseless through the air, might remind them of the suddenness of that punishment which the Scriptures tell us Divine justice will inflict on impenitent sinners." *

* Life and Poems by Lord Surrey, p. 24. Edited by Dr. Nott.

Little did the presiding nobles of that day comprehend this attempt to abash and check the evils which have so baffled wise heads in ours. Surrey, Pickering, one of his companions, and Wyatt the younger, were sent to the Tower, where Surrey wrote his "Satire on the Citizens of London."

Happily for this ardent spirit there was then war with France, and it was found convenient to let these three hot-headed young men free. They joined the forces under Sir John Wallop, and fought, Wyatt and Surrey, like men in firmness, like boys in rashness, at Landrecy. The campaign was not a long one, and Surrey was appointed Governor of Boulogne.

Here he endeavoured to add renown to his country by various skirmishes, and by personally engaging even in single combat. He was badly supported, and ill supplied; and being defeated in an unlucky engagement with the French, was recalled. Lord Hertford was appointed Captain-General over the English pale in France, and Lord Grey deputed to supersede Surrey, and to take the command of the fortress and city of Boulogne.

This was the commencement of that tragedy which ended in Surrey's death.

He was then engaged in finishing a new palace at St. Leonard's near Norwich—the site of a suppressed convent of Benedictine Friars. He received into his family Hadrian Junius, a celebrated scholar, whom he established in his house at Kenninghall as a physician. Churchyard the poet, was also domiciled in Surrey's service; but the peaceful intervals in this gifted man's life were of short duration. Nay, it is melancholy to confess that beneath the seeming prosperity of this noble-hearted being was the gnawing anxiety of debt. On October 19th, 1546, we find the following application to some member of the royal household. It is neither indorsed nor addressed.

The Earl of Surrey to ――――

Y^t may like yow wth my most harty comends to understand y^t I haue vewed the Cloche and Dorter off Chryst churche in Norwiche, whiche is in all thynges as I enfourmyd [informed] you unserviceable to ther churche saving for a memory off the old *superstycyon*, and will extend to discharge me owt off the mysery off debt. and iff it were his most excellent Ma: *pleasure* to gyve it me, I will faythfully promise never to trouble his Ma: wth anny sute of profyght to my self hereafter, and *spende* y^t and the rest in his Ma: s̃vice wth ye old zeale y^t I have s̃vered wth always. beseechyng yow to have my sute soe recom̃ended wherof I can hope but well. having suche a harty main & the thyng beyng in y^t nature y^t his Ma: shall forbeare nothyng nor the churche *defacyd* to suche pourpose as it is now *evected*; and thus wyshyng yow healthe and me relief in this *neceseyt*; I *leve* to trowble you from Kenyngal the 19th off October 1546.

You^r & assuryd loving ffriend
H. SURREY.*

He had, indeed, many claims on his means. After his return from Boulogne, he wrote the following letter:—

"It may like you with my hartie commendacions that wheras yester nyght I perceyved by you that the King's Matie, thincking his liberalitie sufficiently extended towards the straungers that have served hym, I have with faire words done my best so to satisfie them accordingly. Assuring you on my faythe that their necessitie seemed to me suche, as it cost me a hundred ducates of myn owne pourse, and sumwhat els; so that now ther resteth nothing to be doñ, but their paspourte and redy dispatch from you, wherein it may yõ to consider their great chardges here. And now yõ shall

* Rolls: Dom. S. Papers, vol. lxxxiv. No. 818, inedited.

geve me leve to come to myne own matters. Commyng from Boullougne in such sort as you knowe, I left onely two of my servts behynd me, John Rosington and Thomas Copeland. To the saied John for his notable service I gave th' advantage of the play * in Boullougne. To Thomas the profecte of the passage. Whom my Lord Gray put immediately out of service after my departure, notwithstanding the Lres† I obtayned from yō to hym in their favour, and upon a better consideracion John occupieth his rowme, and my Lord to his owne use occupieth th' others, office of the passage, sayeing that I and my predecessors there shuld use the same to our gayne. Which I assure you upon myn honor is untrue, and that it shuld be parcell of th' interteynment of the Deputie, which in Callayes was never used and as me semeth to nere for a deputie to grate; unlesse it were for some displeasure borne to me. Finally Mr. Secretary this is th' onely sute I have made yō for anything touchyng Boullougne syth my depture. Wherfore it may please yō that if my Lord Gray will needes be passinger and that the office was no lesse wourth to the saied Thomas then Fyftie pounds a yeare, being plased ther by a King's Lieutenñt which me thincketh a great disorder that a Capytayne of Boullougne shuld displase for any pryvate gayne; yet at the lest it may please yō to require my Lord Gray to recompense hym wth a sum of money in recōpense of that that he hath lost and pourchased so derely wth so many daungiers of liefe; which my saied Lord of his liberalite cannot refuse to do. And for aunswer that my saied Lord chargeth me to have returned the same to my pryvat profecte, in his so saying he can have non honour, for ther be in Boullougne so many wytnesses that Henry of Surrey was never for singler profecte corrupted, nor never yet bribes closed his hande, which lesson I lerned of my father, and wysshe to succeade hym therin, as in the rest.

* Probably *plage*, on shore.   † Letters.

Further wheras the saied Copeland, was placed ther for his demerites by Mr. Southwell and me of the garde, and that my sayd Lord Gray deteyneth from hym his wages, it may please yõ at my most hartie request to graunt hym yor L$\bar{t}$res for th' obteynyng therof, and of the rest; and to pdon my franckness, for that you know it is my naturall to use it wth . . . And thus wysshing you . . . my friend till I deserve of . . . . trary, I pray to God send yo^u . . . . harte desyreth from . . . . 14th of July 1546.

    You^r assured loving ffrend

            H. SURREY.*

This letter proves how honourable was Surrey's character, and shows the commencement of the cabal against him.

Let us hasten over the martial exploits of his youth at Boulogne, for with them our subject has little to do.

The victim of a conspiracy, he was removed from his post as Marshal of the army by the intrigues of the Earl of Hertford, Jane Seymour's brother; we trace him again, not in the annals of history but in those of poetry; we find him, after the famous campaign of Boulogne, discarded, in disgrace, and a prisoner at Windsor; certain expressions of anger against Hertford had been repeated to that now powerful upstart, and Surrey's disgrace was certain; his ultimate downfall probable.

He made, nevertheless, an effort to extenuate his imputed offence; and addressed a letter to some friend, whose name is not given, but who was apparently in the confidence of Henry; it seems to have been written during his imprisonment in the Tower.

Whilst these machinations against him were going on, Lord Surrey remained at Windsor,—a place, to him, full of pain-

---

* Cottonian MSS. Titus B. II. fol. 58. This letter was written only six months previously to his death.

ful remembrance. Here in the days of his boyhood had Surrey been the companion of the amiable and gifted Duke of Richmond, afterwards his brother-in-law. Few lines on friendship — the true, tender friendship of the very young, before faith in goodness is shaken, and motives of interest are given to acts of kindness — few descriptions of trusting hearts and fond conversation are more touching than the following lines by Surrey. Warton properly calls it more an elegy than a sonnet.*

> "So cruel prison, thou could betyde, alas
> As proud Windsor! where I in lust and joye
> With a kynges sonne my childish yeres did passe
> In greater feast than Priam's sonnes of Troye.
> Where eche swete place returns a tastefull lower.
> The large grene courtes where we were wont to rove.
> With eyes cast up into the mayden's tower,
> And easie sighs, such as men draw in love.
> The stately seates, the ladies bright of hewe,
> The daunces shorte, long tales of great delight,
> With words and looks, that tigers could but rewe,
> Where ech of us did plead the other's right.
> The gravell grounde with sleves tied on the helme
> On formying † horse, with swordes and frendly hartes,
> With chear as though one should another whelme
> Where we have fought and chased oft with dartes.
> The secret groves, which oft we made resound
> Of pleasaunt playnt, and of our ladies praise,
> Recording ofte what grace ech one had found,
> What hope of spede, what drede of long delays."

Only a short time previous to his incarceration Surrey had lost his friend Clere. He had been very liberal to this beloved attendant, and he buried his remains in the chapel belonging to the Howard family at Lambeth; inscribing on a tablet suspended on a wall near to the tomb, the beautiful epitaph already quoted.

Surrey was soon released from his durance in Windsor Castle; but the sunshine of his life was soon to close for ever. On the

---

* Warton's Hist. Poetry, vol. v. p. 12.   † Foaming.

twelfth of December, 1546, he was committed to the Tower — which he quitted only to attend his trial — and, finally, to ascend the scaffold. Various causes have been assigned as the sources of Surrey's disfavour with Henry VIII.: but the old story of jealousy of the succession seems to account both for his attainder, and for that of his father, the Duke of Norfolk. Henry had settled the crown on his son Edward: and was naturally anxious that the establishment both of the Reformation, and of the succession should not be disturbed. Lord Surrey was accused of holding Romanist opinions; and of having set up an altar in one of the churches at Boulogne when he was governor of that city. It is, however, stated by contemporary historians that the hatred of Hertford, and his desire to be the young prince's guardian during his long minority, prompted his hatred to the Howard family.

Under such an influence the noble, admirable, high-spirited Surrey perished.

It is sometimes a man's most venial error that works him the direst mischief. Great family pride was the characteristic of that day, when coats of arms could not be assumed unworthily without condign punishment; and meant, consequently, what they represent. Our ancestors, we believe, were capital genealogists: and Garter King-at-arms had often no very easy office when obliged to uphold the dignity of rank. To that lofty officer of state was application made, so soon as Surrey's fate was decreed in Henry's secret councils, for proof of the misconduct of the earl. The reply of Garter runs thus: — *

To the Kings Most royall Mat[ie] touching the Earl of Surrey's bearing of St. Edw[de] Armes.

"Garter saith that thearle of Surrey a little before he went to Bullein viz the [date omitted] day of the xxxvii[th] yeare of the Kings Mat[ies] most noble Reigne, caused Richmonde

---

* Rolls: Dom. S. Papers, vol. lxxxiv. No. 853, inedited.

herauld to write a Letter to said Garter to cum wth all spede to Lambeth to speake with the s^d Erle in a Morninge & thither he came & tarried there the same morninge ere he spake wth the Erle afores^d. At lenght he sent for ye Garter to cum up to the Gallery in his howse at Lambeth, and there shewed him a Schowchien[*] wherin among other things, were the Armes of Saint Edward and Anjow, and he said he would bear them. And the said Garter asked him by what title. And the said Earle said that Brotherton bare them. And said Garter shewed him that it was not in his Pedigree. And the Earle said that he found it in an house in Norfolke in Stone graven soe, and he would bear it. And Garter told him it was not his honour soe to doe. And so at ye last ye Earle said he would bear it, And that he might lawfully doe it. And after y^t ye said Garter, seeing the Earle soe wilfull, spake to Master Warner in Powles to tell ye said Earle y^t he might not doe it.

"Your most humble Sugett
"GARTER."

Such was Garter's reply. To avoid public indignation, the Earl, it appears, was examined under a false name: the homely one of Baker being substituted for that of Howard. The following interrogatories were therefore addressed to him:—

(*Indorsed*) IN GUILDHALL.

Y^e *Interrogations of Mr. Baker.*[†]

First. Whether you, knowledge yor selfe to be our soveraigne Lord the Kings true subject or not?

Item. Of what Estate and Degree you accept and take yor selfe to be of in this Realme?

Item. What enheritaunce you pretend or thynke that of Right you owe to have wth in this said Relme?

---

[*] Scutcheon.   [†] Rolls: Dom. S. Papers, vol. lxxxiv. No. 844.

Item. What pson [person] and of what estate you know that pson to be off to whom do you suppose yor selfe to be an Inheritor after the decease of yor father?

Item. What pson and of what estate you suppose to be the best of the blodde that you come off and be Inheritor unto?*

The examinations were drawn up in full by Lord Chancellor Wriothesley, and Lord Surrey was tried before the commoners in Guildhall. So anxious was Henry VIII. to convict the Earl, that corrections in his own handwriting appear in the following list of interrogatories taken from the Rolls, and indorsed:

"Fair Copy of the Interrogations prepared for the E. of Surrey drawn out & written by the Ld. Chancellor Wriothesley, & corrected by the King (Henry VIII.), the foundation of the charges brought against the Duke of Norff and the E. of Surrey.

(The words in italics are those inserted by the King.)

(*Indorsed.*)

Interrogations ppared for ye E. of Surrey.

"If a man coming of *the colaterall lyne to the heyre off* ye Crown, who ought to bear tharmes of England *but in* the second quarter with the difference of *theyre* anncestrie, doe *presume to* chaunge his righte place, and beare them in the first quarter, and leaving out ye true difference of thañcestor and in lieu therof use *the very place* only of the heire male apparent; *how this man's intent is to be wayed and whither this* import any danger, perill, or slander to ye Title of the Prince or very heire apparent and howe it wayeth in our Lawes.

"If a man *presume to* take into his armes an old coate of the Crowne *which his ancestors never bare, no he off ryght*

---

* This is an original draft, and altered in some places.

owght to beare, and use it w^{th}out difference, whether it may to the perill or slander of the very heir of ye crowne, or be taken to tendre to his disturbance in the same, and in what pill [peril] they be that consent that he shuld soe doe.

"If a man compassing *hymselfe to governe the realme do actually goe abought to rule the Kynge and* should for that purpose advise his daughter or sister to become his harlott *thynkynge therby to brynge it to passe and soe wolde rule bothe fader and sonn as by the nexte artycle dothe more appere whatt thiss importeth.*

"If a man saye these words ('If the King dye who shuld have the rule of the prince but my father or I') what it importeth.

"The depraving of the King's Counsail.

"If a man shall say these words of a nobleman or woman of the Realme:—'if the King were dead I should shortly sett him up: what it importeth.'

"If a man provoked and compelled by his Dutie of Allegiance, shall such matter as he heareth touching the King and shall hereafter be contynually threetened by the ptie [party] accused to be killed or hurt for it; what it importeth.

"If a man take uppon him to use liberty in his Lordshipp's or to keep plees to make hymself free warren in his groundes without licence: what it importeth.

"If a subject psume [presume] to give without licence armes to straungers what it importeth.*

To these were added another list indorsed, "Interrogations touching Coate Armes. Intended or is likely to examine ye Earl of Surrey uppon."

It is evident from the following letter that the storm was not wholly unexpected by Surrey. His letter to his servant was evidently intended to refer to something in the tablet

---

* Rolls: Dom. S. Papers, vol. lxxxiv. p. 846, inedited.

in which the coat of arms, quartering those of Edward the Confessor, might form an additional proof against the accused.

Therle of Surrey to hugh Elles.

"Hugh Ellys; it will be iij, or iiij days or Catelyn Com who shall bryng yow moneij, I pray delyver this lre [letter] w^t all spede to Mrs. Nevingham whom yew shall fynde at Jeromes Sheltons howse in London)—or els will be ther w^t in iij days comawnd. the paynter to leve ow^t the Tablet wher my Lord off Richemond's picture shuld stand : For I will have nothyng ther now yet the tablet but all dowbet: from Kenyngale this wedensday.

"h. Surrey"

Then follows this fragment:—

"delyver this lter to non but her owne hande.*
yt —aye please yor good lordshippez too exa—n m^{es} henyngham late —Marye shelton of the effects of thearle of Surrey his lettre sent unto her (for y^t ys thought that ye secretis hathe passed betwen them before her maryage & sithens—"

(*Addorsment*)   To my s^rvant hugh Ellis
at Lambeth at the Whyghte Lyon
w^t hast hast hast hast

There were many collateral causes which aided to produce the ruin of Lord Surrey. An attempt was made to charge him with having endeavoured to promote an unlawful passion between the King and his sister, and the widow of Henry's illegitimate son, the Duke of Richmond. This monstrous accusation was not, it seems, brought forward at the trial and the document we have quoted is the only proof of its being started. The abandoned sister, however, swore away her brother's life with as little remorse as if the infamous tale were true. It was also murmured that Surrey had refused the hand of the daughter of his enemy Hertford; but since he was at that time married, that rumour must have been

---

* Vol. lxxxiv. No. 837: Record Office.

unfounded. The Duchess of Richmond was solicited to marry Sir Thomas Seymour, Hertford's brother, but as that union might have saved both her brother and her father from their trial and disgrace, she refused the proposal.

One of the proposed questions, referring to the Duchess of Richmond, namely, "whether he made his father pryvie to the matter of my Lady of Richmond or no," points plainly to the allegation relative to the King.* Surrey's doom was, however, determined; and pardon for any offence was proffered to those who could bring forth any charge against the victim of Henry's tyranny.

Surrey was at Kenning Hall, when he was called from the quiet pursuits of his lettered retirement, to appear before Chancellor Wriothesley and the Earl of Hertford, who presided at the Privy Council. Hertford's subsequent career shows well his character. That of Wriothesley was drawn by Blage, a friend both of Surrey's and of Wyatt's, in the following bitter lines:—

BLAGE OF LORD WRIOTHESLEY.

"From vile estate, of base and low degree,
By false deceit, by craft, and subtle ways:
Of mischief mould, and key of cruelty,
Was crept full high, borne up by sundry stages,
Picture of pride: of papistry the plat:
In whom Treason, as in a throne did sit,
With ireful eye, aye glearing like a cat,
Killing by spight whom he thought good to hit."

It is gratifying to find that the friend of Wyatt was worthy of the esteem of that heart, long since mouldering in the tomb. The impetuous Surrey, denied the charges against him, and challenged him who had framed them to single combat. For himself, conscious of innocence, he declared that he would throw aside his armour, and fight an opponent in his coat of mail, in his shirt. The scene must have been striking and even solemn; for life, human life,

* Rolls: Dom. S. Papers, vol. lxxxiv., No. 840, 841.

hung on a thread. Even the base Wriothesley may have been touched with admiration; for to forego the protection of armour, and to fight only in a linen dress, was, in those days of expiring chivalry, the highest proof of valour. To have fought in a tournament in no other dress than *la chemise de sa dame,* gained a French knight the repute of being the most gallant lover in Christendom.

It was during his imprisonment that Lord Surrey addressed to the Council of State the following letter, which has only been disinterred very recently from the State Paper Office.*

" Yt may leke yor honorable Lp yt sythe the begynning off my durance the dyspleasure off my master (wyche losse of blood w^t other distemperances off nature) w^t my sorrow to see the long aprovyd trewghth of myn old father browght in questyon by añy sturre betwenne Sowthwell & me (hath sore feblyd me as is to be sene) wherfor lest sycknes myght folow by meane wheroff my wittż shuld not be so Freshe to unburden my .... conscyence (conscience of) off suche matter as I have resirvyd in expectation off som off yor Lp, to have bene sent from the Kynges Ma: (majesty) to have takyn my examynacyon; I have resolvyd most humbly to make thys sute: That wher as iiij yeres past yow my Lo. Chawncell^r my L. Privy seale my L. off Wynchester and Sr Antonij Browne had the examynacion off matters towchyng alegẽaunce then layd to my charge,—(wherin God knowyth w^t what Dawnger heskapyd) notw^t standyng my iñocency: for the whyche I most humbly confesse to have conceyvyd no small Jelowzii in yor favo^r and aske yor pardon therfor (my desyer iz now iiij and only yow may be sent to me for so it . . . Ma. servyce) to whom I entend to dyschar . . . in suche matter off importañc as depend . . . formall examyñcyon touchyng (or trustyng) in yor ho . . . w^t respect off

* Whilst this work was in the Press. (*No.* 839, *Vol.* 84, *Record Office.*)

my particular desertes towarde yow, ye will make reporte off my tale to his Ma: (Majesty) (accordyng as yõ shall here) and iff it shall seme to his Ma: y^t I overshote mij selfe to be so bold to chose whom his Ma: shuld sende, I truste his Ma: shall hold him contentyd the w^t when I am hard and albeit Mr Baker[*] wer pšent at the formall examynacyon w^t yor Lp. it shall not stand w^t his Ma: svyce (service) y^t he be present at thys: neverthelesse my matter is preindycyall (prejudicial) to no creature onlesse to mij sllfe (present) and Th' Almyghty pšerve yow: your Lp myserable humbly to comawnde,

"HENRY SURREY."

Addressed To the right honorable my Lorde
and other off the Kynges Majestyes most honorable Councell.

Surrey had demanded a trial, and certain depositions were taken down.

Mrs. Holland, his father's paramour, was the first deponent, for she was resolved to exculpate herself at all events. The Duchess of Richmond was the second.

Young, beautiful, impelled by what she termed true Protestant principles, audacious enough to assume religion as her motive, this fiend, this accuser of her father and brother, complained of the one for his irregular payment of her marriage portion, and hated the other for his (imputed) inclination to Romanism. Her testimony did the work that Hertford wanted; her depositions rendered her the murderess of her brother; — for her father escaped royal vengeance.

Little, indeed, was there to be alleged, except idle, bitter speeches about Hertford and the "new nobility," until at last, she stated that her brother Surrey wore on his arms not a duke's coronet, but what seemed to her like a "close crown" and a cypher, which she took to be the king's H. R., and, on these charges, she judged her brother to be guilty of high treason. Next spoke Sir Edmund Knevett, who, but

[*] Himself, under that name.

for Surrey, would have been a branded, ruined, outcast; but he admitted that he could charge the earl "with no untruth." No, Surrey's honour was unscathed, that was all. Sir Thomas Pope also appeared in court, but no evidence of guilt was elicited.

The Earl was then indicted for high treason, and tried by special commission on the 13th of January, before a jury of Norfolk men. It was a critical day, for at that very instant Henry VIII. lay in the last agonies of death.

The accused spoke well; — too well, according to the chroniclers Hall and Holinshed, who thought that if he had shown less wit "his praise had been the greater." Doubtless he gave his accusers and judges many sharp hits, for a noble imprudence, often the error of those high in station, was one of the leading traits of his dauntless character. But independent men were not appreciated in that day. He reduced, however, the whole burden of the accusations against him to one point — namely, that he had borne the arms of Edward the Confessor. Then a fearful scene ensued. Surrey stood in court, battling for his life on that small point; his integrity, his intellect, his courage, were indeed notable. Meantime — this was at Guildhall — how was the King? Such a question must have been asked by many in a low voice; if he lives, Surrey is doomed; if he dies, Surrey is also doomed. Hertford is Lord Protector, and Surrey has sworn, after the death of Henry, to avenge himself on the "new man."

The fact of bearing the Confessor's arms seriously affected men, who then regarded a coat of mail much as we now do a title, with strange scruples. To bear arms gave, without nobility, the same position as the "De" affixed to surnames does in France. The jury looked upon this matter as a grave offence. In vain did Surrey urge precedence; in the midst of the life-struggle a dastardly witness was permitted to depose to "high words" Surrey had used, and to his own bravado (poor, paid wretch!) in answering them.

Then the flower of chivalry, the friend of Wyatt, started up, all the blood of all the Howards mantled in that long, sharp-featured, most expressive face, as he spoke:—" I leave it to yourselves, gentlemen," he said, "to judge whether it were probable that this man should speak thus to the Earl of Surrey, and he not strike him."

He was, condemned. The Chancellor, the " carrion corpse " described by Blage, pronouncing sentence of death on the noblest of his generation.

Surrey was remanded after his trial to the Tower. There is something solemn in the mystery that hangs over his last moments. We see him, in fancy, small of stature, but incomparably proportioned, with dark, speaking eye, looking back once more at that court;—at the old hall; the Lord Mayor in his robes, the guilty Wriothesley, the craven Knevett. He passes out, and we behold him no more.

The chroniclers, who thought him too witty and too fearless, prudently abstained from details which must have wrung every manly heart had they appeared in their annals.

Henry's last act was to sign Surrey's death-warrant; at all events, if too ill to write, he was able to figure his large initials, the fatal H. R. which had sent so many souls to judgment, on the document.

On the nineteenth, or some say the twenty-first of January 1546, Surrey was beheaded on Tower Hill. His body was buried in the church of Saint Hallows Barking, but removed afterwards, it is said, to Framlingham, in Suffolk. He died in his thirtieth year, having lived in that time double, in one sense, to the lives of ordinary men.

Even Horace Walpole is roused to some natural feeling when he relates that the father, the hateful Duke of Norfolk was spared—spared by the death of the King; whilst Surrey, the lofty, the noble, the pious, the fearless, he who has realised all one's notions of true nobility, *sans peur, sans reproche*, perished on the scaffold.

WILLIAM COWPER AND MARY UNWIN.

BIRTH AND PARENTAGE OF WILLIAM COWPER. — HIS MOTHER. — HER EARLY DEATH. — HIS LINES ON HER PICTURE. — GOES TO SCHOOL. — AFTERWARDS TO WESTMINSTER. — THEN INTO A SOLICITOR'S OFFICE. — HIS ATTACHMENT TO HIS COUSIN. — THE FATHER'S OBJECTION AND DECISION. — COWPER BECOMES INSANE. — INTRODUCED TO MARY UNWIN. — HER CHARACTER. — TAKES UP HIS ABODE WITH HER. — HUNTINGDON DESCRIBED. — UNWIN'S DEATH. — OLNEY. — NEWTON. — LADY AUSTEN. — WESTON. — NEWTON DISAPPROVES OF COWPER'S VISITING THERE. — RELIEF TO COWPER TO REMOVE THERE. — LADY HESKETH'S KINDNESS. — DEATH OF MRS. UNWIN. — DEATH OF COWPER. — VISIT OF MACKINTOSH AND OF BASIL MONTAGU TO DURHAM.

WILLIAM COWPER AND MARY UNWIN.

THE county of Hertfordshire has owned an undue proportion, for its extent, of literary characters. Lord Bacon, at Gorhambury; Sarah, Duchess of Marlborough, at St. Alban's; Cowper, at Berkhampstead; not to enumerate many more dead, and some living, celebrities, are sufficiently notable to glorify a province.

William Cowper, the most unhappy man of his time, was born on the 15th of November, in 1731 (old style), at Berkhamsted, St. Peter's, in this favoured county. His father was the rector of the parish. Berkhampstead — anciently called Bergham stedt, from its being in the hills; *Berg*, being in Saxon a hill; *Ham*, a town; and *Stedt*, a seat — owned at one time a Saxon castle and fort, in which a king of Mercia resided: until William the Conqueror, the Napoleon of his time, came to see and to conquer; and gave Berkhamsted, rated at thirteen hides, to his half-brother, the Earl of Mortaigne.

Many remnants of ancient grandeur remained to attract the early attention of one whose infancy seems to have comprised almost the only happy period of his existence. William Cowper, as he described himself, drawn by the gardener Robert day by day to school, could view the fine old church in which his father preached, with the reverence due to a pile that had received among its worshippers stern Plantagenet crusaders—who succeeded the despoiled Mercians as rulers over the castle and township. Here Cicely, the last of that race, lived and died. Her predecessors, Piere Gaveston and Robert de Vere, the one the favourite of Edward II., the other of Richard II., having held a brief sway here; and the still stately ruin, the ancient church, the peculiarities of the once favoured little town, wanted but the adjunct of a poet's birth to render the place complete in interest.

The lineage of Cowper was thoroughly English, highly respectable, and ancient;—and latterly noble. Yet he took a pleasure in saying that his name was derived from that of a Cooper, or Cow-keeper, or a general dealer (Kooper) Dutch; and that a worthy Scottish bishop, from Fifeshire, had first made the family, as it were, into a family; and there may have been some truth in the notion, for James I. in creating a certain William Cowper, in his reign, a baronet of Nova Scotia, perhaps paid a compliment to some zealous, anti-puritanical Scottish prelate. And James did well in promoting Sir William Cowper, for that worthy man erected a monument to the judicious Hooker, thirty years after that great divine's death. Sir William's son, another Sir William (a confusion of proper names, which there should be a law to prevent), was father of the first Earl Cowper, Lord Chancellor, and of Spencer Cowper, one of the Judges of the Court of Common Pleas.

John Cowper, D.D., the father of the poet, was the son of Spencer Cowper, and was presented to the Rectory of Great Berkhampstead in due time.

The mother of the poet was Anne Donne; she had the honour of being of the same family as Dr. Donne, the friend of Izaak Walton. She was one of the Donnes, of Ludham Hall, in Norfolk; and she appears to have been worthy of the name of Donne.

Her portrait bears some resemblance to that of her son William. She had the same slender form, the same refined features, the same light hair and white complexion; and probably from *her* was inherited the sweet, susceptible nature, the gentle, poetic mind; and—but we hope not—the cruel, incurable malady of later years.

The poet's infancy was happy, for his mother was tenderly affectionate; and that he respected his father is obvious in his famous and exquisite lines to my "Mother's Picture."

Who cannot enter into the feelings of the bereaved child when, many years afterwards, he gazed on his mother's portrait, which had been sent to him by a relation? How many a son could echo those heart-stricken words:

"Life has past,
With me but roughly since I saw thee last."

Mrs. Cowper loved him fondly; and the delicate, petted boy, was born to be beloved. He remembered in after life many little tender cares:

"The fragrant waters on my head displayed
By thy own hand."

Children indeed remember such small kindnesses longer than we think.

We see him sitting by his fond mother's lap, pricking shapes into paper with a pin: and

"Thou wert happier than myself the while,
Wouldst fondly stroke my head—and with a smile."

Alas! the loving child was soon severed from this doating parent, who died at the early age of thirty-four, in childbirth. The beauty of her life, the heroism of her death, were thus described in her epitaph by her niece, afterwards Lady Walsingham:*

"Here lies, in early youth bereft of life,
The best of mothers, and the kindest wife;

---

* Cowper's Life, p. 5.

> Who neither knew nor practised any art,
> Secure in all she wish'd, her husband's heart:
> Her love to him, still prevalent in death,
> Pray'd Heaven to bless him with her latest breath.
>
> . . . . .
>
> Whoe'er thou art that dost this tomb draw near,
> O, stay awhile, and shed a friendly tear;
> These lines, though weak, are as herself sincere."

The sensitive, precocious child was conscious of his loss:

> "I heard the bell toll'd on thy burial day,
> I saw the hearse that bore thee slow away;
> And turning from my nursery window drew
> A long, long sigh, and wept a last adieu."

His was a temperament that "peculiarly required," as Southey expresses it, "the peacefulness and security of home." Yet, at six years of age, he was sent to a school at Market Street, in Hertfordshire; where the fragile child was intimidated by a barbarous lad of fifteen, who frightened the unhappy Cowper so much that he had not courage to look his persecutor in the face. Never did he, he relates, raise his eyes higher than the knees of the tyrant:— "I knew him better by his shoe-buckles than by any other part of his dress. May the Lord pardon him, and may we meet in glory!"

It is difficult, however, for those who love the memory of Cowper to pardon this unknown tyrant, to whose account not only merely infantine misery, but years of wretchedness, may be laid. A child of either sex, predisposed to insanity, should be encouragingly, though firmly treated; whilst no morbid tendencies should, by over indulgence, be evoked, terrors should, at the same time, be kept away. Pleasant images, active exercises, a sense of being loved, all that can cheer, yet not excite, may do much to avert the heaviest calamity with which our heavenly Father chastises His people.

In his anguish, the affrighted William Cowper remembered

that there was a God above—that God whom, in after life, he so often feared had deserted him. Miss Edgeworth, amongst many admirable hints for the young, says, "Never first speak to a child of God as an object of fear." In this poor child's case, whilst his little heart fluttered and throbbed at the very sound of his tormentor's voice, his Maker came into his mind as a refuge—a very present help in trouble.

"One day," he relates, "as I was sitting alone upon a bench in the school-room, melancholy, and almost ready to weep at the recollection of what I had already suffered, and expecting at the same time my tormentor every moment, the words of the Psalmist came into my mind: 'I will not fear what flesh can do unto me.' I applied them to my own case, with a degree of trust and confidence in God that would have been no disgrace to a much more experienced Christian. I instantly perceived in myself a lightness of spirits, and a cheerfulness I have never before experienced, and took several paces up and down the room with alacrity." But these religious impressions were soon effaced: "I cannot recollect," Cowper afterwards wrote, "that until the thirty-second year of my life, I had even any serious impressions of the religious kind, or at all bethought myself of the things of my salvation, except in two or three instances."

Many persons, indeed, of Cowper's intended profession could, at that time, own to the same fact, for he was brought up to the Bar.

During his boyhood, nevertheless, some transient impressions of his Christian responsibility were imparted. Whilst at Westminster school, then the great place for the education of the higher classes, he was confirmed. The head master Dr. Nichols, undertook, of course, to prepare the boys for confirmation. "The old man," Cowper relates, "acquitted himself of this duty like one who had a deep sense of its importance; and I believe most of us were struck by his manner, and affected by his observations. Then, for the first time, I attempted to pray in secret; but being little accustomed to that exercise of the heart, and having very childish notions of religion, I found it a difficult and painful task, and was even then frightened at my own insensibility. I relapsed into a total forgetfulness of God, with all the disadvantages of being the more hardened, for being softened to no purpose." Then, before he had entered life, a warning in the form of a severe attack of the small-pox came; during his illness he had no thought of God, nor of eternity — no contrition. Though he was at that age, he avows, an infernal liar, being able to invent, at a moment's notice, a plausible excuse: "These, I know," he said, "are called school-boy tricks, but a total depravity of principle, and the work of the father of lies are universally at the bottom of them." "Whatever seeds of religion I might have carried thither (to Westminster school), before my seven years apprenticeship to the classics had expired, were all marred and corrupted. The duty of the schoolboy swallowed up every other; and I acquired Latin and Greek at the expense of a knowledge important."

Well might Dr. Arnold declare that public schools (as constituted formerly) " were the nurseries of vice." *

An incident, which would have been received by many with indifference, made a great impression on the excitable, imaginative Cowper.

He was crossing St. Margaret's churchyard one night, when a grave-digger, who was at work by the light of a lanthorn, suddenly threw up a skull, which struck him on the leg. This event "was an alarm," Cowper tells us, "to his conscience, and may be numbered among the best religious documents that I received at Westminster." He became forgetful of mortality. So true is Southey's remark: " Death, indeed, appears to us in boyhood almost as much like a

* Life of Arnold, by Dr. Stanley.

dream — as life, to those who are far advanced in their mortal pilgrimage."

Notwithstanding all his self-reproach, and the too accusing conscience which in after life, under the influence of zealous friends, converted the thoughtlessness of boyhood into a crime, Cowper looked back to Westminster with pleasure, alluding to which, in his Table Talk, he says:

> "The scene is touching*, and the heart is stone,
> That feels not at that sight, and feels at none;
> The wall on which we tried our graving skill,
> The very name we carv'd subsisting still:
> The bench on which we sat while deep employed,
> Though mangled, hack'd, and hew'd, not yet destroyed;
> The little ones, unbuttoned, glowing hot,
> Playing our games, and on the very spot,
> As happy as we once to kneel and draw
> The chalky ring, and knuckle-down at taw;
> To pitch the ball into the grounded hat,
> Or drive it devious with a dexterous pat;
> The pleasing spectacle at once excites
> Such recollections of our own delights,
> That viewing it we seem almost to obtain
> Our innocent, sweet simple years again."

Whilst at Westminster, Cowper formed the acquaintance of several who figured in after life — Richard Cumberland, Impey, famous or infamous in India, and Warren Hastings, were his class fellows. There was one, however, whom he preferred to all: this was Sir William Russell, whose family had been, in former days, intimately connected with that of Cromwell — one of their descendants was bed-chamber woman to the Princess Amelia, the daughter of George the Second. "Ah! Miss Russell," cried Frederick, Prince of Wales, in his sister's room, on the 30th of January, seeing the young lady employed in adjusting some part of his sister's dress; "are you not at Church to try to avert the judgments of heaven from falling upon the nation for the sake of your

* Southey's Cowper, p. 17.

ancestor, Oliver?" "Is it not," she answered, "sufficient humiliation for a descendant of the great Oliver to be pinning up the tail of your Royal Highness's sister?"

Russell alone retained the affection of Cowper. The lines

> "Still, still I mourn, with each returning day,
> Him snatched by fate in early youth away,"

referred to this friend of his boyhood. From Westminster Cowper was transferred into a solicitor's office, to learn the practice of the bar. Here he remained three years, passing his Sundays, however, in the agreeable society of his young cousins in Southampton Row, the daughters of his uncle, Ashley Cowper. In these visits he was accompanied by a fellow-clerk, the great lawyer, who afterwards became Lord Thurlow.

Thurlow had been educated at Canterbury School, "a daring, refractory boy," whose after career certainly carried out the impressions given by his youth.

Southampton Row, then open to the fields, was a pleasant as well as an aristocratic locality; and here the happiest years of Cowper's youth were spent. Instead of studying law — for the pursuit of which he was totally unfitted — he devoted himself to the two young ladies. "There was I," he wrote to Lady Hesketh at a later period, "and the future Lord Chancellor constantly employed from morning to night in giggling and making giggle, instead of studying the law. O fie, cousins, how could you do so!"

One of the culprits who thus allured Cowper and Thurlow from the office was a charming and accomplished girl, Theodora Jane, the ill-fated second daughter of Ashley Cowper. She was intelligent, accomplished, and, as we learn from her after life, of an affectionate, constant nature: an attachment was the result of the long and idle hours of that careless period. William Cowper now became an altered being; his shyness disappeared; he dressed well, he talked well, and he soon avowed his affection for his cousin to his uncle. "And what," asked the young lady's father, addressing his daughter, "will you do if you marry William Cowper?" "Oh, Sir, wash all day, and ride out on the great dog at night!"

Mr. Ashley Cowper, too late to save his daughter's happiness, which became evermore involved in the well-being of her cousin, objected then and for ever to an union. Southey considers the notion that first cousins ought not to marry, as one of the superstitions that has survived the Reformation. He forgets the almost invariable delicacy of health, and decay in the human frame, that is the result of marriages of this kind. The Romish Church, or, as he styles it, the "crafty priesthood," who opposed such ties, were, perhaps, wiser in their generation than we, in ours. In Cowper's case, although the result was most miserable, there were reasons more cogent than ordinary considerations; and the prudent father probably dreaded the insanity which afterwards supervened.

He stated his resolution, and the cousins never met again. They remained still fondly attached, especially Theodora, who never married, nor wished to marry, after this blighting incident of her youth. Her pride in his then developing talents — her constancy to his memory endured to the last. Often did the poet, in sorrow and sickness, receive anonymous proofs that some one absent was thinking of his comforts, and treasuring up the dim image of his first love. All intercourse between the cousins ceased for years. When it had been revived between Cowper and the elder sister, the charming Lady Hesketh, he said: "I still look back to the memory of your sister, and regret her; but how strange it is, if we were to meet we should not know each other."

He had transcribed his early poems for Theodora. She treasured the manuscript for years, committing them at last to an intimate friend, with instructions not to open them till after her death. The once young and gay suitor had by that time become a hopeless maniac. The sight of these relics of former days distressed her who had mourned over the utter darkness of the once vigorous mind. The interesting and constant Theodora survived until 1824.

An engagement to his cousin would, perhaps, have prevented two terrible results — one was a course of "sinful indulgence," to use the poet's own words, during the twelve years that he remained in the Temple, whither he afterwards removed; the other was the state of mind described as darkening this period of Cowper's youth. He was only twenty-one when thus left to himself in the centre of vicious London, his father having bought a set of chambers for him for the sum of two hundred and fifty pounds. The following passage is taken from his own account of his early life:—

"This being a critical season of my life, and one upon which much depended, it pleased my all-merciful Father in Jesus Christ to give a check to my rash and ruinous wickedness at the very onset. I was struck, not long after my settlement at the Temple, with such a dejection of spirits as none but they who have felt the same can have the least conception of. Day and night I was upon the rack, lying down in horror, and rising up in despair. I presently lost all relish for those studies to which I had before been closely attached. The classics had no longer any charms for me. I had need of something more salutary than amusement, but I had no one to direct me where to find it."

Then a volume of George Herbert's poems fell into his hands, and he found in them a strain of piety he could not but admire. Such was the commencement of that religious melancholy which hung over the amiable and unhappy William Cowper. Change of scene was recommended, and he went to Southampton, where, sitting with some friends on an eminence at the end of an arm of the sea, between Southampton and the New Forest, he felt as if the weight of his misery was suddenly taken off his heart. "I could," he said, "have wept with transport had I been alone."

"I think," he adds, "I remember something like a glow of gratitude to the Father of mercies for this unexpected blessing, and that I ascribed it to His gracious acceptance of my prayers. But Satan and my own wicked heart quickly persuaded me that I was indebted for my deliverance to nothing but a change of scene and the amusing varieties of the place. By this means he turned the blessing into a poison."

In this irrational state, Cowper was not proof against what followed. He returned to London;—associated with professed infidels, and with Christians only in name; obtained a mastery over conscience, and even began to doubt whether the Gospel were true or not. This course was assuredly fostering the disease which ensued. He still struggled against vice, and combated Deists, but was growing every day more and more wretched, until at last he was nigh lost for ever.

Meantime, he appears to have overcome his early disappointment. Certain pleasures, besides those of a reprehensible kind, had solaced the heart not, perhaps, so deeply wounded as that of Theodora.

"Sometimes," he writes to a friend and fellow-Templar, Allworthy Rowley, "I go into the adjacent parts of the country to visit a friend or a lady; but it is a short journey, and such as may easily be performed on foot or in a hired carriage: for never, unless compelled to do it, do I mount a horse, because I have a tender skin, which, with little exercise of that kind, suffers severely. I lately passed three days at Greenwich — a blessed three days — and if they had been three years I should not have envied the gods their immortality."

In after times, however, justice was done to the generous-minded woman whose life was devoted to one remembrance. It is not in the hey-day of youth and spirits that women must look to their reward — if reward it is — in the deep regret for their loss. It is when the world palls, when ties are broken, or are disappointing; when health is declining, and nothing but what is true and good seems valuable, that late justice is rendered to the few sincere and tender friends of our youth.

The following lines, addressed to Lady Hesketh, were written in Cowper's middle life; they were enclosed in a letter to Lady Hesketh. The letter was lost, but the verses remain. They were not at first published with Cowper's Poems [*]:—

> "Doom'd as I am in solitude to waste
> The present moments, and regret the past;
> Deprived of every joy I valued most,
> My friend torn from me, and my mistress lost:
> Call not this gloom I wear, this anxious mien,
> The dull effect of humours or of spleen:
> Still, still, I mourn, with each returning day,
> Him snatched by fate in early youth away;
> And her,—through tedious years of doubt and pain,
> Fixed in her choice, and faithful—but in vain;
> O, prone to pity, generous and sincere,
> Whose eye ne'er yet refused the wretch a tear,
> Whose heart the real claim of friendship knows,
> Nor thinks a lover's are but fancied woes:
> See me, ere yet my distant course half done,
> Cast forth a wanderer on a wild unknown."

We must linger a little longer over this perilous period of Cowper's early life before we can show how dependent it made him upon the gentle offices of friendship — how it broke down, during the intervals of reason, his judgment;—a life of excess, falsely called a life of pleasure, being the likely precursor of years of contrition, humiliation, and fanaticism.

Before he for ever left the Temple, Cowper belonged to a club of seven Westminster men, called the "Nonsense Club." Bonnell Thornton, Colman, Lloyd, and Joseph Hill were members, and the company must have been far more amusing than respectable.

Bonnell Thornton was the son of an apothecary, and, as well as Colman, was elected from Westminster to a studentship in Christ Church, Oxford, whence he graduated, in 1754,

---

[*] Southey's Life of Cowper, p. 33.

as a Bachelor of Medicine. He was, however, more of a literary character than a physician. In conjunction with Colman, he wrote "The Connoisseur," a periodical paper, in the conclusion of which the portraits of the two authors were drawn under the character of "The Town," in which that composite individual was stated to be at once "a student of law and a bachelor of physic; to wear his own head and a periwig; to be above thirty years of age, yet not more than four and twenty."

Thornton, who was at once domestic and estimable, had the good fortune to own Dr. Warton as his friend during life, and as his panegyrist on his monument in Westminster Abbey after his death.

The wit of Colman and Thornton was set off by contrast with Lloyd, formerly one of the ushers of Westminster School. Lloyd was content, it was said, "to scamper round the foot of Parnassus on his little Welsh pony, which seems never to have tired. He left the fury of the winged steed, and the daring heights of the sacred mountain," to his friend Churchill. Poor Lloyd! his life was one of trial. Beginning it as an usher — a word which speaks volumes of small miseries — he took, unhappily, to literature; wrote an admired poem called "The Actor," was suspected of being the author of "The Rosciad," got into debt, was cast into the Fleet, and owed his living in that then wretched prison to the friendship of Churchill. Gentle, engaging in manners, too humble and sensitive to cope with misfortune, Lloyd sank into despondency, and, a month after Churchill's death, put an end to his own life.

In sober relief to the others, Joseph Hill, a plain-sailing law-student, showed at these pleasant meetings his practical sense and quiet humour. Cowper's child-like nature instinctively cherished Hill. Bonnell Thornton, Colman, Lloyd, were his boon companions at the Nonsense Club, but Hill, who plodded upwards at the bar, was his friend "for all weathers;" one of those steady-going, safe, certain, and serviceable adherents whom one counts upon as one does on an old coat, which comes in when newer and better-looking garments are worn out, and which cannot be spoiled.

Whilst Cowper, delighting in the country, was spending time and money in running about, Hill despised all recreations. Southey gives this amusing anecdote of his imperturbable, unchangeable nature.

Neither of the friends cared, it seemed, to witness the coronation of George III., but Hill had sisters who expressed far more curiosity than himself, and they were eager to obtain places for the show.

"When Hill's sisters," says Southey*, "obtained, by Ashley Cooper's favour, a good situation for seeing that solemnity, neither their brother nor Cowper could accompany them; and when they returned, full of delight and admiration, 'Well, ladies!' exclaimed Hill—and Cowper joined him in the exclamation—'I am glad you were so well pleased, though you have sat up all night for it.' At the illumination for the King's recovery, in 1789, these old ladies came up again to see the sight. 'Well, ladies,' said their brother, 'I am very glad that you were so well pleased.' 'Why this is just what you said to us, brother, fifty years ago!' they cried."

Cowper held the doctrine that any man might be rich if he would. He despised the love of gain, and went, which was but the logic of his years, into an opposite extreme. One degree of poverty, that in which a man wears clean linen and enjoys good company, he held to be no disgrace; but "if I never sink below this degree of it," he added, "I care not if I never rise above it."

He was at this time in that state which the French describe by the term "*manger son bien.*" His capital was almost exhausted. He began to be afraid of approaching want; his

* Cowper's Life, p. 40.

father having, before his death, which had then taken place, married again.

He had occasionally contributed to periodicals; amongst others he wrote a paper in "The Connoisseur" upon keeping secrets. The effort had so good an effect on his own mind, that he was never again guilty of betraying a secret. But, whilst he kept up his classical knowledge, as well as tried his skill at verse, poverty began to stare him in the face. That there is an ever-recurring retribution in the course of this life, in great as well as small things, every attentive observer of worldly affairs must confess. Cowper had neglected the study of his profession: he had now no stick to lean upon on his road. Despair began to seize upon this improvident, but gentle, suffering being. He applied to his relation, Major Cowper, to procure him a place as Clerk to the Journals of the House of Lords, in case of a vacancy by the death of the clerk. The business of that post, being performed in private, would, it was thought, suit Cowper.

"We both" (Cowper thus relates the truth) "expressed an earnest wish for his (the clerk's) death, that I might be provided for. Thus did I covet what God had commanded me not to covet, and involved myself in still deeper guilt, by doing it in the spirit of a murderer."

His narrative of the transaction is most striking. We read it with compassionate approbation of a man who suffered for a too tender conscience.

"It pleased the Lord to give me my heart's desire, and with it an immediate punishment for my crime. The poor man died; and, by his death, not only the Clerkship of the Journals became vacant, but it became necessary to appoint officers to two other places, jointly, as deputies to Mr. Grey, who at this time resigned. These were the offices of Reading Clerk, and the Clerkship of the Committees, of much greater value than that of the Journals. The patentee of these two employments (whom I pray God to bless for his benevolent intentions to serve me) called on me at my chambers, and, having invited me to take a turn with him in the garden, there made me an offer of the two most profitable places, intending the other for his friend Mr. A."

The result was most disastrous. There was a strong opposition to Cowper's being appointed: that was overruled: and the difficulty now lay in the most vital quarter — his own unhappy condition of mind. It was necessary for him to appear at the bar of the House of Lords; and, to acquit himself properly, to prepare himself, by daily attendance, for his duties. He felt that he could not accomplish his public appearance; and his resolution failed him. A public exhibition was to him like mortal poison: no one, he declares, could have a notion of the horrors of his situation.

"My continual misery," he tells us, "at length brought on a nervous fever; quiet forsook me by day, and peace by night: a finger raised against me was more than I could stand against. In this posture of mind I attended regularly at the office; where, instead of a soul on the rack, the most active spirits were essentially necessary for my purpose. I expected no assistance from anybody there, all the inferior clerks being under the influence of my opponent; and, accordingly, I received none! I read without perception, and was so distressed that, had every clerk in the office been my friend, it would have availed me little."

After suffering agonies of mind, he consulted Dr. Heberden; and was as diligent in the use of drugs as if they could have healed a wounded spirit. In vain did he make an effort to receive consolation in prayer. The mental strength was inadequate; he soon laid aside the sacred volume, and with it "all thoughts of God."

What follows is a fearful narrative of aberration of mind, which might have been averted by the sympathies of home, combined with the faith in God's mercy, by which we regard Him as one who "considereth our trouble." The agonised recital is most powerfully told in Cowper's own words. It furnishes an instance of candour, rare indeed, and very touching. Cowper, in relating this part of his life, years afterwards, deemed it a duty to hold himself up as a beacon. He was haunted, he confessed, henceforth by a thousand terrors. Madness, he began to fear, would be "his only chance." He even looked forward to it, he declares, with impatient expectation; and was afraid "that his senses would not fail him" time enough to excuse his appearance at the bar of the House of Lords, which was the only purpose he wanted his mental malady to answer. Unhappily, as far as he knew, his senses were still able to perform their work.

Insanity, however, had, in fact, then commenced. No man, however morbid, would, possessed of reason, have dreaded an appearance in public, merely to read over a formal document. Cowper's sense of right faltered: he began to consider that his life was his own, and that he had a right to take it away if he chose. He remembered, eleven years previously, having read a paper on suicide aloud to his father, and having argued against it; but his father had given no opinion on the subject. He resolved to take laudanum: but his resolution failed him; he only kept the bottle, which he had purchased from an apothecary with as "cheerful an air" as possible, in his side pocket, as a resource. He then resolved upon drowning, and drove in a coach to the Tower Wharf, intending never to return to the vehicle; but found the water low, and saw a porter seated there on some goods, as if "on purpose to prevent" him from taking that "way to the bottomless pit." He was still bent on self-destruction, and twenty times a day did he put the fatal phial to his lips, when a voice seemed to whisper to him: "Think what you are doing; consider, and live!"

The night previous to his appointed appearance in the House of Lords arrived, and a friend called to congratulate him on a resolution which he heard that Cowper had taken, to "stand the brunt" and keep the office. The poor bewildered Cowper did not contradict his friend; but, when he left the room, said to himself, "I shall see thee no more."

He went to bed to take what he thought his last sleep in this world. He slept till three o'clock, then awoke: found his pen-knife, and lay with it for some hours pointed against his heart. Still resolution failed him; or, rather, let us say, still an angel of mercy watched over him, and guarded the unhappy man from himself.

Day began to break: seven o'clock struck: there was now, the poor maniac thought, no time to be lost. In four hours his friend was to call and take him to Westminster. "This," he said to himself, "is the crisis: let there be no more dallying with the love of life." His next attempt was to hang himself with a garter, made of broad scarlet binding, with a sliding buckle. This he slipped over an iron pin which fastened a wreath of carved woodwork to the old-fashioned bed-post. He mounted a chair; put the loop round his neck, and pushed the chair away. As he hung there, he fancied that he heard a voice say three times, "'*Tis over!*'" He hung so long that he lost all sense, all consciousness of existence.

But God, "whose never-failing Providence ordereth all things both in heaven and earth," willed that the life thus madly endangered should be preserved still for utility to others, though not for happiness to its owner.

The attempt this time was nearly fatal: but the garter broke: the miserable man was awakened to consciousness by falling on the floor. He was able to get into bed, and to call to his laundress, who was opening the shutters of the next room, and beg her to send for a friend, who came directly to him. Cowper confessed the whole affair; a relation was sent for; and it was decided that Cowper could not hold the office, which was instantly resigned. Thus ended all his connection with the Parliament Houses. As an official, his career was at an end: as a poet, it was almost begun.

He suffered the deepest remorse for his attempt on his own life; and the fear of death now superseded his former desire of it. "A sense of God's wrath, and a deep despair of escaping it, instantly succeeded." He believed that he had lost all interest in Christ; all benefits of His passion; all hope in the promises of the great, merciful, eternal Father.

When he went into the streets, he fancied that every one read these thoughts; that people looked at, and laughed at him; that his friends avoided him. He bought a ballad that was sung in the streets, because he thought it was made on him.

At last, his brother found him in this condition, when poor Cowper's first words to him were, "'Oh, brother, I am damned. Think of eternity, and then what it is to be damned!' I had, indeed, a sense of eternity impressed upon my mind, which seemed almost to amount to a full comprehension of it.

"My brother, pierced to the heart with the sight of my misery, tried to comfort me; but all to no purpose. I refused comfort; and my mind appeared to me in such colours, that to administer it to me was only to exasperate me, and to mock my fears.

"At length, I remembered my friend Martin Madan, and sent for him. I used to think him an enthusiast, but now seemed convinced that if there was any balm in Gilead, he would administer it to me. On former occasions, when my spiritual concerns had occurred to me, I thought likewise on the necessity of repentance. I knew that many persons had spoken of shedding tears for sin; but when I asked myself whether the time would ever come when I might weep for sin, it seemed to me that a stone would sooner do it."

Not perceiving that Christ's mission was to arouse repentance, he despaired of ever attaining to it. Martin Madan sat by his bedside, and began to declare to him the Gospel;—to speak of original sin, and the corruption of every man born into this world, whereby every one is a child of wrath! One can hardly imagine taking comfort from such a view, yet a gleam of hope dawned in Cowper's heart. He began to think himself more on a level with mankind.

Well may Southey remark that this was madness in the worst form that madness presents itself. Conviction of sin, and expectation of judgment, never left the poor poet; dreams brought back to him the commission of long-forgotten offences; reflection made him consider even indifferent actions as criminal.

At length it was determined to place the unhappy man with Dr. Cotton, of St. Albans'; a physician with whom Cowper had some slight acquaintance; and who seems, in sweetness of temper and humanity, to have been a precursor of the great benefactor of our own time, Dr. Conolly, to whose introduction the maniac of the nineteenth century owes, under Providence, solace, relief—the chance of a recovery rarely known to occur under the harsh measures of former days.

It is consolatory to think of the amiable William Cowper consigned to so gentle a care as that of Dr. Cotton. We may fancy him sometimes, perhaps, able to enjoy the country he ever so much preferred to the town, around the ancient borough, graced only by its grand Abbey. He draws a veil, indeed, as he says, over the secrets of his prison-house; but that his sufferings were severe may be inferred from these words:

"Let it suffice to say, that the low state of body and mind, to which I was reduced, was perfectly well calculated to humble the natural vain glory and pride of my heart."

About three months after he had been placed at St. Albans' his brother came to visit him. Their interview is most touchingly described by Cowper.

Dr. Cotton having told his brother that he was greatly amended, he was shocked to find poor William as silent as ever. The fact was, the unhappy, demented Cowper looked at his brother's calm face with envy. When alone with him, John Cowper asked him how he found himself. "As much better as despair can make me," was the mournful reply. They went together into the garden. "Here," says Cowper, "on expressing a settled assurance of sudden judgment, he protested to me that it was all a delusion, and protested so strongly that I could not help giving some attention to him. I burst into tears and cried out, 'If it be a delusion, then am I the happiest of beings.'" Hope again dawned in his miserable heart. The brothers dined together. Something seemed to whisper to William that there was still mercy for him—still peace.

That evening the poor stricken one slept well. He dreamed that the sweetest boy in the world came dancing up to his bedside; he seemed just out of leading-strings, but the head was firm, the step steady. He awoke with a sensation of happiness. After his arrival at St. Albans', Cowper had thrown away the Scriptures, as a book in which he had no interest or portion. One day, however, finding a Bible on a bench in the garden, he opened it at the eleventh chapter of St. John, where Lazarus is raised from the dead, and saw "so much benevolence, mercy, goodness, and sympathy with miserable man" in our Saviour's conduct, that he almost shed tears.

Still his heart was softened, but not enlightened; he did not apply that comprehensive mercy to his own broken and contrite spirit, but closed the book without intending to open it again.

The "cloud of horror" which had so long hung over him was, however, every moment passing away. Once more the poor melancholic man had recourse to his Bible. Once more hope was permitted to enter his soul. "I saw the sufficiency of the atonement He (our Saviour) had made; my pardon sealed in His blood, and all the fullness and completeness of His justification."

"Unless the Almighty had been with me," he adds, "I think I should have died with gratitude and joy."

Dr. Cotton now trembled lest joy should prove too much for the fragile invalid;—lest reason should be excited to frenzy. But the amendment was real. For a year after his eventual recovery, Cowper remained near his kind physician; enjoying with that amiable and excellent old man a communion of heart and sentiment rare indeed under such circumstances. No longer, to quote from certain lines which Cowper wrote during his madness, did he view such horrors as these:

> "Hatred and vengeance, my eternal portion,
> Scarce can endure delay of execution,
> Wait with impatient readiness to seize my soul in a moment."

He could, on the contrary, now say, "Blessed be the God of salvation for every sigh I drew, for every tear I shed, that I might not be judged hereafter."

It must have been touching to see the affectionate dependence of the young and afflicted Cowper on the aged and skilful Cotton. Happily that eminent physician was also a man of letters. His "Fireside" has ever been a popular poem with his countrywomen, who can so well appreciate the homely strain, and beloved theme. Many years before Cowper knew him, Dr. Cotton had lost a wife to whom he was devotedly attached. The bereavement had taught him to feel, as well as to think. No system but that of Christianity, the good physician declared, could sustain us in the trials and distresses of life: "But the religion of Jesus, like its gracious author, is an inexhaustible source of comfort in this world, and gives us the hope of everlasting enjoyment in the next."

The value of sound principles in a medical man were never

more fully exemplified in any case than in that of Cowper. Dr. Cotton was as willing to administer to the mind diseased as to the physical ailment. He was the consoler, the spiritual guide, the friend. The result of his gentle care was seen, and at the same time rewarded, when Cowper, rising from the depths of despair to peace, composed the lines entitled "The Happy Change!" beginning thus:

> "How blest thy creature is, O God,
>   When with a single eye
> He views the lustre of thy Word,
>   The day spring from on high.
>
> "Through all the storms that veil the skies,
>   And frown on earthly things;
> The Sun of Righteousness he eyes,
>   With healing on his wings."

It was now requisite for Cowper to choose a place of residence, as he could no longer afford to remain with Dr. Cotton, to whom he was then, as he states, "deeply in debt." He had for some years held a Commissionership of Bankruptcy of the value of sixty pounds a year. He now resolved to resign it, feeling that from his ignorance of the law he could not take the accustomed oath. His income was greatly reduced; and he requested his brother, who resided at Cambridge, to look out for some cheap lodgings for him near that University. London, "the scene of his former abominations," he was resolved to quit for ever. No efforts were made by his relations to change that wise resolution. The poor emancipated lunatic was an object of hope no longer. They acted, however, wisely; and kindly subscribed among themselves means to add to his own scanty income, so that he could live respectably, though frugally.

A poem which he wrote at this time beautifully exemplifies the feelings with which the "stricken deer" rushed into the covert of a country life:

"Far from the world, O Lord, I flee,
   From strife and tumult far;
From scenes where Satan wages still
   His most successful war.

"The calm retreat, the silent shade,
   With prayer and praise agree;
And seem, by Thy sweet bounty, made
   For those who follow Thee.

"There, if Thy spirit touch the soul,
   And grace her mean abode;
O with what peace, and joy, and love,
   She communes with her God.

"There, like the nightingale she pours
   Her solitary lays,
Nor asks a witness of her song,
   Nor thirsts for human praise."

The neighbourhood of Huntingdon was eventually fixed on for Cowper's residence; and by that decision the future colour of his life was tinged.

Mary Unwin, Cowper's "Mary," and the being of all others that may be termed "his destiny," was the daughter of a draper at Ely, named Cawthorne. She was married early in life to Morley Unwin, a clergyman, greatly her senior. Mrs. Unwin belonged to that portion of the hitherto unthinking world in the last century, who had even then begun to assume to themselves the exclusive appellation, "Evangelical." Morley Unwin, her husband, had been master of the Free School at Huntingdon; but having been preferred to the living of Grimstone, in Norfolk, by his College, had married, and taken his young wife there; but Mary, how great soever her piety, did not like the dullness of that retired spot. She persuaded her husband to leave it, and to return to Huntingdon, where, taking a large house in the High-street, Mr. Unwin received and prepared a few pupils for the Universities. His only children were a son and a daughter. The latter being just eighteen years of age, "genteel and handsome," it may be supposed that Cowper would have been more taken with her than with her mother. But no; although Miss Unwin talked, during a long *tête-à-tête* which occurred on Cowper's first call on the family, with " ease and address," he found in Mrs. Unwin " an uncommon understanding;" " she had read much, and was more polite than a duchess." " That woman," he declared in a letter to his cousin, Lady Hesketh, " is a blessing to me, and I never see her without being the better for her company."

Cowper had owed his introduction to this charming family to William Cawthorne Unwin, the son, who had at first been dissuaded by his father from calling on the interesting and elegant stranger, who appeared to avoid society.

When introduced, however, into a circle at once pious, intelligent, social, and lively, Cowper began to wonder how he had liked Huntingdon so much before seeing them. " They are indeed a nice set of people," he wrote to Lady Hesketh, "and suit me exactly." It had been his earnest hope, before he left St. Albans', that, wherever he was, he might meet with such a person as Mrs. Unwin. Cowper's was a clinging and dependent nature; fate had proscribed love, and friendship was the balm of his wounded spirit. His petition to the Giver of all good he believed to have been heard. He was now treated more like a relation than a stranger; driven by the old gentleman in his chaise to Cambridge; allowed to go in and out at all times. " They see," he wrote to his friend Hill, " but little company, which suits me exactly. You remember Rousseau's description of an English morning: such are the mornings I spend with these good people; and the evenings differ from them in nothing, except that they are more snug and quieter." A few sunshiny years were permitted to him whom Mackintosh called the " most amiable and unfortunate of men." Huntingdon, though situated on gently rising ground, on the northern side of the Ouse, has few scenes of striking beauty near it. Yet, by Henry of Huntingdon, the town is declared to have " surpassed all others in pleasantness of situation, beauty of buildings, nearness to the fens, and plenty of game and fish."

Many of its fine old churches,—a priory of regular canons, a house for Augustinian friars, with a castle, and hospital for lepers, had fallen into ruin and oblivion. Camden describes the prospect from the Castle Hill to have been "as glorious an one as the sun ever saw." But Cowper, with the finest instincts of poetry within him, found few charms in the bare flat fields, devoid of trees in the summer, and overspread all the winter with a flood. In old times the foggy, unwholesome fens, whence emanated all the fearful varieties of ague and low fever, were not complained of, because in the then thinly populated and half-cultured country the profits of fishing, the abundance of wild-fowl, the facility of getting twigs for fuel in that waste land, were thought to compensate for maladies to which our ancestors were well accustomed. Cowper was no angler, nor sportsman; he detested every thing like amusement at the expense of humanity. True it was that wherever the Ouse flowed, enamelled meadows showed the effects of the irrigation; still, there was but one beautiful spot, called Hertford, a village at a short distance from the town, where Cowper used to walk and muse over the epitaphs in the churchyard. The long main street of the town of Huntingdon, and its curious churches; the simple, homely character of its inhabitants; the neatness of the streets; the traffic on the river, much changed indeed since Cowper's days, but still navigable, still bearing on its waves craft from Lynn — these were the traits which reconciled him to the sameness of the surrounding country. He soon decided that no place in the world can be devoid of attractions in which congenial minds exist. Mr. Unwin he found simple and original as Parson Adams. His wife was full of energy and animation. The "Mary,"—to whom in after life the poet addressed lines full of pathos, alluding to the unhappiness he had often innocently caused her — was at this time still a young woman, though considerably older than her friend Cowper, who speaks of her hair as then "auburn bright;" she had the spirits that those alone have whose lives have not been overshadowed by some heavy, irremediable calamity. She had the willing sympathies without which woman had better enter a convent, for without them no active mission of domestic life can be well performed.

Her son, at twenty-one, was the "most amiable and unreserved young man that Cowper had ever met with." Both he and his sister were gifted with an attractive exterior.

It may be believed with what delight Cowper, after an acquaintance of some time, found himself received as an inmate in this family. He had tried the experiment of managing his own domestic affairs: it had failed. He found it impossible to continue his mode of life "without danger of bankruptcy." He had managed, in fact, in three months, to spend the income which ought to last a year; and that income was in part made up by generous but not altogether confiding relations.

The rich always expect the poor to live for nothing. His uncle Ashley wrote to him in the gentlest terms, giving him to understand that "the family" were not a little indignant at hearing that he kept a servant: a certain cousin (the Colonel) was the mover of the storm, and threatened to withdraw his contribution; on which Sir Thomas Hesketh, who had by this time married Cowper's cousin, stepped forward, and offered to supply the furious Colonel's place, and make up the deficiency. Whilst this affair was in discussion, one gentle, constant heart bled for the unhappy William Cowper, whose afflictions had rendered him thus dependent, in the very prime of life, on relations. Theodora, for ever severed from him, was his guardian angel still. In this sharp trial, as in the gloomier periods of after days, her spirit was with him; her tenderness, her delicacy of feeling, never rested on any object more dear to her than her lost cousin. He received an anonymous letter, of which he gives the following account, and Southey ascribes the epistle either to Lady Hesketh or to her sister Theodora:—

"While this troublesome matter was in agitation, and I expected to be abandoned by the family, I received an anonymous letter, in a hand entirely strange to me, by the post. It was conceived in the kindest and most benevolent terms imaginable; exhorting me not to distress myself with fears lest the threatened event should take place; for that, whatever deduction my income might sustain, the defect should be supplied by a person who loved me tenderly, and approved my conduct."

Mrs. Unwin performed also a kind office. She generously offered Cowper a home under her roof, and arranged to receive him at half the sum previously stipulated.

It was henceforth his great happiness that he had entered a family " of Christians." Unfortunately for the tender spirit which so easily adapted itself to the views of those whom he loved, the Unwins, like his friend Madan, whom Cowper regarded "as a burning and a shining light," applied this term only to those who, as Southey observes, "approached the rising body of Methodists, in proportion as they departed from the standard of the Church." The Unwins made religion not only the rule but the business of life.

"We breakfast commonly," says Cowper, "between eight and nine; till eleven we read the Scriptures, or the sermons of some faithful preacher of those holy mysteries; at eleven we attend the service, which is performed twice here every day; and from twelve to three we separate, and amuse ourselves as we please. During that interval I either read in my own apartment, or ride, or walk, or work in the garden. We seldom sit an hour after dinner; but, if the weather permits, adjourn to the garden, where, with Mrs. Unwin and her son, I have generally the pleasure of religious conversation till tea-time."

Could any saint of the Romish Church, or ascetic, do more? What a mistake is it to wear holy subjects threadbare — to exhaust religious feelings till they must have wavered between despondency and fatigue. Hymns and the harpsichord went on till tea-time; then, in fine weather, the party prepared for walking, and generally "travelled four miles before they came home again."

To Lady Hesketh he wrote: "My dear cousin, I am a living man!" Great and grievous afflictions had awakened him out of the deep sleep of insensibility to a life of "union and communion with God."

Lady Hesketh, although a woman of practical piety, did not respond to his fervour; nor accord with his certainty of conversion and election. He ceased writing to her about this time, and directed his epistolary attentions almost exclusively to his cousin, Mrs. Cowper, who was acquainted with the circumstances of his sad story.

The first break in a life of peace was caused by the death of old Mr. Unwin, who was killed by a fall from his horse whilst riding to serve his church on a Sunday morning. At nine o'clock on that day he had been in perfect health; at ten he was speechless and senseless, lying on a flock bed in a poor cottage to which he was carried. Cowper received his last sigh. "I heard his dying groans, the effect of great agony, for he was a strong man, and much convulsed in his last moments." The few short intervals of ease were spent in earnest prayer and expressions of faith in his Saviour. Truly does Cowper add: "To that stronghold we must all resort at last, if we would have hope in our death." "Happy is it for us when, the false ground we have chosen for ourselves being broken under us, we find ourselves obliged to have recourse to the Rock that can never be shaken."

It now became a question where Cowper was to reside. That Mrs. Unwin was to continue to receive him as her inmate was at once decided; and after much consideration it was resolved to remove to Olney, to be near the Rev. Mr. Newton, and to receive all the benefits of his ministry. Newton was one of three clergymen to whom Mrs. Unwin and Cowper gave the distinction of wishing to be near them. He had been the captain of a Liverpool slave ship, but, becoming converted, had taken holy orders, and was then the curate of Olney, in Buckinghamshire. Here, accordingly, Cowper and his friend removed, being for some time Mr. Newton's guests, and afterwards settling in a house so near the vicarage that a communication was made through the garden wall between the two houses. Henceforth the small incomes possessed by Mrs. Unwin and Cowper were united; henceforth they enjoyed what was called in the sectarian language of the day, "frequent evangelical worship; that is, not the simple, eloquent service of our church, such as Cowper had enjoyed every morning at Huntingdon, but meetings, addresses, and prayers which sent him from them with an excited pulse, a flushed cheek, a heated and a throbbing head." *

The friendship of Mrs. Unwin gave to Cowper a stay, companionship, and domestic care; but her religious convictions, far more extreme than those of her husband, and the mode of life into which she deemed it her duty to urge Cowper, were the worst for a man recently emancipated from a state of mental aberration that could be conceived. Prayer-meetings, in which the earnest, excitable poet was enjoined to take an active part,— attendance on the sick and dying — Calvinistic views of faith — what was termed "religious intercourse,"— these were the order of each day. Excitement is not devotion. To the wounded spirit there comes healing with the words of holy promise. The faith they witness should be tempered by good sense, which deepens and confirms their impression.

To Cowper the mode of faith and mode of life which he now followed were preparing the fire that was to consume

* Southey.

him; leaving him no chance of long enjoying the calm reason that was perpetually disturbed by feverish imaginations.

Exclusion from all who did not accord with certain views was one feature of the "religious intercourse" between Cowper and his friends. The poet's letters to Lady Hesketh wholly ceased; he wrote seldom to Mrs. Cowper; his tone to his friend Hill was changed. The charming, easy, once gay William Cowper seemed alarmed lest he should relapse into cheerfulness. Rarely could he look forward to death with comfort, for a sense of unpardoned sin lay heavy on his heart, and the decease of his brother about this time (1769), was an event which left him wholly to the influences of those who wished him well, most sincerely, but who were, humanly speaking, his worst enemies. Mr. Unwin, the son of Cowper's friend, had "prayed his brother out of darkness into light;" both the poet and Mr. Unwin were satisfied that a sudden conversion had regenerated a worthy man, whose life had been one of benevolent piety. An account of his brother's death was drawn up by Cowper, and edited by Newton. From that narrative it appears that, even when Cowper first saw him, John Cowper was in a state of humble, devout, patient submission to his approaching fate. His death struck a fearful blow into the heart of William. Cut off from all social intercourse, except that of Mrs. Unwin and Mr. Newton, Cowper had applied himself to poetry, more especially to sacred verse, under the advice of Newton, who saw the despondency which afterwards overwhelmed him, approaching. Melancholy indeed were the efforts of his mournful muse. They speak at once the alarming depression of poor Cowper's mind:—

> " Where is the blessedness I knew
> When first I saw the Lord?
> Where is the soul-refreshing view
> Of Jesus and his word?

"My former hopes are fled,
My terror now begins;
I feel, alas, that I am dead
In trespasses and sins.

"Ah! whither shall I fly?
I hear the thunders roar;
The law proclaims destruction nigh,
And vengeance at the door."

Reasonable friends would have trembled, not rejoiced, at the too tender conscience which was thus expressed; but Mrs. Unwin and Newton saw only in the affrighted lunatic, signs of grace. Alas! they were soon undeceived. In January, 1773, the deep melancholy proved to be a decided fit of insanity. Dr. Cotton was consulted, but too late to avert a terrible and long attack. During this trial Mrs. Unwin, disregarding equally the censorious remarks of the ill-natured, and all personal fatigue, watched him night and day; but no care can assuage the inward wretchedness which madness produces. Only during sleep, when, as Mr. Newton expressed it, "the Lord seemed to visit him," was his agony mitigated. He believed himself to be eternally doomed; and, under that conviction, gave up attending public prayer, or kneeling down in private devotion — both he believed, were to a certainty, wholly unavailing.

In the commencement of his malady Cowper had determined not to enter Newton's house; he was, however, persuaded to do so, and afterwards could not be persuaded to leave it. He passed his days in gardening, and pruning trees, and feeding the chickens. One morning, whilst engaged in the last-mentioned occupation, a smile passed over his countenance; it was the first smile that had been seen there for more than sixteen months — it was the faint dawn of convalescence — and his sudden resolution to leave Mr. Newton's house and to return to his own, shewed the amendment. It had been a great trial to good Mr. Newton to have under his roof so afflicted and anxious a charge; but he "had borne his cross well;" and though his heart had sometimes been impatient and rebellious, thought " he could not do too much for such a friend."

The hapless invalid was now sufficiently recovered to interest himself with some leverets; he examined into their peculiarities of *physique* and character; found that they never were infested by vermin; nursed one of them in sickness, and experienced the greatest gratitude from his dumb friend, whom he immortalised in poetry, both Latin and English. He was thus on the road to convalescence; but nervous diseases, as he himself expressed it, are inveterate foes: "other distempers only batter the walls, but *they* creep silently into the citadel and put the garrison to the sword."

He continued to recover, however, and contributed some beautiful effusions to the " Olney Hymns," before Mr. Newton left Olney to take possession of a London living, presented to him by Mr. Thornton. That event was thus alluded to by Cowper in a letter to Mrs. Newton: —

" The vicarage-house became a melancholy object as soon as Mr. Newton had left it; when you left it, it became more melancholy. Now it is occupied by another family. I cannot look at it without being shocked. As I walked this evening and saw the smoke issue from the shady chimney, and said this used to be a sign that Mr. Newton was there, but it is so no longer."

He felt now a desire to leave Olney. He had "lived in it once, he was buried in it now." He had no business, he thought, with the world, the outside of his sepulchre; and a sepulchre indeed it was, and worse than a sepulchre, for in the tomb there is, at least, peace.

Thus was the cheerful, large-hearted poet chained to a sect peculiarly adapted to foster all his peculiarities, and still more and more to unfit him to return to the society of early friends. That he was not able to leave Olney, that he was not free to visit cheerful relations, or friends more likely to change his thoughts than the exclusive set whom he had learned alone to call Christians, is deeply to be deplored. Olney had little to render it a desirable place for the abode of a delicate, desponding invalid. It is flat, and devoid of any beauty save the winding river. Cowper was indeed buried in it. The affection of Mrs. Unwin had become a jealous, exacting tie; and Cowper's best friends must have wished him to be transplanted from a sphere so contracted to one more congenial.

In the midst of such speculations, Cowper's old friend Thurlow became Lord Chancellor; but this event never benefited the forgotten recluse; and even when Thurlow had an opportunity of obtaining a pension for his former companion, he took no trouble to assist him by so doing.

The simple, excellent recluse resigned himself to his destiny, and tried, when relieved from the pressure of his mortal dread, to make every little thing a pleasure. Gardening, the solace of so many sad hearts, was his daily resource when in tolerable health.

"I am pleased," he wrote to Mr. Newton, "with a frame of four lights, doubtful whether the few pines it contains will ever be worth a farthing; amuse myself with a greenhouse which Lord Bute's gardener would take upon his back and walk away with; and when I have paid it the accustomed visit and watered it and given it air, I say to myself, this is not mine: 'tis a plaything lent me for the present; I must leave it soon."

Then his neighbours, knowing him to have been a lawyer, used to ask his opinion on their own concerns.

"I know less of the law," he wrote to Mr. Hill [*], "than a country attorney, yet sometimes I think I have almost as much business. My former connection with the profession

---

[*] Cowper's Life, p. 279.

has got wind, and though I earnestly profess and protest, and proclaim it abroad that I know nothing of the matter, they cannot be persuaded that a head, once endowed with a legal periwig, can be deficient in those qualifications which it is supposed to cover."

Once or twice he had happened to be in the right, and the "cheapness of gratuitous advice was agreeable." He had long occupied himself in writing verses; but, so long as Newton remained at Olney, his efforts were not allowed to extend to any but religious poems. Mrs. Unwin first induced him to try a subject of greater importance than any that he had hitherto produced. She proposed to him the "Progress of Error" as a theme. He himself confessed, in the following passage, the necessity for some mental occupation:

"At this season of the year, and in this gloomy, uncomfortable climate, it is no easy matter for the owner of a mind like mine to divert it from sad subjects, and fix it upon such as may minister to its amusement. Poetry, above all things, is useful to me in this respect." "I am pleased with commendations, and though not passionately desirous of indiscriminate praise, or what is generally called popularity, yet when a judicious friend claps one on the back, I own I find it an encouragement."

The work was published by Johnson, of St. Paul's Church Yard; and its progress was infinitely beneficial to Cowper: it was something to expect every day a proof, and the arrival of the post brought unwonted interest. Summer drew on, and Cowper had arranged another source of pleasure, which he thus describes in writing to Mr. Newton:—"I might date my letter from the green-house, which we have converted into a summer parlour. The walls hung with garden mats, and the floors covered with a carpet; the sun, too, in a great measure excluded by an awning of mats, which forbids him to shine any where but on the carpet, it affords us by far the pleasantest retreat in Olney. We eat, drink, and sleep where we always did, but here we spend all the rest of our time, and find that the sound of the wind in the trees, and the singing of the birds, are more agreeable to our ears than the incessant barking of dogs and screaming of children."

He was still immersed in his occupations, when one day he happened to be much struck by the appearance of a lady who was calling at a shop opposite Mrs. Unwin's house, in company with a Mrs. Jones, the wife of a clergyman, living at Clifton, near Olney. On asking the name of the stranger, he learned that she was Lady Austen, the sister of Mrs. Jones*, and the widow of Sir Robert Austen, a baronet, with whom she had resided long in France, where Sir Robert died.

Lady Austen was a delightful, intellectual woman of the world: having belonged to the sort of society in which Cowper's early days were passed, she had a ready sympathy in his tastes and feelings. An invitation to tea was promptly sent by Cowper, shy as he was; it was accepted, and he was almost overpowered by the acceptance. A charming evening was the result — he walked back to Clifton with the ladies: the intimacy went on, and Lady Austen was christened by the poet, Sister Ann.

Cowper, in writing to Mr. Unwin, says, speaking of Lady Austen, "she is a very agreeable woman, and has fallen in love with your mother and me; insomuch that I do not know but she may settle at Olney. Yesterday night we all dined together in the *Spinnie*, a most delightful retirement belonging to Mrs. Throckmorton, of Weston. A board, laid over the top of a wheelbarrow, served for a table; our dining-room was a root-house, lined with moss and ivy." At six the party took tea, and then they wandered about into the wilder-

---

* Her maiden name was Richardson.

ness, and returned home, having spent the whole day together without the least weariness of each other's society.

Plans of settling at Olney, on Lady Austen's part, which, as Cowper remarked, "would add fresh plumes to the wings of time," were agitated. "Lady Austen," the poet wrote, " very desirous of retirement, especially of retirement near her sister, an admirer of Mr. Scott as a preacher, and of your two humble servants now in the green-house, as the most agreeable creatures in the world, is at present determined to settle here. The part of our great building which is at present occupied by Dick Coleman, his wife, child, and a thousand rats, is the corner of the world she chooses above all others, as the place of her future residence."

No wonder that Cowper regarded this arrival " as a providential interposition "— words which speak volumes of previous dullness. "We did not want company," he indeed says, "but when it came we found it agreeable." If their life before was " peaceful, it was not the worse for being enlivened." In case of illness, too, his was rather a dreary prospect; but he chiefly rejoiced on account of Mrs. Unwin. Alas! it was Mrs. Unwin who proved the barrier to this scheme, which promised so much happiness to Cowper. For a time, however, all went on smoothly; Lady Austen loved " anything that had a connection with Mrs. Unwin." She had, according to Cowper, so lively a sense of gratitude, that "discover but a wish to please her, and she never forgets it: not only thanks you, but the tears will start into her eyes at the recollection of the smallest service." With these " fine feelings" she had the most " harmless vivacity in the world."

Truly might Cowper say:—

> " Mysterious are His ways, whose power
> Brings forth that unexpected hour,
> When minds, that never met before,
> Shall meet, unite, and part no more:

> His the allotment of the skies,
> The hand of the supremely wise,
> That guides and governs our affections,
> And plans and orders our connections;
> Directs us in our distant road,
> And marks the bounds of our abode." *

In another part of the same poem he says: —

> " Not that I deem or mean to call
> Friendship a blessing, cheap or small;
> But merely to remark, that ours,
> Like some of nature's sweetest flowers,
> Rose from a seed of tiny size,
> That seem'd to promise no such prize."

Cowper was at this time fifty, and Mrs. Unwin fifty-seven years of age. Jealousy and scandal are of no period, and can agitate every age. It had at one time been conjectured whether Cowper and Mrs. Unwin would not have married: but no such idea seems ever to have entered Cowper's mind; and in Mary Unwin's, the most disinterested friendship seems to have existed. But there are jealousies in friendship as well as in love; and a few weeks after the "lines to Anna" were penned, we find Cowper writing to his friend Mr. Unwin, about Lady Austen, in the following terms. After enjoining secrecy, he says: — " My letters have already apprised you of that close and intimate connection that took place between the lady you visited in Queen Anne Street, and us. At her departure she proposed a correspondence, and because writing does not agree with your mother, proposed a correspondence with me." The correspondence, however, was a fatal arrangement; Lady Austen had conceived a romantic notion of her friends, and of their devotion to herself. In *one* of them, perhaps, that devotion existed, but not in the other. Cowper tried to show her her error: he advised her not to embellish any creatures with the colours of her fancy;

---

* Lines on Anna.

his letter gave mortal offence, though approved by Mrs. Unwin.

There seemed still a chance of reconciliation: Lady Austen sent, in spite of coolness, some lace ruffles she had been working, to the poet. Cowper in return, "laid his volume at her feet." Lady Austen was to spend the following summer in the neighbourhood. " Retirement," poor Cowper, probably influenced by Mrs. Unwin, now said, "was their passion and delight." It was to "still life" alone that ne looked for happiness. Nevertheless, a reconciliation took place, and the two parties were soon as happy as ever in each other's society. "We are reconciled:" Cowper wrote to Mr. Unwin. "Lady Austen took the first opportunity to embrace your mother with tears of the tenderest affection." Arrangements were made for Lady Austen's residence at the Vicarage in the autumn. Cowper, who, though he said "his thoughts were clad in a sober livery," like "that of a bishop's servants, yet turned on spiritual subjects," enjoyed thoroughly the careless wit, the blameless high spirits, and graceful ease of Lady Austen. Not so his friend Mr. Unwin, who, on seeing her in London, disapproved. His ideas were that everything like cheerfulness lacked godliness — that one could only escape perdition by a monotonous, exclusive, lachrymose existence.

Cowper, meantime, was far from being in a safe or satisfactory state of health and spirits. In hot Olney, where, in the garden, he felt nothing but the reflection of the heat from the walls, was he destined to spend the passing prime of his days. His two sources of pleasure were writing and conversation. With regard to the first, he says the composing effect was such that he was often so absorbed in rhyming as to forget the past and the future—"themes fruitful to him in regrets at any other time." With regard to the latter, with all Mrs. Unwin's tenderness to his malady, her concern for his comfort, her feeling for his sufferings, one cannot but blame her for allowing, as

Hayley hints she did, jealousies and prejudices to interfere with the communion of mind poor Cowper had enjoyed with Lady Austen. Nevertheless, that evil hour, which came too soon, was still distant. The vicarage door, which had been opened by Newton to Cowper, to pass in and out, was again called in use. Lady Austen was again settled at Olney, and Cowper's letters were full not only of content, but of enjoyment. What mattered it, then, that Thurlow and Colman, his two early friends, had received each a copy of his first poem without vouchsafing even a line of thanks? He had now society so captivating both to him and to Mrs. Unwin, that the friends almost lived together, dining alternately in each other's houses. Cowper was now in excellent health, "and leading the life he had always wished for."

Lady Austen's conversation, indeed, acted on Cowper's mind like David's harp on the troubled spirit of Saul. One afternoon, when he was much depressed, she told him the story of John Gilpin, which had been related to her in her childhood. The next day he said that he could not sleep at night for thinking of John Gilpin, and that he had turned the story into a ballad. This composition, which exhibits the very perfection of quiet humour, was printed at first in the "Public Advertizer." At Lady Austen's suggestion, also, he wrote the "Dirge for the Royal George," which was composed for her to sing to the harpsichord. One day she urged him to try his powers in blank verse. Cowper promised to comply if she would give him a subject. "O," she answered, "you can never be in want of a subject; write on anything; write on the Sofa." The result was that poem, which made Cowper the most popular poet of his day. His enjoyment of life was at this time keen — for all his feelings were keen — but it was of short duration; jealousy, that curse which seems to come direct from the Evil Spirit, broke up the circle, which never formed again.

Lady Austen, it was said, wished to marry Cowper, and a tradition long existed at Olney that she had gone to church with him with that view, but that Cowper, remembering his ties to his earlier friend, repented, and broke off the rash engagement. To contradict this statement, Southey observes that Mrs. Unwin was then three score; and he observes that it was very unlikely that Lady Austen should wish to marry a man afflicted with depression, and occasionally with insanity. Lady Austen has left a kindly, and probably faithful description of her to whom Cowper owed much solace, much care, and some disquietude. Of Mary Unwin she says:—

"She is very far from grave. On the contrary, she is cheerful and gay, and laughs *de bon cœur* upon the slightest provocation. Amidst all the Puritanical words which fall from her *de temps en temps*, she seems to have by nature a great fund of gaiety. Great indeed must it have been not to have been totally overcome by the close confinement in which she has lived, and the anxiety she has undergone for one whom she certainly loves as well as one human being can love another. I will not say she idolizes him, because she would think that wrong; but she certainly seems to possess the truest regard and affection for this excellent creature, and as I before said, has, in the most literal sense of the word, no wish or shadow of inclination but what is his.

"There is something," she adds, "truly affectionate and sincere in her manner. No one can express more heartily than she does her joy to have me at Olney; and as this must be for *his* sake, it is an additional proof of her esteem and regard for *him*."

It is painful — but, to those who know the world, not surprising — to find Cowper writing to Mr. Unwin in the following strain, alluding to the intimacy being again broken, and to Lady Austen's final departure from Olney:—

"You are going to Bristol; a lady not long since our near neighbour is there: she *was* there very lately. If you should chance to fall into her company, remember, if you please, that we found the connection, on some accounts, an inconvenient one; that we do not wish to renew it; and conduct yourself accordingly. A character with which we spend all our time should be made on purpose for us: too much or too little of any single ingredient spoils all." "The dissimilitude," he adds, "between themselves and Lady Austen was too great."

The loss of Lady Austen's society was a grievous one, but it was compensated, in a great measure, by a new acquaintance.

It was to witness the ascent of a balloon that Cowper and Mrs. Unwin were first invited to Weston. Balloons were the wonders of the age, and all the country were assembled to see one ascend. Mr. and Mrs. Throckmorton, the owners of Weston, were a young and most amiable couple, who fulfilled one of the offices incumbent on large proprietors, by making a neighbourhood agreeable to persons of all grades. They received Cowper and Mrs. Unwin most kindly. "We drank chocolate, and were asked to dine," Cowper wrote to Mr. Unwin, "but were engaged."

At that era, to be a Roman Catholic was to be tabooed from the great narrow world of an intolerant hierarchy. The Throckmortons held that faith, and received, consequently, many affronts; but this caused Cowper to treat them with the greater respect. Cowper, indeed, instantly appreciated the courtesy and refinement of his new friends. "I should like exceedingly," he wrote, "to be on an easy footing there; to give a morning call now and then, and to receive one, but nothing more. For though he (Mr. Throckmorton) is one of the most agreeable men I ever saw, I could not wish to visit him in any other way; neither our house, furniture, servants, or income, being such as to qualify us to make entertainments; neither would I on any account be introduced to the neighbouring gentry."

He was soon installed as an intimate acquaintance, and Mr. and Mrs. Throckmorton became "Mr. and Mrs. Frog," — a *sobriquet* indicative of growing intimacy. Cowper was becoming famous in a way he little expected. "John Gilpin" was recited by Henderson, the gentleman actor of the day, at Freemasons' Tavern. The room was crowded. There, amongst listeners and admirers, might be seen the hard face of Conversation Sharp, who had the merit of introducing Johnny to Henderson's notice. There Mrs. Siddons, then in the zenith of her beauty and fame, laughed outright, and, lifting up her beautiful hands, clapped heartily. Poor Cowper! When told of the fame of the "horseman," he wrote to his friend Newton: "I have produced many things under the influence of despair which hope would not have permitted to spring." "Despair made amusement necessary, and I found poetry the most agreeable amusement."

The success of "The Task" had one signal effect. It brought Cowper's relations again around him. During the last twenty years he had had "Unwins, or Unwinisons," he said, almost entirely around him. Amongst the dearest of the ties thus renewed was that with Lady Hesketh. Remembered by many as a brilliant beauty, attracting all eyes on her at Ranelagh, Lady Hesketh was as delightful in mind and character as in person. She regarded Cowper as a brother; and now, a widow of seven years' duration, returning to England, took an opportunity of visiting the much-loved poet, after reading "John Gilpin."

Cowper, when on coming down to breakfast, found a letter, franked by his uncle, and enclosing one from his cousin, said to himself, "This is as it should be. We are all young again; and the days that I thought I should see no more are actually returned." His affection for his cousin, he declared, was unabated. "A thousand times" (no words can equal his) "have I recollected a thousand scenes, in which our two selves have made the whole of the drama, with the greatest pleasure; at times, too, when I had no reason to suppose that I should ever hear from her again." "I have laughed with you," so he adds, "at the 'Arabian Nights' Entertainment;' I have walked with you to Netley Abbey, and have scrambled with you over hedges in every possible direction." The hours he spent with her and poor Sir Thomas were, he adds, among the most agreeable.

He then refers touchingly to Mrs. Unwin's care of him for twenty years. It was to that, under Providence, that he owed his living at all. That care, he said, had injured Mrs. Unwin's health: it would, had she not been wonderfully supported, have brought her to her grave. During that twenty years, he and his friend had had but one purse between them. At first Mrs. Unwin's was double his own; but latterly their humble means had been the same; and much was self-denial requisite to both. He gracefully, and gratefully, entered into these details for the information of that "sweet cousin" who sought only to serve him.

Then he draws a humorous picture of himself—an imaginary one of Lady Hesketh.

"I cannot believe," he says, "but that I should know you, notwithstanding all that time may have done. There is not a feature of your face, could I meet it on the road by itself, that I should not know." "I should say, that is my cousin's nose, or those are her lips and chin, and no woman upon earth can claim them except herself. As for me, I am a very smart youth for my years. I am not, indeed, grown grey so much as I am bald. No matter; there was more hair in the world than ever belonged to me."

"The happiest stage of Cowper's life commenced," says Southey, "when the intercourse with this beloved cousin was renewed."

It had one alloy. The spirit of the Evangelical party suffered no interlopers in its society; dreaded all distraction; repudiated all joy that emanated not from a religious excitement; and Mr. Newton, dreading the effects of worldly contamination, wrote, it seems, to Cowper to warn him of the peril of such mundane communion. Cowper's answer was sensible, moderate, respectful. "He knew not," he said, "a single person among his friends and relations from whom he was likely to catch contagion." "We correspond," says he, "at present on the subject of what passed at Troy three thousand years ago (alluding to his translation of Homer), and they are matters that, if they can do no good, can at least hurt nobody."

No father confessor of mediæval times ever held a penitent in firmer bonds than did the worthy Mr. Newton the amiable and gentle William Cowper.

Mrs. Unwin, happily, entertained no jealousy of the generous, affectionate-hearted Lady Hesketh. "Tell Lady Hesketh that I truly love and honour her," she said to Cowper. Lady Hesketh was an angel of mercy. She obviated her cousin's privations — she consoled — she cheered — she inspirited the delicate, musing invalid. To her he imparted every sorrow, and the remedies for sorrow: the hope, the trust, the prayer, the poetry, the gardening, the carpentering, the making bird-cages, the feeding hares, — all the daily details which formed auxiliaries to the great effort to cast off depression. One passage more, illustrative of the peaceful passages of a life full of innocence, of gentleness, and yet of suffering, and we must then hasten to the darker period of his existence.

Lady Hesketh said she would visit him at Olney. "You have made us," writes Cowper, "both happy by giving us a nearer prospect of your arrival. But Mrs. Unwin says you must not fix too early a day for your departure, nor talk of staying only two or three days; because it will be a thorn that she shall lean upon all the time you are here: and so say I. It is a comfort to be informed when a visitor will go—whom we wish to be rid of; but the reverse of a comfort, my cousin, when you are in question." The good Lady Hesketh was, however, detained in town with her father, then in infirm health and old age.

Theodora was living; still devoted to the one remembrance, which Fate might in vain attempt to banish. An anonymous hand, assuming to be that of a man, sent letters, which Cowper answered to Lady Hesketh; and conferred an annuity of fifty pounds, " wishing it had been five hundred." A small parcel arrived containing a snuff-box and purse. " Again, may God bless him," adds Cowper, to Lady Hesketh. The snuff-box was of tortoiseshell, with a beautiful landscape on the lid of it, glazed with crystal, having the figures of three hares in the foreground, and inscribed there were these words: " Tiney, Puss, and Bess." The letters were full of tenderness. " Who is there in the world," Cowper asked, " that has, or thinks he has, reason to love me in the same degree that he has?" It was evident that those letters, those gifts, came from a woman's heart—that heart dwelling on the past with tenderness and regret.

One would fain linger on the few cheerful years which now remained to Cowper during, what he called, " the absence of Mr. Blue-devil," on his removal to Weston, where he could step out into the grounds of the kind Throckmortons without soiling his slippers: on his escape from the fishy-smelling fumes of the marsh miasma of Olney; on his delight in his new neighbours, in which Mrs. Unwin participated. Lady Hesketh writes, " She *does* seem in *real truth* to have no will left on earth but for his good, and literally no will but *his*. How she has supported herself (as she has done),—the constant attendance, day and night, which she has gone through the last thirteen years, is to me, I confess, incredible; and in justice to her I must say she does it all with an ease that relieves her from any idea of its being a state of suffering."

Consistent with this devoted affection was Mrs. Unwin's total abnegation of self. There she sat, on the hardest and smallest chair, leaving the best to Cowper, knitting with the finest possible needles stockings of the nicest texture. Cowper wore none others than of her knitting for years. "She sits knitting on one side of the table, in her spectacles, and he on the other reading to her (when he is not employed in writing on *his*). In winter, his morning studies are always carried on in a room by himself; but as his evenings are generally spent in the winter in transcribing, he does them, I find, *vis-à-vis* Mrs. Unwin."

One may suppose what an event the removal to Weston was. Hitherto Cowper had been confined at Olney to a gravel walk thirty yards long. A fever of the slow and spirit-distressing kind seemed to have oppressed him and all inhabitants of Olney for years. Nevertheless, his departure from that place, in which putrid fever was the order of the day, seems to have been regarded by Newton and the ultra-saints as leaving a gospel life and going into forbidden paths; and Cowper's return to society as a departure from all hope of enjoying Christian privileges. Well might Mr. Newton say of himself that "his name was up in the country for preaching people mad" *— many of his flock, "gracious people," as he termed them, being "disordered in their minds." These evils are justly ascribed by Southey to excited meetings which "accord as little with the spirit as with the Church of England." †

Mouldering walls and a tottering house warned them, in fact, to leave Olney; yet Cowper felt a pang at leaving them, after thirteen years' residence. The death of Mr. Unwin, the son of Cowper's friend, happened soon after the removal to Weston. Mrs. Unwin had the inestimable comfort of knowing that her son had lived the life and died the death of a Christian, and she bore his loss with submission. The rupture of that bond made her, however, more com-

* Southey's Life, vol. ii. p. 249.　　　　　† P. 150.

pletely dependent for happiness on the affection and wellbeing of Cowper. Sincerely did he mourn for his friend: but "the dead who have died in the Lord," he observed, "I envy always; for they, I take it for granted, can be no more forsaken."

One more reference to happy days whilst the poet's health was comparatively secure, before we sketch the gloomy passage from reason to delusion—from delusion to insanity—from insanity to the grave. He had begun to experience all the inconvenience of being an eminent author; of having odes addressed to him; letters written by a lady to the "best of men;" verses from a Welsh attorney, who begs him to revise them; and asks, most obligingly—

> "Say shall my little bark attendant sail,
> Pursue the triumph and partake the gale?"

When one morning, a plain, devout, elderly figure made his appearance at Weston, and spake as follows: "Sir, I am clerk of the parish of All Saints, in Northampton, brother of Mr. Cox, the upholsterer. It is customary for a person of my profession to annex to a bill of mortality, which he publishes at Christmas, a copy of verses. You would do me a great favour, Sir, if you would furnish me with one." To this I replied (Cowper wrote): "Mr. Cox, you have several men of genius in your town—why have you not applied to some of them? There is a namesake of yours in particular, Cox, the statuary, who, everybody knows, is a first-rate maker of verses. He, surely, is the best man in the world for your purpose." "Alas! Sir, I have borrowed help from him; but he is a person of so much reading that the people of our town cannot understand him." Cowper, his vanity a little piqued, was almost on the point of saying that perhaps, for the same reason, they might not understand *him;* but his good-nature prevailed, and he sent by the waggon that afternoon, to Northampton, his effusion. "A fig," he added, "for poets who write epitaphs upon individuals, I have written one that serves *two hundred* persons!" Seven successive years did Cowper supply the clerk of All Saints in Northampton with mortuary verses.

It was at Weston, in February, 1790, that Cowper received his mother's picture from his cousin, Mrs. Bodham. He " viewed it with a trepidation of nerves and spirits somewhat akin to what he should have felt had the dear original presented itself to his embrace." He kissed it, and placed the treasure where he could see it the last thing at night and the first thing in the morning. Cowper thought he had more of the Donne in him than of the Cowpers. He had been thought in childhood to resemble his mother; in short, he proved himself, by his love of poetry also, "a Donne at all points."

On this valued picture he wrote the most exquisite lines that were ever written to one long lost, ever missed, incessantly deplored.

Mrs. Unwin, meantime, his second mother, made him uneasy by her approaching infirmities. She once narrowly escaped being burnt; then she fell on the gravel walk, and was lame a long time; but she was now afflicted with headaches, which proved the precursors of more serious maladies. Not very long afterwards she was attacked one day with giddiness; she would have fallen down had not Cowper supported her. She was then ill for some time, and unfortunately, Mr. and Mrs. Throckmorton, now Sir John and Lady Throckmorton, left Weston to reside in Berkshire. All their little world, the angelic Lady Hesketh included, were departing.

But fresh interests were at hand. Cowper's literary fame led to his acquaintance with Hayley, who was invited to visit Cowper at Weston. "I will endeavour," Cowper said to Lady Hesketh, "to greet him with a countenance that shall not stiffen him into freestone, but I cannot be answerable for my success."

William Hayley, the guest thus anticipated, had been intended for the bar, but having a fair fortune and literary tastes, had devoted himself to dramatic literature on his outset in life. He was now forty-seven years of age, with a fine, thoughtful, pensive face; with eyes that, as Miss Seward said, " used to sparkle, and melt, and glow, as wit, compassion, or imagination had the ascendance in his mind."

He quickly became a favourite with Cowper, and with the " Muse of Seventy," as Hayley termed her, Mrs. Unwin. One can readily suppose that Cowper, with his delicate appearance, his gentle engaging manners, his natural courtesy, and his cultivated mind, free from all pedantry, must have been indeed a most delightful and interesting host.

Hayley's visit was marked by a sad event. Mrs. Unwin had another paralytic stroke: her speech was now unintelligible; her power of locomotion was gone; she could not keep her eyes open, and the power of her right hand and arm was gone. Electricity was then a fashionable remedy, and Hayley sent for a machine; recovery was hoped for, but it came slowly; change of scene was contemplated, but the axe was laid to the root of the tree, and the sensible, calm mind of Mrs. Unwin was shaken by her attack.

Cowper viewed her state with a despair at which we cannot wonder. He owed to her care even his life; she had watched him when dark delusions would have driven a less tender friend from him, and had, it is alleged, cut him down when he had a second time attempted suicide, and thus saved his *life*. *Her* reason, which had sustained *his*, could now sustain it no longer. She was for a time restored to " charming spirits" by a visit to Hayley at Eartham, but the benefit received was not permanent. Cowper, too, found the scenery around Eartham, after the first days of delight and surprise, too gloomy for his nerves, and pined for the less romantic features of that around Weston.

It is sad to find that in Mrs. Unwin's last days she lent

a superstitious credence to an ignorant schoolmaster, named Teedon, who pretended to certain miraculous revelations, and to whom Cowper imparted his own experiences. These, alas! were the indications of an approaching attack of nervous fever and incipient aberration, which his patient, beloved friend could now no longer alleviate. Her mind had sunk into utter powerlessness, and she sat by his side, mute, nearly blind, a living memento of what Mary Unwin had once been. It was at this time that he addressed to her the lines " On Mary." This was the last original piece that he composed at Weston; and, as Hayley observes, " it is doubtful whether any language on earth can exhibit a specimen in verse more exquisitely tender."

TO MARY.

"The twentieth year has well nigh past,
Since first our sky was over-cast;
Ah! would that this might be our last,
    My Mary!

"Thy spirits have a fainter glow,
I see thee daily weaker grow;
'Tis my distress that brought thee low,
    My Mary!

"Thy needles, once a shining store,
For my sake restless heretofore;
Now rust, disused, and shine no more,
    My Mary!

"But though thou gladly would'st fulfil
The same kind office for me still,
Thy sight now seconds not thy will,
    My Mary!

"But well thou play'dst the housewife's part,
And all thy threads with magic art
Have wound themselves about this heart,
    My Mary!

"Thy indistinct expressions seem
Like language utter'd in a dream;
Yet me they charm, whate'er the theme,
    My Mary!

"Thy silver locks, once auburn bright,
　Are still more lovely in my sight
Than golden beams of orient light,
　　　　　My Mary!

"For could I view nor them nor thee,
　What sight worth seeing should I see?
The sun would rise in vain for me,
　　　　　My Mary!

"Partakers of thy sad decline,
　Thy hands their little force resign;
Yet gently prest, press gently mine,
　　　　　My Mary!

"Such feebleness of limb thou prov'st
　That now, at every step thou mov'st
Upheld by two—yet still thou lov'st,
　　　　　My Mary!

"And still to love, tho' prest with ill,
　In wintry age to feel no chill;
With me is to be lovely still,
　　　　　My Mary!

"Yet ah! by constant heed I know
　How oft the sadness that I show
Transforms thy smiles to looks of woe,
　　　　　My Mary!

"And should my future lot be cast,
　With much resemblance of the past,
Thy worn-out heart will break at last,
　　　　　My Mary!"

It is especially worthy of remark, that no man struggled against insanity so wisely as Cowper. During the intervals of that malady, which made him at once so interesting and so miserable, he displayed in many points marvellous good sense. Previous to his last attack, he sought relief in employment. He improved his garden and orchard; he called around him those whom he loved; he could sometimes, although the conviction of being under sentence of condemnation never left him, find comfort in prayer. Doubtless, the gloomy fanaticism of Mr. Newton, the credulous Puritanical convictions of Mary Unwin, tended to increase his disorder; but it is not owing to those mistaken persons alone that his fine intellect was thus overshadowed by a darkness more dreary than that of the tomb. There must have been a strong hereditary tendency to madness. There was evidently, in those days, a conviction that insanity was a mere mental disease, to be healed by moral means chiefly. Regarding it as a *physical* disorder, much, combined with moral treatment, might have been effected; but as Cowper became older and more feeble, there appeared less hope of recovery.

Mrs. Unwin's state also contributed to render Cowper's last attack permanent. The idea of losing her was ever present to him. She was, in fact, lost to him for several years before his death. Her state gradually sank into that of complete imbecility. Before that mournful relief came she had fallen into despondency. Unable to amuse herself, she looked forwards with dread to the beginning of each day, and longed for the return of night.

Cowper, meantime, to use his own expressive words, " was plunged in deeps unvisited by any human soul but his." He was " never cheerful, because he could never hope; and if he endeavoured to pray, was answered by a double portion of misery." His petitions were, therefore, comprised in these words: " God, have mercy."

And God had mercy. These two desolate beings were not left alone to their helplessness. Lady Hesketh, herself in declining health, took up her abode with them. She found him fixed to his seat, and refusing for six days to take any nourishment except a small piece of bread dipped in wine and water, under a notion of penance for his sins. He was only aroused by Mrs. Unwin's saying, prompted by Lady Hesketh, that she should like a walk: Cowper instantly rose from his chair and took her by the arm. Gratitude, tenderness, friendship, were living to the last in his gentle, afflicted spirit.

Meantime, all his domestic affairs were going fast to ruin, since Mrs. Unwin could no longer control them. Lady Hesketh complains in her letters of a certain damsel, adopted as a servant by Mrs. Unwin, and named Hannah, whose extravagance was involving the unconscious couple in debt, whilst she was herself "sweeping the village in muslin dresses of twelve shillings a yard, and feathers a yard long." All this finery was "only to dine in the kitchen, whilst Hannah must needs put out her clothes to be *mended* as well as made," Mrs. Unwin, poor woman, indulging her in every fancy; whilst towards Cowper, so greatly had disease changed her disposition, "Mary" had become exacting and selfish. His health, his time, his pursuits, were sacrificed to her; and being no longer responsible, she became his bane, almost his tyrant, rather than his companion.

The friendship of Mary Unwin and William Cowper may, therefore, be said to have expired when the once placid and strong mind of Mrs. Unwin became unhinged. They were mercifully removed from Weston into Norfolk, where, in the house of Dr. T. Johnson, Cowper's cousin, Mrs. Unwin, on the 17th of December, 1796, breathed her last. She died without a struggle. Cowper had evidently expected that event; and when the servant opened his window on the morning of her death, said, " Sally, is there life above stairs ? " He went to her bedside, as usual, and returned to the room below, where Dr. Johnson began reading to him Miss Burney's " Camilla," — fiction being then the poet's favourite reading.

Whilst doing so, the kind relative was called out — all was over. He returned into the breakfast-room, and, thinking it a fair opportunity, told Cowper that his friend was no more. The intelligence was received not entirely with apathy, yet without any visible agitation, and Dr. Johnson continued reading. The composure was, however, fallacious. Cowper took it into his head that Mrs. Unwin was not dead, but that she would come alive again in the grave; he wished to see her. When he beheld her well-known features fixed in death he flung himself to the other side of the room with a passionate burst of feeling, the first that he had shown since his return to Weston. Poor Mary! The watching, the forbearance, the devotion — in a word, the friendship of years, were then recalled ere reason, flickering like an expiring light, had for ever sunk in darkness.

The event had a soothing influence; for death is solemn, majestic, and, even to the maniac, rebukes the futile sorrows of the living. Cowper became calm, asked for a glass of wine, and from that moment was never more heard to mention the name of Mary Unwin.

Cowper survived her four miserable years. Never did one ray of hope or happiness visit that despairing heart, thus, for some inscrutable purpose, afflicted even to despair. When visited by Dr. Lubbock, of Norwich, and asked how he felt, "Feel!" was his reply, "I feel unutterable despair."

He was released on the 25th of April, 1800. His cousin, Dr. Johnson, who had watched him with the devotion of a son, seeing his death draw near, spoke to him of hope, of mercy, of the world to come. He was checked by an agonized entreaty on the part of the dying man that he would desist from any reference to those hopes to him; "thus clearly proving," Southey remarks, "that though his soul was on the eve of being invested with angelic light, the darkness of delusion thus veiled his spirit."

When that suffering spirit had departed, the features of one beloved by every human being that had ever approached him assumed, we are told, an "expression of calmness and composure mingled with holy surprise."

He died at Dereham, in Norfolk, and was buried in St. Edmund's chapel; and there Lady Hesketh erected a monument displaying two tablets, one of them dedicated to Mary Unwin. Hayley, unhappily, a warm friend but a wretched poet, wrote the inscriptions.

During the ensuing year (in 1801) two barristers, going their circuit, went out of their way to visit the house where

Cowper expired. These were James Mackintosh and Basil Montagu, both then in the prime of life, of energy, and hope. Dr. Johnson, the relative of the poet, showed them, in the hall of his house, a little spaniel in a glass-case, *Beau,* whom Cowper has celebrated in his verses, "The Dog and the Waterlily":—

> "I saw him with that lily cropped,
> Impatient swim to meet
> My quick approach, and soon he dropped
> The lily at my feet."

The two friends saw the room where the poet died — the bed which he last touched. Then they visited his grave, and that of Mrs. Unwin, at some little distance. Montagu regretted that they were not buried in the same tomb.

"Do not live in the visible, but in the invisible," said Mackintosh. "His attainments, his tenderness, his affections, his sufferings, and his hardships, will live long after both their graves are no more."

With these words we close this narrative of as true, as enduring a friendship as ever ennobled woman, and solaced man.

MARIE ANTOINETTE
AND THE
PRINCESSE DE LAMBALLE.

MARIE ANTOINETTE'S ARRIVAL AT KEHL. — HER RECEPTION. — COURT OF VERSAILLES. — MADAME DE GENLIS. — HER INTRIGUES. — CHARACTER OF THE DUC DE CHARTRES, AFTERWARDS (ÉGALITÉ) DUC D'ORLEANS. — INSULTS TO MARIE ANTOINETTE. — INTERVIEW WITH JEAN-JACQUES ROUSSEAU. — THE COMTE ST. GERMAIN. — DEATH OF LOUIS XV. — THE LITTLE TRIANON. — VISIT OF THE EMPEROR OF AUSTRIA. — BIRTH OF THE DAUPHIN. — THE PRINCESSE DE LAMBALLE. — THE QUEEN'S FRIENDSHIP FOR HER. — THE REVOLUTION. — ANNIVERSARY OF THE FEDERATION. — THE 10TH OF AUGUST. — SCENE AT THE TUILERIES. — THE ROYAL FAMILY REMOVED TO THE TEMPLE. — THE PRINCESSE DE LAMBALLE REMOVED THENCE. — HER DEATH. — EXECUTION OF THE KING. — THE DAUPHIN SEPARATED FROM HIS MOTHER. — MARIE ANTOINETTE REMOVED TO THE CONCIERGERIE. — HER TRIAL AND CONDEMNATION. — HER EXECUTION. — DEATH OF LOUIS XVII.

MARIE-ANTOINETTE

AND THE

PRINCESSE DE LAMBALLE.

It was in the year 1770 that a superb cortége rode up to the entrance of the Bridge of Kehl, at Strasbourg, and arranged itself underneath a spacious tent erected in three compartments, — one for the French, another for the Austrians, a third, the salon which occupied the centre, was considered to be neutral ground, whereon the different members of the two courts, that of the Empress Maria Theresa, on the one hand, and of the King of France, Louis XV. on the other, might assemble.

There stood the principal members of the household of Marie-Antoinette, who, in her sixteenth year, was coming to take up her abode in that country where she suffered on the scaffold for the faults of others.

Great names were heard beneath the sumptuous tent. Here was the Comtesse de Noailles, the chief personage in the group; the Duchesse de Cosse, lady of the bed-chamber; then came the four *dames du palais*, ladies who were to be ready for any occasion of state or service, glittering with diamonds and radiant with expectation; these female courtiers were set off by contrast with the Bishop of Chartres, Almoner to the future Dauphiness; whilst the *chevalier d'honneur*, the officers of the body guard, and the principal equerry in the gorgeous costume of the day, completed the scene.

They all awaited with curiosity the arrival of the young Archduchess of Austria, the ill-fated daughter of Maria Theresa. The alliance was acceptable to the French nation for many reasons. High sounding titles attested the illustrious descent of the princess, who was destined to experience the miseries of the most cruel imprisonment and of an agonised death in the country to which she was transplanted.

Her mother, Queen of Bohemia and Hungary, Archduchess of Austria, Duchess of Milan, Countess of Tyrol, Duchess of Brabant, and of the Low Countries, and of Luxemburgh, and daughter of the Emperor Charles VI., bore all these honours in single dignity since the death of her husband Francis I. Duke of Lorraine and Grand Duke of Tuscany in his own right. The exalted birth of Marie-Antoinette, as daughter of the sole descendant of Rodolph Hapsburg, was enhanced in the eyes of the French by the reputed talents as well as attractions of the princess. She spoke Latin and also Italian perfectly; and had studied French so attentively that before leaving Vienna she had almost forgotten her native tongue. She had been brought up with a simplicity, yet a strictness, which contrasted strongly with the customs of the French Court, but which prepossessed all good subjects in her favour. The Court of Vienna was alternately magnificent to excess when etiquette required it, and simple, on private occasions, in the extreme. Its daily habits resembled those of the most unambitious of the *bourgeoisie*. In the promenade and environs of Vienna, it was no uncommon sight to behold the Emperor and Empress quietly walking in the plainest dress, or driving with their children; no guards, no attendants followed them; and their subjects were accustomed to see them without the slightest demonstration or homage.

The young princesses, the daughters of Maria Theresa,

were permitted to receive no male visitors with the exception of their brothers. Their beautiful and intellectual mother sat amidst them in the homely character of a modest matron and head of a family who were to be the progenitors of kings and queens.

There was something so *naïve* in all this moderation that the courtiers of Louis XV., who, in all his guilty prosperity, still reigned over France, were prepared at once to approve and to ridicule, to admire and despise.

At length the Austrians were seen in procession, conducting the young victim to her doom. She came, and all eyes were riveted on that stately though youthful form, all tongues fain to utter loud praises of the loveliness which broke upon the expectant band of courtiers. Accompanied by the Grande Maîtresse of her maternal home, Marie-Antoinette advanced gracefully towards the French side of the "abounding river." Her complexion was exquisitely fair, with the most delicate tinge of carnation on her cheek. Her blue eyes had an irresistible expression in their lustre. Her features were aquiline and noble, and her mouth, haughty in repose, broke at times into the sweetest smile possible. Even then, young as she was, the future dignified queen and faultless wife and mother, for whom Burke exclaimed "a hundred swords should have sprung from their scabbards," was pronounced to be a worthy descendant of the Cæsars.

She came with her intuitive grace into the salon, henceforth no longer neutral. A pensive expression varying now and then the enchanting gaiety of her countenance, every one would have felt for her, but that all eyes, all French eyes, were intent on remarking the bad taste of her dress,— that dress still being German,— and the French could pardon anything except an error in costume; nor was it until, as etiquette required, she had changed her Viennese dress for a Parisian *toilette*, that they could assent to all the encomiums which had been handed to them on her grace.

It now became necessary to take leave of her own attendants, and to accept those of her new country.

Bursting into tears, Marie-Antoinette threw herself into the arms of Madame de Noailles, a stiff, ill-tempered old lady, who lived but to worship the rules of etiquette, and who did not consider this ebullition on the part of Marie-Antoinette as at all according with her ideas. For this stereotyped specimen of a *grande dame* was the great authority on all questions of *form* at Versailles. "Have you asked Madame de Noailles?" was the constant inquiry of Louis XV. when any difficulty arose; so the old lady was terribly scandalised by this luckless beginning on the part of poor Marie-Antoinette. Madame de Noailles, therefore, retreated in great confusion. A leaf was torn out, as it were, of her book of ceremony. She sank to the ground in deep curtseys, for she was quite incapable of perceiving that it was kindness, and encouragement, and not homage that the young princess wanted. But Madame de Cossé, full of feeling, came to the rescue. She spoke to the poor girl of the mother and sisters whom she had for ever left, and the tears that flowed relieved the head of the princess. In the midst of this never-to-be-forgotten scene, however, a voice was heard: Madame de Noailles spoke:

"Madam," she said, as if to remind poor Marie-Antoinette of her duty, "your royal highness's household are waiting to be presented to you."

"Fulfil all your appointed duties, Madam," was the gentle and graceful reply; "forgive these few tears which I have shed for my country and my family; henceforth I shall never forget that I am a Frenchwoman."

After all this had passed, the cortége entered Strasbourg. There, by mistake, a room which had been prepared was draped with Gobelin tapestry, representing Medea killing her children and the city of Corinth in flames. But during supper the arras was taken down and another substituted.

Another circumstance seemed to cast a shadow on coming events. When, at Versailles, the fishwomen of the Halles came to congratulate Marie-Antoinette, she felt an instinct of fear and disgust. She drew back before these loud-voiced brazen women. Years afterwards, when they were amongst the first to insult her, she called to mind this unaccountable loathing and affright.

Her situation at the Court revived in the remembrance of many the early career of Anne of Austria. That queen had been the victim of the intrigues of Richelieu, Marie-Antoinette was governed by the Abbé de Vermont. Louis XIII. was long indifferent to his beautiful intellectual wife: Louis XVI. was quite incapable at first of comprehending his gay, charming, unaffected bride, whose ease, and perfectly natural character irritated rather than pleased him. Then Madame du Barri, the iniquitous mistress of Louis XV., the grandfather of Louis XVI., endeavoured to allure the Dauphiness, as Marie-Antoinette had now become, to her party; but happily her husband discovered this intrigue, and, to his honour, Louis XVI. forbade Marie-Antoinette to hold any communication with the favourite.

Still the Court of Versailles was a mournful exchange for that of Vienna. The early life of the ill-fated Marie-Antoinette had been singularly peaceful. Every day all the members of the imperial family had risen at the same hour; with prayers the daily duties were begun; a simple breakfast of milk and fruit then followed; then work, reading, and study occupied the morning; at twelve, a frugal dinner was served; then the young princesses walked out; recreation and study divided the remainder of the tranquil day till supper-time; after that social meal the whole household retired to rest. The chief recreation permitted to the young archduchesses was to visit, on foot, with their stately mother, the poor, and to take them provisions and money. Sometimes

Maria Theresa taught her children a sterner lesson. She took them down into the catacombs where lay the bodies of their ancestors. There she pointed out to them the instability of life, the vanity of earthly grandeur. In after life, when surrounded with all that could intoxicate her susceptible heart, Marie-Antoinette used to recall these sepulchral excursions, these maternal admonitions. Alas! she had indeed reason to lay them to heart.

The Dauphiness lived in fact on the very brink of a volcano. Louis XV., the most infamous and profligate of the Bourbons, was still able to throw a grace over his depravity, and to injure virtue by the charm of his manners, conversation, and person. Madame du Barri ruled supreme. The Dauphiness, left in happy ignorance of vice by her mother, asked the Comtesse de Noailles, on her first arrival at Versailles, a singular question. "I know," she said, "from the Abbé de Vermont, the names, the style, and rank of all the different members of noble families who have been presented to me; but the Abbé has told me nothing of Madame du Barri. What office, pray, does she hold at the Court?"

"Her office is to amuse his majesty," was the cautious reply.

"Ah, Madam!" cried Marie-Antoinette, "how I envy her! I should be delighted to assist her in such an office."

The Comtesse smiled, but made no answer; and for some time the young Dauphiness, brought up in all innocence and modesty, did not comprehend that the King was, in truth, a "whitened sepulchre."

It was the aim of Madame du Barri to gain over this young princess to her side if possible, and had it not been for the Dauphin, Louis XVI., the artless girl might have fallen into the snare.

Amongst a host of secret enemies one well-known personage appears prominently on the scene, even at this early period.

Madame d'Adhémar, the faithful attendant of Marie-Antoinette, describes thus her first interview with this famous woman of talent and intrigue.

"I was visiting Madame de la Reynière," says Madame d'Adhémar, "one of my friends, when a young girl of high family made her appearance. She was very poor, and used to play the harp in order to make herself agreeable. The lady of this house supplied her with her dress, her linen, &c., and she repaid the gifts by the ready coin of flattery."

This Parisian sample of the *intrigante* genus contrived to marry the Comte de Genlis without the consent of his parents. Nevertheless, by her address, she managed to get into favour with all her husband's family.

A friend, hoping to serve her, introduced her to the Duc d'Orléans, whose son, then Duc de Chartres, and afterwards known as the infamous Égalité, had several young children. It was to these, amongst whom Louis-Philippe was the brightest constellation, that Madame de Genlis became *gouvernante*. Her intrigue with Égalité, the reputed father of Pamela (Lady Edward Fitzgerald), was the scandal of a later day.

At the time when Marie-Antoinette was first at Versailles, Madame de Genlis was comparatively an obscure individual, creeping in where she could, her sole ambition being to establish herself firmly in court favour. One day Madame d'Adhémar was surprised at receiving a visit from her. Politeness, however, induced the courtly lady to disguise her astonishment. Madame de Genlis apologised for her intrusion; but said she felt so enthusiastic an admiration for the young Dauphiness that she could not resist the desire she had to come and speak to Madame d'Adhémar about it.

"And the same feeling, Madam," replied Madame d'Adhémar, "has, I presume, induced you to go so often as you do lately to visit Madame du Barri?"

Madame de Genlis looked confused, then declared that she

should never have gone near Madame du Barri except to beg that a poor gentleman, "whom she offered to introduce to Madame d'Adhémar, should be released from prison."

She then broke forth into loud eulogiums on Marie-Antoinette, and hinted that she should much like to have a more particular introduction to her than those usually presented.

"I quite comprehend your wishes, Madam," was the coldly civil reply, "but Madame la Dauphine does not, I know, wish to extend her circle, and besides, the Comtesse de Noailles is the only person who has a right to arrange private presentations."

"But will you not have the kindness to speak of me to her royal highness?"

Madame D'Adhémar smiled at this expression, royal highness, a style and title repudiated by Marie-Antoinette who, as Grand-Duchess of Austria, thought herself above it. She, however, the more firmly refused Madame de Genlis, and henceforth that lady scarcely spoke or even bowed to her when they met.

A few days afterwards Marie-Antoinette said to Madame D'Adhémar, "Who is the Comtesse de Genlis who plays so well on the harp, and who is of a high family. I have never seen her."

Madame D'Adhémar told her what she knew of her.

"She is perpetually writing to me," said Marie-Antoinette, "to propose a course of reading for me, and of education for my future children."

"She omits nothing to serve her own purposes," was the sarcastic reply of the *Dame du Palais*.

"I suspect there is some intrigue at the bottom of all this," cried Marie-Antoinette.

Then the faithful D'Adhémar told her how apparent it was that the pretended devotion of Madame de Genlis was assumed only to draw her into the toils of Madame du Barri;

it was agreed that she was not to be admitted; and the result was that Madame de Genlis became one of those secret enemies by whom the web was woven into which Marie-Antoinette was eventually ensnared. Songs and pamphlets against the Dauphiness, when she became Queen, attested the malice of her clever foe; and when the revolution broke out Madame de Genlis showed herself in her true colours. She may truly be termed the evil genius of the wretched Égalité, Duc d'Orléans.

At this period the affection and respect which Louis XVI. had learned to feel for his young wife supported her, however, against every cabal formed against her peace.

One vexation alone dimmed the happiness of the joyous, pure spirit which was destined to be crushed in after years. Marie-Antoinette had no son. Like Anne of Austria, her felicity was incomplete, and her pre-eminence as a princess precarious. Poor Marie-Antoinette! she little thought that the prince so earnestly longed for was to be the innocent source of almost maddening grief.

From the earliest period of her married life Marie-Antoinette had been warned by her mother against the Duc de Chartres (afterwards Égalité Duc d'Orléans), and the suspicions of Maria Theresa were shared by Louis XVI. Égalité, even at that epoch, was endeavouring to ingratiate himself with the public and to injure the reigning family. But the crafty Philippe d'Orléans paid, apparently, the most devoted attentions to Marie-Antoinette, who boasted that she had overcome the prejudice he had entertained towards her. Madame d'Adhémar in vain drew a portraiture of his real character for her benefit.

"The Duc de Chartres," thus wrote the faithful monitor, "although his education has been so much praised, has been badly brought up; he makes, however, a good use of such knowledge as he possesses; having an excellent memory, he is deficient neither in talent nor in sagacity; what ruins him is his mad desire to resemble his great grandfather, the infamous Duc d'Orléans, the Regent, whom Louis XIV. used to call, '*ce fanfaron de vice.*' Brilliant qualities, however, lessened the odium which attached to the licentiousness of the Regent; he had courage, a gift in which his descendant is wanting, if I may judge by certain anecdotes I have heard."

Then she goes on to describe the personal appearance of the wretch who turned against his own kindred, and paid the penalty of his crimes.

" The Duke had once been handsome, but every agreeable attribute had been destroyed by intemperance. His complexion was so bloated that it made one sick to look at him; true, his elegance of deportment was incomparable, his carriage perfect; his manners always those of a *grand seigneur*. Nothing could exceed the politeness, the respect, the delicacy of his behaviour in the presence of modest women. No one could have supposed that under that courteous and proper demeanour the most depraved heart in the world was concealed. In the midnight orgie, however, he threw off that mask, and disclosed all the grossness of his depraved, and impious mind. Penurious, with an air of affected generosity; he was dangerous, not because he had either character or energy, but because he had a vulgar ambition which would attract to him unscrupulous partisans; because he was rich, and had money to spend on the wretched damaged set who formed his circle in the Palais Royal."

He now applied himself to win over the beautiful princess who was so easily made the dupe of her feelings. Marie-Antoinette was extremely fond of flowers. He sent her every day bunches of the rarest Dresden, or Sèvres china, adorned with the most exquisite paintings. One of these porcelain vases was of an antique form, supported by the Three Graces, with figures also of Love and Hymen. One of the faces represented the head of the Dauphiness, encircled with a garland of flowers, which, according to Oriental symbolism, were typical of all the virtues; another of the faces was the portrait of the Dauphin, also crowned with a symbolical garland; his figure was sustained by an anchor, on the points of which rested two doves, emblems of peace and mercy.

A copy of verses, composed by the witty and brave but dissolute Laclos, an artillery officer who had written a romance called by the truly French title " *Les Liaisons dangereuses*," accompanied this exquisite present, which propitiated even Louis XVI. For a time Égalité was received by the Dauphin and Dauphiness, after this attempt to gain their regard, in a perilous intimacy. But Marie-Antoinette was sound at heart. Madame d'Adhémar remarked one day to her that the visits of the Duc de Chartres had become less frequent.

" Yes," was the reply: "Monsieur le Duc receives such bad company at his house that I cannot admit him to mine."

A few days afterwards she confided still more to her *Dame du Palais*. Égalité " had had the effrontery to speak of love to the wife of the eldest son of his king."

" Is it true ? " cried Madame d'Adhémar. It was indeed true; the whole was a political intrigue which the contemptible prince hoped to found upon the infamy of the Dauphiness.

Three men dared to insult her with their addresses: Égalité, as we have seen; the Duc de Lauzun, and the Marquis de Tilly. This last individual was an infamous wretch who was supported by actresses. He dared, however, to give out that the Dauphiness secretly provided for him. The calumnies of this terrible period fell harmless upon the stately and excellent Marie-Antoinette during the life of Louis XV.; but they drove others less courageous from that dissolute court.

Amongst those who experienced the slanderous malice of

Égalité, was the lovely and blameless Princesse de Lamballe. She was then a young widow, in all the brilliancy of a beauty as modest as it was dazzling. Louis XV., pitying her on account of the early death of her young husband, endeavoured by kindness, to console her for her loss. Any attentions from such a man as Louis XV. were injurious to a young and admired woman, but the Court, for once, understood them; and the Duc de Chartres alone, put on royal condescension the construction of a bad mind. He aroused the cabal of the Du Barri from their security; he accused the youthful widow of coquetry; he declared that she wished to rob Madame du Barri of her lover. His envenomed shafts had the effect he desired: Madame de Lamballe indignantly withdrew herself from Court, and returned not till after the death of Louis XV. It was then that Marie-Antoinette, deeply impressed by the propriety of the princess's conduct, bestowed on her a regard which would never have been withdrawn had it not been for the intrigues of others.

Among the wonders of that day, Jean-Jacques Rousseau, the "disciple of truth and of nature," as he styled himself, was the theme of a certain party. The persecutions he had endured from the Encyclopædists had gained him notoriety.

It was after the death of Louis XV., when Marie Antoinette had become Queen, that Rousseau's fame rose to its height. She was anxious to see him, but an interview was impracticable, for Rousseau declined all court favours, and was resolved not to present himself at the Tuileries.

One day, however, as the Queen, very simply dressed, was walking in the gardens of the *Petit Trianon*, Madame d'Adhémar who attended on her saw a man looking in at the iron gate, and recognised Jean-Jacques. She told the Queen, and the enthusiastic Marie-Antoinette rushed instantly to the gate, and calling the porter, ordered him to let in the person who was walking there, but on no account to say that she was at the Trianon.

The porter was a Swiss, and knew Rousseau by sight, so he was resolved to play *his* part well. "*Notre ours*," as Madame d'Adhémar calls the unconscious lion of the day, entered the grounds, looking uneasily around him: at this instant two strangers arrived and inquired of the porter if they could see the house; they were answered in the affirmative; and Rousseau, reassured, asked the same question and was answered by the porter, who offered to conduct him through the grounds. They got into conversation, and as they approached the Temple of Love they perceived two ladies seated on the steps, the Queen and Madame d'Adhémar.

"Who are those ladies?" Jean-Jacques inquired.

"Two German ladies, who are allowed to walk here whilst her majesty is absent."

Rousseau approached the ladies; the Queen then spoke to him: her voice trembled, for genius has an imperative influence even over royalty.

They spoke of the difference between English and French gardens.

"I delight not in French gardens," Rousseau observed. "Their regularity, their stateliness; these alleys of which one cannot see the termination, these immense parterres, these marble basons containing water, all these points show me that such gardens were not made for me—that I am scarcely authorised to enjoy them. I scarcely dare to abandon myself to pleasure, lest whilst I gaze a brilliant Court should take me by surprise. In an English garden, on the contrary, the free growth of the trees, the flowers, the enamelled grass, the shining rivulets, the thick, shady groves, the rocks, the dark grottoes, inspire me with the idea that I am in the country, and far from the rich and great." The Queen listened to him with deep interest.

"And why," she asked, "do you avoid the great? are they not human beings like yourself? do they not deserve to receive kindness from you?"

"I like nothing that inspires me with fear; I am afraid of the great and powerful."

"What you say, Sir, is sad — what! are the great never to be beloved?"

"We give our respect to the Crown — that is all that it can receive."

The Queen was vexed. She wished, as most sovereigns do, to possess the love of her subjects.

"You are a republican, Sir, I perceive," she said, "hence your horror of kings."

"Ah! Madam! I hate no one! on the contrary, in spite of my injuries, I love my fellow-creatures."

"That is creditable to you, Sir. May I ask your name," replied the Queen.

"My name," Rousseau replied, somewhat vexed that so great a man as himself was not known to a lady of rank, "my name is Rousseau. I am Rousseau, of Geneva."

"Rousseau, *the* Rousseau of the world!" the Queen, with a sweet smile, replied.

"Madam, you are too kind. I am an obscure individual."

"And somewhat prejudiced against monarchs." Something flashed across the mind of Rousseau: he started up, looked around him: there was a gloomy expression in his eyes as he said;

"I thought these gardens were open to every one: I heard that the Queen was not here."

"The Queen does not wish to be here."

"Ah! but that makes all the difference. Never shall I forget this day! Madam, you are right; monarchs may be loved, not loved alone, they may be adored."

"Monsieur Rousseau! That is flattery!"

"Ah," he cried, "do not prohibit my freedom of speech and thought; what I have said has come from the bottom of my heart. You are right, Madam; sincerity can never exist in the precincts of a Court, and kings as well as queens are right in suspecting Rousseau."

He made a deep bow and retired.

"Ah!" cried the Queen, after some moments of confusion, "these philosophers are dreadful; they prevent our subjects from loving us, when we so much need their affection."

Rousseau died shortly afterwards; but Marie-Antoinette henceforth distrusted and discouraged men of letters, who, she thought, and perhaps at that æra, with justice, were inimical to the throne.*

The Court of Versailles contained, nevertheless, amid its most ardent votaries, one of the most accomplished men of his time; a man of rank, talent, and fortune, endowed with rare perfections of person, yet a compound of charlatanism and ability.

This singular being appeared to have the gift of perpetual youth; and he dealt largely in the mystic sciences which the superstitious, though infidel character of the times adopted. In 1743 news was spread about Versailles that a stranger of enormous wealth — at least if one might judge by his jewellery — had arrived there. Whence did he come? What was his origin? These were questions that no one could answer. His exterior was perfect; a graceful form, tall and supple, small hands, a *mignon* foot, an elegant leg, which was perfection with its fine silk stocking; these were no vulgar attributes; but his fine, lofty, sagacious, intelligent face was peculiarly striking. Then his costume was so tasteful; his light doublet showed his exquisite figure; his dark hair also was so carefully arranged; his teeth, which the sweetest smile in the world showed to advantage, were so white and regular, his eyes were so black and piercing; that even Madame D'Adhémar the prudent, the proper, exclaims, "*Oh! quels yeux; je n'ai vu nulle part leurs pareils!*"

* See the Memoirs of Madame la Comtesse d'Adhémar, vol. i. p. 292.

He appeared in 1768 to be about forty or forty-five years of age; no one remembered him younger. The old evergreen Comtesse de Georgy used to say: "Fifty years ago I was ambassadress at Venice; I remember the Comte de St. Germain *there*; he looked the same age then as now, perhaps he is now a little younger than then."

"At all events, Madam," was the Comte's reply, "I was always enchanted to make myself agreeable to ladies."

"You were then styled the Marquis Balletti," resumed Madame Georgy.

Like all pretenders to science of that, and the preceding century, St. Germain turned silver into gold. Then his way of living was singular. He had two valets de chambre, one of whom, he said, had served him for the "*last five hundred years.*" He was never known to partake of food in any house but his own; and never to invite a single guest to his table.

In spite of all his peculiarities, St. Germain was made Minister of War, 1775. He then formed a royal guard of fifty gendarmes and fifty horse, as an escort to their majesties; these were not disbanded till 1787. Notwithstanding royal favour, the mysterious St. Germain was suspected of being at the bottom of the fatal conspiracies which eventually ruined France. He is reported to have died in 1784 at Schleswic, in the dominions of the Elector of Hesse Cassel; nevertheless, the Comte de Chalons, a Venetian ambassador, declared that he had met him on the Place Saint-Marc in 1788.

Many wonderful anecdotes of his second sight are preserved. He cast the nativity, and foretold the death of Madame de Pompadour; and it happened as he had predicted. He was generally the hero of his own histories, which he told in such a manner—sometimes relating how he had even called spirits from their dread abode—as to strike awe into his listeners. Then this accomplished charlatan used to turn to his valet Roger.

"Am I right, or not, Roger, in what I state?"

"Monsieur le Comte," was his confederate's answer, "you forget that I have been in your service only five hundred years; therefore I cannot have been present at the event you are describing; *ce doit être mon prédécesseur.*" So M. Roger acquired the sobriquet of Monsieur "*cinq cents ans.*"

Let us pause for a time on the brief and happy period of Marie-Antoinette's life. There was something of mournful presage in the commencement of her reign. When the young couple heard that Louis XV. was dead, they threw themselves on their knees: "O God! guide us, protect us; we are too young to reign!"

During the period of mourning, the King and Queen were seen walking out together, she leaning on his arm; of course, matrimonial happiness became the fashion; and many couples who had long been separated, were now beheld pacing along the terrace at Choisy in the same fashion.

Louis and Marie-Antoinette received condolences from the Court at La Muette. Little black bonnets with great wings, shaking old heads, low curtsies, keeping motion with the hand, in fact, a general routing out of the venerable ladies of the *ancien régime* appeared. Marie-Antoinette with difficulty kept her countenance, but she managed to do so, and received the crowds with infinite dignity, until, observing one elderly dame, the Marquise de Clermont-Tonnerre, seated on the floor, concealed behind the hoops of the ladies, playing of certain childish pranks, she was obliged to conceal a smile behind her fan.

The next day, the following verse of a song was circulated by the Anti-Austrian party.

"Little Queen, you must not be
So saucy with your twenty years,
Your ill-used courtiers soon will see
You pass once more the barriers!
Tal lal lal, fal la la."

More than fifteen years afterwards, Madame Campan, bed-chamber woman to the Queen, heard it said in Auvergne, among the remote French circles there, that the Queen had laughed in the faces of the duchesses, and sexagenarian princesses. No opportunity was lost of blaming the young Queen; for instance, Louis XV. had died of small-pox. When Louis XVI. and his brothers resolved to be inoculated, the Queen was blamed for advising them to submit to it. The Queen wished to see the sun rise, and was accompanied by her ladies; but the infamous Égalité was also of the party, and the coarsest abuse was the result.

Hitherto, Marie-Antoinette had been simple in her dress. Louis XV. himself, the most perfect gentleman, as far as manners went, in Europe, had been enchanted with her girlish attire. When she wore a dress of gauze, or taffeta, she was compared to the Venus de Medici. She was styled the Atalanta of Marly. Painters linmed her lovely face; one of them placed it in the heart of a full blown rose; and Louis XV. rewarded him for the conceit: everything had conspired to dazzle her.

No spot on earth has witnessed such various scenes as the quaint old palace of the Tuileries. Soon after her entry into Paris, Marie-Antoinette was called by the clamours of the multitude into the balcony of that palace. On seeing the vast crowd beneath: "Heavens," she cried, "what a concourse!" "Madam," said the old Duc de Brissac, Governor of Paris, "I may tell you, without offending the Dauphin, they are so many lovers." Yet, even then, a certain faction aimed at a divorce, and the indifference of Louis XVI. was the theme of all tongues. Still, until the death of Louis XV. Marie-Antoinette had preserved a tolerable popularity in France.

The Little Trianon, which had been built for Louis XV. was bestowed by his successor on Marie-Antoinette. Everything there, even to the faded beds in which Madame du

Barri had slept, was in the same state as heretofore. The queen, delighted in visiting this lovely spot — so great a contrast to Versailles — attended only by a valet; these traces of her simple pleasures, her few transient enjoyments, sadden even the visitors of the nineteenth century. There she received her brother, Duke Maximilian, and was overwhelmed by his blunders. When Du Buffon, for instance, presented him with his famous work, the Archduke refused it, saying he should be sorry to deprive him of it; but this error of an unformed youth was nothing compared to that of the Emperor Joseph II. who afterwards visited Paris. When the Queen told him that she had prepared apartments for him in the Château of Versailles, he replied that he "always lodged at a public house when he travelled." The Queen, nevertheless, *insisted* on his being her guest, and assured him he should be at perfect liberty. The emperor replied that he knew the Palace of Versailles was large enough for him, as well as for others, and that *he* might as well be there as the numerous *mauvais sujets* who were lodged in it; but his valet had already made up his camp-bed in a ready-furnished house, and there he should stay.

Poor Marie-Antoinette! She had been talking continually of her brother; and had boasted of his intellect, his energy, and simplicity of character. There were, however, times in which Joseph II. appeared to advantage. He dined daily with the King and Queen, who, when alone with their own family were attended, as Madame Campan relates, by women only; the Emperor then spoke with wit and fluency in French, ridiculed the severe etiquette of the court, made flattering observations on the sights of Paris, and reproached his royal brother-in-law for being ignorant of them, and advised him to see not only Paris, but France.

Then he taxed his sister for wearing rouge. One day, when she was laying it on, he said, "a little more under the eyes, Marie; lay on the rouge like a fury, as that lady does," pointing to a court lady who was highly painted: then he made the most injudicious observations. Even to the comedian Clairval, he remarked: "Your young Queen is very giddy, but you French people don't mind that." He abused the French government to Monsieur Campan, at that time secretary librarian to the King; told improper stories of the King and Queen of Naples, and even of his own court; and showed, indeed, all the want of *tact* that so strongly marks the German character.

The return of Voltaire in 1778 to Paris, after an absence of twenty-seven years, seemed to many a prelude to all the spirit of disaffection and revolution which soon followed that event.

Scandal, in truth, never ceased, whilst Marie-Antoinette innocently enjoyed herself. When she gave a fête at Trianon, and lighted up the gardens, it was said that she had had a whole forest destroyed to make this illumination. When, before the birth of her son, she sat on a bench placed on the terrace of Versailles, listening to music, and enjoying the evening breeze, or walked, arm in arm with her sisters-in-law, an imitative yet calumnious crowd, all the *beau-monde* being there likewise, invented or perverted incidents.

Dressed like the other princesses, in cambric muslin gowns, and in large hats with muslin veils, Marie-Antoinette was sometimes mistaken for a *bourgeoise;* and people, to her great amusement, used to come and sit down by her. One night a young clerk in the war office pretending to mistake her, began talking to her of the beauty of the night, and the effect of the music. The Queen, fancying she was not recognised, replied encouragingly; of course the young man boasted of the interview until desired to hold his tongue. Another time one of the body-guard of *Monsieur* had the effrontery to speak of her in the same manner. In vain did Madame Campan remonstrate with the Queen, and persuade her to give up these evening amusements; in vain did she tell her that she saw, one night, two women deeply veiled, seated near her, in profound silence; that these women were Madame du Barri and her sister-in-law; in vain did she relate to the Queen the infamous libels circulated respecting these innocent diversions: her majesty was too much delighted with them to abandon them, too conscious of innocence to be prudent.

A few days before the birth of the first Dauphin, a bundle of songs was thrown into that part of the Palace of Versailles, called the Bull's-eye. It was taken up, and found to contain the most disgusting slanders, and was put into the hands of the King.

On the 11th of December, the heir apparent to the crown, Louis, Dauphin of France, was born. Often had Marie-Antoinette before the birth of her first born, a daughter, shed tears that she was childless. She might, indeed, have wept in extreme anguish could she have foreseen that the infant welcomed so fondly was to die at an early age. The Princesse de Lamballe was beside her when the exclamation, "*La Reine va s'accoucher!*" brought a rush of persons into the royal chamber. No one could move about for the crowd. Marie-Antoinette nearly sank under the announcement that a son was born at last. "Give her air," cried the physician. "Warm water! she must be bled at the foot." She had fainted. The windows were fastened up with strips of paper; the King, with the force of affection opened them; the lancet was plunged into the foot; the Queen opened her eyes; but the alarm was too great for the loving friend who afterwards showed such heroism, and who met death for herself so calmly. As the Queen, snatched from the jaws of death, asked, unconscious of having been bled, why her foot was bandaged—whilst the princes of the blood and minister stood by, the Princesse de Lamballe was carried insensible from the chamber.

Madame Campan, meantime, was shedding tears of delight at the safety of her beloved mistress, yet as she mournfully observes: "When recalling those bursts of happiness, those transports of delight, that moment when Heaven gave us back again a princess beloved by all about her; how often have I reflected upon that impenetrable and wholesome obscurity by which all knowledge of the future is concealed from us. What should we not have felt, if in the midst of our joyful delirium, a heavenly voice, unfolding the secret decrees of fate, had called to us: Bless not that human art which calls her back to life; weep rather for her return to a world fatal and cruel to the object of your affections. Ah! let her leave it, honoured, beloved, regretted; you can now weep over her grave — you can now cover it with flowers." The day will come when, " all the furies of the earth will deliver her over, prematurely old, heartbroken, to the executioner."

The Princesse de Lamballe had been for some time appointed superintendent of the Queen's household when the Dauphin was born. It was during one of the very severest winters ever known in France that this ill-fated woman had first become the intimate friend of Marie-Antoinette. The sledge parties which the Queen had enjoyed in her youth, were introduced into France that winter; and it became the fashion for all *grands seigneurs* to drive their sledges, their horses caparisoned with white feathers, and bells ringing at their heads. During six weeks the snow remained on the ground, and the park of Versailles was the scene of the sledge races, in which large sums were won and lost. Amid the most admired was the Princesse de Lamballe, her sweet face the emblem of spring — the spring of her short life, " peeping beneath sable and ermine[*]," inspired the greater interest from her story. She was at that time living with her father-in-law, the Duc de Penthièvre, who treated her as his adopted daughter, and the most devoted gratitude, the tenderest respect was felt by her towards that venerable prince. The Queen, however, full of kindness, perceived that the house of the

[*] See Campan.

aged prince did not afford the amusements suitable to youth, nor ensure such an establishment as the Princesse de Lamballe ought to possess. She, therefore, revived for her sake, the office of superintendent of the household, which had been discontinued, and the young widow removed to Versailles. Differences eventually arose respecting the official prerogatives of the superintendent; but everything was so amicably arranged, that the friendship of the Queen and Princess was never disturbed.

It was on the 27th of March, 1785, that another infant prince was born; and in 1789, his elder brother, commonly styled the First Dauphin, died at Meudon. The younger son, whom Louis XVI. used to call his "little Norman," was, after the execution of the King his father, entitled by Legitimists, Louis XVII.

A brief reference to the tragic events for which France has suffered a retribution unknown in the annals of modern history, must bring us to that tragedy in which Friendship like a guardian angel, pointed to a heaven of rest, and sustained Marie-Antoinette and her friend in their hour of doom.

As yet their unequal intimacy was in all its serenity. From her first entrance into France, the Queen had longed for that union of heart which she enjoyed with the pure and amiable Madame de Lamballe. There was a truth, a gentleness in the character of the princess that made the Queen earnestly desire to secure not merely her allegiance, but her love and respect. Marie-Antoinette could not endure women of mere brilliant qualities; she used to call them "*girandes de feu d'artifice*," and she was right; it was those who professed little, but who felt much; it was the gentle, the modest, the pious who adhered to her in the stern anguish of the Hundred Days; and followed her from prison to prison with their prayers, whom she valued, and by whom she was really beloved.

It became the fashion in the Court for every lady to have a friend, an inseparable, who went with her everywhere; to whom one note at least was written in the morning, and who spent the rest of the day with her chosen favourite. For a long time, Marie-Antoinette had been the only lady at Versailles who had not enjoyed that privilege; at last it was announced, without scandal for once, that the Queen had selected a friend, and that that friend was Madame de Lamballe.

There was something almost angelic in the feelings of Marie-Antoinette for this lovely victim to her friendship for the poor Queen: Marie-Antoinette loved her as an elder sister would cherish a younger; she admired, she respected the unfortunate princess.

Let us forget the pleasant days of their first intimacy when the Queen loved to drink tea uninvited in the rooms appropriated to the princess, lest the gloom of the closing scenes should by contrast be too mournful, too dreadful to any heart not devoid of human pity. Let us pass over the terrible antecedents of the Revolutionary Fever.

Farewell to Versailles! The royal family then on the throne of France have quitted it for ever. They are arrived at the Tuileries: June has passed; July is drawing to its close. It is the summer of the year 1792.

The revolutionary fever was at its height. "Majesty," says Montaigne, "falls less easily from the summit to the middle, than from the middle to the bottom."

The anniversary of the Federation had arrived. Petion was the idol of the populace; as the King and Queen drove from the Champ de Mars to the Tuileries, the little prince Louis-Charles dressed in the uniform of the national guard, said indignantly to his mother: "Is Monsieur Petion king to-day?" He was answered by a mournful gaze. "No, no," cried the precocious child; "it is you who are king, for you are just and merciful, papa." Nevertheless, the shouts of "King Petion" resounded through the air. The aim of this famous leader of the French Revolution was in fact to place his son on the throne as king, and to establish a council of regency of which he was himself to be the president and ruler.

Expiring efforts were made on the part of Louis XVI. and the Queen to win over some of the leaders of the revolution to their side. The Girondist Guadet had a secret interview at night with the Queen and her consort. "The Queen," Monsieur de Beauchesne relates, "brought to it * her noble attributes and her disquiet heart; Louis XVI. his confiding goodness." It was less as king than as husband and father that the unhappy prince depicted to the deputy for Bordeaux the anguish of his position. Commencing coldly, the conversation became pathetic; republican inflexibility became less inflexible, royalty had shed tears. As Guadet was about to withdraw, the Queen asked him if he would not like to see the Dauphin; and herself taking the candle she led him into the contiguous chamber, which was that of the young prince. "How tranquilly he sleeps," said the Girondist in a melancholy tone, whilst the Queen leaning over the Dauphin's bed, murmured, "Poor child! he alone in the château sleeps thus!" Marie-Antoinette's accents touched the Girondist's heart; he took the child's hand, and without awakening him kissed it with an air of emotion, then, turning to the Queen, he said: "Madame, educate him for liberty. It is the condition of his life." It is a singular coincidence, that the day on which the King was guillotined, was soon followed by the execution of Guadet at Bordeaux.

Towards the end of July, a Swiss officer in the service of the King, wrote to a friend thus: "They have quietly contrived to send all the armed force out of Paris. Here are the five regiments of the line, and two-thirds of the Swiss guards that they so feared, put out of the way of harming the factions. We shall soon see the tragedy begin."

* See "Louis XVI., his Life, his Sufferings, and his Death," by Mons. A. de Beauchesne, vol. i. p. 148.

The 10th of August was the day fixed upon. Two projects for escape had been suggested to the King, but he rejected them. The failure of his flight to Varennes was not forgotten by him; besides, the Queen, with her hereditary courage, observed: "We might as well die here, as suffer the fate of James II." Alas! she did not, she could not foresee, that a fate worse than immediate death was contemplated by the fiends who composed the majority of the National Assembly.

Three sections of that body now declared that they no longer considered Louis XVI. king, and that it was time that the people should rise in a mass, and govern themselves. It was, therefore, decreed that if by twelve o'clock on the night of the 9th of August, the deposition of the King had not been declared, the whole body of the Federates should proceed, armed, to the Château of the Tuileries, whilst the tocsin was sounded and cannon were let off, to enforce the edict.

The royal family within the palace, had retired after supper to the council chamber; the ministers and some other persons had decided on passing the night there. The ancient pile stood apparently in repose; in the early part of that summer's night the placid stars shone on its glistening roofs, the night winds blew over the now neglected flowers and perishing shrubs of the young Dauphin's private garden, where the poor child had for some time been precluded entering. The waters of the Seine flowed peacefully along, untinged till a later hour by the blood of victims; towards eleven, however, force was opposed to force on the Place du Carrousel and in the courts of the Tuileries, and in its now smiling, then crowded, gardens. A brave ex-captain of the French Guards, named Mandat, had made this last endeavour for his sovereign. For ever honoured be his name! He was summoned before the Council of the Commune in the Hôtel de Ville, where Danton and Tallien and others sat. He was then accused of cutting off the colours of the people:

he became confused, and defended himself badly. He was ordered off to the Abbaye. Scarcely, however, had he quitted the Hall, than he was killed by a pistol shot, and his body thrown into the Seine.

The troops, therefore, which he had summoned were wavering and disorganised; and whilst this scene was going on outside the Tuileries, one still more heart-rending was taking place in the chambers of that palace which has witnessed such various revolutions, such scenes of despair and peril. Marie-Antoinette was going from one privy councillor to another endeavouring to inspire each with hope that she no longer had herself. As the attendants were preparing to take off her son to bed, she burst into tears. "Mamma," said the child, "why do you weep now when you bid me good night? I wish I might stay with you this evening; do not send me to bed." She embraced him as she said: "Be easy, my child, I shall be near you."

The poor child retired to bed. Fate was now to be counted not by hours but by minutes. The midnight hour struck. As the last stroke was heard, the tocsin was sounded from the Cordeliers, the *générale* (call) was beaten in every quarter. The sections rose, the revolutionists armed with pikes, glided into the ranks of the royal troops left by Mandat. The artillery of the insurgents was planted near the Château. Day broke upon that fearful host, the deeds of which France has not yet expiated. Marie-Antoinette, dreading lest the swords of the Federates should penetrate the hearts of her sleeping children in their beds, had ordered that the Dauphin and his sister should be roused and dressed, and brought unto her. She and the King pressed them to their hearts. "Mamma," said the Dauphin, "why should they hurt my father? he is so good." Then the King visited every post of the Château, he showed himself to the grenadiers, to the volunteers, the bourgeoisie, and the gendarmes, who crowded every room and staircase of the Tuileries.

A mournful cortége accompanied him. Marie-Antoinette, her children with her, and her sister-in-law, the incomparable, the ill-fated Princess Elizabeth, and the Princess de Lamballe followed her closely. Thus they passed along; Louis, heavy in countenance, yet with a certain majesty of demeanour, was calm. An heroic dignity marked every movement of the Queen's. In happier days she had been celebrated for the grace with which she used to walk down the galleries of Versailles, and the address with which she bowed from side to side as she passed on, forgetting no one, her sweet smile playing on her fair young face. That night the grace, the majesty, of her step were impressed on the memory of those who saw her for the last time. The modest, lovely, "good Madame Elizabeth," as she was styled, was composed, firm, gently courageous. Then came the *belle des belles*—alas! her name was written already in the book of doom—"Marie-Therese, Louise de Savoie de Bourbon Lamballe." She who bore those high-sounding names, she whom Marie-Antoinette most loved, could not be saved. The victim was lovely, innocent, adored, and a Bourbon. The more need that she should perish, and perish in agony.

We have seen, of late, that grand old gallery, the floor of which was, even on the accession of the present Emperor, notched by swords, and stained with blood, we have seen that gallery illuminated, resplendent, filled on either side with all that the city of Paris can boast of wealth and political distinction.

Still do the old legitimist nobility shun its gilded walls, and why? they cherish the memories of the dynasty that then expired in misery. They gaze upon the lovely Empress, pale as the delicate primrose in the shade, as she passes out, and retire, and say: "Our forefathers knew one as fair, and more majestic." Many of the remnants of the old loyal-hearted class will not even cross the Place Louis Quinze*, as they

---

* Place de la Concorde.

still call it, desecrated by the blood of Louis XVI. New names, not old ones, are heard resounding in that gallery now. Those sentiments are indeed fast dying out; it is well perhaps they should. On the night of the 9th of August, 1792, they were not all crushed by the demon revolution. The old chivalry glimmered then, sank in the socket like a light burnt out, and has never been wholly rekindled. Tears filled the eyes of those who watched the royal procession; many blessed the Queen, some did more; a band of gentlemen, two hundred in number, had hastened to the Tuileries on hearing of the King's danger. They wore no uniforms, and carried their arms under their clothes; thus were they called the "Knights of the Poignard." As the Queen passed them, some of these gallant gentlemen begged that she would touch their weapons to make them victorious, others entreated that they might kiss her fair hand, to make death sweeter to them. Then shouts arose to the roofs of the gallery. "Long live the King of our fathers!" cried the young men, "Long live the King of our children!" cried the old ones, and the Dauphin was lifted up to them, "a living standard for which they vowed to die."

The Queen, Madame de Lamballe, and the children had returned to their own apartments when other sounds than those of "Vive le Roi," broke on their ear,—"Deposition or death! *Death!*"

"Madame," said a *chef de légion*, entering the apartment of the Queen, "the last hour is come; the people are the strongest, a fearful carnage must take place."

"Sir," cried Marie Antoinette, "save the King and my children."

Then, ere the tears of anguish were wiped from her streaming eyes, that fatal step was taken which placed the royal family for ever in the power of the merciless Federates.

The erection of the Rue de Rivoli has effaced the slightest trace of the spot where the Couvent des Feuillants and the temporary hall of the Assembly once stood. It was there that Louis and his Queen, his sister, his children, and Madame de Lamballe were conveyed.

Their transit was attended with threats and execrations, and in a narrow passage the royal family were separated for some minutes. Marie-Antoinette trembled for her son; a grenadier, however, carried him and held him high above the crowd. As the child was deposited in the hall of the Assembly cheers rang through the room. They were succeeded by these words: "Take him to the King, near the President, he belongs to the nation; the Austrian is unworthy of the confidence of the people." The child wept and clung to his mother.

Then the Assembly began their discussion; the King and all his family, with Madame de Lamballe, being removed into a box where the reporters for the press sat, as the constitution, it was pretended, could not legally act in the presence of the sovereign. Behind Madame Elizabeth and the Princess de Lamballe several of the Knights of the Poignard stood, resolved to die if they could not defend the young and beautiful objects of their pity. Meantime a general massacre was filling the courts of the Tuileries with blood. As the King heard the first cannonade, he said, "I have given orders not to fire." He was powerless. Murder reigned around the riding-school, where the Assembly sat; the shrieks of victims, the sound of blows drowned the voices within; the hall and galleries were crowded with people coming and going; the heat was excessive, and the *loge*, where the royal family sat, had become a furnace. Men covered with blood brought in spoils from the Tuileries, and rouleaux of gold, portfolios, and diamonds were laid on the table; the savages greeted them as trophies. The Dauphin silently looked into his mother's face for comfort, found it not, and wept. Marie-Antoinette sat in proud dignity; her royal husband was calm; the Princess Elizabeth bent her head in pious submission; the little

Princess Marie-Thérèse was bathed in tears. Madame de Lamballe was pale and beautiful in her distress. At length an assassin, one of the artillery of the National Guard, entered; he bared his blood-stained arm; "I offer," he said, "to take the King's life if necessary." It was the signal for a doom never reversed. The act for the provisional suspension of royalty was hurriedly drawn up and read.

The massacre outside went on, and fires were lighted to consume the dead bodies. The King and his family meantime were lodged for the time in the old convent of the Feuillants. The Dauphin then remembered his favourite dog, and fretted lest it should have been killed. "Dear child," cried the saintly Elizabeth, "there are sorrows more cruel than the loss of your dog. Pray to God to preserve you from them."

After three days and nights passed at the Feuillants the unhappy prisoners were conveyed to the Temple. Their journey thither lasted two hours, during which they were subjected to every species of insult. It was seven o'clock in the evening before the royal family arrived at that monument of misery and popular tyranny.

Of this ancient edifice, Monsieur de Beauchesne, the able biographer of Louis XVII., thus writes, in eloquent and touching terms:—

"The ancient edifice of which we are about to speak disappeared at the commencement of the present century. Built in an age of faith, it was demolished in an age of impiety. It held an important place among the historical monuments of Paris. With its name, for the past six centuries, were associated, from age to age, recollections which already deserved perpetuation, when the French Revolution came to give it a solemn consecration, by making it the witness of a great and prolonged martyrdom. One might, before that time, have set oneself down at the cradle of the Temple, and interrogate its infancy as to the destinies of its founders, the Knights, and the Temple would have recounted their bravery, their power, their wealth, the persecutions they went through, their frightful death, and the end of that illustrious order which had filled Christendom with its services and the world with its renown."

But these reflections, as the admirable author just quoted observes, have given place to a still grander recollection; its walls have been indeed "disgraced by the darkest drama that has ever disgraced human annals; the burning of the grand master is henceforth, in history, masked by the scaffold of the King." These meditations have yielded to those of a darker and still more impressive character; the darkest deeds that have ever sullied modern times supersede all previous associations in the memory of man.

It is conjectured to have been about the year 1128 that the Templars, the first of all the military and religious orders (founded at Jerusalem in 1118), came to Paris. They settled themselves in the midst of marshes near Paris, and, by their industry, transformed these pestilential environs of the city into fertile gardens and meadows. A vast tract of land, planted with horn-beams, was thus cultivated to the northeast of Paris; it was called the *Culture du Temple*. Enclosed by walls which were fortified at intervals with turrets, this tract extended as far as the Montagne de Bellevilles, where some pleasure-houses, called *Courtilles*, were erected by the Templars; that name still marks the place where the French resort on holidays, for recreation.

In the centre of the *Culture du Temple* there stood, until the commencement of the present century, the chief residence of the Order. It was a solid massive square tower, with walls nine feet thick, and it was flanked at each of its four angles by a tower of smaller dimensions, surmounted each by a low turret. A broad ditch encircled all this edifice, and separated it from the garden. Such was the building which Hubert, a powerful Knight Templar, the treasurer of his Order, erected; the large tower was the treasury of the Knights; three of the four smaller towers were their prisons, in case of infringement of discipline—the fourth contained the staircase. There was also, of course, a church, which was built on the model of the Church of St. John in Jerusalem. In this church the proud, high-born, chivalric Templars were received and installed as knights with imposing rites and ceremónials.

In the year 1792 the old precincts of the Temple had been greatly encroached upon, and the streets of Paris encompassed it on all sides; the Temple, however, still formed a small town by itself, and its gates were closed every evening. Hence it was called *La Ville Neuve du Temple*. Here were narrow streets crowded with *ouvriers*, and debtors, and old clothesmen, " an immense bazaar, serving as a boudoir for the toilette of poverty." *

In one of the angles of the enclosure of the Temple stood the hotel which was called *Le Palais du Grand Prieur*, though nothing but a low small house; above this building rose a lofty tower, of a square form, flanked with turrets. It was here that the commune of Paris resolved to incarcerate the royal family; and, for the first time, regrets were expressed that the people had destroyed the Bastille.

The Temple was, however, gloomy and miserable enough. The rooms wherein the royal family were confined were approached by a winding staircase. Madame de Lamballe occupied a dark ante-chamber, to the left of which was an apartment appropriated to the Queen and her daughter, overlooking a garden; and here the royal family generally passed the whole day.

They had arrived at the Temple destitute of the commonest necessaries for comfort or cleanliness, and any external communication would have exposed them to suspicion.

Late in the evening of the 17th of August two municipal officers presented themselves at the Temple, commissioned " to bring away all persons who were not of the *Capet* family."

* De Beauchesne.

The edict was aimed at the Duchesse de Lambelle. The blow was overwhelming. In vain did the poor Queen entreat that her beloved friend might remain with her; in vain did she urge the plea that the princess was her relation, — a Bourbon. Alas! they knew it too well. "A special fate awaited," Monsieur de Beauchesne tells us, "this unfortunate princess. In the gaoler's book the words 'de Savoie and de Bourbon-Lamballe' were written in emphatically large characters. An exceptional destiny was reserved for her." A heart-rending farewell took place. As the Queen and her friend were exchanging their last adieus, the children, awakened by their sobs, wept, and caressed those who were about to quit them for ever. Madame de Tourzet, the governess of the Dauphin, was also ordered to leave the Temple for a still gloomier prison. The municipals could only separate the weeping prisoners by assuring the Princess and Madame de Tourzet that after their examination they would be permitted to return. Monsieur Hue, and other faithful servants of the King, and several other ladies, amongst whom was the daughter of Madame de Tourzet, were then led out by torchlight through the garden to the Temple gate, whence they were taken in hackney-coaches, first to the bar of the commune, and afterwards to the Hôtel de la Force.

It was not until the 20th of August, that any news of their friends reached the King and Queen. Hue returned that day, and told them that the Princess de Lamballe and those with her of the royal household would return to the Temple no more. Manuel, one of the Municipals, observed with some astonishment, the Queen and Madame Elizabeth beginning to prepare linen for their beloved friends in La Force. As they made up bundles of linen, he perceived that what the King had said was true: "The race that has governed others is able to assist and provide for its own wants."

They were again left to such repose as breaking hearts can feel; and the character of these august personages rose under the pressure of suspense and terror.

Deprived of power, they became, in that dreary prison, private individuals, and they graced their now low and adverse fortunes. The following brief account of the rising occupations of the royal captives is interesting. Between six and seven o'clock, Louis dressed himself, and passing into the turret next his chamber, there prayed for strength for himself and safety for others. The Queen rose even earlier, and heard her son say his prayers. At ten o'clock Louis gave the Dauphin lessons in Latin, French, Geography, Writing, and History, whilst the Queen instructed her daughter. At one, they all went into the garden, attended by the jailer, Santerre. They dined at two. The afternoons were passed in work, or reading; but silence was rarely broken; sometimes the sound of a child's laugh dispelled the gloom; sometimes they played with the poor doomed Prince at ball, or battledore and shuttlecock, in Madame Elizabeth's room. Towards evening, the Queen and her sister-in-law read aloud history or fiction; often pausing to compare what they read with their own fate. Miss Burney's "Cecilia," a book full of beautiful and noble sentiments, touched them deeply.

At eight, the mournful parents of the child, whose destiny could not have presented anything but sorrow to their view, sought to amuse the captive bird, gay in his cage as French children can be everywhere. They even proposed charades taken from the *Mercure de France*.

As he prayed one evening, the little Prince called to mind the Princess de Lamballe, and his innocent petition was proffered for her. It was affecting to hear him lower his voice when the municipal guard, always in attendance, drew near him.

Meantime the 3rd of September arrived. Madame de Tourzet, her daughter, and the other women of the Queen's household had been released. One captive alone remained in the Hôtel de la Force, the blameless, heroic Princesse de Lamballe.

It has been stated that she was interrogated before *Grands Juges du Peuple*, as the sanguinary tribunal of La Force was entitled. Other accounts say that on the 3rd of September, she was conducted to the gate of the prison, and there the ferocious villains who slaughtered the finest and fairest of her sex awaited their prey. On being questioned about the Queen, the Princess is reported to have said: "I have nothing to say to you; to die a little sooner or later has become indifferent to me; I am prepared." She was then, according to one account, dragged over dead bodies through the courts, and there killed. Other reports stated that, being brought before the bar of the commune, she fainted; she could not utter a word. Then a man in a tricoloured scarf, cried: "Let *Madame* go!" Under these words was couched the sentence of death.

It is further alleged that she was then hurried to the Rue des Ballets, which in those days separated La Force from St. Antoine; dragged up a blind alley called the Cul-de-sac des Prêtres, and there struck by a sabre on the back of her neck.

At all events, peace came at last! she died as a heroine, scorning life, if it were to be purchased by betraying her friend. She died like a Christian, amid a host of demons. Fain would we be silent on what followed. Whilst her spirit went to Him who gave it, her corpse, pierced with pikes and sabres, was the sport of the accursed infuriate crowd; women and children in rags howled and blasphemed.—Let their cries resound; they cannot harm her more. Let her murderers cut out that heart which so lately throbbed with piteous fear from that poor frame; let them separate that head from the loveliest of forms. She knows it not. Not to her! not to her! O God of this world, is the torture, or the wail, or the life-long woe. She is with Thee!

Amid the populace in their tricoloured rags, one female figure stands transfixed; one grateful heart is well nigh broken by the shrieks and curses. It is Madame de Lebel, the wife of a celebrated painter. The Princesse de Lamballe had been kind to her, and she was going to inquire after the fate of one once raised so high above her, now fallen so low in misery.

"What," she asks, "is happening?"

She is answered: "The head of Lamballe is being paraded through Paris."

Astounded, alarmed, Madame de Lebel rushed into the Place de la Bastille and took refuge in the house of a hair dresser whom she knew. She was scarcely there when the procession stopped and one of the mob ordered the *coiffeur* to dress the hair of Madame de Lamballe. Madame Lebel was between the shop and the partition behind; she fainted, and the hairdresser, thrusting her into his back room, concealed her from view. He then took into his hands the head, streaming with blood, and quickly, and with an address which none but a Frenchman could show, disentangled the fair, admired tresses, matted with blood, washed the delicate ringlets, then powdered them *à la mode*. "Antoinette will know it now," said one of the pike-bearers; and placing it again on the pike's point, he resumed his progress.

The prisoners in the Temple had not been allowed to walk that day in the garden. Before dinner time, a sound of drum beating, and a booming noise in the distance, showed that revolutionary fury was kindled. A crowd, a blood-stained crowd, with reeking hands and torn garments, composed of drunken women, who sang,— wretched children, hootings of ragged men shouting curses, arrived before the Temple. Amid their shrieks, the words "La Lamballe! La Lamballe!" were heard distinctly above all other cries. Like a mighty torrent, the procession rushed, as it were, onwards, until it stopped before the Temple. Then arose to the insulted Heavens a "deafening clamour, that acted as a summons to all the furies of the district."

The dense crowd opened, and a headless body, dragged by ropes, fiends disputing which should have the honour of that horrible charge, was visible.

It was now evident that the populace meditated forcing an entrance into the Temple itself, in order to show the bleeding body, covered only by a linen chemise, to the Queen. This demoniacal intention was, however, frustrated by a barrier of tricoloured ribands, which the Municipals on duty had erected to impose respect on the mass; but at the very threshold of the great door, stood two men — watchmen — called searchers; wretches selected for the inquisitorial office from the dregs of the people. One of them, a strong man, with a sabre placed in a tricoloured belt, and a scarlet cap on his head, was on the point of admitting the crowd, when the Municipals interfered. Amongst the populace stood a wretch with the bleeding heart of the Princess in his hand. Amongst them was the headless body, which had been bathed in the fountain of the Temple,—white as marble.

Let us pass over the horrors that ensued. No English reader could tolerate such details as a too faithful historian has transmitted to his countrymen. To them the narrative of Monsieur de Beauchesne furnishes a lesson which, thanks be to heaven and to the stable faith of Britain, we need not.

Amid the cries that were heard that day these words were distinct:—"We want a *pendant* for la Lamballe! Give us the Austrian!" The Austrian! the Austrian! resounded from the lowest and most wretched of both sexes.

Meantime the royal family had risen from their dinner and entered the Queen's room. Clery, the valet-de-chambre of the king, had gone down to the room of Tison, the guard. Suddenly the head of Madame de Lamballe was seen at the window; Tison's wife uttered a scream; it was responded to with hideous laughter from the crowd without; then a report was got up declaring that the King and Queen were not in the tower; a demand was made that they should appear at the window; the poor little Dauphin burst into tears; one of the municipal guards mercifully endeavoured to keep the poor captives from appearing, but the cries outside increased; four men sent by the crowd entered to inquire whether the Capet family were or were not there; and one of them insisted on them showing themselves at the window. The cries redoubled; the Queen's name was heard; the most humane of the guards, placing himself before the King, said, "Do not look, do not go; it is too horrible." "They want," said the head of the deputation from the crowd, "to hide from you the head of La Lamballe, which we are bringing to show you how the people treat tyrants; I advise you to appear, if you do not wish the people to come up."

The Queen fainted. Then her family, weeping, collected around her, but consolation was impossible. The tender friendship of their happiest years, a friendship as sincere if it had existed between equals, had risen into heroism; it was thus rudely wrenched, dissolved in anguish; its last throb announced with curses; the anguish aggravated by peril. The popular statement, that the Queen saw and recognised the fair hair, is not borne out by the careful researches of Monsieur de Beauchesne, the latest historian of that fearful period. Yet, had she seen it, Marie-Antoinette might, it is said, have known the sweet face that had once adorned the gay galleries of Versailles, and enhanced the intimacy of the Trianon; that lovely countenance though pale, like sculptured marble, was not disfigured;—the fair tresses that hung on the bloody pike, were still glossy, and flowing.

Not least agonising is it to know that the Duc de Penthièvre, the father-in-law of the murdered princess, was alive. By his care, the body and the head were recovered, but they had been the sport and derision of the *Sans Culottes* for hours before rescued from the mob.

After the death of her best beloved friend, the deepest gloom overspread the Queen and the captives of the Temple. On the 29th of September, Louis XVI. was separated from his family; he was confined in the great tower of the Temple. "Your master," said one of the Municipals to the faithful Clery, "will not see his children again."

When the unfortunate King next saw his family, it was to bid them farewell on the morning of his execution.

On the 3rd of July 1793, an order arrived in the Temple that the son of Capet be separated from his mother and family. When the Queen heard these words, the forbearance, the heroism, that had raised her character to sublimity, forsook her. "Take my child from me!" she cried, pale as death, "it is not possible. Gentlemen," she added, addressing the officers, "the commune cannot think of separating me from my son, he is so young, he so wants a mother's care; for Heaven's sake let not this terrible trial fall upon me."

The anguish, the thrilling tones, the deep abasement of one once so elevated, touched not the hearts of those who heard her. They began to use force. "Mamma," the poor child shrieked, "mamma! do not leave me." Then she clung to him, catching hold of the bed-post, caressing, soothing the poor doomed boy. "Let us not fight with women," said the wretches. "Citizens, call in the guard."

Then the gentle Madame Elizabeth interposed; the child was soothed; the mother was tranquillised. She dressed him with her own now wasted hands, and then, seating herself in a chair, gathered up all the strength still left in her breaking heart, and tearless, without heaving a sigh, said to him: "My child, we are about to part; remember your duty when I shall not be near you; never forget God who tries your faith, nor the mother who loves you." The words were uttered with the mournful and solemn tone of one who felt that with the presence of that child hope, comfort, desire of life, would depart. "Be good, patient, sincere, and your father will bless you in heaven." She kissed him on the forehead, and gave him to his jailers. Then the bitterness of death had passed. For a time she resumed the dignity of the daughter of Maria Theresa. When the door closed, and she was left alone with her sister-in-law and her daughter, the Queen threw herself on the vacant bed of her son and gave vent to her anguish.

One scene more, for this is no chronicle of those horrors which have been so often told, but a mere portraiture of character,— of friend and friend,— and then let us close a theme so full of torture, even though years and years have passed away since those dreadful days electrified Europe.

On the 1st of August (1793) it was decreed that Marie-Antoinette was to be committed to the Concièrgerie. As she passed out she struck her hand against the gate of her prison. When asked whether she was hurt: "Oh! no!" was her answer, "nothing can hurt me now."

She passed the door of her son's former room; she turned upon it her last look. Let us now follow her, in retrospective sadness. As she issues from the Temple to the grim Concièrgerie, we behold her as she passes. She is leaving the gentlest and most sensitive of children in the hands of the fiend Simon; but she gathers up her courage, and goes on. She enters that prison still standing by the river's side, still containing the room in which hours that had begun to madden her, were spent. We see her there alone, unemployed. One boon she asked, her knitting, that she might finish a pair of socks she had begun for her son,— it was refused.

After two months of confinement in a damp dungeon, the heroic captive is brought to trial. We behold her in majestic silence, listening to a libel called by the revolutionary prosecutors, her accusation. Then comes in Hébert, who had collected materials in the Temple— wrung from a beaten, intimidated boy, her son— to form the chief pretext of her doom. She is still silent; then Hébert declares he has a document to prove his charges — the confession of the young Louis XVII. She turns on him a look that flushed even his cheek with shame or remorse. No matter. Her answer is demanded: "If I answer not," she said, "it is because nature refuses to answer such an accusation! I appeal to all mothers present here!"

What can be finer than her last words when asked if she had anything to say in defence. "Nothing in my defence," were her words, "but much, for your remorse, to feel. I was a queen, and you have dethroned me; I was a wife, and you have murdered my husband; a mother, and you have torn my children from me. I have nothing left but my blood; hasten to shed it, that you may satisfy your thirst with it."

They hoped either to weaken her courage by repeated examinations, or, perhaps, — one would fain think so, — to find some plea for her acquittal. The staircase whence she issued for the last time from before the "Committee for Public Safety" is still shown to the calm visitor to Paris, by his commissionaire, after he has inspected that part of old Paris. We can picture her — a dreamy, wild look on that superb brow — her light hair tinged slightly with grey, her step, nevertheless firm, and something there is not of this world in those glistening, blue, clear eyes, that see above her the pure heavens, as she breathes for an instant the fresh air; then she enters the vehicle which bears her back to the Concièrgerie; she is admitted into her cell, cold, perhaps, — trembling. She throws herself on her pallet, then wraps herself in a blanket, and sleeps.

The handwriting in which she wrote her last letter to Madame Elizabeth, is firm and clear.

"I have been condemned," such were her words, "not to a shameful death — death is only shameful to criminals — but to rejoin your brother, like him, innocent. I hope to manifest the same firmness that he did in these last moments."

"I have to speak to you," she resumes in another part, "on

a subject most painful to my feelings. I know the child must have occasioned you much distress; but forgive him, sister; think of his age, and how easy it is to make a child say whatever one wishes, even what he does not himself understand."

Poor, poor Marie-Antoinette! She trembled for her child; she dreaded lest he might have given pain to his aunt; she had the terrible and singular dread — terrible for a mother to feel, lest the words of her affrighted child might be adduced in calumny against herself. In the conclusion of her letter, she bade adieu, a last adieu, to her brothers, her sisters, her beloved sister-in-law, the ill-fated Elizabeth; their sorrow caused her infinite grief: these were her last written words except those addressed to her son. "Farewell, farewell! My remaining moments I shall occupy solely with my religious duties. As I am not free in my actions, they may, perhaps, bring me a priest; but I here protest that I will not say one word to him, and that I will treat him wholly and entirely as a stranger." She kept her word.

Her son she enjoined not to avenge the enemies of his parents. "She forgave," thus she wrote, "all the injuries her enemies had done her." On the 16th of October the roll call was sounded throughout the whole of Paris. All the armed force was mustered. At eleven, Marie-Antoinette was found by the officials talking to a priest of "constitutional" principles. He had begun to say: "Your death is about to expiate —" "Yes, Sir, — to expiate my faults, but not a single crime." The priest then exhorted her to take courage.

"Ah, Sir!" was the heroic reply, "I have served my apprenticeship to it for several years. At the moment that I am going to the scaffold it will not fail."

She was placed in a very dirty cart, with a plank for a seat, with no hay or straw in it; a white horse to draw it; a man with a stern repulsive face was the driver. Everyone turned to the gate of the prison, awaiting her appearance. At last,

Grammont, an actor, who commanded the national guard, gave the signal, and forth came the Queen, pale, but stately, with a slight flush on her temples; her eyes bloodshot, her eyelids stiff and motionless as if already those orbs had been sealed in death. She had on a kind of night jacket over a white skirt, and beneath the latter a black petticoat; black ribbon round her wrists, a neck kerchief of white muslin. Her hair was white—cut close: it had changed colour in a night; on her head was placed a small cap with a black ribbon; her elbows were bound with a thick rope, the ends of which were held by the executioner Sanson. As she entered the cart, Sanson offered his hand to help her up the steps. The Queen made a sign in the negative, and turned her head gently away. The constitutional priest—I borrow the term of the day—accompanied her to the scaffold.

It is only to rend the heart to repeat the insults offered to her progress. She spoke once to the priest to ask him to read to her a bill stuck up in the Rue des Jacobins. "Manufactures of Republican weapons for dethroning Tyrants." To the last, friends concealed in the crowd were in hopes of assisting any attempt that might be made at a rescue; when they saw that all was hopeless, they retired with averted faces that they might not see the death of the heroic, unhappy Queen.

As the fatal cart moved along, Marie-Antoinette gazed calmly on the crowd around her; nothing could take away from her the stately bearing which was natural to this ill-fated being: the committee, seeking in every form to debase her, had tried her as a citizen, and sent her in a vile cart to the place of execution, and, whilst Louis XVI. had been conducted to the guillotine in a carriage, she was unprotected from the public gaze, and exposed to every insult. She had twice to encounter the utmost insolence from Grammont, the comedian. "There she is," he cried, in the course of the fatal drive—"that infamous Antoinette!

she is done for!" And again at Saint Roch, the procession stopped in order that the multitude collected on the steps of the church might utter their profane insults. There a crowd of abandoned women in red caps, whose office it was to pursue the victims of that period to their doom, called out that they wished to drink the Queen's blood, and addressed her with the name of Messalina. They were paid by the commune for their exertions.

As Marie-Antoinette heard them and gazed on them, an expression of mournful compassion passed over her ever noble features. "Alas!" she said, "my sorrows will soon be over, but yours are only begun." Every house as she passed was closed; but in the Rue Saint Honoré a little child held up by his mother, kissed his hand and bowed his little head to the insulted Queen. On seeing this tears started into the eyes of Marie-Antoinette.

But her passage from anguish to rest was now nearly accomplished. When she reached the spot where her husband had suffered before her, her fortitude was shown in a firm step, her piety in short, but fervent, prayer. She turned a fixed and mournful gaze on the Tuileries; then her eyes were raised to heaven. "Make haste!" she said to the executioner, and bent her head. The blow was given, and the hapless sufferer was at rest.

Many persons, it appears, did not expect that this act of iniquity would have been perpetrated. Even the wife of Simon, the barbarous guardian-jailer of the miserable son whom Marie-Antoinette left in the Temple, ignorant that the *rappel* had sounded and the victim gone forth, said to her husband that day: "*La Veto,*" thus they styled the Queen, "will not go to the guillotine!" "And why not?" was the reply. "Because she is still beautiful, and she can talk, and will soften her judges."

"Justice is incorruptible," Simon rejoined; and it was not until night that they knew the truth.

On the 10th of June, 1795, two civic commissioners of the Temple section ascended to the second story of the Temple tower, wherein lay an emaciated form, on a wooden bed without a mattress. It was that of the only surviving son of Marie-Antoinette, proclaimed, even during the Reign of Terror, Louis XVII. Yet, as his accomplished historian says, he had borne "the title of King only beneath the thatched roof of La Vendeé, and within the tents of our exiled nobility." His nominal reign had lasted two years; his life ten years, two months, and twelve days. Yet in that space what agony, what desecration, what solitude, affright, starvation, disease, had blighted his childhood. Serene, with unclosed eyes, that had looked, whilst the soul neared eternity, on some far off invisible object, that child had seemed almost to taste of a new existence even before his departure to the world of spirits.

"Do you not hear music?" he had said to his compassionate attendant, Gouin; "listen! listen! Amongst the voices I distinguish that of my mother." Then his large eyes glistened with delight. "I have something to tell you," he said to another of his attendants; but no accents were heard from his lips. The keeper took his hand, the child's head rested on the man's shoulder, no struggle marked the release: — without a sigh the son of Marie-Antoinette and of Louis passed away —"Little Capet" was dead. It was an event scarcely worth the mentioning. The commissioners performed the last duty — the emaciated corpse was put into a coffin made of deal—and buried it in the cemetery of St. Marguerite, near the Rue Saint Bernard. As the keepers were leaving the room, one of them said to the other, who was walking behind: "You have no need to shut the iron door now."

No — the last captive of the Temple was free; the bird was uncaged: the soul was with its Creator, Sanctifier, Redeemer.

The very scene of misery so unparalleled is changed. At one time, indeed, so versatile are the French, the Temple became a sort of sanctuary to which the public repaired — some from reverence, more from curiosity. In the house, inhabited by the Princess Royal, Marie-Thérèse, were found these words in pencil, written on the table —

"Oh! mon père, veillez sur moi du haut du ciel!"

And a little below,

"Oh, mon Dieu! pardonnez à ceux qui ont fait mourir mes parents!"

After a time it was resolved to sell the Temple. Napoleon, however, prevented its becoming private property: yet he determined to leave no memento of the sufferings of fallen monarchy. The tower was therefore doomed; first dismantled, then the materials were advertised for sale; in October 1808 the auction took place, the men who assisted in the demolition being the only persons allowed to enter that which the Legitimists regarded almost as sacred to the memory and sufferings of Louis XVI., and Marie-Antoinette.

But the remembrance of the beautiful and devoted friends remains. That inequality of station precludes perfect friendship, the sad history of Marie-Antoinette and of Madame de Lamballe refutes. "There may be love," says Bishop Hall, "where there is the most inequality; but friendship supposes pairs." Yet a holier, a more disinterested, a more heroic devotion than that which has been here described cannot be imagined, nor has ever been known to exist.

JOSEPH ADDISON AND RICHARD STEELE.

ACCOUNT OF ADDISON'S FAMILY. — HIS FATHER, LANCELOT ADDISON. — EARLY FRIENDSHIP BETWEEN STEELE AND ADDISON. — DIFFERENCE IN THEIR CHARACTERS. — STEELE'S "CHRISTIAN HERO." — HIS COURTSHIP OF MRS. SCURLOCK. — THEIR MARRIED LIFE. — QUARRELS WITH ADDISON. — STEELE IS MADE A MEMBER OF PARLIAMENT. — EXPELLED THE HOUSE. — HIS DEBTS. — ADDISON'S CAREER. — FELLOW OF MAGDALEN. — GOES TO BLOIS. — PATRONISED BY GODOLPHIN. — RECEIVES ROGER BOYLE IN HIS GARRET. — THE "SPECTATOR." — PLAY OF "CATO." — STEELE PACKS AN AUDIENCE. — ADDISON PROSPERS. — MARRIES LADY WARWICK. — HIS DEATH-BED. — STEELE'S DEATH. — DAUGHTERS LEFT BEHIND HIM. — THE TWO ELIZABETHS.

JOSEPH ADDISON and RICHARD STEELE.

The father of one of our most valued writers was a poor youth on the foundation of Queen's College, Oxford. There Lancelot Addison, to whose son Joseph we owe the never failing delights of the "Spectator," laid the basis of future eminence for himself and his family.

Numerous, indeed, are the instances of good effected by those ancient institutions, whose great founders are reverently remembered each Sunday in the "bidding prayer" at St. Mary's, Oxford, a prayer in which gratitude assumes the form of adulation as it turns from dead benefactors to living chancellors, and vice-chancellors.

Lancelot Addison, the son of an English clergyman, was a sprightly youth, whose loyalty to Charles I. appeared prominently at an inconvenient moment both for himself and others. In 1658 he was chosen, owing to his wit, to be one of the Terræ Filii in the act then celebrated. Now a Terræ Filius at the Oxford commemoration was a sort of privileged jester, after the manner of Shakespeare's fools, an office neither very complimentary nor safe, as it proved, and long since abolished; the gibes and jests of tempestuous undergraduates in the theatre being the only remnant of the old jollity that was let loose at the last day of discipline, the first of safe impertinence.

Lancelot—honoured be his memory!—hated the Protector, and lamented the dead King Charles I., who, of all monarchs was suited to the spirit and opinions of Oxonians. So when the youth — for, though he had taken his Master's degree, Lancelot was only twenty-five — satirised the worldliness, hypocrisy, avarice, and ignorance of the Roundheads, he was sternly reproved, and, in imitation of obsolete discipline, made to ask pardon on his knees. He did as he was ordered, but left the University in disgust, and so ended his hopes of a college tutorship or benefice.

Lancelot was rewarded, after the Restoration, by the chaplaincy of Dunkirk, where an English garrison was then placed. But when that port was ceded by Charles II. to the French, he went to Tangiers, and remained there eight years; but coming home, was superseded in his chaplaincy, but presented to the living of Milston, near Ambrosebury in Wiltshire, and thereupon he married his wife, and the mother of Joseph, being Mistress Jane Gulstone, the daughter of a doctor in divinity, and the sister of the then Bishop of Bristol.

Lancelot was now comparatively rich upon 120*l*. a year. He was also appointed one of the chaplains to Charles II., and at Milston his life of innocence and homely neighbourship in the good old pastoral way was not only happy, but useful. An octavo, called "West Barbary," brought him into notice as a writer; he was made a prebend of Salisbury, and became a doctor of divinity in that very theatre in Oxford where he had played the fool, and asked pardon on his knees. It was at Milston that Joseph Addison, his eldest son, was born, on the 1st of May, 1672; and here the good Lancelot maintained, upon his living, four children, who were born to him during the lifetime of his first wife; and fulfilled, as well, those duties of hospitality and charity of which a rectory house ought to be the centre. Here he lived in friendship with the most eminent persons of the county, and here, it is not improbable, his gifted son may have found materials for those delightful pictures of country life which he has given us in the papers on Sir Roger de Coverley. One interruption to this peaceful and useful career had almost ruined the good man; there was a fire at Milston. However even this turned to good account, for the Ecclesiastical Commissioners made it a plea for compensation, and this faithful son of the Established Church was made dean of Lichfield in 1683. Meantime he wrote various works, which, one is almost ashamed to say, are scarcely known to divines who are familiar with the lightest papers in the "Spectator." Yet they must have been interesting, from the zeal and learning of the writer. How inviting are the titles, to wit: "The Primitive Institution, or a Seasonable Discourse of Catechising;" then again, "A Modest Plea for the Clergy," much wanted in those days; then, among eleven works, all theological, "An Historical Account of the Heresy denying the Godhead of Christ," and "An Account of the Millennium."

Lancelot Addison was on the high road to a mitre when the Revolution broke out. He was too sincere to like its church principles, and remained, therefore, dean of Lichfield and rector of Milston till, in 1703, he died at the good old age of seventy.

Joseph, meantime, seemed to be treading closely in his father's steps, and to the conversation and writings of the dean we may ascribe many of those admirable "Saturday" papers which form a manual of religious instruction.

The life that became so valuable flickered in its commencement. Hurriedly was the name of Joseph given to the infant Spectator. He was christened on the day he was born, not being expected to survive that birthday. Sent to school, first to Ambrosebury, then to Salisbury, and lastly to the Charter House, Joseph Addison was ready at fifteen years of age to be entered at Queen's College, Oxford, where he signalised himself for writing good Latin almost before most boys wrote good English. But he was not destined to end his academical days at Queen's. His Latin verses were appreciated by Dr. Lancaster, the provost, who exerted himself to get the promising scholar made a demy of Magdalen College; and, accordingly, in 1689 he was elected at what was called the Golden Election, there having been none the previous year, owing to the quarrel between the College and James II. Sacheverel the red-hot churchman, was elected at the same time as Addison.

It is pleasant to think of the author of the "Spectator" walking through the delicious vistas of Magdalen gardens; the Cherwell sparkling beneath the trees, whilst now and then a glimpse of the grand old building, grey and majestic, is detected; or the bells of Magdalen tower, full, loud, imperious in their tones, call the loiterers to prayers in the richly sculptured chapel. There exists not even in Oxford, the prince of academic cities, a college with which one would so gladly associate the name of Addison as the stately fabric where Bonner preached. Still is the walk by the river side pointed out as having been the favourite haunt of Addison, and some of the trees are stated to have been planted by his hand. Here he listened at spring time to the notes of birds, in the varieties of which he delighted; here he strolled to dissipate the nervous tendencies which even then marked the young undergraduate's manner; here he read, and in yonder ancient chambers made himself master of the art of criticism and studied moral philosophy and theology. He had at this time an intention of going into holy orders. Addressing a poem to Sacheverel, he says:—

> "I've done at length; and now, dear friend, receive
> The last poor present that my Muse can give;
> I leave the art of poetry and verse
> To those that practise them with more success;
> Of greater truths I'll now prepare to tell,
> And so, at once, dear friend and Muse, farewell."

Tickell, Addison's friend, referring to these lines, says, that Addison's "remarkable seriousness and modesty" proved the chief reasons for his not going into orders. The duties of the priesthood appeared too responsible for the sensitive, conscientious Joseph Addison; he resigned them from a distrust of himself. Whilst at Oxford he studied chiefly after dinner (which was probably at that time at noon). His Latin poetry was greatly admired, both at Oxford and Cambridge. He was, however, twenty-two years of age before he published anything in his own language.

Meantime, before he went to Oxford, Addison had formed an early friendship with Richard Steele, an Irish youth of good family; strange to say, the date of Steele's birth is not known. His father, a barrister, was private secretary to the Duke of Ormond. The affection thus formed was life long, and yet never were two characters more different. The one cautious, gentle, retiring; the other impulsive, excitable, even reckless, and often blamable. Steele, in after life, described these contrarieties between himself and Addison in the following beautiful words:—" There never was a more strict friendship than between these gentlemen; nor had they any difference but what proceeded from their different way of pursuing the same thing. The one with patience, foresight, and temperate address, always waited and stemmed the torrent; while the other often plunged himself into it, and was as often taken out by the temper of him who stood weeping on the bank for his safety, whom he could not dissuade from leaping into it. These two men lived for some years last past, shunning each other, but still preserving the most passionate concern for their mutual welfare. But when they met they were as unreserved as boys, and talked of the greatest affairs; upon which they saw where they differed, without pressing (what they knew impossible) to convert each other."

What a candid, what a complete, what a sensible view of friendship, and that friendship between two men of the world of strongly marked opinions, both in politics and, in what were then closely connected with politics, on Church matters!

Whilst Addison was writing Latin poems, Steele was leading a gay, disreputable life in the guards; nevertheless, Dean Addison looked favourably on the friendship between his son Joseph and Steele; and it appears from a letter of Steele's to Congreve that all Addison's family shared the partiality of the eldest son. "Were things of this nature," he wrote to Congreve, "to be exposed to public view, I could show, under the dean's own hand, in the warmest terms, his blessing on the friendship between his son and me; nor had he a child who did not prefer me in the first place of kindness and esteem, as their father loved me like one of them."

Gay, frank, generous, Steele must have been a delightful accession to the limited society of a country rectory, or even of a Lichfield deanery; and Lancelot Addison appears, like most men who know the world well, to have been very indulgent to high spirits and youthful indiscretions; besides Steele, not unlike many men of strong passions and weak judgment, had deep and fervent religious convictions and aspirations.

The family circle at Milston must indeed have been delightful, to say nothing of the dean himself, one of the most benevolent, as well as industrious and learned men of his day. There were, besides Joseph, two sons, Gulstone and Lancelot, and a daughter, Dorothy. Gulstone was only a year younger than Joseph; he became governor of Fort St. George in the East Indies; Lancelot, also eminent in his career, was afterwards a fellow of Magdalen College Oxford, and was highly esteemed in that university. Dorothy was a wit. Swift, speaking of her, says: "Addison's sister, Mrs. Sartre, is a sort of wit, very like him: I am not fond of her." She married first Dr. Sartre, formerly chaplain at Montpelier, and afterwards Prebendary of Westminster; and afterwards Daniel Coombes, Esquire. Anne, another sister, died young.

It may readily be conceived how delightful the various

characteristics of this family party must have been. Addison's chief quality was *humour*, not a bitter personal satire like that of Swift, but a kindly cheerfulness that never pained. Steele's wilder satires must have, been exquisitely appreciated; for he had to deal not with a stiff pedagogue in the old dean, but with a clergyman who had been in a garrison, who had mixed with diplomatists and officers at Tangiers, and who could pardon much that he might wish to alter in "Ensign" Steele. In person, as far as we can judge from portraits, they were greatly contrasted, Addison in his full-bottomed wig, his velvet coat, his long cambric neck-tie edged with delicate lace, with his regular, handsome, placid features, and *blond* complexion, was personable in the extreme. One rarely sees paintings of him except in full dress; the Secretary all over. Steele, in his cap, turned up and bound, it is true, with gold lace, his broad, short, somewhat vulgar face beneath, bare of all moustache or whiskers, as indeed is Addison's, though redeemed by the wig,—does not convey to the mind of him who gazes on those small fierce eyes, and somewhat contemptuous mouth, any notion of the author, who, full of sentiment and feeling, could write the exquisite tale of Constantia and Theodorus, or the charming play of the "Conscious Lovers." But so it was; Addison, correct to a fault, handsome, wellbred, devout, and elegant, was inferior to the short-faced, vulgar-looking Steele in elevation of taste and warmth of feeling, in enthusiasm and animal spirits. Cut out for an under Secretary of state, Joseph never committed himself to an imprudence or impertinence; whereas Steele went wrong all his life. He had that charming *abandon*, which so often characterises his countrymen.

Both these then, young and gifted men, had sterling qualities. Addison was eminently and almost unexceptionably good. Of that fault, a weakness, sometimes excusable,—always pitiable, ofttimes in consequence of a broken heart, at all events of disappointed views, or betrayed affections,—of that propensity to inebriation with which his memory has been charged, there was then no known indication; he was the life, the pride, the solace of his family. Steele, wild as any Irishman in youth, had a fund of conscience in his noble thoughtless head; he was affectionate and faithful both to man and woman; and had the rare merit of being in private, the patriot and Christian philosopher,—in his matured years,—that he avowed himself to be in public. Then they had both many recollections in common to turn to in those days of ease at Milston:—not only the Charter House, but the gardens and meadows of Oxford had witnessed their early attachment. Addison, as we have seen, had entered Queen's College in 1687; Steele, at the age of sixteen, had matriculated at Christ Church, and became, in 1691 a postmaster of Merton College; this was whilst Addison was a *probationary* Fellow of Magdalen. What days must they not have seen together! what proctors and bull-dogs must not Steele have encountered; what chapels escaped; what Dons bearded; yet carried all off by his over-mastering talents, his invariable good nature, and by a fund of sound morality at the bottom of his wayward impetuous impulses.

They both entered into the career of literature, Addison dedicating to Dryden — then in the decline of life — his first poem; and thus securing to himself the rare prestige of being highly praised by "Glorious John." Steele, who at first rode as a private in the guards, wrote a poem on the funeral of Queen Mary, consort of William III., and called his performance "The Procession."[*] It was very characteristic of Steele that, whilst an ensign in the guards, being unable to restrain himself from the excesses of youth, he wrote a poem, chiefly in order to impress on his own erring heart principles of religion and self-control. It was at first

---

[*] See Nichols's preface to Steele's Correspondence, vol. i. p. vii.

an anonymous work, and was called the "Christian Hero." Still the mad young Ensign did not improve; so, in 1701, he printed the work with his own name, hoping that such a standing testimony against himself would make him ashamed of judging and feeling so rightly, and of acting so ill. Alas! even this failed. He had been reckoned a good boon companion; but now his comrades shunned the man who was better than themselves; some showed their notions by passing off sorry jokes, which so moral a soldier was expected to bear patiently; others, when he fell,—and his life was one perpetual fall,—compared Ensign Steele with his own "Christian Hero." So he found himself unpopular, and to repair the mistake, he wrote a play, called "The Funeral, or Grief à la Mode." It was acted in 1702. Nothing makes a man so popular as a successful play, and Steele had the good fortune to attract the favour of grim King William, who put down his name, as amongst those to be provided for, in the last "Table Book" he ever wrote in; it was like Steele's luck that it *was* the last.

Not that King William or Mary did anything for literature or learning. It is only our native monarchy that encourage letters; and except, inasmuch as Mary with her ladies, all in masks, listened, blushing we hope, to Congreve's comedies, —there is no record of much enjoyment, even of the highest dramatic excellence, in that queen's dull life.

Addison was following out his course of life all this while, in writing an Essay on Dryden's Translation of the Georgics of Virgil, and in planning a translation of Herodotus himself; but he was soon called into public life, and besides, like Steele, he fell in love: and the object of his affections is stated to have been the sister of his friend Henry Sacheverel.

This famous partisan divine had been Addison's Chamber Fellow at Magdalen College; and had afterwards become a Fellow and Tutor of that society. Sacheverel was a native of Marlborough, where his father, the rector of St. Peter's

Church in that town, left at his death a numerous family in indigent circumstances. Sacheverel set out in life with the character of a well-bred man: and had the charge, on that account, of most of the young men of rank who entered at Magdalen, where, until our own time, all were gentlemen commoners, or noblemen, except the demys. Nevertheless, he lived to be called by Bishop Burnet, a "bold, insolent man," and by the Duchess of Marlborough, "an ignorant, impudent incendiary: a man who was the scorn even of those who made use of him as a tool." Of course, his being the friend of Addison, the polished, the moderate Addison, is almost an answer to these attacks on the character of Sacheverel.

In 1694, when Addison, intending to enter holy orders, wrote his "Account of the Greatest English Poet," he dedicated that work to Sacheverel, his dearest friend and colleague. Addison was then, it appears, attached to the sister of that beloved companion whose opinions afterwards so widely differed from his own. The cause of the love passages not ending in marriage, does not appear. Sacheverel, to whom some credit is due for a sort of eloquence, which had, at least, boldness to recommend it, professed the extreme of High Church opinions: in 1709 he preached at Derby, and at St. Paul's, in London, that famous sermon in which Lord Godolphin, under the name of Volpone, was supposed to be aimed at; whereupon he was impeached before the House of Commons, his trial lasting nearly a month, and suspended from preaching for three years. Bishop Atterbury is said to have written his defence. An estate at Callew, in Derbyshire, was bequeathed to him afterwards by a relation, and Sacheverel died in good circumstances.

Of Steele's youthful engagement we know much more than of Addison's; for he has left some of the most amusing love letters in the world.

He rushed early in life into matrimony; and was united to a lady of Barbadoes, of whom little is known, except that she died a few months after she became Mrs. Steele; of her maiden name, her character, or the time of her death, not even the accurate Nichols, who edited Steele's correspondence, could find any record. The lively Ensign became, however, possessed of a large estate in Barbadoes, upon the death of his first wife's brother, who was taken by the French during his voyage to England, and died in France.

The funeral of Mrs. Steele happened to be attended by a beautiful and charming woman of about twenty-nine years of age: she was the daughter of Jonathan Scurlock, Esq., of Llandunno, Carmarthenshire; and Steele testified the great respect he bore her, in his dedication to the "Ladies' Library." By his first marriage, Steele had no children: two sons and two daughters were the offspring of the second.

His letters are addressed to Mrs. Mary Scurlock, all ladies after the age of ten being styled Mistress, the term 'Miss' being after that age, somewhat disrespectful and derogatory, as indicating that a person so designated must be giddy or light in conduct. In the Muses' Mercury for January 1706-7, Steele wrote the following song:—

> "Me, Cupid made a willing slave,
>   A merry wretched man;
> I slight the nymphs I cannot have,
>   Nor doat on those I can;
> This constant maxim still I hold,
>   To bafle all despair,
> The absent ugly are and old,
>   The present young and fair."

These lines were symptomatic. In August the same year, the following formal letter of proposal to Mrs. Mary Scurlock, is extant.

"MADAM,

"Your wit and beauty are suggestions which may easily lead you into the intention of my writing to you. You may be sure that I cannot be cold to so many good qualities, as all that see you must observe in you. You are a woman of a very good understanding, and will not measure my thoughts by any ardour in my expressions, which is the ordinary language on these occasions.

"I have reasons for hiding from my nearest relations any purpose I may have of waiting on you, if you permit it; and I hope you have confidence from mine as well as your own character, that such a condescension should not be ill used by Madam, Your most obedient servant,

"RICH. STEELE." *

In number thirty-five of the "Tatler" (Aug. 11, 1707), Steele made use of his love effusions in his works, for an epistle is introduced by these words:

August 11th, 1707.

"MADAM,

"I sent to you on Saturday by *Mrs. Warren*, and gave you this trouble to urge the same request I made then, which was, that I may be admitted to wait upon you." Then he proceeds to say, that he shall not trouble her with his sentiments till he knows how they will be received; that he knows no reason why difference of sex should make "their language to each other differ from the ordinary rules of reason."† "I shall affect plainness and sincerity in my discourse to you, as much as other lovers do perplexity and rapture. Instead of saying, 'I shall die for you!' I prefer 'I should be glad to lead my life with you.'" *Mrs. Warren* is changed in the "Tatler" to *Mrs. Lucy*, as well as in the manuscript of the following address again, to Mrs. Mary Scurlock.

"You are as beautiful as witty," he proceeds, "as prudent and as good-humoured as any woman breathing, but I will

---

* Steele's Correspondence, vol. i. p. 92.   † Ibid. p. 93.

confess to you, I regard all these excellencies as you will please to direct them for my happiness or misery; believe me, Madam, the only lasting motive to love, is the hope of its becoming mutual. I beg of you to let *Mrs. Warren* send me word when I may attend you. I promise you I will talk only of indifferent things, though, at the same time, I know not how I shall approach you in the tender moment of first seeing you, after this declaration has been made by Madam, your most obedient, and most faithful, humble servant,

"RICHARD STEELE."

The style of these letters reminds us of the epistolary effusions of Sir Charles Grandison; ladies were prompted in those days by parents not to capitulate until proper conditions had been made. Mistress Scurlock, it is true, had not any fortune on her marriage; yet she seems to have been fearful of opposition from her mother. She kept her ardent lover, therefore, at a respectful distance; he went to her house, but she refused then to see him. Nevertheless her answer must have been favourable, since three days afterwards, it appears that Steele had visited Mrs. Scurlock "to wait on her." He was a true lover of the old school.

"I am now," he writes (Aug. 14) "under your own roof while I write; and that imaginary satisfaction of being so near you, though not in your presence, has in it something that touches me with so tender ideas, that it is impossible for me to describe their force. All great passion makes us dumb: and the highest grief as well as highest happiness, seizes us too violently to be expressed by our words."

"You are so good as to let me know I shall have the honour of seeing you when I next come here. I will live upon that expectation, and meditate on your perfections till that happy hour. The vainest woman upon earth never saw in her glass half the attractions which I view in you. Your air, your shape, your every glance, motion, and gesture, have such peculiar graces, that you possess my whole soul, and I know no life but in the hopes of your approbation. I know not what to say, but that I love you with the sincerest passion that ever entered the heart of man. I will make it the business of my life to find out means of convincing you that I prefer you to all that is pleasing on earth."

The attachment which he professed proved sincere, and stood many irritations, and a certain amount of lectures from his beloved Mary. When we condemn this letter as somewhat fulsome, the fashion of the day must not be forgotten; nothing, however, can be more tender or more beautiful, than Steele's letter to his Mary on the morning when she was to receive the sacrament. He had abstained from seeing her on the previous day.

August, 16th, 1707.

" MADAM,

"Before the light this morning dawned upon the earth, I awaked and lay in expectation of its return; not that it could give any new sense of joy to me, but as I hoped it would bless you with its cheerful face, after a quiet which I wished you last night. If my prayers are heard, the day appeared with all the influence of a merciful Creator upon your person and actions. Let others, my lovely charmer, talk of a blind being that disposes their hearts; I contemn their low images of love; I have not a thought which relates to you that I cannot with confidence beseech the All-seeing Power to bless me in. May He direct you in all your ways, and reward your innocence, your sanctity of manners, your prudent youth and becoming piety, with the continuance of His grace and protection!"

But mothers were to be consulted; and we find Mistress Mary Scurlock addressing hers in the following terms:—

"Dear Madam,

"The matter in hand is this: your frequent declarations of your earnest wishes that I might happily please you by obliging myself by my choice of a companion for life, has emboldened me, now Fate has put it in my power, to give so far encouragement as to promise speedy marriage upon condition of your consent, which I do not question having when I tell you I not only make use of the most weighing consideration I am mistress of, but also hope my inclination is in the direction of Providence, whose guidance, in every particular of this nice affair more particularly, I cease not to implore continually."

Mary Scurlock's heart soon surrendered to one whom she described as, "as agreeable and pleasing a man as any in England." She was reluctant to confess how short the siege had been—one month only.

"I cannot recommend the person to you," she continues, "as having a great estate, a title, &c., which are generally a parent's chief care; but he has a competency in worldly goods to make easy, with a mind so richly adorned, as to exceed an equivalent to the greatest estate in the world, in my opinion; in short, his person is what I like; his temper is what I am sure will make you, as well as myself, happy."

This letter has no date, but it may be presumed from the following epistle of Steele's that it was in September 1707. On the third of that month he wrote from Whitehall, and gave a flourishing account of his prospects. His friends, he said, were then in great power, "so that it would be highly necessary for him and his future wife to be in the figure of life they might think it convenient to appear in, as soon as possible," in order to profit by favour whilst the wind was

* Vol. i. p. 99.

with him, being assured that in a "court it would not long blow one way." He had then the appointment of Gazetteer to the State, with a salary of 300*l.* a year, paying a tax of 45*l.* He was gentleman waiter to His Royal Highness the Prince of Wales, with a salary of 100*l* a year. This made his income, including the estate of Steele's first wife, who had, he takes care to say, a great value for him, after certain deductions, 1025*l.* a year.

Mrs. Scurlock's estate, on the other hand, gave about 400*l.* a year; so that, with such expectations, it is marvellous that difficulties such as Steele was plunged into should ever occur. In conclusion, he promised to himself, in his letter to the mother of the dearest creature on earth, "the pleasures of an industrious and virtuous life." In addressing his betrothed he predicted such a "fulness of conjugal bliss, that angels, so far from being their superiors, would become their attendants." But felicity so perfect is not the lot of man, more especially not of a man so impulsive as Richard Steele.

All was not yet smooth sailing. Mary Scurlock appears to have wished her marriage to be kept private until her mother's arrival, from Wales, in London. She insisted on the letters Steele wrote to her being addressed, even after the ceremony had taken place, to "Mrs. Warren," the name she assumed. He was resolved to write to her by her proper name, and directed to Mrs. Steele; and this at Lord Sunderland's office where every letter was franked by the minister.

In the following letter to his wife, to whom he had been privately married on the seventh of September, there is evidence of wounded feeling.

To Mrs. Steele.

September 9th.

"Madam,

"I hope your denying what I urged with so much passion, and which I complained of in too vehement a manner, has not been a grief to my tender companion, for, upon reflection this morning, I extremely approve your conduct, and take your behaviour to proceed from an inclination to come to my arms hallowed by a parent's blessing. I comply with your measures in bringing that happiness about, and shall behave myself as if only in the beginning of a sacred love made at the altar."

In conclusion, "I beg of you to show my letters to no one living, but let us be contented with one another's thoughts upon our words and actions, without the intervention of other people who cannot judge of so delicate a circumstance as the commerce between man and wife. I am eternally yours,

"R. Steele."

Then some slight variance ensued; Steele writing to his wife begging her pardon for *every act* of rebellion he had ever committed against her, still styling her "dear Madam," and signing himself her "most obliged husband, and humble servant;" and she replying thus:—

"It is but an addition to our uneasiness to be at variance with each other. I beg your pardon if I have offended you. God forgive you for adding to the sorrow of a heavy heart, that is above all sorrow but for your sake." Then she sends him these lines, more affectionate than poetic:

"Ah! Dick Steele, that I were sure,
Your love, like mine, would still endure;
That time, nor absence, which destroys
The cares of lovers and their joys,
May never rob me of that part
Which you have given me of your heart;

> Others, unenvyed, may possess
> Whatever they think happiness.
> Grant, this, O God, my great request,
> In his dear arms may I for ever rest!"

Steele's next epistle was addressed to "the dearest being upon earth;" and now domestic life commenced. A house in Bury Street, St. James's was taken, and furnished with Mrs. Scurlock's goods, for the mother was to live with her daughter and son-in-law. Nevertheless, Steele continued to subscribe himself to his wife "her most *obedient* husband;" an expression strange to the ears of Englishmen.

Once settled, the happy pair led a life, desultory indeed, yet seemingly full of confidence. "Dick," as Mrs. Steele termed him, dated his letters somewhat too often, it must be allowed, from coffee houses; but then he writes to "dear Prue," his wife's name now, to join him in the coach, to bring his best periwig in the coach-box and his new shoes, and tells her they are to take "the fresh air in free conference;" for "it is a comfort to be well dressed in agreeable company." "You are vital life," he adds "to your obliged, affectionate, husband and humble servant." She was the "beautifullest object that could present itself to his eyes." Nevertheless, he sometimes begs her to consult her cool thoughts, and then she would know that it is a woman's glory to be her "husband's friend and companion, and not his sovereign director;" and in a subsequent letter he returns her one of her epistles in order that she may see how "disrespectfully" she had treated him. She seems indeed to have tormented him by her suspicions, and her over-control of his actions. One specimen more of the almost weak fondness expressed by the most candid and affectionate of men to a wife who seems to have had the most powerful influence over him:—

September 13th, 1708.

"DEAR PRUE,

"I write to you in obedience to what you ordered me, but there are not words to express the tenderness I have for you, *love* is too harsh a word for it; but, if you knew how my heart aches when you speak an unkind word to me, and springs with joy when you smile on me, I am sure you would place your glory rather in preserving my happiness, like a good wife, than tormenting me like a peevish beauty. Good Prue, write me word you shall be overjoyed at my return to you."

After this the picture is darkened. Sometimes he writes to her "a little in drink," as he avows; then he thinks it necessary on another occasion to assure her "he is going very soberly to bed." He is "busy about the main chance," which is evidently a losing affair in Steele's hands. He now writes to Prue, "you cannot think what difficulties I am put to." The death of Prince George of Denmark, which took place in 1708, did not lessen his income; Queen Anne continuing his salary by way of amity. Steele had to sit up by the royal corpse of that prince, who like himself was often, as he owns "a little fuddled." About this time, Steele's difficulties came to a crisis and he was arrested. Addison on this occasion refused to bail him; but money was obtained for that end elsewhere.

His wife meantime was miserable and anxious at her house in Bury Street, where that "*insufferable brute,*" as Steele calls the landlady, passed some affront on her. And now, difficulties produced their too frequent effect, dissension. Steele writes to his wife that she was "cruel to generous nature," and that after "short starts of passion, not to be inclined to reconciliation was against all Christianity and justice." In another letter he begged of her to add to her other charms a fearfulness to see a man that loved her in pain and uneasiness. "Rising a little in the morning, and adding a little cheerfulness, would not be amiss." However, he soon writes to her in an altered strain—as thus: "Thou art such a foolish tender thing, that there is no living with thee. I have broke my rest last night, because I knew you would be such a fool as not to sleep." Things began to brighten. "She was to be cheerful and beautiful;" he would have her "go out and divert herself." He "doated on her so, that he could not hide it." Prices were improving, Steele was made governor of the Theatre Royal; he had built, meantime, an elegant house adjoining the palace at Hampton Court: he called it the "Hovel at Hampton Wick:" and furnished it with his usual extravagant profusion.

He was soon obliged to borrow a thousand pounds on the security of his house and furniture. Addison lent him the money, and it was to be repaid at the end of a twelvemonth, Steele giving a bond to that effect. But, at the end of the time, no money was forthcoming, and Addison's attorney proceeded to execution. The house and furniture were sold, and the surplus remitted to Steele by Addison with a "very genteel letter," according to the received account, "stating the friendly reason of this extraordinary procedure to be to awaken Steele, if possible, from a lethargy that must end in his inevitable ruin." Steele received the letter with his accustomed composure and gaiety — and met his friend as usual. Nothing but a few bickerings between them betrayed a soreness of feeling, which pride on Steele's part concealed, and which prudence, on that of Addison forebore to elicit. Addison it is well remarked, acted by Steele as he did with his favourite in Roger de Coverley, whom he killed through fear that somebody should murder him. It must, however, have been grievous to Steele to leave Hampton Wick, in the neighbourhood of which his great patron Lord Halifax assembled all the wits of the day. But Steele had had worse things to encounter than the surrender of a house which he could not afford to live in; and had recently been locked up at the Bull's Head in Vere Street.

Hitherto Steele had fulfilled his office as Gazetteer "according to order, without ever erring," as he said, "against the rule observed by all ministries, of making the paper very innocent and very insipid;" but in 1713 he lost his place for writing in the Tatler against Harley (afterwards Earl of Oxford), who had not only given him the post, but augmented the salary from 60*l*. to 100*l*. a year. By good authority Steele has been acquitted of ingratitude to Harley; and Swift, whom he attacked for his writings in the Examiner, and who distinctly denied writing in that periodical, was an actual contributor to that paper even at that time. So little principle of truth has there been from time immemorial, in public men, for whom a new code of honour has been, it seems, expressly invented! Steele, according to Swift's allegation had called the dean, "a clergyman," says Swift, "of some distinction, an infidel: a clergyman who was your friend, who always loved you, who had endeavoured at least to serve you, and who, whenever he did write anything, made it sacred to himself never to fling out the least hint against you."

Steele had taken it for granted that to Swift and Mrs. Manley all the offensive papers in the Examiner were attributable. In allusion to this Swift says, "I have several times assured Mr. Addison and fifty others that I had not the least hand in writing any of these papers, and that I had never exchanged one syllable with the supposed author in my life, that I can remember, nor even seen him above twice, and that in mixed company, in a place where he came to pay his attendance."

The supposed author to whom Swift refers was Oldisworth. The able editor of Steele's letters, Mr. Nichols, regards it however certain that Swift was an "accomplice of the Examiner and a writer in it long after the time usually supposed." It is, as he observes, melancholy to reflect to what lengths party will bring two such men as Steele and Swift. "He is the vilest of mankind, and you may tell him so," was Swift's infuriated speech to Addison about Steele; to which Steele answers, "as to the vilest of mankind, it would be a glorious world if I were; and I would not conceal my thoughts in favour of an injured man, though all the powers in the earth gainsaid it, — to be the first man in the nation." This was truly one of those occasions in which Addison might be supposed "to stand weeping on the bank," unable to save his friend from the torrent of his own imprudences. On the fourth of June, 1713, Steele wrote to the Earl of Oxford resigning his place as commissioner of the stamp revenue. "I should," he wrote, "have done this sooner, but that I heard the commission was passing without my name in it and I would not be guilty of the arrogance of resigning what I could not hold." Lord Oxford had, he owns, treated him with great liberality of heart: but Steele's convictions with regard to the public welfare were stronger either than private friendship, or his own interest; and he trembled, he avowed, to see the country in "the hands of so daring a genius as his lordship." The cabals of that day of political intriguing are now almost forgotten: and the struggles between Whig and Tory are almost puerile in our eyes. But we must remember that during the last years of Queen Anne's reign, the greatest dread existed of Jacobite ascendency. The cry that the Protestant Church was in danger kept from the throne of England the exiled Stuarts; and no measures were deemed unworthy by the two great rival factions,— Godolphin and the Duke and Duchess of Marlborough representing the Whigs; Harley Earl of Oxford, aided covertly by Atterbury and Swift, being at the head of the Tories.

Queen Anne's health was manifestly failing, when Steele was attacked in the House of Commons. On resigning his commissionership, he had been elected member for Stockbridge. In March, 1713-14, the storm burst over his head.

On the tenth of that month, Mr. John Hungerford complained to the House of divers scandalous papers, published by Mr. Steele, and was seconded by Mr. Auditor Foley, cousin to Lord Oxford, and by Mr. Auditor Harley, the earl's brother. The names of the objectionable works were the "Englishman," and the "Crisis," which had been corrected by Dr. Hoadley, Bishop of Winchester, and by Addison, so that Steele's dearest friend had not merely "stood weeping on the bank" this time. At this juncture Lord Halifax stood Steele's friend; he told the House of Lords, that he believed if they would recommend the "Crisis" to her Majesty's perusal, she would think quite otherwise of the book than they did. Steele had been for many months leading a reckless, rambling, unsatisfactory life, which seems to have vexed his poor wife to the very heart. Sometimes he wrote to her from Bow Street, a suspicious address, indicative of his having been taken up to a police station when "fuddled;" sometimes from Buttons, where perhaps Addison, himself at this time an unhappy man, sat with him; he was often sending to the goldsmiths to discount bills; promising his wife, however, to come home early, and writing to her because he heard she had given herself up to lamentation. In vain did he beseech her to repose confidence in him: it was of no use. Who could have confidence in so rash a man, whose life was spent in sinning and repenting, in recommending to others what was right, and for ever failing himself to act well, or wisely? It has, indeed, been well said, that in speculation Steele was a man of piety and honour; in practice, he was much of the rake and a little of the swindler."

His wife was sitting, full of fears, at home on the day when the charge against her husband came before the House. He endeavoured to reassure her; "there is nothing can arise to me," he wrote, "that can afflict you, therefore, pray be a Roman lady, and assume a courage equal to your goodness."

On the eighteenth of March he was heard in his defence.

Being asked whether he acknowledged the writings that bore his name, he answered that he did, frankly and ingenuously, own those papers to be part of his writings, that he wrote them on behalf of the House of Hanover, and owned them with the same unreservedness with which he abjured the Pretender. He afterwards spoke for three hours, assisted by Addison, then member for Malmesbury, by whom he was prompted. The debate lasted till eleven o'clock, and amongst others, Robert, afterwards Sir Robert Walpole spoke in his behalf. The "Englishman" and the "Crisis" were, however, judged to be scandalous and seditious libels; it was, therefore, resolved that Mr. Steele be expelled the House.

After making his defence, poor Steele was ordered to withdraw. Addison followed him out, begging him not to be seen till he heard the result of the debate. Steele went to the Temple, and wrote to his wife, what he meant to be consolation: "Nothing can happen to my condition in private life, and I have busied myself enough for the public." Then the next day, "Pray let nothing disquiet you, for God will prosper and protect your innocence and virtue:" in another note he signs himself "your reprehended spouse, and humble servant." What a model for husbands! "Learn from Mr. Steele how to write to your wife," was Lady Mary Wortley Montagu's admonition to her husband; "but it is only the erring who write as Steele did to his 'Prue.' You and Betty, and Dick and Eugene, and Molly, (his children,) shall be henceforth my principal cares, next to keeping a good conscience," was his vain assurance." In the hurry of a life not only strongly agitated by party spirit, but we fear often "degraded by loose pleasures," Steele's attention to religious duties would be marvellous did we not know the inconsistencies of man's nature, he writes: "I am going this morning to a very solemn work, and invoke Almighty God to bless you and your little ones, beseeching Him to spare me a little life to acquit myself to you and them, whom of all the world I have hitherto endeavoured least to serve." "Dear Wife," he adds; "I honour, I love, I doat on you;" yet he left her for the tavern and the gaming table.

Steele now occupied himself with "A Roman Ecclesiastical History," which he addressed to Daniel Finch, eldest son of Daniel, Earl of Nottingham, and called by his political opponents "Young Dismal." To the "Roman Ecclesiastical History," was prefixed an "Account of some collateral circumstances and secret passages, joined to an account of the ceremony of the last inauguration of saints by his Holiness the Pope;" and this preface was written by Bishop Hoadley, a fact which gave Swift occasion to say afterwards, that

> "Steele, who owned what others writ,
> And flourished by imputed wit,
> From perils of a hundred jails
> Withdrew to starve and die in Wales."

Steele's acquaintance with Lord Finch had the following origin: Lady Charlotte Finch, the sister of his lordship, had been attacked coarsely and rudely in the "Examiner" for alleged misbehaviour in church; and Steele had written a spirited defence of her in the "Guardian." When the question of Steele's expulsion was mooted, Lord Finch stepped forward, and attempted to speak in behalf of the accused, but was overcome by modesty, and by deference to that assembly in which he had not hitherto spoken a word. As he sat down covered with confusion, he was heard to say, "It is a struggle; I can't speak for this man, though I could readily fight for him." His words being whispered from one to another, operated in an instant like electric fire; and a sudden burst from all parts of the House of "Hear him! hear him!" with ineffable marks of encouragement, Lord Finch rose, and, with astonishing recollection and the utmost propriety, spoke a speech on the occasion, in which, as it was related to this writer, in the language of the theatre, "there was not one word which did not *tell*." The eyes of the whole company were upon him, and though he appeared to have utterly forgot what he rose up to speak, yet the generous motives which the whole company knew he acted upon, procured him such an acclamation of voices and cheering, that he spoke with clearness and magnanimity.

After Steele had ceased to be a member, he complained of loss of liberty, and of all that makes life agreeable. He had long discovered that since the death of his mother, he had been "prone to melancholy;" it was in fact his affairs, and the unprovided state of his family that produced that condition. "Prue" had brought him no fortune, and a little "frowardness" on her part had contributed, with other cares, to the troubles of life. Steele was now solicitous to know how affairs stood with his mother-in-law to a "farthing." He wished evidently, to get some settlement made by Mrs. Scurlock on his children; "assignments for debts" the good lady had paid, covering Prue's share of her paternal property. Hot words seem to have passed, Steele, as usual, begging pardon for being passionate. At last, in October after his expulsion, he made up his mind to go to the club and ask for a subscription for the "Crisis."

"It frets my proud heart to do this, but it must be done," he wrote to Mrs. Steele. Alas! an extravagant man has nothing to do with pride. Steele had still to encounter reproaches, where, indeed, he probably fully deserved to meet with them: still meantime, he signs himself, "your faithful obsequious husband."

Addison had, in common with his friend, experienced the stings and arrows of outrageous fortune.

"To Addison," says a modern writer, "we are bound by a sentiment as much like affection, as any sentiment can be which is inspired by one who has been sleeping a hundred and twenty years in Westminster Abbey.* And,

---

* This was written in July, 1843. See Edinburgh Review for that year.

it must be confessed, in spite of a weak leaning to Steele, it is impossible to disallow the higher moral attributes of Addison.

His first entrance into a literary career was fortunate. Having addressed a poem to the Lord Keeper Somers, on one of King William's campaigns, Addison gained the goodwill of that able lawyer, and by his mediation, a pension of three hundred a year was procured from the crown, and the result was that he was enabled to travel. It was at one time intended that he should have been appointed to attend on Prince Eugene, who was in Italy; but the death of King William broke up this scheme, and happily for us the young author returned to his own country, and lived to adorn her literature with that unspeakable boon to every English home, the " Spectator."

Let us see him, however, in fancy, for a short time, at all events in his travels, and participate in the excitements and advantage which he fully prized.

A Fellow of a College,—and Addison was still a Fellow of Magdalen,—must have made a strange figure in the Court of Louis XIV. Addison was fortunate enough to see that great king and little man, in all the pomp and ultra-superstition of his declining life. The English stranger was introduced under very favourable circumstances at Versailles. The English Government had interfered in his behalf with the head of an Oxford College. When the pension was granted to Addison, the Ministry were afraid lest the Fellowship should be a matter of complaint; the Chancellor of the Exchequer wrote therefore to Hough, afterwards Bishop Hough, to say that the State could not spare Addison to the Church. The public service, he added, was to be recruited from men like Addison, instead of filling every civil post with adventurers utterly devoid of talent and knowledge.

Under the banner of Charles Montague, soon afterwards Lord Halifax, and with the patronage of Somers, therefore, did Addison appear at the French Court. He was then, in 1699, just twenty-six years of age.

A more bashful man never landed on the flat, bare shore of Calais. He studied much, talked very little, had long fits of absence, and seemed protected either by shyness or some previous entanglement of the heart, from all love affairs. A more genuine fellow of a College in the placid, perfect composure of a reserved Englishman, never visited the most charming capital in the world.

But underneath this calm wave which seemed to hide beneath its clear waters nothing but frivolous pebbles, and washy sand, there was ore of no ordinary value. The round fair face, with its Saxon complexion, betrayed, indeed, no impression; the sly humour which afterwards delighted a circle at Button's, was bottled up, but effervesced in private. The steady-going, unprejudiced observation which gave to his mind so philosophic a range, was never dreamed of in that courtly, formal, and sophisticated sphere to which he was now presented.

His impressions were briefly conveyed in the following letters to Charles Montague, Lord Halifax.

"HONOUR'D SIR,

"I am now in a place where nothing is more usual than for mean people to press into ye presence and conversation of great men, and where modestie is so very scarce, that I think I have not seen a blush since my first landing at Callice, which I hope may, in some measure, excuse me for presuming to trouble you with a letter. However, if I may not be allow'd to improve a little in ye confidence of ye country, I am sure I receive in it such effects of your favour in ye civilities "My Ld. Ambassador has bin pleased to show me, that I cant but think it my duty to make you acquainted with them; I am sorry my travels have not yet furnisht me with anything else worth your knowledge. As for the state of learning, there is no book comes out at present that has not something in it of an air of devotion.

"Dacier has bin forc'd to prove his Plato a very good Christian before he ventures on the Translation, and has so far comply'd with ye taste of ye age, that his whole book is overrun with texts of Scripture; and ye notion of pre-existence supposed to be stol'n from two verses of the prophets. Nay, ye humour is grown so universal, that it is got among ye poets, who are every day publishing Lives of Saints and Legends in rhime."

He soon perceived that to speak French indifferently is a positive misfortune in Paris; and he hastened to Blois, where he understood that French was spoken in its greatest purity (a distinction now allotted to Tours), and where there was not then a single Englishman. Blois has still the reputation of containing the best Legitimist society of any city in France some years ago; though now, the gratitude expressed by the natives there to Napoleon III. would imply that the old traditions were dying out. At Blois, Addison, who was talking for improvement, probably talked more than he ever did in his life, either before or afterwards; yet he was thus spoken of by a certain Abbé Philippeau, who gave the following account to Mr. Spence.

"Mr. Addison stayed above a year at Blois. He would rise as early as between two and three in summer, and lie abed till between eleven and twelve in the depth of winter. He was untalkative while here, and often thoughtful; sometimes so lost in thought, that I have come into his room and stayed five minutes there before he has known anything about it. He had his masters generally at supper with him, and kept very little company beside."

VOL. I.   S

His enjoyment at Blois, consisted, as he told Congreve, chiefly in recalling the interesting sights which he had beheld before his seclusion—Versailles, and especially Fontainebleau, which he preferred to all in remembering.

"The King," he says, "has humoured the genius of the place, and only made use of so much art as is necessary to help and regulate Nature without reforming her too much. The cascades seem to break through the clefts of rocks that are covered over with moss, and look as if they were piled upon one another by accident. There is an artificial wildness in the meadows, walks, and canals, and ye garden, instead of a wall, is fenc'd on the lower end by a natural mound of rock-work that strikes the eye very agreeably."

He came to the conviction, during his residence at Blois, that the French are the happiest people in the world. It was not in the power of want and slavery to make them miserable (nor is it now). "There is nothing to be met with in the country but mirth and poverty. Ev'ry one sings, laughs, and starves. Their conversation is generally agreeable; for if they have any wit or sense, they are sure to show it. They never mend upon a second meeting, but use all the freedom and familiarity at first sight that a long intimacy or abundance of wine can scarce draw from an Englishman. Their women are perfect mistresses in this art of showing themselves to the best advantage."

In another letter (to Bishop Newton) he remarks that he never thought to have seen so much magnificence or so much poverty as he met with together in France. The king's splendour caused half his subjects to go barefooted. Fogs, and German counts, were the drawbacks to his enjoyment of Blois; the fogs were ascribable to the Loire, the Counts were a kind of gentlemen just come wild out of their own country, "and more noisy and senseless than any he had yet had the honour of being acquainted with."

He now began to think of returning to Paris, having

mastered the French tongue, which had, he confessed, been a "rub in his way harder to get over than the Alps."

It was about this time that Addison formed the acquaintance of Edward Wortley Montagu, the husband of the celebrated Lady Mary Wortley Montagu; he was, indeed, a companion worthy of Addison; a zealous Whig, a learned, accomplished and earnest man. Edward Wortley Montagu travelled to greater advantage than most youths of family who make the grand tour. He spoke French perfectly, a rare accomplishment in England in those times, for when George I. sat in council on his accession, Wortley Montagu is said to have been the *only* person who could converse with his sovereign in French, and George I. spoke no English.

It is curious to find the character of the French so like then, what we observe it now to be; their national vanity, that feature which is, in some few, elevated into patriotism, was exalted now to an intense degree by the advancement of Philip Duke of Anjou, the nephew of Louis XIV., to be king of Spain. "There is," Addison says, "scarce a man that does not give himself greater airs upon it, and look as well pleased as if he had received some considerable advancement in his own fortunes." He turned gladly to men of letters; but to those he is not in his account very favourable. "Their learning," he says, "for the most part lies among old schoolmen. Their public disputes run upon the controversy between the Thomists and Scotists, which they manage with abundance of heat and false Latin." He visited Malebranche, whom the literary society of the day scarcely valued, looking on his deep researches with indifference, and regarding all new philosophy as visionary or irreligious. He much praised Sir Isaac Newton, but deemed Hobbes " un pauvre esprit."

Boileau, Addison found old and deaf, and so ignorant of English literature, that he had scarcely ever heard the name of Dryden; but the classical tastes of the aged *savant*, his enthusiasm for Homer and Virgil, his hatred to all who did not adequately value those poets, his critiques upon Fenelon and Corneille interested Addison greatly.

Addison then proceeded on his journey with Wortley Montagu as his companion; his acquaintance with that gentleman being, as he states, one of the most "fortunate accidents of his travel." The great author of "The Spectator" appears to have had a much more keen sense of moral, than of material beauty. The noble scenery of Geneva, which he visited on his return, was thrown away on him; and he complains that in the Tyrol he had *very little* to amuse him, *except* the "natural face of the country."

He returned to England confirmed, by what he had seen in France and Italy, in his liberal opinions. Foreign travelling, he always said, was the best cure for Jacobitism. In one of his papers in "The Freeholder," he makes a Tory foxhunter ask what travelling is good for, except "to teach a man to jabber French, and to talk against passive obedience."

Addison was at Geneva when the news of King William's death crushed all his hopes; his pension was stopped; but he had still his fellowship, to which he added by becoming tutor to a young Englishman with whom he travelled in Switzerland and Germany. He returned through Holland to England in 1703, having heard of his father's death on the way; and that event was the forerunner of many privations and of much anxiety.

We now behold him, his pension stopped, in a garret up three pairs of stairs, over a shop in the Haymarket. He had published his travels and his work on "Medals;" but no signal fame ensued; and the young author sat down dispirited, poor, and, as it seemed, forgotten. But at this juncture Lord Halifax remembered him.

Lord Godolphin, then Lord Treasurer, was not a reading man; Newmarket, the card table, and a lounge in the Friery where the far-famed Sarah of Marlborough then lived, filled up his scanty leisure. But he was too sagacious not to appreciate poetry, and to comprehend the influence of literature, and the advantages which had even then been derived by the Whigs in their patronage of letters. Nothing could exceed the bathos of most of the poems which the battle of Blenheim, which took place in 1704, elucidated; witness the following lines, still extant in proof of the statement:—

> " Think of two thousand gentlemen at least,
> And each man mounted on his capering beast;
> Into the Danube they were pushed by shoals."

Godolphin could negotiate war, he could lead the House of Lords, he could equally well judge of race-horses and game-cocks, cock-fighting being amongst his minor delights; but of poets he knew little. A poet, however, he thought must be found to do justice to the battle of Blenheim, and he consulted Halifax on the subject. "I do know," answered Mouse Montagu, "a gentleman who could celebrate the battle worthily, but I will not name him." He had done his best, he added, to encourage literature; but his power to do so no longer took the desired effect,—he declined giving advice. After some discussion, however, he was prevailed on to name his pet poet, and he named Addison. But, he added, as the matter to be propounded was task-work, the poet, paid as he must be, should be propitiated with courtesy. Godolphin sent off the Hon. Henry Boyle, then Chancellor of the Exchequer, forthwith to that locality, the first notice of which Cunningham says is in these lines of Suckling's ballad on a wedding.

> "At Charing Cross, hard by the way,
> Where we (thou know'st) do sell our hay,
> There is a house with stairs;
> And there I did see coming down,
> Such folks as are not in our town,
> Forty, at least, in pairs."

The Hay-market, since removed (in 1830), must have been just before Addison's garret, on the east side of the street. And here Boyle visited him. It was a curious sight: Addison in his garret receiving the high-born Henry Boyle. The result was Addison's poem " The Campaign," the great merit of which, Dr. Johnson remarks, is the manly and rational rejection of fiction. It was in this poem that the famous similitude of Marlborough to an angel guiding the whirlwind appeared. Allusion was also made to a terrific storm,

"Such as of late o'er pale Britannia pass'd"—

the storm of November 1703. Whole fleets were cast away in that tempest; large mansions blown down; a prelate buried under the ruins of his palace;—London and Bristol half in ruins; trunks of huge trees and the shattered walls of houses showing in many places the fearful destruction caused by the blast: such was the reference to fact, and the success of the "simile seems but," says a writer in the Edinburgh Review, " a remarkable instance of the advantage which the particular has over the general in rhetoric and poetry."

Never was poetry so forgotten, as Addison's "Campaign," so promptly rewarded. In 1705 he was made Under-secretary of State, and accompanied Lord Halifax to Hanover, in order to carry the decorations of the Garter to the Elector.

In 1708 Addison sat in the House of Commons as member for Malmsbury. Athough he was accounted even by the fastidious Lady Mary Wortley Montagu to be "the best company in the world," yet he was the most silent of silent members. In his extreme reserve, that reserve which came over him like a blight in the presence of strangers, Addison must have resembled the late Lord Cockburn, the most eloquent, the most charming, the most playful and humorous of men among those whom he knew and understood, the most taciturn among strangers. Addison — Steele, who so well appreciated him, said—"was above all men in that talent we call humour, and enjoyed it in such perfection, that I have often reflected, after a night passed with him apart from all the world, that I had had the pleasure of conversing with an intimate acquaintance of Terence and Catullus, who had all their wit and nature, heightened with humour more exquisite and delightful than any other man ever possessed." He alludes to "that smiling mirth, that delicate satire and genteel raillery," which rendered so delightful—he wrote after his friend's death—"hours that could return no more." "I say," Steele adds "when he is as free from that *remarkable* bashfulness which is a cloak that always hides and muffles merit."

Addison, in fact, thought that there was no real conversation but between two persons. He called talking "thinking aloud;" of display he had no conception. To be the wit of a dinner-table would have been gall and wormwood to one of his sensitive and shrinking nature; nevertheless, even Pope could allow that Addison's conversation had something in it more charming than that of any other man. "This," he adds, "only with familiar friends; before even a single stranger he preserved his dignity by a stiff silence." It has been said that he was never easy with his inferiors. Yet Young speaks of his being full of vivacity in company, and going on in a "noble stream of thought and language," so as to rivet the attention of all hearers.

He had now, "without high birth, and with very little property, risen to a position which," observes a writer of our own day, "dukes, the heads of the great houses of Talbot, Russell and Bentinck have thought it an honour to fill." In 1709 the Marquis of Wharton, being appointed Lord-Lieutenant of Ireland, constituted Addison his Secretary. He was also made Keeper of the Records of that kingdom, in order to augment his salary. So much had literature done for him. Yet one of his recent works had then been the unsuccessful opera of

"Rosamond;" it failed on the stage of the opera-house. He published it, and dedicated it to the Duchess of Marlborough, "a woman," Dr. Johnson remarks, "without skill or pretensions to skill, in literature or poetry." Addison's rise would be unaccountable did we not consider that the pen was in those days a more formidable engine than the tongue. It was the only mode of communicating opinions to the country, when the meagre reports of debates confined the most spirit-breathing eloquence almost wholly to the Houses of Parliament. Hence, the chiefs of parties not only sought for able auxiliaries in pamphleteering, but wrote indefatigably themselves. Walpole and Pulteney, the Pitt and Fox of an earlier period, were laborious writers in periodicals and pamphlets. Pulteney edited the "Craftsman;" Walpole wrote ten pamphlets; Addison, therefore, rose by those abilities which were essential to the state, and which were then essential to public men. Previously to the elevation of Addison, he had assisted Steele in his play of the "Tender Husband;" and had written a humorous prologue to that piece. Steele, on the other hand, surprised him with a dedication of that play to him. In after life Steele honestly declared in the concluding paper of the seventh volume of the "Spectator," that many of the "applauded strokes" in the "Tender Husband" came from the pen of Addison; "and that he thought very meanly of himself that he had publicly avowed it." It is pleasant to observe, at this time, the even flow of friendly converse which was maintained between Addison and Steele. So long as they were votaries chiefly of the Muses, they were linked to each other in the firmest bonds; but politics in that era could sever the tenderest friends. Addison had, however, a softness of address, a sweetness and courtesy which gave his great colloquial powers an infinite charm. He was also Steele's truest, fondest, most anxious and judicious friend. The old proverb, "short accounts make long friends," was never, however, violated with impunity. Addison lent Steele long sums; and, as usual, was severely censured when he wanted them back again. You are an angel when you lend, a demon when you ask to be paid. We have seen how Addison reclaimed the thousand pounds lent to Steele in 1708. For that apparently harsh measure those who weakly rely on *ex parte* evidence, have blamed the best friend that ever lent his hard earnings to another. There can be but little doubt that Addison saw that the most reckless waste, and endless dissipation, precluded all hopes of his being repaid except by severe measures. From tavern to tavern went Steele, when he could as well have stayed at home; and money which it had cost Addison days of labour to accumulate, was, no doubt, lavished on unworthy objects by a man of the best resolutions and the worst actions possible.

In the spring of 1709, the first idea of the "Tatler" was formed by Steele. Periodical writing was then chiefly confined to politics, and was low in value: Steele's old occupation as Gazetteer suggested to him something better than the meagre papers of the day, productions long since forgotten in our time. Steele, therefore, thought of something on a new plan,— a paper which should contain not only the foreign news, but dissertations on the stage and the gossip of the taverns and the clubs. Three times a week only did the post leave London for the country, and on those three days, Tuesdays, Thursdays, and Saturdays, was the "Tatler" to leave also. What a boon to the country squire by his fireside! What a hope for the solitary spinster in her lodging in Bath or Tunbridge! What an excitement for the very clubs and taverns, which furnished so great a part of the material of which Isaac Bickerstaff, Esq., Astrologer, the supposed editor of these new papers, constructed his essays and criticisms! But then there was no one in that, or perhaps in any other time, so fitted for the "Tatler" office as Steele. He knew many phases of that which was, *par excellence,* called society in those days. He consorted with the learned at the table of Lord Somers; Halifax supplied him with the opportunity of meeting with the witty and the fashionable; the *crême de la crême* was to be enjoyed at Congreve's parties: Lady Burlington, to whom he addressed the "Ladies' Library," and Mrs. Katherine Bovey, supplied him with models of the cultivated English female; whilst with Lord Wharton and at the Kit-Cat Club everything good and bad was to be found. But not only in this highly intellectual and courtly society was Steele initiated fully, but in what was called the "town"—for an acquaintance with which he had bartered peace of mind and ease of circumstances. The "town" comprised all that under-current of social life in which the daily wants of the genteel poor comes commingled with their scrambling pleasures, and hourly difficulties. The "town" took in also "all pleasant vices," had little to do with crimes, much with absurdities and peculiarities. Tavern life, theatre life—the pulpit also, as well as the stage, all came under the denomination of the "town," which comprehended all classes, from the jaunty milliner to the man in office.

Isaac Bickerstaff was a personage already partially known to the public, Steele having assumed the name to head a satirical attack on Partridge, the almanac maker.

The publication of the paper had not been imparted to Addison, but, as soon as he knew of it, he resolved to give the scheme his best help. Steele generously acknowledged the immense advantage of this assistance. "I fared," he said, "like a distressed prince who calls in a powerful neighbour to his aid. I was undone by my auxiliary. When I had once called him in, I could not subsist without dependence on him. The paper was advanced indeed. It was raised to a greater thing than I intended it." In so generous a spirit did these devoted friends act, at this time, in concert; their freedom from rivalry, their courteous tributes to each other, form a model of chivalric authorship, as one may term it, and present a strong contrast with the spirit of our own time. If Addison conferred a benefit on Steele, Steele did a service to Addison; for he drew forth those powers so rich, so various, so precious, even now, for Addison's works are never obsolete, which shone dimly in the "Tatler," compared with the radiance of genius which breaks forth in the "Spectator." In pure, easy, elegant English, Addison was unrivalled. Still it is only to a limited degree to *language* that he owes his eminence. On this point it has been truly said that "had he clothed his thoughts in the half French style of Horace Walpole, or in the half Latin style of Dr. Johnson, or in the half German jargon of the present day, his genius would have triumphed over all faults of manner."

Dr. Johnson observes, "for instruction in common life, nothing is so proper as frequent publication of short papers, which are read not as a study, but amusement. If the subject be slight, the treatise likewise is short. The busy may find time and the idle may find patience." We believe it is impossible to conceive the good done to society by the "Tatler" and "Spectator," the latter more especially, since it has less of the coarseness of the age; it holds out nobler motives, it contains a purer morality, it is, with infinitely more wit, far more earnest than its predecessor. The learned Dr. Parr used to say to young men introduced to him specially for advice on literary subjects, or, with a view to education, " Sir, read the 'Spectator,' you can never be weary of doing so. It is incomparably the best book of the language."

It is true that with the Augustan age, as it was called, there appeared a greater restraint of wit, a greater decency of manners, a higher standard of morals, than the world in England had known since the days of Charles I. Anne was eminently proper. Every woman ought to admire her, every man *will*; for men are stricter (when gentlemen) than women in such matters, in that she would not consent to have her image dispersed among her subjects with the bare neck and shoulders usually assigned to regal ladies. She ordered her bust on the coin to be draped, and in like manner she abhorred indecency, and countenanced the homely ways which tend to virtue, if they do not constitute it. Her favourites among her own sex were women of character. She was strict in her requirements from men of a general respectability. So far, part of the land was cleared for Addison and Steele when they came, not with sermons, but with real and invented characters to reform with playful satire the corrupted condition which had succeeded the Restoration. The mirth of Addison was ever innocent, fresh, and kindly. "The mirth of Swift," it is remarked, "was that of Mephistopheles. The mirth of Voltaire is the mirth of Puck;" but that of Addison is "consistent with tender compassion for all that is frail, and with profound reverence for all that is sublime."

"Every morning," says a writer in the "British Journal," [*] "were the readers of the 'Spectator' instructed in some new principle of duty;" good nature and good sense became habitual to them, through the medium of that single half sheet, "which did more good than all the pulpit discourses in a year put together." We quote from the opinions of a contemporary.

In order to prevent mistakes Addison's papers were always marked by some letter in the word CLIO. The "Spectator" was regarded as an expansion of the "Tatler," and among other stipulations made by Addison in undertaking it, it was arranged that no ephemeral matters should appear in it, and that all political allusions should be avoided, whilst the general line should be liberal. The "Spectator" himself was the conception of Addison; an imaginary gentleman, who, after studying at the University had travelled on

[*] For Sept. 13th, 1729.

classic ground, and become a classical antiquary. On returning to London he sees every variety of life; he has been an *habitué* of Willis's, where wits congregated; he has smoked with the philosophers at the Grecian, and mixed with politicians and fine ladies. You see the "Spectator" in the Exchange, you may watch him every evening in the pit of Drury Lane; but his shyness is invincible, and he never speaks to you; in fact, the bashful man is Joseph Addison himself.

He lives—so to speak—with a small circle of intimate friends, whom Steele sketched, and whose portraits Addison finished. Four of them fill up the background; to wit, the clergyman, the soldier, the Templar, and the merchant, and the background is good enough for them; but two of the friends are those inimitable characters, Sir Roger de Coverley and Will Honeycomb, whom, to our dying day we cannot but recall with pleasure.

Will Honeycomb, Esq., the old beau, with jaunty air, easy motion, sudden laugh, management of snuff-box, and white hands and teeth, gained the admiration of the fair, was supposed to be Colonel Cleland, a friend both of Addison and Steele; and a letter prefixed to the eighth volume of the "Spectator" is said to have been written by Eustace Budgell. His character was taken in hand by Addison, through the conception of Steele.

Sir Roger de Coverley was Addison's favourite conception, and he was especially annoyed when Steele, taking the old knight into his own hands, vulgarised him by making him commit an act of immorality; on which Addison went to Steele and made him promise that he would not meddle with Sir Roger again; and as he expressed it to an intimate friend, resolved to move Sir Roger out of the way,—and that no one else might murder him, he resolved to kill him himself.

Whilst every essay in the "Spectator" can be read with pleasure in its distinct form, the whole constitutes a consistent narrative, and that whole delineates the manners of every-day life in England at that time, with a perfection that is the more astonishing when we consider the number and variety of the papers. Hitherto the familiar novel with which our own day abounds, existed not. Richardson was then a compositor, not an author; so that the masterly insight into English life which his works afford was unknown to the envied readers in the Augustan age. The events in the "Spectator" are such as happen to us every day. The most trifling incident elicits stories or reflections; the girl's face half seen over the window blind; the parish clerk, who, being a gardener, dresses up Covent Garden Church till he makes it a grove, and till no one can flirt at church between the evergreens; the poultry yard at Sir Roger de Coverley's,—are all touches of familiar life which continually recur to remembrance in our daily existence. The "Spectator" ever lives with us, is our friend, our associate, our storyteller, one to whom, were he living, we could give our confidence:—and betray—a great proof of liking—our weaknesses.

Then what a master in manners he was. No one condemns prudery so much as Addison: no one so deprecates levity, or draws the line between too great vivacity and too great reserve. It is curious to find him dreading the effects of peace and the contamination of French morals in 1710–11, and wishing that there were an act of parliament to prevent the importation of French fopperies. "What an inundation of ribbons and brocades," he cries, "shall we be exposed to! What peals of laughter and impertinence?" It appeared that very strong impressions, from what Addison calls the "ludicrous nation," had been received by English women even in his day.

He remembered the time when well-bred ladies employed a *valet de chambre* instead of a waiting-maid, because, forsooth, a man was more handy about them than a woman; and, simultaneously with this practice was the custom for ladies to receive visitors in bed. "It was then looked upon as a piece of ill-breeding for a woman to refuse to see a man, because she was not stirring;" and a porter who refused to admit the male visitor would have been deemed unfit for his place. "As I love to see everything that is new," he writes, "I once prevailed upon my friend Will Honeycomb to carry me along with him to one of these travelled ladies, desiring him, at the same time, to present me as a foreigner who could not speak English, that so I might not be obliged to bear a part in the discourse. The lady, though willing to appear undressed, had put on her best looks and painted herself for our reception. Her hair appeared in a very nice disorder, as the night-gown, which was thrown upon her shoulders, was ruffled with great care."

The *fast* young lady of the nineteenth century is only, it seems, a descendant from one of the same species in the eighteenth; when to speak loud in public, and to let every one hear you speak of things that ought only to be whispered, were parts, says the "Spectator," of a refined education. This also he deduces from the French. A blush was unfashionable, and silence more ill-bred than anything that could be spoken. Discretion and modesty were considered as betraying narrowness of mind. Then his description of a lady of quality at a theatre, exemplifies what he thus decries.

"Some years ago I was at the tragedy of 'Macbeth,' and unfortunately placed myself under a woman of quality that is since dead, who, as I found by the noise she made, was newly come from France. A little before the rising of the curtain she broke out into a loud soliloquy, '*When will the dear witches enter?*' And immediately, on their first appearance, asked a lady that sat three boxes from her, on the right hand, if those 'witches were not charming creatures?'"

How true it is that Addison restored virtue to its dignity, and taught innocence not to be alarmed.[*] The dregs of that

[*] Dr. Johnson.

cup, which was pledged to gallantry and vice in the days of Charles II., were not cleansed away when the "Spectator" came forward "to dissipate the prejudice that had long connected gaiety with vice, and easiness of manners with laxity of principles."

That such a mission was requisite as that of a social reformer, was manifest;—that it was acceptable, is proved by the unprecedented popularity of the "Spectator." To Steele, likewise, is due much of the credit of that gentle revolution, or rather improvement in our view of common matters, and also in our notions of the all-important subjects of love and marriage, which the "Spectator" introduced. Before the era we now describe, marriages among the higher classes were conducted as in France, on a principle of *convenance;* and to this antiquated system may be ascribed most of the immorality which was only a part of a fine gentleman's character in the eighteenth century; and much, I write it in solemn sadness, of the married infelicity of the French. There is something so affectionate in the French nature, as we see in the parental and filial tie,—(stronger there than in England,) —something so kindly, that when a Frenchman marries for love, he makes the best husband in the world. As it is in France now, so it was in England until after the Augustan age commenced. Love, as portrayed by De Grammont and other writers of the bygone age, was sensual, inconstant, and therefore selfish and remorseless. It was a scourge, not a passion; and the coarseness in which all allusions to marriage are couched, and the debased views of that tie, continued until holier and higher sentiments came into fashion. There had been a time when such degraded ideas of marriage and love were not universal. Surrey and Wyatt have taught us that delicacy of sentiment existed even under the Tudor Harry; but a long interregnum of very different convictions had intervened between the age of those two chivalric and noble-hearted men, and that of Queen Anne.

To Steele are owing some of the most refined notions of love that have ever been expressed in the language.

> "I tell thee, love is Nature's second sun,
> Causing a spring of virtues where he shines;
> And, as without the sun, the world's great eye,
> All colours, beauties both of art and nature,
> Are given in vain to men; so without love
> All beauties bred in women are vain;
> All virtues bred in men lie buried;
> For love reforms them as the sun doth colours."*

Such were Steele's sentiments. How exquisite is his tale of Theodosius and Constantia; how grateful to the feelings the respectful, pure attachment of his "Conscious Lovers."

We forgive Steele his touch of coarseness in the character of Sir Roger de Coverley, and are willing to believe that with the kindest, tenderest heart that ever woman commanded, he combined the most delicate conceptions of love, and the most earnest and holy views of marriage.

To the improvement in manners and morals the advance of good taste and the restoration of true art to the stage may have contributed. To this both Addison and Steele contributed.

A hundred years had indeed passed away since Henslowe's Diary (dated March 1598–9) had given an account, each item stated with grave simplicity, of the properties used in the Miracle Plays: rock, cage, tomb—*hell-mouth* especially was one of the oldest properties in the miracle plays and moralities; in Addison's time the taste which delighted in the "descending of a god, the rising of a ghost, or the vanishing of a devil," was as general as ever. A ghost, especially if in a blood-stained shirt, was an especial favourite with an English audience. "A spectre has very often saved a play, though he has done nothing more than stalked across the stage, or rose through a cleft of it, or sunk again without speaking one

---

* From George Chapman's comedy of "All Fools." See Collier's History of Dramatic Poetry, vol. iii. p. 257.

word." So Addison tells us. The sounding of the clock in "Venice Preserved" shook the hearts of the audience more than words could do, whilst the ghost in "Hamlet" he holds to be a master-piece.

Still he deprecated these appeals to the senses, both in tragedy and in comedy. A lover running about the stage, with his head peeping out of a barrel, was, he observes, thought a very good joke in the reign of Charles II., and invented by one of the greatest wits of that time.

The sale of the "Spectator" was great, yet Swift declares that the "Spectator" had begun to weary his readers before he retired: and ridiculed his endless mention of the "fair sex." The year 1713, in which was produced the tragedy of "Cato," is reported to have been the grand climacteric of Addison's reputation. The notion of this celebrated play was the characteristic scheme of Addison, in his University days. One may easily conceive him meditating upon it in what is still called Addison's Walk, in Magdalene Gardens: the tall trees interlacing overhead: the noble towers of Magdalene Chapel seen at intervals through the openings in the avenue; the placid stream beyond in the meadows — all these were the calm accompaniments of Addison's projects and aspirations.

Whilst on his travels he put his scheme into execution, and brought back "Cato" in manuscript, to be read to a few chosen friends, who persuaded Addison to bring it on the stage, as they thought the notions of liberty seasonable. Colley Cibber was then manager of Drury Lane, where it was brought out, and a young actor, the celebrated Booth, made his fortune by his appearance in the part of Cato. It had a run of a month, and was then stopped only by the inability of one of the actors to perform. The Queen, hearing of its great success, sent to say she would like to have the play dedicated to her: but Addison had already destined that compliment for the Duchess of Marlborough, and therefore declined.

"Cato" was brought on the stage at much expense: for Addison made a present of the proceeds of the representations to Cibber; and Cibber felt himself bound to do it every justice. It must have been very interesting to have seen Addison, night after night, wander through the whole exhibition behind the scenes, with restless and unappeasable solicitude. "Cato," Pope wrote to Sir William Trumbull, "was not so much the wonder of Rome in his days as he is of Britain in ours; and though all the foolish industry possible has been used to make it thought a party play, yet what the author once most properly said of another may the most properly in the world be applied to him on this occasion:

> "'Envy itself is dumb, in wonder lost,
> And factions strive who shall applaud him most.'

The numerous and loud claps of the Whig party on the one side of the theatre were echoed back by the Tories on the other; while the author sweated behind the scenes with concern to find their applause proceeding more from the hand than the head."

Steele, as he himself relates, undertook to pack an audience, a measure which had been for the *first time* tried for "The Distressed Mother." The least attractive parts of the play were the love scenes, which are said to have been added by Pope, in compliance with the popular taste; but Dr. Johnson throws a doubt on that statement.

Meantime, Steele's fortunes were brightening. The death of Queen Anne brought the Whigs again into the ascendant, and George I., on his accession, appointed Steele Surveyor of the Stables at Hampton Court, and governor of the Royal Company of Comedians. In April 1715, Steele having been put into the commission of the peace had to present an address to his Majesty; he was then knighted, and shortly afterwards elected member for Boroughbridge, in the new Parliament.

Steele had still every possible reason for being prudent. Nevertheless, in compliment to the King, he made a grand display on the birthday of the sovereign, and treated above a hundred ladies and gentlemen at his house, the day on which his royal master entered his fiftieth year.

Previously to Steele's festivities, Steele, introduced by the Duke of Newcastle, had presented to George I. an address framed in language which must have excited the liveliest passion in the Jacobite ladies; for that "faction," as Steele styles it, was then *haut ton* of that period.

"Most Gracious Sovereign," it begins, "it is impossible for us to express to your Majesty our just grief and indignation at the unnatural efforts which have been made by wicked men, to disturb your government, and prepare the way for an outlaw, who disputes your right,"[*]—and ends thus: "That your Majesty may always enjoy the glorious character of being the father of your people, and the friend of mankind, while all your faithful subjects contend to have it said of them, that they lived and died freemen, is the hearty prayer of your Majesty's most faithful subject,

"R. S."

The birthday entertainment consisted of all manner of sweetmeats in pyramids,—of the most generous wines, such as Burgundy and Champagne, and was ushered in with a prologue, written by Addison's friend Tickell, and spoken by Mrs. Younger; and concluded with an epilogue written by "Sir Richard" and spoken by Wilks the actor, who was very merry and free with his own character. Two hundred ladies and gentlemen were assembled; and after the "entertainment," which seems to have been partly musical, partly dramatic, was ended, a large table that stood in the area of the concert-house, was taken away, to make room for dancing, which was performed "with great decency and regularity."

[*] Steele's Letters, vol ii. p. 385.

Minuets, doubtless, opened the ball; it was probably ended with Sir Roger de Coverley, a dance which, Addison says, was named after the grandfather of his hero. An ode of Horace was set to music for this occasion.

The means for these gay doings, were, it seems very probable, found in the large sum of 500*l.* given to Welsted, a clerk in one of the offices of state, a *protégé* of Steele's. In the notes on the Dunciad, Welsted was censured for having received 500*l.* for writing anonymously for the ministry. The following letter clears the fame of Welsted; and shows, at the same time, how low political men in that day stood. Steele's terms " outlaw " and " pretender," in the address, were well paid for.

"Speaker's Chambers, Aug. 14th, 1715.*

" Dear Prue,

"I write this before I go to Lord Marlborough's, to let you know that there was no one at the Treasury but Kelsey, with whom Welsted left the order, and he is to be at the Treasury to-morrow between two and three, when, without doubt, the money will be paid."

" I have no hopes from that or anything else, but by dint of riches, to get the government of your ladyship.—Yours,

" RICHARD STEELE."

Relating a story in the " Englishman," of a poor man with a torn neckcloth, who received the intimation of a 10,000*l.* prize in the lottery with perfect *sang-froid*, he adds: — " I would much rather have had his temper than his fortune, for had it happened to me, I should have given it, like a slave as I am, *to a woman who despises me without it.*" Again, Sir Richard sneers at his wife's love of money in the following postscript.

"Your man Sam owes me threepence, which must be de-

* Steele's Cor. vol. ii. p. 383.   † Ibid. p. 384.

ducted in the account between you and me; therefore, pray take care to get it in, or stop it." It would be well if he had imitated his wife's prudence. Debt pursued him through life, and poisoned all the happiness he had in looking on children whom he feared would be paupers; and on a wife who had his fondest affections. Like most public men he met with ingratitude: he had, he owned, a quick sense of ill-treatment, yet he strove to keep up his own spirits and good humour. "Whenever I am a malcontent," writes this most amiable of thoughtless men, "I will take care not to be a gloomy one, but hope to keep some stings of wit and humour in my own defence." He had, when he wrote that letter (undated), "not twenty shillings from court favour." Poor Steele; never was he so happy as in the society of his children—himself a child. "Your son," he wrote to Lady Steele from Hampton Court, "is mighty well employed in tumbling on the floor of the room, and sweeping the sand with a feather. He grows a most delightful child, and very full of play and spirit." "We are very intimate friends and playfellows; he begins to be very ragged, and I hope I shall be pardoned if I equip him with new cloaks and frocks, or what Mr. Evans and I shall think for his service."

It was the old story; devoted to his wife, Steele had many differences with her on money matters. What she called *thoughtless* expenditure he termed suitable generosity; doubtless *she* was right. Steele had an immense love of display; he reproached his wife that she was not fond enough of dress; that she had no wish to shine out, even at his expense. "Condescend to be," he adds, "what nature made you, the most beauteous and most agreeable of your sex." Then he puts in a significant postscript: "A quarter of Molly's schooling is paid." Though "he abhorred debt as much as treason," he was for ever writing to his dear, honoured, lovely Prue, either that he would search Pall Mall for a house, or about a new carriage and traffic in horses; all of which news seems always to have given sincere vexation to "Prue." Gout was coming on; he owns to a little intemperance and to much repentance; he would work his brains and fingers to procure plenty of means, and would ask nothing of Lady Steele in return but "to take delight in agreeable dresses, cheerful discourses, and gay sights, attended by him." Then, about his children, one extract more from the letters of this most good-natured man and fond parent:—

"Mrs. Moll grows a mighty beauty, and she shall be very prettily dressed, as likewise shall be Betty and Eugene; and if I throw away a little money in adorning my brats I hope you will forgive me. They are, I thank God, all very well; and the charming figure of their mother has tempered the likeness they bear to their rough sire."

The trial of the Earl of Oxford, the Bangorian controversy, and the profits and business of his commissions, are the subjects of many of Steele's letters at this time. An amusing account of his visit to the Duke and Duchess of Marlborough at Blenheim diversifies the biography of this most agreeable man.

In the summer of 1718 Sir Richard Steele, in company with Bishop Hoadly and Dr. Samuel Clarke, paid a visit to Blenheim. The great duke had some months before been attacked with palsy, but was still well enough to take much interest in the representation of "All for Love," which was got up by Lady Bateman, his granddaughter, by Lady Sunderland, and several persons in the neighbourhood.

Lady Bateman had asked Sir Richard Steele to write a prologue for the occasion; but he had not at that time complied. She expressed her disappointment; upon which Bishop Hoadly asked one evening for pen, ink, and paper, and the next morning presented a prologue to the lady, who spoke it in the evening, before the Duke and Duchess, the former shedding tears as he listened to a compliment from the child of his favourite daughter to himself. When the Bishop and Sir Richard were passing through the hall of Blenheim House to take their departure, Steele whispered to Dr. Hoadly, seeing an array of servants in rich liveries, " Does your lordship give money to all these fellows in laced coats and ruffles?" " No doubt," said the Bishop. " I have not enough," Steele whispered; then turning to the servants, he accosted them in a speech, saying, as he had found that they were "*men of taste*," he invited them all, as such, to Drury Lane, to see whatever play they chose, " he having then a share in the patent," which he owed to the friendship of the Duke of Marlborough.

All the contentions and doubts, the remonstrances on one side, the promises and professions on the other, so long marking the correspondence between Sir Richard and Lady Steele came to a sudden termination. In December 1718 he thus writes to Alexander Scurlock, the cousin of Lady Steele:—

Dec. 27th, 1718.

" Dear Cousin,

" This is to let you know that my dear and honoured wife departed this life last night.

" I desire my Aunt Scurlock and Mrs. Bevan, and you yourself, would immediately go into mourning, and place the charge for such mourning of those two ladies and your own to the account of, Sir,

" Your most affectionate kinsman,

" And most humble servant,

" RICH. STEELE."

The loved and tormented " Prue" was buried in Westminster Abbey, with this inscription merely on her gravestone:—" Dame Mary Steele, wife of Sir Richard Steele, Knight, daughter and sole heiress to Jonathan Scurlock, Esq., of the county of Carmarthen, died Dec. 26, 1718, aged 40 years, leaving issue one son and two daughters, Eugene, Elizabeth, and Mary."

The letters to which so copious a reference has been made, with the endeavour to present Steele's character in a domestic point of view, were fondly treasured by Sir Richard's eldest daughter, Elizabeth, afterwards Lady Trevor. At her death they came into the possession of her relative and executor, the Rev. David Scurlock, of Lovehill Place, Langley, Bucks; who, in writing to Mr. Nicholls, the editor of Steele's Letters, mentions the following fact:—

"Steele and Addison wrote the 'Spectator' chiefly in the room where I now write; they rented the house from my father. Though I have lately built a new house, I have religiously reserved the old part which is attached to it, and have made it my *sanctum sanctorum*. Oh! that it would inspire me with the genius that once inhabited it.

"Yours, &c.
"DAVID SCURLOCK."

In spite of this aspiration, Mr. Scurlock does not appear to have been a literary character; for he never found time to collect and edit Steele's letters; and at his death, the correspondence was found mixed up with some of his own letters, and was sent to Mr. Nicholls by Mrs. Scurlock with permission to publish. Steele survived his wife eleven years. It was during the year 1718, and most likely after the death of his prudent Prue, that he obtained a patent for bringing fish to market alive, and published an "account of his fish pond." Yet, projector as he was, he wrote, in 1720, against the South Sea scheme, two pieces, one called "The Crisis of Property," the other, "The Nation a Family."

He was always poor, and had the elements of poverty within him. Speculative, generous, fond of show, somewhat dissipated, at all events, very convivial, what hope was there of his being rich? He was also unlucky. In 1721, his patent as Governor of the Royal Company of Comedians was arbitrarily revoked by George I., and poor Steele lost 10,000*l.* He produced, however, in 1722, his play of the "Conscious Lovers," and the King made him a present (that beautiful comedy being dedicated to his unimaginative Majesty) of five hundred pounds.

Few letters of Steele's, except some short and tender ones to his children, now display those feelings which had been frankly poured out to Prue. In 1721 he thus commenced a diary for the perusal of his three children.

"*April 4th*, 1721.—I have lately had a fit of sickness which has awakened in me, amongst other things, a sense of the little care I have taken of my own family. And as it is natural for men to be more affected with the actions and sufferings and observations upon the rest of the world, set down by their predecessors, than by what they receive from other men, I have taken a resolution to write down in this book, as in times of leisure I may have opportunity, things past, or things that may occur hereafter, for the perusal and consideration of my son Eugene Steele and his sisters Elizabeth Steele and Mary Steele, my beloved children.

"*Easter Sunday, April 9th*, 1721.—After repeated perusal of Dr. Tillotson's 'Seventh Sermon,' and after having done certain acts of benevolence and charity to some needy persons, I went this day to the Holy Sacrament. In addition to the proper prayers of the church, I framed for my private use on this occasion the following prayer:—

"O Almighty God, I prostrate myself before Thy Divine Majesty, in hopes of mercy for all my former transgressions, through the merits of thy Son, Jesus Christ.

"Thou art my Maker, and knowest my infirmities, appetites and passions, and the miserable habit of mind which I have contracted through a guilty indulgence of them." Then, after a beautiful prayer for grace, he concludes: "Lord, O Lord, receive a broken and contrite heart."

Another entry is very characteristic of poor Steele; sanguine and imprudent in every stage of his life.

"*April* 29*th,* 1721.—I this day purchased fifteen assignments in the Fishpool, undertaking with a promissory note to deliver to Mr. Robert Wilke (who sold them to me), a bond of five hundred pounds upon demand, the said bond to be payable two years after this date."

To his daughters he recommended the example of their mother: they were placed under the care of Mrs. Keck, an excellent friend of Lady Steele's. He was most solicitous for their welfare, even to their handwriting, warning his "Betty" against flourishes — the fashion of the day, yet enforcing on them the rare merit of exactness in writing. In these children certain trials awaited him. Elizabeth, indeed, grew up beautiful and intelligent; she became after her father's death the wife of John Lord Trevor, and was universally beloved and respected.

Steele had one sister, Katherine, who was insane for some time before her death; to her he allowed thirty pounds a year, and ten pounds a year for her companion. But the chief object of his distress, in the latter part of his life, was the diseased condition of his son Eugene, who suffered dreadfully from an internal disorder. In October 1723, Richard writes from Bath to his daughter that he had gone to that place with a very heavy heart; in November, the news of Eugene's death reached him. "Do you and your sister," he wrote to Elizabeth, "stay at home, and do not go to the funeral. Lord grant me patience."

His letters were now chiefly dated from Hereford, where he lodged in the house of a mercer who received his rents; these amounted to 600*l.* a year, and after the death of his wife came to Steele. His debts, it appears, from a memoranda on a slip of paper, in his handwriting, amounted to 608*l.* for the liquidation of which he set apart a portion of his income. Besides his three children by Lady Steele, Sir

Richard had a claim on his parental offices, which few men would have regarded in the light in which he viewed it.

This was a natural daughter, whose mother was a relation of Tonson's the bookseller. Steele brought up this child with his own daughters, so that Elizabeth Steele imbibed the strongest affection for her; he educated her carefully, and gave her the same name (Elizabeth) as that of her legitimate sister. At one time Steele had destined *this* Elizabeth to become the wife of Richard Savage, and had intended to give her a *dot* of a thousand pounds; but the vicious, ungrateful conduct of the reprobate poet disgusted him, and Elizabeth became the wife of Mr. Arguston. ✳

Chequered as was Steele's private life, it was far less infelicitous than that of his friend Addison. In middle age, just before the beginning of that great work the "Spectator," Addison lost, as he wrote to Wortley Montagu, both his place, an estate in the Indies, and his mistress; his place was worth 2000*l.* a year; who or what his mistress was, whether Mistress Sacheverell or some other lady, does not appear. This, however, is certain, that Addison married for ambitious motives, and was wretched. "Of the estate in the Indies," Miss Aikin remarks, "no other notice has been found; and concerning the mistress he complains of having lost nothing has been discovered."

The following letter from Addison to Charles Earl of Halifax, is very characteristic of the prudent complaining man, whose delicacy did not interfere to prevent his pressing claims which a man of his station would in these days hesitate at any rate to prefer:—

"Nov. 30th, 1714.

"My Lord,

"Finding that I have miscarried in my pretentions to the Board of Trade, I shall not trouble your lordship with my resentments of the unhandsome treatment I have met with from some of our new great men, in every circumstance of that affaire, but must beg leave to expresse my gratitude to your Lordship for the great favour you have shown me on this occasion which I shall never forget. Young Cragges told me about a week ago that His Matie, tho' he did not think fit to gratifie me in this particular, designed to give me a recompense for my service under the Lord Justices, in which case your Lordship will probably be consulted. Since I find I am never to rise above the station in which I first entered upon publick businesse (for I now begin to look upon myself like an old sergeant or corporal), I would willingly turn my secretaryships in which I have served five different masters, to the best advantage I can, and as your Lordship is the only patron I glory in and have a dependence on, I hope you will honour me with your countenance in this particular. If I am offered lesse than a thousand pounds I shall beg leave not to accept it, since it will look more like a clerk's wages than a marke of His Majesty's favour. I verily believe that H. M. may think I had fees and perquisites belonging to me under the Lord Justices, but though I was offered a present by the South Sea Company, I never took that nor anything else for what I did, as knowing I had no right to it. Were I of another temper, my present place in Ireland might be as profitable to me as some have represented it. I humbly beg your Lordship's pardon for the trouble of such a letter, and do assure your Lordship that one of the greatest pleasures I shall receive in what ever I get from the government will be its enabling me to promote your honour and interest more effectually. I am informed Mr. Yard, besides a place and an annual recompense for serving the Lord Justices under King William, had considerable fees, and was never at the charge of getting himself elected in to the House of Commons.

"I beg your Lordship will give me leave to adde y^t I believe

I am the first man that ever drew up a P. of Wales's preamble, without so much as a medal for my pains.

"My Lord,
"Your Lordship's most obedient, and most humble servant,
"J. Addison."*

Addison had acted, as many men of talent at either university often do, as a tutor in a noble family. It happened that one of his pupils was Sir John Rushout, the second baronet of that name, and ancestor of the Northwick family. The original portrait of Addison by Kneller was painted for that pupil, who died in 1705.

In spite of Addison's losses, nevertheless, he found means, in 1711, to purchase the house and grounds of Bilston, near Rugby, his brother Gulston assisting in the purchase money.

Addison had, for some time, fixed his abode at Kensington, in order, it is said, to be near Holland House, and to attend at once to the education of its young occupant, Richard Earl of Warwick, and to engage the favour of his mother the Countess. Be that as it may, his friend Wortley Montagu seems to have been unable to induce him to leave the neighbourhood. That he was the young Earl's tutor is extremely doubtful: there seem, indeed, to have been but two periods in Addison's busy life in which he could have regularly fulfilled such an office; that of his residence in Oxford, and that of his travelling in Italy; now, whilst Addison was travelling, Lord Warwick was in his cradle. Even Dr. Drake, who could have discovered anything, had there been anything to discover, has been unable in his "Essays illustrative of the 'Tatler,' 'Spectator,' and 'Guardian,'" to bring any one fact to bear upon the question.

* Additional MSS. 7121, pp. 15 and 16. From a volume of MS. letters to Charles Montagu, Earl of Halifax, from various people of the time.

Addison was, at all events, an admirable friend and guide for the wild young nobleman; and he was solicitous to attract his childish tastes to the best mental food for children — natural history. He hunted out birds' nests for the boyish peer, and sent a hen's nest with "fifteen eggs, covered over with a broody duck," which might satisfy his lordship's curiosity a little. Then he invites him to a "concert of music, found in a neighbouring wood;" "a lark, that by way of overture, sings and mounts till she is almost out of hearing, and afterwards falling down leisurely, drops to the ground as soon as she has ended her song." The whole finished by a nightingale that had something of an Italian manner in her diversions. But write as he did, and talk as he might, and probably Addison *was* talkative with children, he could not elevate the character of the young scapegrace to any high standard.

Woe was the day when Addison first liked the child, as it appears he may have done, for the mother's sake; for that mother was wholly unworthy of being the companion of this superior being. It was said by Johnson that Addison long sought her ladyship's favour. "The inequality of their respective stations made *him* timorous and *her* contumacious." To our ideas no such great inequality in the conditions of this infelicitous couple appears to justify *her* pride or *his* submission. Title is an arbitrary distinction, separating the classes in foreign nations, because there the higher orders of professional men are educated merely to their profession, not generally as gentlemen. In England it has always been otherwise. The aristocratic professions, the church, the bar, medicine in its higher branches, the army and navy, comprise the bulk of our younger sons of peers, baronets, and esquires. Addison, as the son of a clergyman, was a gentleman by birth. As Addison he was much more. A member of parliament, Under-secretary of State, may match with any widowed peeress in Great Britain, and feel her equal. We are speaking of mere conventional distinctions, of ranks as they then stood and as now they stand. On the 2nd of August, 1716, he took the step which is popularly believed to have been fatal to his peace, and was united to Charlotte Countess-Dowager of Warwick, daughter of Sir Thomas Middleton, of Chirk Castle, Denbighshire, by a co-heiress of Sir Orlando Bridgman. He had solicited her, according to Dr. Johnson, by a very "long and anxious courtship," and she had returned it by "playing with his passion." "His advances," adds the doctor, "at first were certainly timorous, but grew bolder as his reputation and influence increased, till at last the lady was persuaded to marry him, on terms much like those on which a Turkish princess is espoused, to whom the sultan is reported to pronounce, 'Daughter, I give thee this man for thy slave.' The marriage," Dr. Johnson states, "neither found nor made them equal."

Miss Aikin disbelieves this statement; but, in the absence of evidence, we cannot but adopt the belief of those who were almost contemporary with Addison, and the result almost establishes the fact. One daughter, it is true, blessed this joyless marriage, survived Addison, and became the mistress of Bilston Grange. But neither her infantine attractions, nor the society of his lady wife, could keep Addison at home. Yet greater prosperity than ever was Addison's portion the year after his marriage; and in 1717 he was made Secretary of State, an office which he afterwards resigned upon a pension of 1500*l.* a year. He now took up his abode at Holland House, that fine old structure which once belonged to the gallant Earl of Holland, the handsome lover of Henrietta Maria. The vicinity was then resorted to for the air; even in the time of Sir Walter Scott it had a great seclusion about it, giving it, the author of Waverley thought, its greatest charm, in spite of what he calls "its tumble-down look, its bastard Gothic, and its heavy front." Here formerly stood a gateway, now separated and the piers only standing, the work of Nicholas Stone, master-mason to James I. Addison had long made Kensington his occasional abode; he now tempted the dangerous splendours of the countess's home. He only tried them three years. His health must have been declining even when he was married; and asthma had rendered his labours at the Treasury almost insupportable. Many things are laid to the account of hard work which ought, with more justice, to be set down to errors of diet or to intemperance. In 1718 we find him writing to Dean Swift that he had been drinking the waters at Bristol. One of his latest traits was his kindness to Mrs. Clark, Milton's last surviving daughter. On hearing that she was still alive, he sent for her, requesting that if she had any papers of her father's she would bring them with her, as evidence of her being Milton's daughter. On seeing her, however, he said, "Madam, you need no other voucher than your face," alluding to her resemblance to her father's picture; he then presented her with a purse of gold, promising to provide for her in future, but his death frustrated this design. Addison had blessed God for his ability to retire from office, but peace was not to be his lot; an odious political quarrel separated him from Steele, to whom he had been accustomed to pour out his inmost soul. Among the old friends with whom Addison, rushing from the thraldom of his countess, used to drink a bottle of claret, or perhaps, a bumper of brandy, the once light-hearted Steele no longer appeared. He had joined the opposition to the Peerage Bill and attacked it in a paper called "The Plebeian." Addison was then still in the ministry, and called upon by Lord Sunderland, retorted in a paper designated "The Old Whig." Addison, on this occasion, rose superior to his opponent, in courtesy as well as wit. He was accused, however, but unjustly, of calling Steele "Little Dicky." Steele, however, retorted by some personalities, especially in reply to "The Old Whig," that Addison was so old a Whig that he had quite forgotten his principles. With these, and similar animadversions, did the former schoolfellows part, and part for ever.

Addison was now sinking into his grave. Dropsy had come on; he bore up with fortitude; perhaps the hardest effort is in such a case to resign oneself to life. At length, finding all chance of prolonged existence at an end, he sent away his physicians, and prepared to meet death with calmness. It was said, and a tradition has always existed, that he was habitually intemperate. The room, we believe the library, in Holland House, is still pointed out wherein he wrote, a table being placed at either end, and a bottle of brandy, and as the author of the immortal "Spectator" walked to and fro, sometimes thinking, sometimes dictating to others, he found a glass always convenient to his hand: it may have been a medical precaution, for spasms sometimes come on, which nothing but stimulants can relieve, in dropsy. Yet the general impression is that Addison exceeded even the least temperate of his time; and it was a time of intemperance.

His death-bed was, however, touching, and almost sublime. Party feeling seemed to have yielded to the enlarged views of a Christian on the confines of a higher state. He sent for Gay, a needy author then, and asked him his forgiveness. Gay could not imagine what there had been in Addison's conduct towards him to forgive. In Anne's time there had been great political differences between them, but in Anne's grave they seemed to be laid. Some wrong there was, however, to Gay, that lay in the very depths of Addison's conscience. He was in a condition of extreme debility, and thus kindly, forgivingly, they parted. We wish he had sent for Steele.

"With his hopes of life," Dr. Young, author of the "Night Thoughts," relates, "he dismissed not his concern for the living." After his interview with Gay, he sent for the young Lord Warwick, "a youth," Young says, "finely accomplished, but not above being the better for good impressions from a dying friend." The youth came; life was glimmering in the socket; Addison was silent. "Dear Sir, you sent for me. I believe and hope," cried the young man, "that you have some commands for me: I shall hold them most sacred." Life was ebbing fast; Addison grasped the hand of the young Earl. "See," he faintly said, with a last effort, "in what peace a Christian can die." He spoke feebly these last words, and soon expired.

Thus died one to whom the English nation owes the formation of mind and character in its youth of modern times. A gentler monitor never wrote for the delight of ages; a truer friend never existed; a more religious man—his faith being as pure from Calvinism as it was from superstition, —never combated with this world's sins and temptations than Addison. We would willingly draw a veil over his reported habits of intemperance; but if that cannot be done, we may plead that they were the effect rather of unhappiness than of criminal self-indulgence. He died on the 17th of June 1719, having just entered his forty-eighth year.

In the dead of the night his remains were conveyed to Westminster Abbey, and by torchlight the procession, in front of which walked Bishop Atterbury, moved round the shrine of Edward the Confessor to the Chapel of Henry VII. Gladly would we record the name of Steele among the mourners, and, amid so much that was obscure, we may hope that his form, wrapped in funereal garb, may have followed his earliest friend to his resting-place, but there exists no statement of the fact.

Steele survived Addison ten years. In one of his works he refers, in a beautiful passage, already quoted, to the friendship between himself and Addison, and speaks of their alienation in mournful terms.

The death of Steele was comparatively obscure. He became paralytic, and retired to his estate, left by his wife, at Llangunno, near Carmarthen, where he died on the 1st of September 1729. He was buried, according to his own wish, privately. He was, said the prelate who preached his funeral sermon, "a coquet to virtue; made continual advances, and seemed just on the point of yielding himself up to the comely dame who courted him, as she once did Hercules, when, on a sudden, he would flounce off, flirt back, and sink into the arms of pleasure."

"He would have been," the panegyrist adds, "what he was, had Addison never been born, but Addison would have died with narrow fame had he never had a friendship with Sir Richard Steele, whose compositions have done eminent service to mankind."

From that opinion many will differ, but all who know Steele's works well will allow that "he had an art to make people hate their follies, and he showed gentlemen a way of becoming virtuous with a good grace."

His writings, in truth, still insure our love for his memory, whilst his errors are long since forgotten.

Of the daughters who survived Steele, the two Elizabeths alone lived to any mature age. Mary, his youngest daughter, died at the hot-wells at Bristol, soon after her father, of consumption. The right Elizabeth and the wrong lived on. Elizabeth the legitimate, as Lady Trevor, occupied a high position in society. She had her father's wit, his good-nature, his extravagance, and some portion of his talents. Her only child, Diana Maria, was remarkably beautiful, though, strange to say, an idiot, who died at four years of age.

Elizabeth the illegitimate, Mrs. Ayreton, was of a poetic turn; she was very amiable as well as intellectual, and the affection of Lady Trevor for her was marked not only by her sisterly regard for her, but by her adoption of her two children after her death, and receiving them into her family as her own, a trait strongly symptomatic, in Lady Trevor, of the *Steele* nature. Mrs. Thomas, the elder of these orphans, was

Lady Trevor's companion till her death. To her son the letters of Steele's which have been so largely quoted were intrusted.

Besides the *wrong* Elizabeth, Sir Richard Steele left a natural son, named Dyer, who is said to have borne a very strong resemblance (as such sons generally do, nature thus marking out the shame and the exposure) to his gifted, erring, repentant father.

MAGDALEN HERBERT AND DR. DONNE.

QUOTATION FROM LORD HERBERT OF CHERBURY. — THE NEWPORTS AND HERBERTS. — STATE OF MONTGOMERYSHIRE. — LORD HERBERT OF CHERBURY. — ANECDOTES OF HIM. — HIS CHARACTER. — MAGDALEN HERBERT'S PRIDE IN HER SONS. — SHE IS CALLED THE AUTUMNAL BEAUTY. — GEORGE HERBERT. — DR. DONNE'S HISTORY. — IZAAK WALTON. — BISHOP ANDREWS. — MAGDALEN'S SECOND MARRIAGE. — DONNE CALLED THE PSEUDO-MARTYR : MADE DEAN OF ST. PAUL'S. — GEORGE HERBERT IN HIS PARISH. — DEATH OF MAGDALEN HERBERT, AND OF HER SON GEORGE. — DEATH AND MONUMENT OF DR. DONNE.

MAGDALEN HERBERT AND DR. DONNE.

"My mother," proudly says Lord Herbert of Cherbury in his autobiography, "was Magdalen Newport, daughter of Sir Richard Newport and Margaret his wife, daughter and heir of Sir Thomas Bromley, one of the privy council and executors of Henry VIII. By these ancestors I am descended of Talbot, Devereux, Grey, Corbet, and many other noble families, as may be seen in their matches, extant in the many fair coats the Newports bear."

There spoke the most accomplished man of his time,— a traveller, an ambassador:—according to his own ideas a philosopher, yet an idoliser of old names, noble races, and chivalric distinctions.

The world has some sympathy with such tastes in this our day: half a century ago it had none, and, if you asked a man who or what his grandfather was, he scarcely knew and cared not one whit, content if he had, like Bishop Watson, the power of simply saying that his "forefathers were not hewers of wood, nor carriers of water."

To acknowledge that the Newports could confer any dignity on the Herberts was an avowal of no small amount of candour, more especially in a Welshman. To our notions, however, Magdalen, as the mother of Lord Herbert himself, and of George Herbert the poet, added far more to the family lustre than generations of Greys, Talbots, and the like, though with reverence be it spoken. The exemplary matron who was honoured by the friendship of Dr. Donne, was the youngest daughter of Sir Richard Newport, in Shropshire; her husband, Richard Herbert, was one of a fearless, hot-tempered race, nearly related to the Earls of Pembroke, but living in the wilds of Monmouthshire, at Colebrook. Richard himself, a "black-haired" and "black-bearded" man, as his son describes him, was as hot and valiant as any of his family; stern and manly, of compact, handsome limbs, he was famed for having defended himself, with the aid of one friend only, John ap Howell Corbet, against a band of ruffians in the churchyard of Lanvroil, and, though prostrated by a wound from behind with a forest-bill, for walking home to his own house at Llyssyn. Meantime his skull was "cut through to the *pia mater* of his brain" (I quote his son, Lord Herbert); yet he recovered — for Welshmen had then nine lives — and offered single combat to the chief of the family by whom the attack had been instigated. The challenge was refused; and Richard, cooled down, espoused the fair, the pious, the learned Magdalen Newport.

Two races which may really be termed noble in the best acceptation of the word, were thus conjoined. The Herberts had anciently held a grand position in Montgomeryshire; the Castle of Montgomery had once been their seat. Various accidents had reduced their possessions; and Sir Richard, the grandfather of Lord Herbert of Cherbury and of George Herbert, had retired from the lofty castle to a lowlier seat, named Blackhall, so famous for its hospitality that it was a common saying among the country people when they saw any fowl rise, "Fly where thou wilt, thou wilt light at Blackhall;" for each day, at that lavish board, was the table twice spread for every meal. Old Sir Richard had been a soldier, a poor one, it is true, at first, but so brave, so loyal, that he was well paid for his services in the times of Edward VI. and of Mary, and bought, with his gains, estates which descended to his grandson Lord Herbert. It was a fine school for a swordsman, that same county of Montgomeryshire; day and night there was skirmishing with the outlaws and thieves who infested the wild mountain district; Sir Richard could scarce eat his dinner without taking half a score of prisoners; and the knight's power became so great, and his character stood so prominent for courage and honour, that "divers ancestors," says Lord Herbert, "of the better families now in Montgomeryshire were his servants, and raised by him."

Magdalen, when received as a bride into this time-honoured family, brought, it appears, little portion; for her family, Izaak Walton relates, "had suffered much in their estates, and seen the ruin of that excellent structure where their ancestors have long lived and been memorable for their hospitality."

It must have been somewhat a trial of faith to have seven sons and three daughters born to burden the estate of Edward Herbert with the needful provision for sons, who, being nobly descended, could not, as in our more practical times, resort to commerce as a means of subsistence; yet Magdalen, meekly, and piously, remembering that seven sons and three daughters were Job's number, was grateful for her share of these blessings, and thankful that they were defective neither in their shapes, nor in their reason. Often indeed would she reprove her offspring for not sufficiently praising God for this mercy.

To enumerate the names, and to describe the career of Magdalen's sons is almost her best panegyric; for, by an early widowhood, the charge of their career chiefly devolved on her.

Edward, afterwards Lord Herbert, was, says Horace Walpole, "a man of a martial spirit and a profound understanding, one of the greatest ornaments of the learned peerage." In the ancient house at Charlecote, near Stafford-on-Avon, the seat of the famous Lucys, there hangs a portrait of this "noble author." A short, somewhat insignificant nose, a small mouth encompassed with a black beard, and dark eyes, more peering than pleasant, do not carry out the grand description of Lord Herbert's personal advantages given by Walpole. "Had he been ambitious, the beauty of his person would have carried him as far as any gentle knight can aspire to go." "His valour," to quote the same authority, "made him a hero; his sound parts made him a philosopher." It was for his rare endowments, which James I. appreciated, that Herbert was made Knight Banneret when Henry Prince of Wales was installed Knight of the Garter. This was in 1603. After that early "initiation into the forms of chivalry, the spirit of which he drew from the purest founts of the 'Fairy Queen'" (our Horace again!), what an important, what an intellectual career he led! An ambassador in France, in order to advocate toleration to the Protestants, how good was his reply to the Duc de Luynes, who had the meanness to conceal behind a curtain a gentleman of the reformed religion, who was to hear and to judge how little would be done by James I. for the French Protestants. When the haughty De Luynes exclaimed, "We are not afraid of you," Herbert, smiling, promptly replied, "If you had said you had not loved us, I should have believed you, and given you another answer. In the mean time, what I will tell you is, that we know very well what we have to do." Whereupon De Luynes, rising, cried out, "By Heaven! were you not Monsieur the ambassador, I know very well how I would use you." "As I am the ambassador from the King of Great Britain," Sir Edward answered, "so am I also a gentleman; and my sword" — laying his hand on it — "shall give you satisfaction if you wish it. No ceremony! no ceremony!" he added, seeing De Luynes prepare to accompany him to the door; "after such language, ceremony is needless."

After this Herbert went off to Cognac, where he was told

by the Maréchal St. Geran that he was not in safety. "I am safe," answered Herbert, "whenever I have my sword by my side." He was afterwards recalled; but, the gentleman who stood behind the curtain, testifying that De Luynes had given the first affront, Sir Edward's conduct was placed before King James in its proper light, and he was again sent as ambassador into France. He continued to enjoy royal favour, and, in 1625, was created a baron of the kingdom of Ireland by the title of Lord Herbert of the Castle Island. He seems, by his loyalty during the civil wars, to have been reduced to great poverty, and obliged to sue for a pension from parliament, by way of compensation for losses, in 1644. His castle at Montgomery was demolished, for which also he claimed satisfaction. During all this life of business, and vicissitude, Lord Herbert never neglected study. "As a public minister," says Horace Walpole, "he supported the dignity of his country even when its prince disgraced it; and that he was qualified to write its annals as well as to ennoble them, his 'History of Henry VIII.' proves, and must make us lament that he did not complete, or that we have lost, the account he purposed to give of his embassy. These busy scenes were mingled with and terminated by meditation and philosophical inquiries. Strip each period of its excesses and errors, and it will not be easy to trace out and dispose the life of a man of quality into a succession of employments which would better become him." [*]

Such was Lord Herbert: valour in youth; the business of the state in middle age; repose, and science, and letters in later life. Unhappily for himself, and perhaps for those who were exposed to the influence of his great abilities, and attractive manners, during his life, Lord Herbert of Cherbury was a deist. Leland calls him a most "*conscientious* deist." In his work "De Veritate," Lord Herbert asserted the sufficiency, universality, and absolute perfection of natural re-

[*] Royal and Noble Authors, vol. iii. p. 22.

ligion, with a view to discard all revelation as needless; and this book was his favourite production: it was the effort of his eccentric mind on which he placed the greatest stress,—the work, and the only one, which was recorded as his on his tombstone. So justly was it said by Grainger, "that he was at once wise, and capricious; a man who redressed wrongs, and quarrelled for punctilios; hated bigotry in religion, and was himself a bigot in philosophy; exposed himself to such dangers as other men of courage would carefully have declined, and called in question the fundamentals of a religion which none had the hardiness to dispute except himself." Of his superstition, the following account of his inducement to publish the "De Veritate" is a sufficient proof.

"Being thus doubtful in my chamber, one fair day in the summer, my casement being open to the south, the sun shining clear and no wind stirring, I took my book 'De Veritate' in my hands, and, kneeling on my knees, devoutly said these words: 'O Thou eternal God, author of the light which now shines on me, and giver of all inward illuminations, I do beseech Thee, of Thine infinite goodness, to pardon a greater request than a sinner ought to make. I am not satisfied enough whether I shall publish this book: if it be for Thy glory, give me some sign from heaven; if not, I shall suppress it.' I had no sooner spoken these words but a loud, though yet gentle noise, came forth from the heavens, for it was like nothing on earth, which did so cheer and comfort me that I wot my petition was granted."

His "History of the Life and Reign of Henry VIII.," a book scarcely ever perused in our days of rapid reading, was published in 1649, a year after his death; and, however the accomplished Lord Herbert may have judged of his own works, it is certainly that by which he is still best known.

With all his acquirements Lord Herbert must sorely have grieved the believing and religious mother to whom he owed the care of his youth and his great attainments. She superintended the education of her sons, and had them, until they went to public schools, instructed by her chaplain. But if Edward disappointed maternal hopes, in so far as the all-important question of *belief* was concerned, there were many sources of satisfaction, as well as of pride, in the others. Richard, her second son, distinguished himself in the Low Countries, and fell bravely at Bergen-op-Zoom. It is recorded of this gallant young soldier that he had the scars of four-and-twenty wounds on his body. William was also brave as a lion, and was famed likewise for gallant exploits in Flanders. Charles, the next of the seven, became a fellow of New College, Oxford, where he died young. George, the poet, deserves more especial notice when this list is completed. Henry, the next brother to George, went to court, was made Master of the Revels, and a gentleman of the King's Privy Chamber: he accumulated a good fortune. Thomas, the youngest, was a naval officer of a very high reputation; but thinking himself neglected, after many eminent services, he retired in disgust and melancholy, the only one whose life had been unprosperous, a circumstance fully accounted for by the neglected state of the navy at that period.

George, the poet and divine, whose simple and beautiful verses, for many a long year forgotten, have of late years been the delight of reflective minds, was a king's scholar at Westminster, and then elected to Trinity College, Cambridge, in 1608. He was chosen orator of the university, and held that post eight years. Acquirements in modern languages were then esteemed almost essential for an aspirant youth; and George, hoping to become secretary of state, like Naunton or Nethersole, learned Spanish, — the fashionable language in James's time, — as well as Italian, and French. It seems strange that a fellow of a college should leave his learned seclusion, as George Herbert often did, to follow the court. Yet George Herbert was to be seen in the gay resorts of Whitehall, at Theobalds, or Windsor: Buckingham was then in all his splendour, Ben Jonson was writing the Masques, and Henry Herbert at his post as Master of the Revels. Even the worldly and vitiated court seems never to have sullied the holy, gentle spirit of George Herbert. After the death of the Duke of Richmond and the Marquis of Hamilton, his hopes of preferment were ended; he took orders, married, and became a prebend of Lincoln, and rector of Bemerton, near Salisbury.

It was now that his mother saw the good fruits of that care which had guarded her sons from much evil. When they went to college, and during her widowhood, she went to reside first at Oxford, where she remained four years, in order to watch over the youth that requires so much judgment, and more especially so much tenderness, to keep it right, or to reclaim it when wrong. She used to say, "As our bodies take a nourishment suitable to the meat on which we feed, so our souls do insensibly take in vice by the example of conversation with wicked company." Ignorance of vice she wisely deemed "the best preservative of virtue;" and yet how madly we allow our sons to see, to know, even to become familiarised with, all that is coarse, self-indulgent, extravagant, and sometimes criminal, in public schools, and elsewhere!

At Oxford, Magdalen, still handsome, was styled "the autumnal beauty;" that designation being given to her by one in whose society she took infinite delight when at the university, the famous Dr. Donne. At Oxford, Izaak Walton tells us, "her great and harmless wit, her cheerful gravity, and her obliging friendship, gained her an acquaintance and friendship with most men of any eminent worth, and learning, that were at that time in or near the university."

Donne, afterwards Dean of St. Paul's, became the firm and attached friend of Magdalen Herbert. It was a friendship cemented by the delightful power of conferring favours with delicacy on her side, and by a grateful yet independent spirit on his part. Burdened with a wife and seven children, Donne yet refused to enter holy orders, merely because such a step would have afforded him a living. When eventually he became a clergyman, he devoted himself to his calling with the truest zeal and piety that man could ever evince. On leaving Oxford he wrote these lines descriptive of the intelligent and high-minded Magdalen Herbert, in whose society many of his happiest hours were passed:—

"No spring nor summer beauty has such grace
As I have seen on an autumnal face."

Then, in respect to her conversation, he adds:—

"In all her words, to every hearer fit,
You may at revels or in council sit."

Poor Donne was doomed to many privations; and as far as his own sufferings were concerned, he might have borne them with that patience which distinguishes the clergy of this country. But his heart often bled to witness, in the early part of his career, the sufferings of his wife, and to behold his children in want almost of the necessaries of life.

"It is now spring," he writes, "and all the pleasures of it displease me; every other tree blossoms, and I wither. I grow older and not better; my strength diminishes, and my load grows heavier; and yet I would fain do or be something, but that I cannot tell what is no wonder in this time of my sadness: for to choose is to do, but to be no part of anybody is to be nothing; and so I am, and shall so judge myself unless I could be so incorporated into a part of the world as by business to contribute some sustentation to the whole."

Donne was eccentric through life. A picture of him at Lincoln's Inn is mentioned by Grainger: it is, says that writer, all enveloped with a darkish shadow, his face and features hardly discernible, with this ejaculation and wish thereon: "Domine illumina tenebras meas." This wish, adds Grainger, "was afterwards accomplished when, at the persuasion of King James, he entered into holy orders."

He became an admirable preacher, but was more known as a poet than a divine; yet of his poems it has been said:—

> "'Twas then plain Donne in honest vengeance rose,
> His wit harmonious, but his rhyme was prose."

Satire was Donne's forte; but, as Dryden observed, his "thoughts were debased by his versification."

Donne, on becoming Dean of St. Paul's, was also vicar of St. Dunstan-in-the-West. Amongst the congregation who sat beneath him was a humble shopkeeper, who during the week exercised his calling in the Royal Burse in Cornhill, built by Sir Thomas Gresham. The shops over the Burse were scarcely seven feet and a half long, and only five wide; yet here, day after day, toiled Izaak Walton, "the common father of all anglers," and the most charming writer of biography in our language.

During the seven days of labour, Walton's delight was to steal out on an afternoon, with two friends named Roe, whom he has celebrated, to the river Lea in Hertfordshire, rising just above Ware, and falling into the Thames below Blackwall. But on Sundays Walton steadily, and much to his own benefit, attended Dr. Donne's sermons, and became, what he terms it, his convert.

Fly-fishing was known to Walton only through a friend, whose name would have long ago gone into oblivion had it not been connected with that of Walton; this friend was no less a person than the chief cook of the Protector Cromwell, Thomas Barker by name, a gossiping old man who lived in an alms-house near the Gate House in Westminster, and an enthusiast who had spent much money as well as time in fly-fishing. He published a work called "Barker's Delight, or the Art of Angling;" and he had, like Walton, a vein of humour in his work, that rendered what one cannot call a *dry* subject, highly amusing.

To Walton we owe the completion of a biography of Dr. Donne, which had been commenced by Sir Henry Wotton. On the death of the Doctor he wrote also some verses, beginning, " Our Donne is dead." Walton was also the biographer of George Herbert, although he had no personal acquaintance with the poet, but derived his information from others; yet the memoir is singularly complete and graphic.

Notwithstanding the wit and knowledge of the human mind displayed by Dr. Donne, he was, during the whole of his life, an eccentric being. The following letter from him to Lady Magdalen speaks at once of his obligations, and of her kindness, whilst at the same time it attests the confidence he had in her judgment, and the opinion he entertained of her piety, in intrusting his hymns to her care. These productions were unhappily lost.

" MADAM,
"Your favours to me are everywhere. I use them and have them. I enjoy them at London and leave them there, and yet find them at Mitcham. Such riddles as these become things inexpressible, and such is your goodness. I was almost sorry to find your servant here to-day, because I was loth to have any witness of my not coming home last night, and indeed of my coming this morning. But my not coming was excusable, because earnest business detained me, and my coming this day is by the example of your St. Mary Magdalen, who rose early on Sunday to seek that she loved most, and so did L And from her and myself I return such thanks as are due to one to whom we owe all the good opinion that they whom we need most have of us. By this messenger and on this good day I commit the enclosed holy hymns and sonnets (which for the matter, not the workmanship, have escaped the fire) to your judgment and to your pro-

tection too, if you think them worthy of it; and I have appointed this enclosed sonnet to usher them to your happy hand." *

Amongst other learned men, Lancelot Andrews, Bishop of Winchester in the reigns of James I. and Charles I., was a staunch friend of the Herbert family. Andrews afforded a proof that the acquirement of general knowledge and of modern languages is not incompatible with the most profound learning. Secretary Walsingham, knowing his superior attainments, brought him to court, where, as one of the royal chaplains, he preached to the fastidious, yet, in his case, approving Queen Elizabeth; yet he was, nevertheless, and especially by one of the learned compilers of the "Biographia," accused of introducing bad taste in his sermons, which were overloaded, according to that critic, with pedantic allusions. Posterity, however, thinks otherwise, and Andrews' sermons are deemed a model of orthodox composition, and a treasury of thought.

The personal character of Lancelot Andrews made his friendship a proud distinction. He was a bishop who realised one's most exalted ideas of the prelacy, viewed in its relation to society. During the last six years of his life, his private alms, given in secresy, were found after his death to amount to 1500*l*. alone. One of his bequests was a sum of 200*l*., which was to be distributed immediately after his death among maid-servants " of good report " who had lived seven years in one service. His munificence to all public institutions was on a splendid scale; his hospitality so noted that it used to be said that Bishop Andrews kept Christmas all the year round; and his abundant table was open to all, — to scholars and men of worth, of whatever degree, as to noblemen and prelates; and his courtesy, his " gravely facetious " discourse, were the theme of all praise. He dined at twelve o'clock, spending the intervening time

* See Miss Costello's " Celebrated Englishwomen," vol. i. p. 385.

in study. Like all hard-working men, he hated morning visits: "Those are no scholars," he used to say, "who come to me before noon." Several hours in the afternoon were, however, always allotted by him to conversation.

Such was Andrews, who, with Dr. Donne, formed the intimate circle around Magdalen Herbert: so pure in morals and in mind, that King James, rebuked by his loftiness of character, refrained, in the presence of Andrews, from his coarse and undignified jokes; so wise that Lord Clarendon thought that, had he succeeded Bancroft in the primacy, the infection of schism would never have been known in the Church; so above all reproach, so entitled to all praise, that Milton, differing from him in principle, wrote a Latin elegy on his death.

No wonder that, under these influences, George Herbert, during the first years of his residence in Cambridge, declared that his poor abilities should ever be consecrated to the service of God. "I beg of you," he adds, "to receive this as one testimony:—

> "My God, where is that ancient heat towards Thee
>   Wherewith whole shoals of martyrs once did burn,
> Besides their other flames? Doth poetry
>   Wear Venus' livery? only serve her turn?
>
> . . . .
>
> Or, since Thy ways are deep, and still the same,
> Will not a verse run smooth that bears Thy name?
>   Why doth that fire which, by Thy power and might,
> Each breast doth feel, no braver fuel choose
> Than that — which one day worms may chance refuse?
>
> . . . .
>
> Each cloud distils Thy praise, and doth forbid
>   Poets to turn it to another use;
> Roses and lilies speak of Thee: to make
>   A pair of cheeks of them is Thy abuse."

One anxiety alone possessed the mind of Magdalen Herbert in regard to her son George. She dreaded contamination from the court life into which he was often led. She opposed his desire to travel, and, submitting to her maternal wishes, George Herbert gave up his wish to visit foreign lands. Probably the deistical tendencies of her eldest son alarmed the mother, whose greatest solicitude was for the immortal welfare of her children. In the lines called "Affliction," George Herbert pointed to the disappointment which duty had imposed on him.

> "Whereas my birth and spirit rather took
>   The way that takes the town,
> Thou didst betray me to a singing book,
>   And wrap me in a gown.
> I was entangled in a world of strife
> Before I had the power to change my life.
>
> . . . .
>
> Now I am here, what thou wilt do with me
>   None of my books will show.
> I read, I sigh, and wish I were a tree:
> To fruit or shade, at least some bird would trust
> Her household with me, and I would be just." *

A second marriage on the part of a mother is generally followed by alienation, if not by a total rupture of the filial bond. A woman, it has been said, may love the children of her husband; a man seldom loves those of another man, the first husband of his wife. To this saying the second marriage of Magdalen Herbert forms a notable exception. Young as she was when she became a widow, it was not until her youngest son had attained his sixteenth year that she married again. Her choice fell upon Sir John George Danvers, the brother of Henry, Earl of Danby in the time of Charles I., by whose death in 1643 the title became extinct, but the estates devolved upon Sir John, the second brother. Danvers Street, in Chelsea, still recalls the family to whom Magdalen Herbert now allied herself, Danvers House having been situated near, or in Cheyne Walk.

There was a considerable difference of age between Magdalen Herbert and her friend Donne, whose qualities she prized so highly; her sympathies were engaged in his behalf by the misfortunes of his early life. Donne was descended, by his mother's side, originally from Sir Thomas More, and his family were of the Romish faith; many endeavours had been made by his mother to keep him in that belief, but Donne, at nineteen, examined into controversial matters, and the result was a sound and lasting Protestantism. Many anecdotes are recorded of him which show how conscientious was his mind. Amongst others, he refused, for some time, to take orders, alleging previous irregularities of life which might bring dishonour on that sacred calling. His early life had been marked by misfortune. Having married privately the daughter of Sir George More, then Chancellor of the Garter, Donne was not only dismissed from a place he then held as secretary to Sir Thomas Egerton, Lord Keeper, but committed to prison; at the same time Samuel Brooke, who afterwards became Master of Trinity College, Cambridge, and who married the runaway couple, and his brother, Christopher Brooke, were similarly treated — the three being sent to separate prisons. Donne was released first, and made every effort to get his friends liberated. A long separation from his wife, and a tedious lawsuit, in order to recover her, ensued. The erring couple then suffered poverty and dependence, but were eventually forgiven, and a moderate provision made for their support.

Donne soon became eminent, and his "Pseudo-Martyr," written to prove that Romanists ought to take the oath of allegiance,— a work which Warburton calls "absurd and blasphemous trash,"—procured him the deanery of St. Paul's. King James conferred the deanery upon him in his usual singular manner. Sending for Dr. Donne, he began thus — before eating, though dinner was served — "Dr. Donne, I have invited you to dinner, and though you sit not down with me, yet I will carve to you of a dish that I know you love well; for knowing you love London, I do therefore make you

Dean of St. Paul's, and when I have dined, then do you take your beloved dish home to your study, say grace there to yourself, and much good may it do you."

Dr. Donne died of consumption, which came on after a fever, in his fifty-ninth year. His person was graceful and comely, whilst there was so delightful a combination of gaiety and sentiment, or what was then termed "melancholy," in his conversation, that he must have been one of the most fascinating of men. "His aspect," we are told, was "cheerful, and such as gave a silent testimony of a clear-knowing soul, and of a conscience at peace with itself." His melting eye showed too a soft heart, "full of noble compassion; of too brave a soul to offer injuries." Yet, like many men, chastened by after life, he was of a nature highly passionate, yet very humane, and of so tender a spirit that he never beheld the miseries of mankind without pity and relief.

His work on Self-Homicide was dedicated to Lord Herbert of Cherbury; it is called "Biathanus," and, later in life, was bitterly regretted by its author, and he often was so nearly suppressing it, that it "was only not burnt." "Know the date of it," he wrote to Lord Antrim, "and that it is a book written by Jack Donne, and not Dr. Donne. Reserve it for me if I live, and if I die I only forbid it the press and the fire. Publish it not, yet burn it not, but between those do what you like with it."

Thus did the chastened and purified man regard the learned, but questionable production of his youth. One of Dr. Donne's letters to Magdalen Herbert shows his devotion to her matronly and beautiful character, and is also very characteristic of himself.

"*To the worthiest lady Mrs. Magdalen Herbert.*

"Madam,

"As we must die before we have full glory and happiness, so before I can have this degree of it as to see you by a letter, I must also die; that is, come to London — to plague London, a place full of danger, vanity, and vice, though the court be gone. And such it will be till your return to redeem it. Not that the greatest virtue in the world, which is you, can be such a marshal as to defeat or disperse all the vice of this place; but as higher bodies remove, or contract themselves, when better come, so at your return we shall have one door open to innocence. Yet, Madam, you are not such an Ireland as produceth neither ill nor good, no spiders, no nightingales, which is a rare degree of perfection. But you have found and practised that experiment, that even nature, out of her detesting of emptiness, if we will make that our work to remove bad, will fill us with good things." *

With such friends and so gifted a family, Magdalen Herbert might be supposed to have been pre-eminently happy. But she had her cares: especially did she regret that her son George should delay his ordination. The court still had its charms for him; and there were not wanting friends who, in the then degraded state of the Church, did not hesitate to represent to him that it was a profession beneath the rank which his family held. To this, prompted by his mother, he replied: —

"It hath formerly been judged that the domestic servants of the King of Heaven should be of the noblest families on earth; and, though the iniquity of late times hath made clergymen meanly valued, and the sacred name of priest contemptible, yet I will labour to make it honourable by consecrating all my learning and my poor abilities to advance the glory of that God which gave them, knowing that I can never do too much for Him that hath done so much for me as to make me a Christian; but I will labour to be like

---

* Costello, vol. i. pp. 391-2.

my Saviour, by making humility lovely in the eyes of all men, and by following the merciful and meek example of the dear Jesus."

Stimulated by these high views, George Herbert became a deacon, and in 1626 a prebend of Layton Ecclesia, in the diocese of Lincoln.

He soon began the task of restoring the church, on which his mother sent for him to Chelsea, and addressed him thus:—

"George, I sent for you to persuade you to commit simony by giving your patron as good a gift as he has given you; that you give him back his Prebend, for it is not for your weak body and empty purse to build churches."

But George Herbert was resolute. He begged, indeed, for time for reflection; then, after asking her blessing, he begged her to forgive his being, at the age of thirty-three, for the first time an undutiful son to her, for he had made a vow to God that he would rebuild that church."

The result was that he brought his mother to his way of thinking. Subscriptions were then collected from friends. William Herbert, Earl of Pembroke, gave a hundred pounds, and other friends contributed; and thus, under the superintendence of Herbert, the most remarkable parish church that the country then afforded was completed.

It was a costly mosaic, in the form of an exact cross; and Herbert, as Walton relates, lived to see it "wainscoted so as to be exceeded by none." The reading-desk and pulpit he placed at a little distance from each other, and he made them of the same height; for neither, he said, should have precedency one over the other; "but that prayer and preaching, being equally useful, might agree like brethren, and have an equal share of estimation."

He had now to witness the decline of his admirable mother's life, and to console her in her last days.

"Comfort yourself," he wrote to her, "in the God of all

comfort, who is not willing to behold any sorrow but for sin. Madam, as the earth is but a point in respect of the heavens, so are earthly troubles compared to heavenly joys. Therefore, if either age or sickness lead you to those joys, consider what advantage you have over youth and health, who are now so near those true comforts."

The thread of life he observed to be like all other threads or skeins of silk, "full of snarls or incumbrances." Sickness he had always feared worse than death, because sickness would have interfered with his functions; but she had abundantly played her part in life. Her children were in the years of discretion and competent maintenance; her responsibilities for them were therefore ended. Did she trouble herself with temporal cares? For "those of estate," as he calls them, "of what poor regard ought they to be! since, if we had riches, we are commanded to give them away; so that the best use of them is, having, not to have them." Or did their rank enforce splendid living? "But, O God! how easily is that answered, when we consider that the blessing in the holy Scripture was never given to the rich, but to the poor. I never find Blessed be the rich! or Blessed be the noble! but Blessed be the meek, and blessed be the poor, and blessed be the mourners, for they shall be comforted."

Yet even to this faithful and holy man it had been a struggle to cast off his sword and fine clothes, yet he became the pattern of a parish priest, and left in his works the memorial of a saintly life.

Music, sacred music, was his delight. Who can ever visit Salisbury Cathedral without seeing, in imagination, his face upturned to heaven as he listened to those sacred strains that, he declared, so elevated his soul, that it was his heaven upon earth?

The Holy Apostolic Church was associated, in his mind, with her who was at rest in heaven long before he was summoned from earth. When asked by a clergyman, who visited him about a month before his death, what prayers he wished to have read to him, his answer was, "O Sir! the prayers of my *mother*, the Church of England; no other prayers are equal to those."

He died in 1635. Some years previously Dr. Donne had preached Magdalen Herbert's funeral sermon in Chelsea Church. Tears had denoted the true feeling with which the attached friend recorded the virtues of her who had indeed been all that was generous and kindly. She died in 1627, not having the happiness of witnessing her son's marriage with a cousin, one of the nine daughters of a Mr. Danvers, after an acquaintance of three days only.

Dr. Donne survived his friend, Magdalen Herbert, four years only. The last fourteen years of his life were saddened by the death of his wife, which took place in 1617, after the birth of her twelfth child. The calamity overwhelmed Donne with grief; it happened, as such sorrows often do happen, just after signal good fortune. Donne had then recently been created a Doctor of Divinity at Cambridge, on the special recommendation of King James I.

Such were these two friends, gifted, exemplary, sincere, constant. Their friendship was of that old-fashioned sort which modern times, improving us so greatly in many things, have never seen equalled. Society now is on too vast a scale; interests are too diffused; expediency is too much cherished, for the same single-hearted, trustful, and unvarying friendships to be frequent; though we will hope they are not unknown, even under the disadvantages of counter influences.

Dr. Donne's monument in St. Paul's is still the most striking of the tombs in that cathedral; nor is it to be wondered that it is so when we learn its history. Some time before his death, when he was emaciated by consumption, Donne caused a sheet to be wrapped round him, and gathered

DR. DONNE'S MONUMENT. 317

over his head like a shroud. He then closed his eyes, and, in that position, and covered in that manner, had his portrait drawn. It was from that likeness that Stone modelled the singular and startling monument. This tomb was taken out of Old St. Paul's, and is now in the crypt of the present cathedral.

SIR KENELM DIGBY
AND
SIR ANTHONY VAN DYCK.

CLARENDON'S REMARK ON SIR KENELM DIGBY. — BROUGHT UP BY LADY DIGBY AS A PROTESTANT. — LAUD HIS PRECEPTOR. — SIR KENELM'S PERSONAL AND MENTAL QUALITIES. — HIS ATTACHMENT TO VENETIA STANLEY. — HER PARENTAGE. — OBSTACLES TO THEIR UNION. — RECITAL OF SIR EVERARD DIGBY'S FATE. — MEMOIRS OF SIR K. DIGBY. — VENETIA AS BRIDESMAID TO ELIZABETH OF BOHEMIA. — DANCING IN THOSE DAYS. — MEMOIRS CONTINUED. — STORY OF ABDUCTION AND ESCAPE. — DIGBY'S SYMPATHETIC POWDER. — SEES VENETIA'S IMAGE. — HIS ENTERPRISE ABROAD. — CHARLES'S FAVOUR TO HIM. — HIS INTRODUCTION TO VANDYCK. — VANDYCK'S MARRIAGE. — SUCCESS, AND MODE OF LIVING. — VENETIA'S DEATH. — SIR KENELM'S GRIEF. — HE BECOMES A ROMANIST. — TROUBLES OF THE CIVIL WAR. — VANDYCK'S DEATH. — DEATH OF SIR KENELM DIGBY.

SIR KENELM DIGBY
AND
SIR ANTHONY VAN DYCK.

"Sir Kenelm Digby," Lord Clarendon remarks, "was a person very eminent and notorious throughout the whole course of his life, from his cradle to his grave." In this opinion Sir Kenelm himself did not concur. Born of an ancient race, although his father, Everard, was considered one of the most respectable of the Gunpowder Plot traitors, he remembered through life that his family was under an attainder. "I inherited," with bitterness he used to say, "from my father, only a foul stain in my blood." This was, however, more mournful than true: two of Sir Everard's manors being entailed, the crown was defeated in its efforts to confiscate them; and the infant Kenelm, only three years of age at his father's death, was secure in the possession of an income of 3000*l.* a year.

Gothurst, in Buckinghamshire, was Sir Kenelm's birthplace, his mother, Mary Mulsho, being one of the coheiresses of that property. With his attainder Sir Kenelm inherited another disadvantage,—his parents were Roman Catholics. It was a most unfashionable faith, and its professors were as certain of every kind of persecution as if they had been heathens. Recusancy, in fact, was far more dangerous in the seventeenth century than unbelief. With this cloud over the family, attainder and Romanism, the widowed Lady

Digby sacrificed her conscience to the safety of her son. She brought him up as a Protestant, and he was placed with Laud, afterwards Archbishop of Canterbury, for education.

Laud was then Dean of Gloucester, but was rapidly rising in the favour of James I.; he had also been President of St. John's, Oxford, and was well versed in all the peculiarities of youthful character; and a valuable man must he have been to form the intellect of a boy of ability. He was merry, which boys like; quick and hasty, which boys seldom dislike; sincere to an extent; zealous to a fault; and boys soon see through insincerity: the candid and fearless always carry the day with them; and, with their excitable natures, they sympathise with the zealous, and generally out-herod Herod. But one scarcely knows whether, as an anxious parent, one would have placed a son hereditarily disposed to Romanism, with Laud. He had then been fiercely attacked on account of his supposed papistry; and when, in 1617, he accompanied, as chaplain, King James to Scotland, had tried, with more zeal than discretion, to bring the church of that stiff-necked people into uniformity with that of England. "But the Scots were Scots," as Heylyn in his life of Laud expresses it, and chose to go their own way; and the energetic champion of what a vast number of Christians now deem the true Apostolic Church, was obliged to bide his time. His tragic death, of noble martyrdom, was subsequently the result of his early and late exertions.

Kenelm Digby must, however, have derived much of his learning, his taste, and the laudable ambition, without which a man of high birth is almost culpable, for *noblesse oblige* not in the mere sense of making high marriages, of squaring scutcheon to scutcheon, counting quartering against quartering, as the Germans do, but in maintaining with honour the name that destiny has given.

Laud was a man of vast designs; an aspirant that never quailed beneath an obstacle. Nothing is so infectious as half worldly, half holy aspirations; at all events he gave the young tyro an excellent education; for Clarendon, his friend, tells us, Sir Kenelm had every advantage; and one result of a well-considered training was apparent in "a great confidence and presentness of mind;" wisely specified by Clarendon, for without those advantages the most brilliant abilities are apt to be obscured. As he grew up, it became easy to prophesy that Kenelm, in spite of his father's crime, would distinguish himself in a court, wherein, except as working men, on whom James relied for what he called statecraft, the talents of society were all-essential. We cannot find a better description of this favourite of nature, than by adopting the words of Digby's friend.

"He was a man," Clarendon tells us, "of a very extraordinary person and presence, which drew the eyes of all men upon him, which were more fixed by a wonderful graceful behaviour, a flowing courtesy and civility, and such a volubility of language as surprised and delighted; and though in another man it might have appeared to have somewhat of affectation, it was marvellous graceful in him, and seemed natural to his size and mould of his person, to the gravity of his motion, and the tune of his voice and delivery."

At fifteen Digby was sent to Oxford, and entered at Gloucester Hall, well prepared for distinction. Thomas Allen, who was his tutor, thought so highly of his acquirements as to compare him to the celebrated Picus de Mirandula. After staying at Oxford two years, Kenelm proposed, according to custom, to travel, and from the years 1621 to 1623 there has been an hiatus in his annals, which is, in some measure, supplied by the following letter in the State Paper Office. By this, Digby, it appears, was employed by James I. in some office relative to the crown jewels; possibly he was intended to be the bearer of them to Spain, but afterwards deemed too young for so great a trust.

"Right Ho^ble Cosen,

"The 10th of this month I receaved in a l̃re of yo^rs commaundm^ts from his Matie to solicit the choice and dispatch of those Jewells, wch his will was to have sente him by M^r T̃rer (Mr. Treasurer). The next morninge earlie I wrote to understande my Lords pleasure, and to morrow afternoone is ye tyme appointed for the takinge them owt. In the other p̃te of yor l̃re I received for my selfe, a Jewell of greater valew p̃chance then my sourraigne conceaves; I mean his care to transporte thes Jewells sent for, by another; as paleinge* that iorney, with my yeeres, and state of bodie, in a most tender care, then I am, or can heereafter be worth to him. But it hath ever byn the pleasure of greate and good hartes to add more and more to their owne worckes; wch makes my Soueraigne (who gave me this otium cum dignitate) thus to confirme, and please me in y^t. On the other side S^r: if there be any latitude lefte betweene pleadinge merit, and showinge thankfullnes; it may please you to take knowledge from me that I have failed noe meatinge since the dep̃ture of that wistlie-lovinge Prince* in the first, and in the second place, that ingenious dutifull adventurer†; In wch coorse however I (neither havinge office, nor p̃ticuler direcc̃on) may seeme to have sailed alonge by the cautious and provident compass of my sup̃io^rs: yet beleeve y^t S^r, I ever kepte my harte, and one eye confident uppon that steddie motion of our North starr‡, the infallible prosp̃itie of whose wisdome grows (as I conceave) owt of the little variac̃on it hath.

"Lastlie S^r in accompt of p̃ticulers, the comission of trade wth the uttermost of o^r diligences, and powers; yet are the branches so many, and of so greate waighte, as doe rather concurr wth a Kinge, then a merchante harvest; the one expectinge not shorte but sounde retornes for his peoples good: the

---

* Charles I.   † Buckingham.   ‡ James I.

other returnes from hand to mouth, wth an end accordinglie, rather self, than the publique. The Commission of Fees continues still in an obscure destinie, once past the Seale, and recald; and now (for ought I know) either deade, or forgotten. This audit I presume to make, in respecte it hath pleased his Matie to comhaunde my service in both. Good S^r I humblie crave leave to kiss his hands from me, and profess that the remnant of my days, are dedicated to serve him, and give (besides prayers) wth Love, and the best discrecõn I have, till it shall please him to printe any of his own, more excellent characters into the humble harte of

"His faithfull Vassall
"& your true friend
"F. Brooke.

"Brooke House, March 6, 1622."*

The young courtier, whose studied phrases, in the letter thus quoted, recall the days of euphuism, appears, in spite of his father's sad fate, to have enjoyed the favour of King James. The earliest mention of the name of Digby occurs in a letter of news, addressed by Chamberlain to Carleton, remarking, that though Buckingham "hates the name of Digby, the King had knighted Sir Kenelm." This was in December, 1623, and it was on the thirteenth of that month James gave to the world the first proof of that signal favour which he exhibited to the son of one of the conspirators against his life. Possibly the King believed in the innocence of Sir Everard Digby.

Previously, however, to his travels, Sir Kenelm had formed, almost in his boyhood, the attachment which decided his fate in life. The object of his passion was Venetia, or, as she has been called by some, Anastasia Stanley, who realised in all but her

---

* Indorsed "To the right honorable his verie lovinge cosen Sr Edward Conway, Knighte, principal Secretarie to his Mat^{ie} at the Coort." — State Paper Office, No. 44, vol. cxxxix. Jas. I. Domestic Papers.

purity the notions that one forms of a true heroine of romance. Her birth, not an indispensable but an advantageous circumstance, was noble; her father, Sir Edward Stanley, of Tonge Castle in Shropshire, being the grandson of Edward, third Earl of Derby: her mother, Lucy, was the daughter and coheiress of Thomas Percy, seventh Earl of Northumberland. Such a marriage would have gratified even the most susceptible old lady in Germany, where requirements that the blood on *both* sides should be pure, so as to accomplish the great fact—eben-bürtig—are far more stringent than on the point of amiability, or sense, or principle, and are almost ludicrous in some localities where railroads and traffic are unknown.

The Stanley family were, at that time, not only some of the most illustrious in birth and employments, but the handsomest of the great aristocratic families: the family portraits of the time displaying symmetry of face, and commanding forms. Sir Kenelm Digby, in his memoirs, thus describes Venetia's origin, designating as " Stelliana " the lady of his love.

" Stelliana," he writes, " being born of parents that in the antiquity and lustre of their houses, and in the goods of fortune, were inferior to none in Peloponnesus; it pleased Heaven, when she was not many months old, to take her mother from her, deeming, as I think, the earth, and too negligent a husband, not worthy of so divine a blessing: who dying, left the goodness of her soul and the beauty of her body, in both which she surpassed all others of her time, to her infant daughter."

Some of her ancestors, he also wrote, had exalted and pulled down kings of England: and " their successors still have right to wear a royal crown upon their princely temple," alluding to the sovereignty of the Isle of Man, then possessed by the Earls of Derby.

Sir Edward Stanley, to whom Sir Kenelm gives the *nom*

de plume of "Nearchus," had no sooner lost his wife, than he learned to regret her, and to honour her memory. He fell into a deep melancholy, in which, perhaps, remorse had no small share; and plunging into solitude, gave full scope to his "melancholic fancies." His daughter, lovely and promising as she was, became an incumbrance to his determined sorrow; it was necessary, he knew, for one of her high birth to have persons around her who could educate her suitably; he therefore resolved to send the motherless child to a grave and virtuous lady, the wife of a kinsman of his, who promised that no care should be wanting to cultivate the intellect which already gave indications of superiority. The discreet matron (whose husband Aubrey, in his detracting spirit, calls a "tenant" of Sir Edward Stanley's) happened to be an intimate friend of the widowed mother of Kenelm Digby. There was something peculiarly mournful in the fate of Lady Digby, who lived on her own property, at Gothurst, in great retirement. Sir Everard (knighted by James I.) was considered by his contemporaries to be a "man of fair fortune, pregnant abilities, and court-like behaviour;" religious fanaticism was, however, the Familiar which haunted his home and lured him to his destiny. Even for that influence there existed this excuse, that Elizabeth and James had held down the Catholics with the iron hand of intolerance. The one would not, though she hated Puritans, ameliorate the condition of the Romanist party: James, more disposed, dared not make even an attempt to do so. Sir Everard, mild, prosperous, the happiest of fathers and of husbands, was the last, his friends thought, to become a desperate man. He always denied his participation in the Popish plot, and nobly refused to implicate others. That he gave 1500*l.* towards it, that he entertained Guy Fawkes at his house, could not, however, be denied. When the plot was defeated, he was taken in open rebellion with others of his faith. His end was very touching. He pleaded not entire innocence, but stated, in extenuation, his faith; and urged convictions, which, under happier circumstances, might have assumed the colour of patriotism. That King James had broken his compact with the Catholics, that fresh oppressions of that persecuted sect would be imposed, could not be in fact gainsaid. As a Romanist, Everard deemed it his duty to restore to supremacy, if possible, the Church to which he adhered; and he believed that, for that end, all consideration of national tranquillity, life, fortune, even the welfare of his family, should be set aside. With regard to the open rebellion with which he was charged, he frankly avowed it. He requested, that as he had been alone in that crime, on him alone might the punishment fall; he prayed that his debts might be paid, his family be spared the confiscation so mercilessly enforced by a plunder-loving monarch. But he spoke in vain. On sentence of death being passed upon him, he was deeply affected; he bowed to those on the bench, and said: "If I could hear any of your lordships say you forgave me, I should go more cheerfully to the gallows." The lords, with one accord, replied, "God forgive you, and we do."

It was in undying remembrance of one whom she doubtless considered as a martyr, that the widowed Lady Digby lived in deep seclusion at Gothurst. The sympathies of her neighbours, even of those connected with the then Protestan house of Stanley, must have gone along with her and her sons. The country long rang with the current story of Si Everard's death: alas! he was hanged, drawn, and quartered, — no barbarity being omitted to mark him as a criminal of a deep dye: the tragedy was played out at the west end of St. Paul's Church, in London. On the gallows, the unhappy, mistaken man asked forgiveness of God, of the King, the Queen, and all the parliament, and in deep penitence submitted to his doom. Wood relates, that when the executioner plucked out from the still heaving body the quivering heart, and, holding it up, said, "Here is the heart of a traitor," Sir Everard, still living, made answer, "Thou liest;" and this ghastly tale was long credited by the ignorant and credulous, who, in that day, certainly predominated over the reasonable portion of society. His wife remained to bear the brunt of suspicion, and to suffer, as appears from some inedited letters in the State Paper Office, from an incessant surveillance; nothing, however, was proved against her.

When she received in her desolate home her eldest son, Kenelm, she welcomed back not a docile boy, but a growing youth, whose form, afterwards termed gigantic, was then almost manly. On this son her affections were fondly riveted, and, during the interval of his college life, she looked eagerly for his return in the vacations. Her estate was only thirty miles from Euston Park, where Venetia Stanley, a playful child, was then domiciled: frequent meetings took place. But we must let Sir Kenelm tell the tale in his own words, premising that in his memoirs Lady Digby is called Arete,—himself Theogenes.

"The affection of the one to her son, which would not suffer her to be long without him, and the respect of the others to their charge, which made them glad to satisfy her though yet childish desires, in anything they could, as in the fondness of going abroad and the like, was the cause that they seldom came together but that the two children had part in the meeting; who, the very first time that ever they had sight of one another, grew so fond of each other's company, that all that saw them, said assuredly that something above their tender capacity breathed this sweet affection into their hearts. Whereas other children of like age did delight in fond plays and light toys, these two would spend the day in looking upon each other's face, and in accompanying these looks with gentle sighs, which seemed to portend that much sorrow was laid up for their understanding years,— they demeaned themselves so prettily and so affectionately, that one would have said, Love was grown a child again and took delight to play with them. And when the time of parting came, they would take their leaves with such abundance of tears and sighs as made it evident that so deep a sorrow could not be borne and nursed in children's breasts without a nobler cause than the usual fondness in others."

Troubles, however, came. These "first innocent" years were clouded; and scarcely, says Sir Kenelm, had they arrived "to the maturity of judging why they loved, and ready to love still only because they loved, when she (Fortune) turned about her inconstant wheel in such sort that, if their fates had not been written above in eternal characters, even then their affections had been by a long winter of absence sapped and destroyed in their budding spring. For what is not that able to do in so young hearts, that immediately after have the aventures and pursuits of new and advantageous love? Yet these kept their first fire alive."

Sir Edward Stanley, in the midst of all this childish wooing, hearing of his lovely daughter's growing attractions, or perhaps alarmed at her intimacy with the Romanist Digbys, sent for her home. Stelliana, as Kenelm still styled her in his memoirs, was, even then, so "small, that she could scarcely reach to gather the lowest fruit of the laden boughs;" the love-making between her and Kenelm must, therefore, have indeed begun betimes; and we cannot but consider the father as perfectly right in separating her from her juvenile admirer. Delighted with her surpassing beauty, Sir Edward resolved to introduce her at the court of James I.; and no opportunity could be better. Elizabeth Stuart, the darling of the nation, was at hat time on the eve of marriage with the Count Palatine of Bohemia; and Whitehall was in all the excessive commotion of court revels. The magnificence displayed on that occasion, notwithstanding that only three months previously all had been mourning — " outward show," at least — for Prince Henry, was extraordinary: "it were of no use to write," says one chronicler, "of the curiosity and excess of bravery of both men and women, with the extreme *daubing* on of cost and riches."

Dresses which cost fifty pounds a yard (but it may here be observed, not many yards were used in those wise days of tight dresses),—a blaze of jewels, such as Elizabeth's court had never displayed; embroidery of gold and silver enhanced the enormous cost of dress. Yet a gloom hung over the court; and there was a sort of presage of evil times in many minds.

Amongst the twenty noble bridesmaids of the young Princess, Venetia Stanley probably walked after the Princess to the altar:—whether she were conspicuous or not in that procession, at all events, her acquirements (which, Sir Kenelm records, were so extraordinary for her age, as to induce "men to doubt that the heavens meant not long to lend her to the earth"), and her "beauty and *discretion*" (an old-fashioned word, implying then what we now call tact, or *savoir faire*), "did soon draw the eyes and thoughts of all men to admiration: so that in this the example of her was so singular, that whereas the beauty of other fair ladies used to grace and adorn public feasts and assemblies, hers did so far exceed all others, as well in action as in excellence, that it drew to her not only the affections but also the thoughts of all persons, so that all things provided with the greatest splendour and curiosity passed by unregarded and neglected."

Venetia's heart, in fact, pined in secret for her first love, who, like Paul, left by Virginia, fretted at the idea that she was surrounded by admirers, whilst he was far from her in seclusion. Nor were his fears chimerical. The Masques and Banquets of James's court were so many occasions of licence, either in gallantry, or intemperance; the latter being the favourite excess of James and his queen. One evening a nobleman of the court, whom Digby has styled Ursatius, addressed the beautiful Venetia in the most flowing Euphuism of the day; she was spared the awkwardness of reply at that moment by another masque, who claimed her hand for a corrento. Ursatius, therefore, was obliged "to resign all his spirits, rub his eyes," for the corrento began, and it was impossible to withdraw his regards from Venetia as she mingled with the dancers.

One word about dancing in James's day, before we give the beautiful description of Venetia's dancing, which Sir Kenelm penned in all a lover's enthusiasm.

Dancing, in the reign of Elizabeth and her successor, was an almost daily amusement at court. No slovenly steps, no careless demeanour were permitted. Elizabeth rewarded good dancers with her especial notice. Witness Sir Christopher Hatton's owing his promotion in a great measure to his dancing. Gray, referring in his "Long Story" to Stoke Pogeis, once the seat of the Hattons, brings in this fact thus:—

> "Full oft within the spacious walls,
> When he had fifty winters o'er him,
> My grave Lord Keeper led the brawls,
> The seal and maces danced before him.
>
> His bushy beard and shoe-strings green,
> His high-crown'd hat, and satin doublet,
> Moved the stout heart of England's Queen;
> The Pope and Spaniard could not trouble it."

The Brawl, the Pavin, and the Canary dance were all comprised under one generic name, the Corrento. The French Brawl was regarded by the very scrupulous as not altogether proper; there was a shaking of the foot in it that required, however, great dexterity. But it was probably in the Pavin (from *pavo*, a peacock) that the young Venetia made her *début* as a belle, and a dancer. The Pavin came from Spain, and had much of the Spanish state and gravity in its slow and majestic measure. Ladies never danced it except in trains,—"the motion whereof resembled a peacock's tail." Their partners—if princes, wore their robes; if gentlemen, their caps and swords; if lawyers—for lawyers were the greatest dancers in the court—their gowns. The Canary was a dance for two, with strange fantastic steps, very much, says Mr. Douce, "in the savage style." It must, therefore, have been in a Pavin that Venetia made the impression of which Sir Kenelm tells us.

Ursatius, he relates, was constrained by the fascination of her grace, "to contemplate her motions that were so composed of awful majesty and graceful agility, that all the beholders, being ravished with delight, said, surely one of the Graces was descended from heaven to honour these nuptials. Which was the cause that when they had seen how skilfully she kept time with her feet to the music's sound, she was suffered no more to return unto her former seat; for every one in their turn beseeched the like favours of her that she had done to their companion, before he could lead her back unto her first place; yet in this they deceived themselves; for her excellency that would brook no partner, engrossed to herself all the commendations, while they scarce had any notice taken of them. But she was wearied with her much exercise, before the beholders could be satisfied with delight, which made time glide away so swiftly and unperceivably, that they heard from abroad the watchful cock warn men to rise up to their daily labours, before they could persuade themselves it was time to go to rest."

Venetia went home, and was attended, as was then the custom, by an aged gentlewoman—a sort of half governess, half lady's maid, half nurse:—above the French *bonne,* below the English governess; an excellent maternal friend, nurse, counsellor in all domestic and even in matrimonial matters, if good—a dangerous inmate if bad; and so poor Venetia's *gouvernante* proved.

Sir Kenelm indignantly calls this attendant "Faustina;" he hates her with as vigorous a hatred as Byron felt for her who—

"Born in a garret, in a kitchen bred,"

stood, he believed, between him and reconciliation with a

wife whom he respected and regretted. Faustina was already in the interests of Ursatius: and, when Venetia related to her the events of the evening, praised the discretion, the courtesy, the generosity of Ursatius; and, of course, following out her preconcerted line of conduct, imputed to Sir Kenelm gross neglect and inconstancy. Venetia, however, stood firm to her first flame; she had neither seen him nor heard from him during the last four years, yet she confided in his constancy; she ascribed his silence to the wishes of their parents. She saw it was ordained by Heaven that she should remain faithful to him, since her attachment had not been stifled either by absence, or persuasion.

Finding arguments unavailing, Faustina formed a diabolical plan of delivering her young charge into the hands of Ursatius. She appeared to acquiesce in Venetia's wishes, and informed her that her lover, Sir Kenelm, or, as he styles himself, Theogenes, was then in London, and wished to meet her in the park, three miles from the city: and Venetia, falling into the snare, consented to go forth by the back door, where a hired carriage with four horses awaited her. This carriage belonged, in fact, to Ursatius, whose coachman, in a disguised livery, drove it. The rest of this singular incident, which is adopted as true, and not merely romantic, by the biographers of Sir Kenelm Digby, is told in these words:—"She was scarcely gone halfway to the appointed place, when five or six horsemen, well mounted, overtook the coach; who speaking to the coachman, that was instructed what to do, he stayed his horses, and two of them alighting came into the coach unto her, and, drawing their poignards, threatened her with death if she cried out or made any noise, assuring her withal that from them she should receive no violence if she would sit quietly, and therewithal drew the curtains that none might see who was in the coach as they passed by. In this agony of distracted thoughts, and fearing the worst that might happen to an undefended maid that was fallen into rude hands, she travelled till morning, when, the coach staying, she was taken out, and led into a fair lodge that stood in the middle of a pleasant lawn environed with rich groves; and there an ancient woman, entertaining her with comfortable speeches, brought her into a richly adorned chamber, advising her to repose after so tedious and troublesome a night. After she had helped her to bed it was some time before sleep could take possession of her fair lids, but at length her heart yielded to the weight of so heavy a burden, and Death, himself grown tender in seeing her affliction, sent his brother Sleep to charm her eyes, that else would have turned into a flood of tears." Towards evening she heard one come into the chamber, rose halfway up in her bed, and then, by the glimmering of the light that stole in between the chinks of the drawn curtains, she perceived, as he came near her, that it was Ursatius. Ursatius then knelt down, "and pleaded his love as an excuse for the terrible and almost fatal dilemma in which he had placed her." After blaming Faustina for the whole conspiracy, Ursatius retired.

The good angels, therefore, and more especially that guardian spirit who, according to the belief of the times, was supposed to attend each individual man or woman on the face of this earth, from the moment of birth to that of death — nay, even to the gates of heaven, — seem to have watched that night over Venetia. Scripture does not, theologians declare, warrant the doctrine in which Shakspeare believed; the general ministry, only, of angels is recognised by our Church. The good angel who under different forms, sometimes in sleep, sometimes in special revelations, or by invisible angelic agency; and the bad angel or demon who followed the doomed or marked man in this world, were nevertheless, in the days of Kenelm Digby, as strongly believed in as any other point of religious doctrine. "There is a good angel, but the devil outbids him too," *—"You follow the young prince up and down like his ill angel," † were popular quotations. Venetia, thus innocent and believing, and, like others of her generation, only just shaking off the old superstitions of Romanism, probably believed that

> "Millions of spiritual creatures walk the earth
> Unseen, both when we wake, and when we sleep."

She acted as if she did, with a courage that is rarely supported without a conviction of God's prescience and mercy. The instant Ursatius disappeared, she resolved to escape. Tying her sheets together, she let herself out of the window and escaped through the garden, over the wall, into the then uncultured tracks and "horrid woods," somewhat like an American prairie, and also full of wolves. Attacked by one of them, her shrieks brought to her aid Mardontius, a young nobleman to whom that *nom de plume* was assigned, and who afterwards made a conspicuous figure in her history.

Mardontius falls in love with her, of course, and Venetia is safely harboured in the house of a respectable matchmaker, named, in the memoirs, Artesia, — a lady who designs to bring Sir Kenelm and a favourite granddaughter of her own together. Nothing so surely rivets love's charms as the appearance of a rival, and Venetia's feelings became rather more engaged in the affair than heretofore. Besides, Artesia, unconscious that she was fanning a forbidden flame, spoke to her, first of Lady Digby, and afterwards of Sir Kenelm and his brother John, in the following terms. — "She spoke," Sir Kenelm tells us in his memoirs, "much in commendation of that lady, extolling with what admirable wit and understanding she was endowed, and how, being left a widow in the flower of her youth, accompanied with a flourishing beauty and a plentiful estate, yet she was so wedded to

---

* Scot's Discourse on Witchcraft. † Henry IV.

her dear husband's love that she neglected all the advantageous offers of earnest and great suitors, that she might with more liberty perform the part of a careful mother. 'For by him,' said Artesia, 'she had two children. The eldest Theogenes, although the great strength of his body make him apt for any corporal exercises, yet he pleaseth himself most in the entertainments of the mind; so that having applied himself to philosophy and other deepest sciences, he is already grown so eminent that I have heard them say who have insight that way, that if a lazy desire of ease or ambition for public employment do not interrupt him in this course he is like to attain to great perfection. Their mother was ever dear to me,' continued she, 'and if I can effect what I have affectionately endeavoured and solicited, we shall be able to leave to our posterity the inheritance of our affections as well as of our estates; for I have laboured long, and Arete hath not been wanting on her part to join in marriage her eldest son and my grandchild, that you see here.'"

These words, addressed to Venetia, we may readily believe "shot her heart through;" but she was quickly consoled: Theogenes was to visit Artesia in a few days; so the conclusion of Artesia's speech was to her "like a gale of wind that, in a burning day, creepeth over sweet and flowery meads, and breathes upon the languishing face of the faint traveller that is almost dead with heat."

According to Aubrey, the obstacles that Lady Digby had originally offered to the marriage of her son with Venetia Stanley, were owing to the bad repute in which Venetia's moral character stood; but Sir Kenelm imputed her objections to a paternal and maternal quarrel between Sir Edward Stanley and his mother. A middle course was pursued; no contract was allowed: Sir Kenelm was allowed to travel for three years, in the hope of returning, when older, to offer his hand to Venetia. A farewell interview in London closes the novel for a period at this point, and Digby sets out for Paris.

Sir Kenelm was obliged to fly from Paris, on account of the plague. He retired to Angers. Here Marie de' Medici had retreated after the battle of the Pont de Cé, in 1620. Whilst waiting here for her troops to arrive, she amused herself with balls and Masques, when one night she met Sir Kenelm, or, as he calls himself in his memoirs, Theogenes. He thus records the incident * : —

"Theogenes coming one Masque night to the court, with the company that importuned him to go along with them, was, by one of the ladies that had known him at Athens, taken out to dance, in which he behaved himself in such sort that, whether it were the gracefulness of his gesture, wherein the commendations of art was the least thing he aimed at, or that the heavens had ordained he should be the punisher of the Queen's affections, she felt at the first sight of him a secret love, which soon grew so violent that it made her forget her own greatness, and compelled Theogenes, in order to preserve his constancy for Stelliana, to quit the court; and he caused it to be reported that he was murdered in the tumult which arose in consequence of the queen having disbanded her forces, upon her reconciliation with the king, her son, after the battle of Marathon."

From France Digby proceeded to Italy.

Whatever may have been the defects of the education given him by Laud, one good result remained; Digby had imbibed that love for the arts which pervaded all refined minds more or less in the reigns of James I. and Charles I. until crushed by civil commotion. To Laud, Oxford owes that beautiful inner quadrangle of St. John's College, with the exception of the south side,—which was the old library. By Laud, who determined to adorn the University with fine buildings, the Convocation House, with Selden's library above, were erected. Sir Kenelm went therefore into Italy, with a

* Private Memoirs of Sir K. Digby, p. 87.

certain foundation of enthusiasm, without which all the treasures of art are but the objects of the vulgarest sightseeing.

There was, at this time, in Venice a young painter studying his art with all the energies of genius, and trying to catch the almost matchless and imperishable tints of Titian. Handsome, generous, naturally courtly, endowed with strong passions, yet far more skilful in conveying to his canvas all the minuteness of still life than the turbulence of excited emotion, this youthful artist was patiently working his way up to the highest position among the great masters of a great time: this was Anthony Vandyck; a name so honoured and so familiar in England, that it seems to recall a countryman, not a foreigner, to our minds.

Born at Antwerp in 1598, he could only have been twenty-five years of age, when Sir Kenelm Digby, still under twenty, had passed from Genoa, his first resting-place in Italy, to Venice. Although a Fleming, Van Dyck did not, as most Flemings are said to do, see Italy with only Flemish eyes. His impressions of Italian art had been received early, for, as a boy, he had been sent by his father, an Antwerp merchant, to learn drawing from Van Balen, a countryman who had studied in Rome. The fame of Rubens drew, as Horace Walpole relates, "the young congenial artist to a nobler school." Rubens soon perceived his genius. One night that great master went out, leaving a picture unfinished: his pupils took the opportunity of sporting about the room; one of them, striking at his companion with a maul-stick, threw down the picture, on the canvas of which the colours were still wet. It fell on the floor, and was nearly spoiled. Van Dyck, who was at work in the next chamber, was prevailed upon to repair the injury done. The next morning Rubens, on coming to continue his work, looking on his picture at some distance, exclaimed "that he liked it better than he did the night before." This unconscious compliment to Van Dyck was the foundation of all his after success.

Rubens then advised him, not only to go to Italy, but also to confine his attention chiefly to portraits. The advice is said to have originated in jealousy; but we agree with Walpole, that the generous nature of Rubens was incapable of such a motive. He took, there can be no doubt, the just view of Van Dyck's especial gifts; some men's minds and hands are destined to work on a large scale; some minds take broad views. Michael Angelo and Rubens may be compared in art to Milton, and Dryden, in poetry. Van Dyck's strength lay more in detail; perhaps his mother's talent, displayed in her painting flowers "in small," and her wonderful embroidery in silk, descended, in that especial observance of minutiæ, to him. He made a portrait of the wife of Rubens, a masterpiece of colouring, and then went to lay himself at the feet of Titian, and of Paul Veronese. He soon equalled the carnations of Titian, and became famous for satins; still, we are told, he "had not much idea of the saints, or their expression." Walpole thinks he had no due conception of female loveliness, and that his Madonnas were homely. " He has left us to wonder that the famous Countess of Carlisle could be thought so charming; and had not Waller been a better painter, Sacharissa would make little impression now."

In spite of these strictures, Sir Kenelm found in Van Dyck, not only a rising painter but a congenial spirit in other points. Their familiar intercourse must have been very interesting to lookers-on. Beside the almost gigantic figure of Digby, stood the small form of Anthony Van Dyck; but that form was admirably proportioned; the face of the painter was full of animation; his manners were kind to a degree; he knew not a mean or harsh sentiment. Richly dressed, his carriage and equipage magnificent, his retinue numerous and well appointed, his table splendid, and always attended by persons of high rank, Van Dyck kept state like an ambassador rather than a painter; and, in fact, his assemblies resembled a court. For painters, in those days, ranked with diplomatists, associated with princes, and were often employed in state affairs. Their noble art was thought to raise them to the higher orders of society; and Van Dyck, as we shall see, was considered not an unsuitable match even for the daughter of an Earl. Venice, as well as Paris, was the source of fashion on dress at that time; the French hood, such as we see in all pictures, was Parisian; it consisted of a long strip of muslin, reaching from the back of the head down over the forehead, and leaving the hair exposed; but the caul, or net of gold thread, was probably Venetian. The high shoe, almost a stilt, and sometimes a foot high, was an imitation of the Venetian chopine. We may imagine the "bravery" in which Van Dyck delighted, and how greatly Sir Kenelm added, by his nobleness of deportment, his *prestige*, and his costly attire, to the splendour of the painter's receptions. It was probably at Venice that Van Dyck's first unsuccessful visit to England was planned, but the painter had still much to do in Italy. He went to Rome, and, avoiding what he deemed the low conversation of his countrymen, lived in such state that he was called "*il Pittore Cavalieresco*." At Rome he painted his famous portrait of Cardinal Bentivoglio; that prelate had been nuncio in Flanders, and was partial to Flemish artists. From Rome Van Dyck went to Palermo, where he completed portraits not only of Philibert of Savoy, viceroy, but of a female artist, Sophonisba Anguisciola, then ninety-one years of age. The plague, however, drove him back, and he returned to Antwerp.

His altar-pieces now gave him a new reputation; in them he introduced the heads of brother painters. The patronage of the arts extended by Charles I. eventually drew him to England; but this was at a later epoch in our narrative.

Sir Kenelm Digby meantime, though happy in the society of Van Dyck, was tasting of some of the miseries of an attachment to which friends object; his letters to Venetia were intercepted, and, whilst uneasy at this inexplicable silence, news of her approaching marriage with the young nobleman whom he calls Mardontius, were brought to him at Florence. Nor was this intelligence the most painful that was imparted. The good name of his mistress had been tampered with; "that monster, which was begot of some foul fiend in hell," Digby relates, spread abroad a scandalous rumour of a too great familiarity between her and Mardontius. Much prejudice to her honour was therefore coupled with the details which an English friend from London imparted. Digby thus describes his own state of perturbation on the occasion: —

"Theogenes then quite forgot the noble temper of his mind, which being by nature composed of an excellent mixture, and, besides, richly cultivated with continual study and philosophical precepts, did formerly stand in defiance of fortune; but now he was so overborne with passion that he might serve for a clear example to all who may promise most of themselves, that none may be so completely perfect in this life, nor armed against the assaults of passion, but that some way or other there is an entrance left unguarded, whereby he may be humbled and put in mind, at his own cost, of the frailty of human nature. For his soul was so overburdened with grief, that his reason and all that he knew availed him nothing in his own behalf; but sinking under that insupportable weight, he, as soon as his shrunk heart began to dilate itself, broke into a torrent of fury, cursing all womankind for Stelliana's sake; and was so possessed with anger and disdain, that, if nature had been in his power, he would have turned the world again into a dark chaos. 'Injurious stars, why gave you so fair an outside to so foul and deformed a mind? And what secret sin have I committed so great that I must be made the idolater of such a dire portent?'"

Miserable and indignant, Sir Kenelm tore from his arm a bracelet of Venetia's fair hair — a love-token which she had sent him — and threw it into the fire.

At this period of his history, Digby's "actions became mingled with those of great princes." Prince Charles and the Duke of Buckingham were then on their journey to Spain: the Prince, as the "wooer" of the fair Infanta Maria, the sister of Philip IV.; Buckingham, as his friend and adviser. John Digby, first Earl of Bristol, a distant relation of Sir Kenelm, was at this time ambassador in Madrid, and, hearing of his young relative's accomplishments, invited him to visit him, with a view to introducing him to a court noted for taste, for splendour, for a love of the arts, and, as far as the Queen Isabella and the Infanta were concerned, for feminine virtue, as well as for beauty. Sir Kenelm gladly obeyed the summons, and although he professed that all places were indifferent to him now since the tidings had reached him of Venetia's alleged inconstancy, he resolved to "employ for the advantage of others' profit, those talents which God and better nature had bestowed on him."

This visit to Madrid involved Sir Kenelm in all the famous intrigues and quarrels which afterwards agitated both the Spanish and the English courts, and from which his own dexterity and prudence alone extricated him.

His relation, Lord Bristol, was well aware, it appears, not only of the favour which Sir Kenelm enjoyed at the court of King James, but also of his ability, and of the wonderful and seemingly intuitive knowledge of the world, which were likely to prove so useful in the mazes of diplomacy.

That Bristol regarded Sir Kenelm as a mediator between him and Buckingham will be shown hereafter. Meantime we return to Sir Kenelm's personal narrative, a narrative which has far more the features of romance, than those of real life.

It was whilst he was on his journey to Madrid that an adventure, which he relates very fully, took place: he fell in with a Brahmin, how or where exactly he does not specify, "which man," he however relates, "as his name giveth him out to be, was one of those that the Indians held in great veneration for their professed sanctity and deep knowledge of the most hidden mysteries of theology and of nature," to enlarge which he had passed from the East into the West, "to partake of what sciences flourished there."

The mystical opinions of the Brahmin, and his profound metaphysical meditations, were far from being devoid of interest to Sir Kenelm; and from this era of his life we may date his own singular and fanciful notions. The perfect courtesy of the Brahmins is proverbial; and the most intimate confidence was soon established between the young Englishman, in all the vigour of life, and the aged sage, one of whose tenets enforced a state of frequent abstraction and of silent contemplation of things above the ken of man.

The Brahmin, however, had human sympathies; he remarked the sadness of Sir Kenelm; he inquired its source, and received the confessions of a deceived and disappointed man.

The Brahmin took his own method of offering consolation. "No events," he told the pensive Sir Kenelm, "could be so adverse in his life but that the influence of the celestial bodies had power to turn them into good." Upon this followed a long argument upon free will and necessity; upon the agency of spirits, both angelic and diabolic, and on the power of man to avail himself of their instrumentality.

In this discussion, Sir Kenelm was reasonable and incredulous, the Brahmin mystical and incomprehensible; nevertheless, according to Digby's account, after asking the young man what spirit he would like to see, he promised to show to him her whose misconduct had so deeply affected Sir Kenelm's happiness.

Sir Kenelm then relates that, as they travelled through a dense wood, they had not gone far when he, of "a sudden stopped, and held the priest that was going forwards, and pointed to him with his hand to that object which stayed his steps. It was a body sitting upon a broken trunk of a dead and rotten tree, in a pensive posture, so that but part of her face was discovered to them. Her radiant hair hung dishevelled upon her white shoulders, and, together with them, was covered with a thin veil that from the crown of her head reached to the ground, through which they shined as the sun doth through a pale cloud, and sometimes, without that eclipsing shade, did send out direct and unbroken beams, and so doubled the day of beauty; which was caused by a gentle air, that, as being jealous of that senseless veil, did blow it ever and anon away, and played with those bright hairs, adding new curled waves to those that nature made there. In her fair face one might discern lilies and roses admirably mixed; but in her lips the rose alone did sit enthroned in sweet majesty; her eyes, as being niggardly of casting away their heart-piercing beams, were hid by her modest lids."

When they approached this beautiful vision, the figure arose; a deep melancholy overspread that lovely countenance; Sir Kenelm stooped down to take her snowy hand; he tried to hold it; his hand grasped nothing but air; thrice did he endeavour to catch the hem of her garment, "as many times did he find himself deceived." Then the magician told him that this was the effect only of magic; his art had called forth the semblance or spirit of Venetia; his agency had shown him, instead of being gay and faithless, that she mourned his absence. Then Sir Kenelm declared that he was convinced that spirits, even infernal ones, could take upon themselves the appearance of angels of light.*

Henceforth his mind, constituted for greater things, was obscured by superstitions, even exceeding those cherished in an age of strong intellects, and yet of great credulity.

A compact with the devil, entered into by witches, was a matter of popular belief in that day. The magician, however, in this instance, differed from his class. Witches, according

* Private Memoirs of Kenelm Digby, p. 147.

to Reginald Scot, being generally old women, "blear-eyed, pale, foul, full of wrinkles; poor, sullen, superstitious, and papists;" they "were doting scolds, mad, devilish, not unlike those possessed with spirits." Witches, it was believed, "could pull down the moon and stars, and, with wishing, send needles into the livers of their enemies; they could raise spirits, dry up springs, turn the course of running waters, and stay both day and night, changing the one into the other" (to quote Reginald Scot again). Then the learned King, James I., who wrote a work on witchcraft*, gravely assures his readers that one sign of witches was their movements on the water: "For," he writes, * "as in a secret murthur, if the dead carkasse bee at any time handled by the murtherer, it will gush out of blood, as if the blood were crying to heaven for revenge of the murtherer: God having appointed that secret supernatural signe, for triall of that secret unatural crime, so it appears that God hath appointed (for a supernaturall signe of the monstrous impietie of witches) that the water shall refuse to receive them in her bosome that have shaken off the waters of baptisme, and wilfully refused the benefite thereof. No, not so much as their eyes are able to shed teares (threaten and torture them as you please) while first they repent (God not permiting them to dissemble their obstinacie in so horrible a crime), albeit the womankind especially be able other wayes to shed teares at every light occasion when they will, yea, although it were dissembling like the crocodiles."

"Such," Dr. Nathan Drake informs us, "was the creed of the country from the throne to the cottage. Men of learning arranged themselves on the side of King James and his Demonologie,"† with few exceptions. Among the opponents of the system was Bacon, who, in the "Tenth Century of his Natural History," attributes the achievements and confessions of witches to the effects of a morbid imagination.

---

* The Demonologie, vol. ii. pp. 485, 486.   † Drake's Shakspeare.

Shakspeare availed himself of this popular superstition to give mystery and solemnity to his dramas; but Sir Kenelm Digby seems really to have believed that "the earth hath bubbles as the water has."

Digby, however, proceeded to Madrid, where he attached himself to the service of Prince Charles. Whilst in that capital, he was piqued by a remark of Lord Kensington on his indifference to the charms of Spanish ladies, and, though now convinced of the constancy of Venetia, he devoted himself to a certain beauty of the Spanish court, of whom Lord Kensington was really enamoured. Young, handsome, and, as the world thought, free, Digby's suit might have ended in marriage; but the remembrance of Venetia was still dearer to him than any new object. He rejected the advice of friends, and even, he avows, the solicitations of the fair Spaniard herself, and resolved to remain constant to Venetia. Thus the spirit whom the Brahmin had summoned had acted for once a friendly part.

Digby returned to England with Charles, landing at Portsmouth on the 5th of October, 1623.

The joy with which the young Prince was welcomed home, the festivities that followed, the almost immediate improvement in manners and in costume; the taste for the arts which Charles and the accomplished Buckingham introduced, must have rendered the first few months after the return of the travellers one of deep interest; but dissensions were the canker that secretly ate into all the enjoyments of the court, and the following letter shows that Sir Kenelm was regarded as an arbitrator between the two discordant factions.

" Good Cosen,

"I giue you thankes for your paynes in my businesse, in wch whatsoever the successe shall bee my obligation to you shall bee the same.

" I was in hope by your letter that ther had bene expected

from mee an answer only to those points wch were brought mee by you from my Lo. Duke, but it seemes, by a letter I have receaued from his Gr: as likewise by a message sent mee since from him by Mr. Gresley, that nothing will serue the turne but that I make y^r accknowledgment that is required by subscribing the paper that was sent mee; and so likewise the libertye wch I besought of his Matie, to follow freely myne owne affayres (for that was my request and not to come to London) wch I understoode had bene graunted mee by his Matie. My Lord Duke now sendeth me word that if I come to London I must understand myselfe to bee a Restrained man, untill I have made such an accknowledgment as is required. My present request I hope shall bee but modest wch is only that I may know cleerly what his Maties pleasure is to the end I may not fall into errour, and I shall most willingly and readily obey it, whatsoeuer it shall bee, no way doubting but his Matie in his owne dew tyme will afford mee a gratious and an equall hearing. In the interim I haue sent you my answer to the propositions, wch I intreate you to present vnto his Matie and to his Grace; if they may bee accepted, as I can no way doubt but they will, for I conceaue it will seeme so hard and so vnjust a course under his Maties gratious Gouerment to haue it injoyned to a gentleman to accknowledg' faults hee is no way guiltye of.

" I shall intreate you further as you haue already taken much paynes in this businesse, that you will deliuer this message from mee to the Duke, That as I have since applyed my selfe to bee reconciled vnto his Graces fauour, I omitted nothing that might expresse my respect vnto him, so I doe really still poursue the desire of regayning his good opinion and friendshipp, and if I shall bee soe happy as to obtayn it I will honestly endeauour by my best seruices to deserue the continenance of it, and therefore I entreat his Gr: not to insist or presse mee to those thinges wch would make mee for the future uncapable of his Maties fauour and unworthy of his friendshipp, but that if hee intend in any kinde to fauour mee that hee would doe it in a noble manner, whereby I may bee obliged trewly and hartely to loue and serue him. For otherwise I shall in respect of myne honor and defence of myne innocencye vndervalue any earthly regards whatsoever, and trust to God's protection, his Maties Justice and the goodnesse of my cause and so desiring to heare from you with all conuenient speede, I recoṁend you to God and rest

"Yr. affectionate Cosen,
"to doe y^r seruice,
"BRISTOL.

"Sherborne, 16th of March, 1624." [*]

The justice of King James was, however, only a broken reed when his likings and prejudices intervened; and although the disgraceful story of Carr was not enacted again, and though there was a certain nobleness in Buckingham's nature that preserved him from servility, James refused to see matters in a fair light; and the hopes of Bristol, and the mediation of Sir Kenelm, proved alike fruitless.

The romantic events of Sir Kenelm's existence were continually recurring. Amongst those which had the greatest influence on his future life, was his meeting, on his return to London, with Venetia. She was seated in her carriage when he beheld her, radiant in her youth and loveliness.

"Yes, she sat," so he tells us, "pensively on one side of the coach by herself, as Apollo might have taken her counterfeit to express Venus sorrowing for her beloved Adonis." A report of Digby's death had reached the court, and been partly credited by Venetia; her joy, therefore, in his appearance was rapturous: a reconciliation was soon effected, explanations were given, but still, there were obstacles to their union. The confidence of Digby had been shaken by

[*] State Paper Office, No. 59, vol. clxxxv., Jas. I. Domestic Papers.

the reports affecting Venetia's character, and he somewhat basely resolved not to commit himself to wedlock, but to make the fair girl his mistress if he could. She resented the insult, then pardoned it, and Digby was again restored to favour, and their attachment placed upon the footing of a platonic regard. Notwithstanding his unworthy and incomprehensible conduct, Venetia, with all a woman's generosity, when her lover was afterwards selected to accompany the Duke of Buckingham to the French court, pawned her plate and jewels, and sent him a large sum, entreating him to make use of it without encumbering his estate by borrowing. This act sank deeply into a heart which was, in spite of all its inconsistencies, warmly devoted to Venetia. Her character was, it is true, by that time, almost blasted in the estimation of the virtuous. In spite, however, of the world's

> "dread laugh,
> Which scarce the firm philosopher can scorn,"

or of the still more painful fact of his mother's opposition, Digby resolved to make Venetia his wife. To this, however, Venetia at first objected. She had been induced by a report of Digby's death, and by a suppression of his letters, to give Mardontius a promise of marriage, and her portrait. A marriage contract, or what we call an engagement, is often wantonly broken in the present day, and, if with little feeling, with little remorse. But the notions of those times were far more strict, and Venetia refused to marry Digby while her portrait remained in the possession of Mardontius. Digby was, therefore, obliged to challenge Mardontius, in order to get the portrait back. They met; Mardontius, without drawing his sword, placed the portrait in Digby's hand, and with it a written declaration, that if ever he had uttered a word derogatory to Venetia's honour, it was false.

The slanders, however, have lived: they are extant in the pages of Aubrey. Venetia, he states, " had one, if not more children by the Earl of Dorset, who settled on her an annuity of £500 per *annum*, which, after Sir Kenelm Digby married, was unpaid by the Earl. Sir Kenelm sued the Earl after marriage, and recovered it. Sir Edmund Wylde had her picture, and was very familiar with her. After her marriage she redeemed her honour by her strict living; she and her husband were invited once a year by the Earl of Dorset, when with much desire and passion he beheld her, and only kissed her hand, Sir Kenelm being still by."

This statement cannot be reconciled with the delicately scrupulous conduct imputed by Digby to Venetia; nevertheless, public rumour, as well as the plain-spoken Aubrey, had laid grave charges at the door of the beautiful, intellectual Venetia; neither does Digby stand up for her honour as valiantly as one would expect. Many parts of Aubrey's account, however, have been proved to be perfectly false; for example, there is no notice of any trial against Lord Dorset's heirs and executors, for the annuity he is stated to have allowed Venetia: again, the story of Venetia and Digby dining with his lordship once a year, and of his kissing her hand, must have been an invention, since Dorset died before Venetia's marriage to Sir Kenelm. The age of James I. was notoriously scandalous; the manners were gross; the notions of the time latitudinarian on moral points; but what has been alleged against Venetia fell to the ground upon her marriage with Digby. No one, in fact, so greatly contributed to injure her fame as her husband. Instead of resting manfully on her innocence, and defending her from slander, he throws out hints that "indiscreet, unstayed youth, or rather childhood," may have caused innocent error in her actions, "and whoso marryeth her, that, being past her years of innocent ignorance," must expect, he conceives, many faults. It must be remembered, he adds, " that the clearest brooks that are have some mud, but which will not at all defile the pureness of the stream if it be not *indiscreetly* stirred, and then too it hath so shallow a bottom, that it quickly slideth away." Since Sir Kenelm took this view of the subject, no one can be surprised at his marrying Venetia, blighted as was her reputation.

They were married privately, in January 1625, and the union, although a suspicion of it added to previous reports, was kept rigidly secret. Sir Kenelm, meantime, was busily engaged in proclaiming to the world his application of the celebrated Sympathetic Powder, the knowledge of which he acquired, as he stated, from a friar to whom he had done some essential service. Many diseases were deemed incurable in those days, but were manageable by miraculous agencies. A dead man's hand drawn over a tumour dispelled the swelling; the royal touch cured the evil, and had cured it since the days of Edward the Confessor, until Dr. Johnson, a sickly child, received its supposed benefit from the hand of Queen Anne, in her black hood and diamonds.

"Such sanctity had Heaven given her hand."

"To each succeeding royalty" was left the healing benediction, until the heavy, incredulous Hanoverians came to the crown. Touching and praying were the medicine for a malady most prevalent when insufficient animal food, want of drainage, and constant intermarriages fostered the cruel disorder in this country. A split tree, into which a child was placed for a few minutes, and drawn thrice through the fissure, naked, cured rickets; the tree was bandaged up, and, as it united and grew again, so grew the child. Sympathetic indications are perpetually insisted on by the writers of the seventeenth century. That a murdered corpse bled at the touch of the murderer, or even at his approach, Shakspeare and Dryden imply: the first in his Henry VI., when Richard III. approaches the royal corpse, the latter, in his forty-sixth *Idea*.

"In making trial of a murther wrought,
If the vile actors of the heinous deed
Near the dead body happily be brought,
Oft 't hath proved the breathless corps will bleed."

God, it was thought, had appointed that secret supernatural sign for the discovery of crime. It is not then surprising that when Sir Kenelm Digby imparted to James I. his secret of the famous Sympathetic Powder, the idea was quickly taken up. James Howel, generally called the Letter-writer, was wounded in the hand in endeavouring to part two friends in a duel. James sent to the busy court gossip, Howel, his own surgeon, but a gangrene was expected, and Howel sent to Digby for his powder. Digby instantly paid him a visit.

"I asked him," Digby relates, "for anything that had the blood upon it; so he presently sent for his garter, wherewith his hand was first bound; and as I called for a bason of water, as if I would wash my hands, I took a handful of powder of vitriol, which I had in my study, and presently dissolved it. As soon as the bloody garter was brought me, I put it within the bason, observing in the interim what Mr. Howel did, who stood talking with a gentleman in a corner of my chamber, not regarding at all what I was doing; but he started suddenly as if he had found some strange alteration in himself. I asked him what he ailed? 'I know not what ails me,' he said, 'but I find that I feel no more pain. Methinks that a pleasing kinde of freshnesse, as it were a wet cold napkin, did spread over my hand, which hath taken away the inflammation that tormented me before.' I reply'd, 'Since then you feel already so good effect of my medicament, I advise you to cast away all your playsters; only keep the wound clean, and in a moderate temper betwixt heat and cold.'" This was presently reported to the Duke of Buckingham, and a little after to the King, who were both very curious to know the "circumstance of the businesse, which was that after dinner I took the garter out of the water, and put it to dry before a greate fire. It was scarce dry, before Mr. Howel's servant came running, that his master felt as much burning as ever he had done, if not more; for the heat was such as if his hand were 'twixt coals of fire. I answered, that although that had happened at present, yet he should find ease in a short time; for I knew the cause of this new accident, and would provide accordingly, for his master should be free from that inflammation, it may be, before he possibly could return to him; but in case he found no ease, I wished him to come presently back again; if not, he might forbear coming. Thereupon he went, and at the instant I did put again the garter into the water, whereupon he found his master without any pain at all. To be brief, there was no sense of pain afterwards, but within five or six dayes the wounds were cicatrized and entirely healed."

The doctrine of sympathetic cures and indications was very common in the reigns of Elizabeth and James I.; otherwise one can hardly imagine a man of sense, still less, of a philosophic mind, relating, so gravely, an incident which not only borders on the marvellous, but on the impossible.

This, one might suppose, was wonderful enough. Dr. Drake, with good sense, ascribes the cure to the plasters being taken off the wounds. A sympathetic power was supposed also to subsist between the wounds and the instrument that inflicted them. If the weapon that had dealt the blow, was anointed with a salve, or stroked in a particular manner, great relief was felt by the wounded person.

"They can remedie," says Reginald Scot, "anie stranger, and him that is absent, with that *verie sword* wherewith they are wounded. Yea, and that which is beyond all admiration, if they stroke the sword upwards with their fingers, the partie shall feel no paine; whereas if they draw their finger downwards, thereupon the partie wounded shall feele intolerable paine."

The superstition of the sympathy relating to the mandrake, a vegetable, the root of which is supposed to be endued with animal life, is referred to by Shakspeare:

"—— what with loathsome smells,
And shrieks like mandrakes torn out of the earth,
That living mortals, hearing them, run mad;
Oh! if I wake, shall I not be distraught?"

Sir Kenelm's reputation for science, and its application to practical purpose, was considerable. Still, however, he committed the injustice of keeping his marriage secret, although, to judge by his language, he fondly appreciated the felicity of possessing as his wife the lovely Venetia. Of love he thus writes (let his enthusiasm produce a smile in the faces of lovers of modern days, when the *impassive* style has become fashionable): "And this joy and content of lovers, besides that it is the highest and noblest that we can possess, is also the securest, and placed, as it were, in sanctuary, out of the hands of fortune and change, for the ground of it is in ourselves, and we need the help of no exterior thing to make it complete; it dependeth upon our wills which we govern as we please: therefore, this is the true happiness, which a wise man ought to aim at, since that himself is master of it, and he can give it to himself when he list."

"The love of a virtuous soul in a fair and perfect body" he believed to be "the noblest and worthiest action that a man is master of;" yet he imperilled the life of Venetia from fear of the world.

Whilst Sir Kenelm was in London, Venetia remained in seclusion at the house of her father in the country. In due time her first confinement was drawing near: still, the marriage was kept a profound secret, being confided to one female servant only — a young and inexperienced person. One day, however, Digby was summoned to his wife; she had been riding out one evening and had been thrown from her horse. She was brought speechless to her chamber; the pains of childbirth came on, yet still Venetia kept her secret. No cry nor expression betrayed the cause of her suffering, and in peril, in secresy, a son was born.

The part which Sir Kenelm took in political affairs appears to have been at once kind and honourable. But he had, in consequence of his father's religion and treason, many difficulties to overcome.

Chamberlain writes to Carleton: "The Papists of Cheshire and Lancashire, who, by mediation of the Spanish ambassador, had obtained respite till Lady-day from payments for recusancy, are sent for to answer their doings. A secret society, first formed in Lord Vaux's regiment in the Low Countries, has spread to England; they weare blue and yellow rebbons in their hats, have a prince called Ottoman, and nicknames as Tityse, &c."*

Notwithstanding various speeches in parliament, in which the members declared that the Spanish treaty of marriage between Prince Charles and the Infanta of Spain should take place in "spite of all the devils in hell, and all the Puritans in England," that negotiation had failed. On the return of his son from Spain, James knighted Kenelm Digby—"son," as Chamberlain calls him, "to him that was a prime man in the Powder Plot." The distinction thus conferred was followed by many proofs of confidence on the part not only of James I. but of his successor. The following extracts from a letter written by Sir Kenelm to his cousin, the Earl of Bristol, show how disposed Charles was to excuse that ill-used nobleman, whose failure in the Spanish marriage he imputed rather, as it appears, to an error of judgment than to want of zeal in the cause.

Charles was grieved to hear of the illness and depression of the disgraced ambassador.

"Truely, my Lord," Sir Kenelm wrote, "he did receaue the newes of yor ill state wth much tenderness, and asked me many p̃ticulars how you weare; and bad me hasten to let yor Lo^p knowe he was verye sorrye for yor sicknes and protested

---

* Domestic Papers for 1627: State Paper Office.

in the deepest manner that might be, that he had no personal displeasure or grudge (these were his words) against yor Lo^p: but that he held you to be an honest and sufficient man and one that loved him and had endeavoured his service really, and should be glad of any good that arrived vnto you. And in the other point concerneninge yor busines, he would not have yor Lo^p. conceaue that he thinketh you to be a delinquent and to have offended in any matter of honestye or not p̄formance of what was com̄aunded you, for if that had bin then this course that hath bin should not have bin used wth yo^u but you should have beene com̄itted to the Tower, and brought to a publick trial, but the true cause why yor Lo^p: is thus in suspence and remoued from the Court is because yor Lo^{p.} in the treatye of the Spanish Match (he thinketh) was soe desirous of it and soe passionate for it (as he confesseth himselfe was alsoe after hee had seene the Ladye), that you trusted more to the Spanish ministers and their promises then was fittinge in discretion. . . . His Matie alsoe told me that though yo^u much desired the match, yet he thinkes you did not labo^r so effectually as yo^u might haue done to effect what he soe extreamely desired, wch was to haue the Infanta then alonge wth him; and whilst the Duke and the Conde O. Oliuares were good friends, and that you were fallen out wth the Conde (wch he saide was indeede for beinge an honest man to him) you weare verye cold in Sollicitinge that particular; but that as soone as the conde and the Duke were fallen out, wch was not p̄sonall betweene them, but caused by the busines and for His Maties seruise, yor Lo^p. was instantly freindes wth the Conde wthout recapitulateinge any busines of the quarrell or receaueinge satisfaction for the wrongs he had done you; wherin His Mat^{ie} saith he discouered much ill will in you to the Duke, and an apt-es in you to be euer confident in the Spaniardes when their promises concurred with yor desires. The summe and conclusion of his Maties discourse was, that p̄sonally he hath a very good affection to yor Lõp and the error wch he conceaves to be committed by yo^u is such that the least acknowledgment shall expiate it, and then yo^u shall haue his fauo^r againe as before. I hope this relation will bringe much content vnto yor Lop̃. especially I tellinge y^o that the Kinge seemed to me to speake it verye affectionately and lamentinge yor sicknes, wch pray God soone to free you of, that you may in due time take notice to his Matie of what I write to yor Lop̃ as yo^u shall thinke fitt. And goe wth remembraunce of my humble seruice to yor Lop̃.

"I rest,

"yor Lop̃s most faithfull servant,

"London, 27 May, 1625."*   " KENELME DIGBYE.

This gracious reception on the part of the King seemed to augur for Sir Kenelm a future career of great success, whether as a courtier and soldier, or in maritime affairs; yet it is evident from some of the letters lately brought to light in the State Paper Office, that the jealousy of Buckingham, and consequently of his secretary Nicholas, impeded one of the most ardent desires of Sir Kenelm, that of nautical distinction.

Sir Kenelm himself asserts, that it was his wish to prove to the world that his love for Venetia had not lessened his courage and ambition, which induced him to entreat King Charles to send him on a voyage.

The objections made to a request seemingly so advantageous to the country as well as honourable to himself, appear, indeed, singular to our modern ideas.

The first obstacle is stated to be inferiority of rank. Nicholas, secretary to the Duke of Buckingham, thus states that point:—

"First, that it is graunted to a private gent, whereas such com̃^s (commission) haue not bene used to be graunted to † . . under the degree of a Baron unlesse it were for ye Kinges service.

---

* State-Paper Office.—Domestic Papers, Chas. I., vol. ii. No. 100.
† A word erased.

"Secondly," he proceeds to say, "that it doth not only licence S[r] Kenelme, but all such as he will answere for, w[ch] is more then was graunted to y[e] D. of Cumberland. (That this com͠n * graunted to that knt: and his deputies and officers, whereas y[e] s[d] D[ke] had it only to him selfe and his officers) He hath power to himselfe and his deputies to execute marshall Lawes w[ch] none eu[r] had before (but y[e] E. of Warwick that went not in an im͠ediate service for his Mat[ie]) He doth anticipate power to take the thingges and goods of anie that shall not be in amity wth his Mat[ie] w[ch] large irregularity and Latitude was unheard of, till my lo: of Warwick's Com͠n whereof I . . . . . . and my lo; was p̄mised it should be amended. fst his passe, and that he take duty or valew, he is not I thinke to pay damages, for when he is att sea he cannot tell whether the King be fallen out wth the States or noe.

"This Com͠n Thoughe there be noe menc̃on in it for y[e] King's svice, doth require all officers by sea and Land (in w[ch] my lo: Ad[ll] is comp̄hended), to ayde assist & further him & his officers in anie thinge he or his officers shall require and stande in neede of for the furtheraunce of his sv̓ice, wch is S[r]. Kenelme & his adventurers only.

"I should be satisfied from you on the behalf of my Lo: Ad[ll] (Admiral) what you thinke of these points & of ye Com͠n in geñall (General.) And whether you cann remember that the like at anie time hath bene graunted to any private man of his ranke that hath not bene imployed for his Maties sv̓ice. My lo. thought much that the E. of Warwicke had such a com͠n as was graunted to him, and will take it for a greate remissness in those he trusteth here in adm[ly] businesses when he shall heare of this graunt to S[r] Kenelme of this Com͠n hath no relac̃on to their Lop̄[s] † att all I pray lett."

"I knowe," he adds in another letter, "my lo: will thinke

---

* Commission.   † Words erased.

his officers wondrous negligent, when he shall heare that such a Com̃n is graunted: My lo: of Warwicks canne be noe p̃sident (precedent) to warrant this, and I am confident my lo: would never haue Given way to that to passe had but he had leasure to consider the consequence hereof, or had it not bene in the puzle of the greate pparaćons as where then in hand.

"I honor Sir Kenelme Digby, and thinke him worthy of encourag̃mt, Soe as it be not at my lords cost, and to ye dishonor or diminućon of the rt. priviledges of his graces place; wch I hope shall be p̃vented by yor care and industry wch I shall not fayle to make knowne to my Lo: as being truly, &c.

"25e Fbris, 1627."* "E. NICHOLAS.

The commission, with very full powers, was, however, granted; Charles styling Sir Kenelm in that document our "trustie and well-beloved friend."

Thus we see, that whilst all were bred up to arms, a previous nautical education was not thought essential to the naval service; and a military man, and even a civilian of influence, often took the command of a squadron. The object of Sir Kenelm's expedition was to intercept the trade in silks of the French in Spain and Portugal, and by this means to insure that trade to the English.

Before leaving England he imparted his marriage to Digby, Earl of Bristol, who promised to befriend the suspected and injured Venetia.

Sir Kenelm's expedition was triumphant, and his favour at court was now permanently insured. Sir Kenelm, in spite of his absence, not only retained his post as gentleman of the bed-chamber, but was also appointed a Commissioner of the Royal Navy, and Governor of Trinity House. About this time, also, a reconciliation was opened for the return of Van Dyck to England, but the painter, as it appears from

* Domestic Papers, State Paper Office. Nicholas's Letter Book, 1627, p. 64.

the following letter, translated from the Italian, in which he seems sometimes to have written,—at first drew back from the overtures made to him, conceiving that Sir Balthazar Gerbier, the English agent in the affair, had not promoted his interests at the English court.

To Sir Balthazar Gerbier.

" To the Agent of England.

" Your excellency will do me the favour to hold in suspense the treaty with the Queen Mother of France, as well as her Highness, respecting my voyage to England, until such time as I may speak with your excellency in my own person and not through another. I kiss your hand and remain, &c.,

" ANTO. VAN DYCK."

(*Translation*) *Postscript to a letter (in French) from Sir B. Gerbier to the King (Charles I.)*

" Van Dyck is here, and says he is resolved to go over into England: he pretends to be very ill pleased with me, because that babbler Geldorp has written that I had orders to speak to the said Van Dyck on the part of your Majestie, and that I concealed it from him.

" Your Majesty so commanded me, consequently I was not called upon to give an explanation to any one, neither do I intend.

"Dated from Brussels, March 13, 1632." *

Let us view Digby now, for a brief space, the ornament of that staid court, into which Charles I. introduced his own refined tastes, and where none were patronised who did not, in some measure, contribute to the pleasures of intellect and to the love of art.

Henrietta Maria was then in all the bloom of her almost

* State Paper Office, No. 2.

infantine loveliness, gay as a bird, fond of pleasure as a Frenchwoman was likely to be, easily prejudiced, easily won by talents which took her fancy. Sir Kenelm spoke French well; he was suspected to be inclined to Romanism, which he afterwards avowed; he was voluble, and had *savoir faire*, and a careless elegance of manners, so that it seemed as if he had been brought up in a court. Henrietta Maria delighted in his society; Charles respected his abilities; their tastes were in unison, and Digby employed his influence in one way calculated to insure the gratitude of posterity; he brought Van Dyck to England.* It was from Sir Kenelm that Charles I. learned what a treasure had been sent away when Van Dyck, chagrined and scarcely noticed, had, after his first visit, left England in disgust. But the slight was repaired. The great painter was received with distinction, and lodged among the King's painters in Blackfriars, or, as the Frenchman Felbien, with what Horace Walpole calls "the dignity of ignorance," terms it, *L'Hôtel de Blaifore*. Striking scenes had been enacted in this same "*Hôtel de Blaifore*" before Van Dyck took up his abode there. A church, precinct, and sanctuary had once composed the monastery of the Black or Preaching Friars, founded by Hubert de Burgh in 1221. Various great personages had largely endowed this monastery, the hall of which, before its suppression in 1538, was used for various occasions. Blackfriars had been honoured in the reign of Henry VIII. by being appropriated to the reception of the Emperor Charles V. In the hall of Black Friars poor Katharine of Arragon made that passionate and fruitless appeal, which after the lapse of centuries is never read, even in the obsolete language of the chroniclers of the day, without emotion; the Friary, as it was called, contained

---

* An entry occurs in the State Paper Office, dated March 20, 1630-31, by which it appears seventy-eight pounds was paid to "Monseur Vandyck of Antwerp, for a picture of Reynaldo and Armida." The money went through the hands of Endymion Porter.

many separate dwellings within the "site, circle, or compass of Blackfriars;" the convent was dissolved and the church pulled down, but the sanctuary still remained, and existed until merged into the ward of "Farringdon Within." It was probably in part of the old convent, granted by Edward VI. to Sir Thomas Cawarden, Master of the Revels, that Van Dyck lived from 1632 to 1641. The rent of his house was stated, in 1638, to be twenty pounds a year, the title, one pound, six shillings, and eightpence. It appears from several entries and warrants that fifteen shillings a day was allowed for the painter's board and lodging. Here Charles I. came frequently, not only sitting to the painter for his own picture, but often working himself at the easel. What an assemblage must have been seen from time to time in that antique edifice:—Charles himself, his coronation robes, or his suit of white satin, hanging over a chair-back ready for the painter when he employed himself on them; or the King's young wards, "dear Steenie's" children, George, second Duke of Buckingham, and his brother Lord Francis Villiers, handsome boys, who sat to Van Dyck by the King's wish; or graver company sometimes, to wit, Archbishop Laud, upon whose beaming face the clouds of care had not then lowered:— Inigo Jones, all the Wharton family, and last, not least, the stately Sir Kenelm and his beautiful, his doomed Venetia. One would like to have peeped in at that old lattice, and taken a survey of that chamber: the artist, with his eye full of fire and genius, his fine features, in a dress too rich for work, but setting off his figure to the best advantage, working at his satins, on the excellence of which,—he is said to have painted one white satin dress fourteen times over before he could satisfy himself,—he used to pride himself.

Here Venetia in all her bloom was depicted; she is represented as treading on envy and malice, unhurt by a serpent that twines round her arm, a delicate compliment to her implied justification. It was no slight undertaking to sit to

Van Dyck for a portrait, he was so slow and fastidious; Lanière the painter sat to him seven whole days and evenings. Nothing would induce the painter to let his sitters see their portraits when in progress. Often the great and the learned stayed to dinner, which was then at noon, so that, after studying their faces, he could retouch the likeness in the afternoon:—and how delightful must have been those impromptu dinners; the talk, not all of painting, but of the sister art of music. For Van Dyck loved music, he was generous to musicians. His receptions were splendid, and at last, though he died at forty-one, both his fortune and his constitution were injured by this princely style of living. He began to take less pains with his portraits, and, being asked the reason, answered, "I have worked a long time for reputation, and I now work for my kitchen."

Van Dyck, says Walpole, sought to repair his fortune, not by the laboratory of his painting-room, as Rubens had done, but by that "real folly, the pursuit of the philosopher's stone, in which, perhaps, he was encouraged by the example of his friend Sir Kenelm Digby." It is stated that Van Dyck sympathised in Digby's tastes, believed in the sympathetic powder, and appreciated his friend as one of the greatest philosophers of his time, whilst Sir Kenelm proved the most valuable patron that any painter could desire.

It was not only by the luxuries of his table and style that Van Dyck became poor; he had other expensive pleasures. The highly-finished portrait of his mistress, Mrs. Lemon, still attracts, by its beauty of outline and colouring, many a connoisseur's eye. This person lived openly with Van Dyck, yet she also received the attentions of Endymion Porter, gentleman of the bed-chamber to Charles I., and a protégé of the first George Villiers. Towards the end of Van Dyck's short life, he married, by the King's desire, the Lady Maria Ruthven, one of the beauties of the court. She was the daughter of the Earl of Gowrie, a house famous for its treasonable attack upon James I. Beauty and rank were her only portion, and Charles, it is thought by some, sought to lower the Ruthven family by thus marrying its brightest ornament to a painter. But this surmise, springing from the small mind of Horace Walpole, a liberal in profession, an aristocrat in his inmost heart, is unworthy of the more generous views of Charles I., who, probably, with juster views of the relations of society, thought a man of eminence in a noble profession equal to match with the daughter of an ancient house.

Sometimes Van Dyck retired at Eltham, near the old palace of the Tudors, over the ruins of which Evelyn lamented when he beheld the devastations made by Rich during the rebellion. But the usual tenor of Sir Anthony's life was passed at Blackfriars, whither Charles rowed in a royal barge, delighted to see his portraits of the ill-starred royal family.

The King had granted him an annuity of 200*l.* a year, and the sums paid for Van Dyck's paintings, though they may seem small in our days, were considerable in that state of the value of money. Charles, it appears, from several entries discovered in the State Paper Office, did not disclaim the foreign custom, to which the English have so strong an objection, of offering less prices than those asked; for there is a list of pictures delivered about the year 1628, in Van Dyck's handwriting, with the diminution of prices marked by the King.

It makes one's heart ache to think how dispersed these treasures of art were, in after days, when the decree of Parliament caused them to be sold, as Horace Walpole terms it, by "inch of candle." After the execution of Charles, a twelfth Roman Emperor, painted by Van Dyck to complete the set by Titian, was purchased by the Spanish Ambassador. A portrait of Charles in armour,—in which Van Dyck excelled,—and riding on a dun horse, found its way, somehow, to Munich, where the great Marlborough bought *it*, and placed it in Blenheim House. For his portraits **Van Dyck** received according to their size, for a half length 40*l*., a whole length 60*l*.; a family portrait, including several figures, cost 100*l*.! Among his sitters, Sir Kenelm,—to whom Van Dyck owed his establishment in England,—with **Venetia** and her children, were more frequently seen at Blackfriars than any other friends.

In the following letter addressed by Van Dyck to Mr. Francis Junius, reference is made to the famous print of Sir Kenelm Digby, engraved by Van Voorst from a portrait by Van Dyck. The original letter (of which that here given is a translation) was in Dutch.*

" *To Mr. Francis Junius* †, *London.*

" Sir,

" The Baron Canuwe ‡ has returned to me, by sea, the copy of your book 'De Pictura Veterum,' which he values very highly, and considers it a most learned composition; I am confident it will be as acceptable to the public as any hitherto published, and that the arts will be much elucidated by so remarkable a work, which must materially promote their regeneration, and insure a great reputation and satisfaction to its author. Lately I communicated the same to a very learned gentleman, who came to visit me, and I can hardly describe in what favourable terms he spoke of your book, which he considered to be as curious and learned as any he had ever met with.

" The before-named Baron Canuwe wishes to receive a copy of it as soon as the printing shall be finished, persuaded

---

* Harl. MSS. No. 4936, and numbered 26 in the volume.

† Francis Junius was librarian to the Earl of Arundel (the first English patron of Vandyck) and tutor to his children.

‡ Edward, 2nd Viscount Conway.

that everybody will take a particular interest in the same, and be anxious to see it.

"As I have caused the portrait of the Chevalier Digby to be engraved, with a view to publication, I humbly request you to favour me with a little motto by way of inscription at the bottom of the plate*, by which you will render me a service, and do me great honour; the present tending chiefly to offer you my humble service.

"Believe me always to remain, Sir,
"Your unworthy servant,
"This 14th August, 1636." "ANT. VAN DYCK."

Sympathetic powder, and the philosopher's stone, were not the only themes that were discussed in the Friary— or worn threadbare as the friends paced the then delicious neighbourhood of Eltham. Sir Kenelm was now in a state of transition from the Anglican to the Romish Church. Early predilections had, perhaps, never been wholly effaced from a mind full of romance, and devoted to old-world literature. Before 1636, he had begun to have religious scruples: in that year, he reconciled himself to the Church of Rome.

He wrote an apology for his conversion to his old tutor Laud: the archbishop returned him an answer full of tenderness and good advice, but expressing little hope of retain-

* There is a plate, engraved by Van Voorst from a portrait by Van Dyck, of Sir Ken. Digby, inserted in the "Centum Scones," in the background of which is a broken armillary sphere, beneath it the words "Impavidum ferient," supposed to be an allusion to a naval victory gained over the French and the Venetians in the Bay of Scanderoon, by a squadron under the command of Digby. This was probably the device and motto furnished by Junius. In the early impressions of this plate Sir Kenelm Digby is singularly enough styled "Astrologus Caroli Regis Magnæ Britanniæ." This action is recorded in a poem of Ben Jonson's, entitled "An Epigram to my Muse the Lady Digby, on her husband, Sir Kenelm Digby," wherein he writes this couplet,—

"Witness thy action done at Scanderoon
Upon thy birth-day, the eleventh of June."

ing him in the Protestant Church. Laud well knew that when once a conversion of that nature takes place, the mind refuses to see the light: implicit acceptance is accorded even to points of faith which have not the remotest foundation in Scripture, and all free discussion is for ever relinquished.

Sir Kenelm replied to the archbishop, and endeavoured to convince him that the change had not been made without great consideration. He afterwards published at Paris his " Conference with a Lady about the Choice of a Religion."

The studies of Van Dyck must have been a succession of *tableaux* of the great characters of the day. Mistress Lemon, with her soft fair face and voluptuous beauty, had vanished from the scene, and the high-born wife had succeeded her: and now, when Van Dyck had become respectable, Charles would permit his lovely queen and her ladies, in their tendril-like curls and satin dresses, to pass their judgments upon the portraits. Here stands the dark-browed Wentworth, Earl of Strafford, haughty, unpopular, yet of a grand presence and striking mien. Strafford was inimitably depicted by Van Dyck. It is a face so full of strong determination, so little capable, one would fancy, of changing that expression, that one can hardly imagine the doomed earl melting into tears during his trial when he spoke of his children. Strafford, with the shadow on his brow, was Van Dyck's masterpiece. "I can forgive him," says Horace Walpole, "any insipid portraits of perhaps insipid people, when he showed himself capable of conceiving and transmitting the idea of the greatest man of the age." One would hardly have expected that sentence from Horace Walpole.

Sometimes in that studio the burly figure and diseased visage of Ben Jonson might be seen, and we may imagine him uttering some sentences of Dutch, of which he had picked up a smattering when he was a soldier in Flanders. Gerard Honthorst has left us a living likeness of "poor Ben"—

what a head it is; so broad a forehead; such hard and massive features; one eye askance:—the form so bulky that it must have almost filled up the small old-fashioned chamber. What a contrast his rough attire and very ugly face to the handsome Van Dyck, *point devise* even in his studio, and *petit maître* whilst at his easel! But Ben had the patronage of Sir Kenelm, and celebrated the virtues of Venetia in his Eupheme, a long poem which he published in her praise after her death.

It was about this time, and before the death of Venetia, that a letter in the State Paper Office indicates at once the unwarrantable interference of King Charles in university matters, and the resistance of the college authorities. Either Charles was ignorant of Digby's actually being married, or, he considered his sovereign powers sufficient to set aside the statutes, when he made known his pleasure that Sir Kenelm should be chosen a fellow of St. John's College, whether at Cambridge or Oxford is uncertain: it appears from the following letter that Sir Kenelm had been prosecuting certain studies at Cambridge (since Christ's College is here spoken of), and that he was desirous of having a permanent post in that University; yet he had been originally at St. John's, Oxford. Both Oxford and Cambridge were, in those days, the residence frequently of the learned, long after their term of pupilage was over. But an interference like this on the part of Charles seems without precedent; though accepted as for the good of their society, by the Master and Fellows of St. John's.

"Right Hon[ble] our most noble Chancellor,

"At our late Election of Fellowes his Ma[tie] was pleased by diverse letters (out of his Princely care for the good of our Colledge) to recomend diverse persons to our Choyce, and in two of them a faculty was expressed of full liberty to execute his gracious Comands. The third on the behalfe of one Sr Digby of Christs Colledge, did the more p̄plex (perplex) us for that it was no way in our power to giue to all satisfaction therunto. However p̃tye (partly he) forgatte himselfe so farr as neyther to attend the three public dayes of Examination; wherin tryall was to be taken of the sufficiency and capabillitye of all suitors; nor after, to shewe himselfe to any one of the Senio^rs, nor yett to haue his name given up to the Electo^rs all the tyme previousely appoynted by Statute under payne of Ineligibility to the end his partes and qualityes might be Inquired after; yet his sacred Mat^yes request would haue ben tye ynough uppon us, his most dutyfull and obedient servants, to haue indeavored the accomplishment of his Royall desyre, had wee bene inabled thereunto, by a dispensation wth those opposite Statutes, vnto wch otherwise wee stand obliged by oathe:—Pardon us therfore most Honble S^r that wee presume thus to molest yor public affayres wth the relation of our poore Collegiate occasions: and we hope you will give us leave in all humility to implore yor mediation, by a Candid and fayre presentement of our loyall affections to his most gracious Matie and with all of our just excuse, for omitting that wch was not in our possibility to p̄forme. We know our owne thoughts best; and should much reioyce yf that yor Lo^pp would vouchsafe to vnderstand them from our selves, wch will be a new obligation binding us ever to pray for the Increase of yor Lop̄p̄s health and happines.

"Yo^r Lop̄p̄s suppliant Orrato^rs and Servants,
"The M^r & Senio^rs &c."*

It is evident, by one part of his "Eupheme," that Ben Jonson had seen the lovely Venetia in the act of sitting for her picture; hence the following lines, entitled by him

---

* Domestic State Papers, 29th March, 1633, No. 238. Indorsed, "Copy of a l^re (letter) of St Johns Coll. to the E^rl of Holland, excusing their not chosing Sr Digby according to his Maties lr̄es. d̄d̄ by Dr. Beale."

"The Picture of her Body," seem to be suggested by such an occasion:

"THE PICTURE OF HER BODY."

"Sitting, and ready to be drawn,
What make these velvets, silks, and lawn,
Embroideries, feathers, fringes, lace,
Where every limb takes like a face?

"Send these suspected helps to aid
Some form defective, or decayed;
This beauty, without falsehood fair,
Needs nought to clothe it but the air.

"Yet something to the painter's view
Here fitly interposed; so new;
He shall, if he can understand,
Work by my fancy, with his hand.

"Draw first a cloud, all save her neck,
And out of that make day to break;
Till like her face it do appear,
And men may think all light rose there."

Before Sir Kenelm had changed his mode of faith, she who was ever his idol — his Venetia — was no more. On the first of May, 1633, this beautiful, gifted woman, whom Ben Jonson called "his Muse," was found dead in her bed. As she was only thirty-three years of age, and did not appear previously to be ill, the darkest hints were thrown out, and Digby was accused of having poisoned her out of jealousy. Her head was opened, and the portion of brain within it found to be very small — a fact which Sir Kenelm ascribed to her drinking viper's wine; but Aubrey observes, that "spiteful women would say it was a viper's husband who was jealous of her." One explanation was, perhaps, as rational as another.

Digby, however, acted the bereaved widower to perfection: he retired to Gresham College; assumed a long mourning cloak, a high-cornered hat, and let his beard grow; lived like a hermit, and conversed chiefly with the professor there, devoting his days to chemistry. It is not unlikely that Venetia's death, his seclusion, his passion of grief, and some remorse—for he had not been the most faithful of husbands—led him to think more deeply on religious subjects than a man of the world has time to do. The early impressions of infancy recur in that season when the spirit is bowed down by anguish. He turned, perhaps, with a certain feeling of relief, to the Romish faith, which allows to those who die in error the process of a purgatory to refine the dross of their carnal natures. It is the very weak, or the very unhappy, or the very sinful that are most easily led to adopt the tenets that promise so much, and exact so little of what it is much more difficult to give than offerings and masses.

He proved, however, his love for Venetia, who thus, in her thirty-third year was taken from him, by employing Ben Jonson to write his "Eupheme." Efforts of that kind were usually well paid in those days. No "In Memoriam" was written for mere friendship. Ben Jonson, however, wrote from his heart; we cannot believe it otherwise when such verses as these are penned.

"THE PICTURE OF HER MIND.*

"A mind so pure, so perfect fine,
As, 'tis not radiant, but divine;
And so disdaining any crier,
'Tis got, where it can try her fire.

"There, all exalted in the sphere,
As it another nature were,
It moveth all, and makes a flight,
As circular as infinite.

"Whose notions when it will express
In speech, it is with that excess
Of grace, and music to the ear,
As what it spoke, it planted there.

"The voice so sweet, the words so fair,
As some soft chime had parted there,
And though the sound were parted thence,
Had left an echo on the sense.

---

* Jonson's Works, 722.

"But that a mind so rapt, so high,
So swift, so pure, should yet apply
Itself to us, and come so nigh
Earth's grossness; there's the how and why.
* * * *
"Thrice happy house that hath receipt
For this so lofty form, so streight,
So polished, perfect, round, and even,
As it slid moulded off from heaven.
* * * *
"In action, wingèd as the wind;
In rest, like spirits left behind
Upon a bank, or field of flowers,
Begotten by the wind or showers."

Lady Digby was buried in Christ's Church, Newgate, in a brick vault, over which were three steps of black marble, with four inscriptions in copper gilt affixed to it; over this was her bust of copper gilt. The material seemed intended for durability, but in the great fire of London all was destroyed, except the vault, and the bust, which was stolen about 1675-6:" "I saw," Aubrey writes, "as I was walking through Newgate Street, Dame Venetia's bust, standing at a stall at the Golden Cross, a glazier's shop. I presently remembered it, but the fire had got off the gilding; but taking notice of it to one that was with me, I could never afterwards see it exposed to the street. They melted it down."

Ben Jonson owed, he declares in undying verse, his best inspirations to the accomplished and courteous Venetia. Lowly born as he was, he honoured her ancient lineage; coarse—he appreciated her refinement; thus he speaks that sorrow which, in him, found words so full of pathos:

"'Twere time I dy'd too, now she is dead,
Who was my Muse, and life of all I said,
The spirit that I wrote with and conceiv'd;
All that was good, or great with me, she weav'd,
And set it forth:—"

The rest of his ideas he compares to "fine cobwebs," of no value nor permanence.

> "I murmur against God for having taken
> Her blessed soul hence, forth this valley vain
> Of tears! and dungeon of calamity!
> I envy it the angels' amity,
> The joy of saints, the crown for which it lives,
> The glory and gain of rest, which the place gives!
> * * * *
> Was she then so dear when she departed?
> You will meet her there,
> Much more desired and dearer than before.
>
> There, all the happy souls that ever were,
> Shall meet together, in one theatre,
> And each shall know there one another's face,
> By beatific virtue of the place;
> There shall the brother with the sister walk,
> And sons and daughters with their parents talk,
> But all of God."

The character of Venetia drawn by this poetical pen, would lead us wholly to discredit the rumour that early in life she had been frail. After describing her as having all nobility except pride, as possessing a mind as calm as she was fair,—

> "Not tost or troubled with light-lady air,
> But kept an even gait, as some straight tree
> Moved by the air, so comely moved she,"—

he speaks of the influence Venetia exercised in her household: He says—

> "She was in one, a many parts of life,
> A tender mother, a discreeter wife,
> A solemn mistress, and so good a friend,
> So charitable to religious end
> In all her petite actions, so devote,
> As her whole life was now become one note
> Of piety and private holiness."

Ben, crippled by debts, humbled by perpetual adversity,

felt the beauty of that evenness of character so rare in *les grandes dames*,— Venetia was not uncertain in manner, not one day overflowing with emotions, the next, tired of a *protégé*, imprudent enough to be always in trouble: the fine-lady impulse dying into coldness, or excited to impatience.

Venetia's character is so graphically, so affectionately pictured by Jonson, that we cannot but believe he wrote from an intimate knowledge of its gentle nobleness. His " Eupheme " is ended with these lines, alluding to that early death for which he believes she was prepared:

> " In this sweet extasy she was rapt hence.
> Who reads will pardon my intelligence,
> That thus have ventured, these true stands upon,
> To publish her a saint. My Muse is gone."

Little is known of Digby's movements for some time, except that on his friend Van Dyck's return from Paris, whither he had gone soon after his marriage to Lady Maria Ruthven, Sir Kenelm was the medium of proposing to King Charles that Van Dyck should make designs for the embellishment of the banqueting house at Whitehall. The ceiling of that room, which is now used as a chapel, had already been adorned by Rubens with the history and procession of the Order of the Garter. With that beautiful fragment, known still as the Banqueting House at Whitehall, the name of Van Dyck is so connected that a short account of it may not here be unwelcome.

Whitehall was, in the reign of the Tudors, a building of the style of architecture which bears the name of those monarchs, with a succession of galleries and courts, a hall, chapel, cockpit, tennis court, orchard, and banqueting house. James I. resolved to build a new Whitehall, and Inigo Jones designed one worthy indeed of its purpose and architect. Nothing, however, was finished except the banqueting house. Charles I. also intended to complete Whitehall, but an empty treasury impeded that project. Before the civil wars began, Charles, however, stimulated by Sir Kenelm Digby, asked Van Dyck what sum he would require to carry out the embellishments. "I would not," Horace Walpole writes, "specify the sum, it is so improbable, if I did not find it in Fenton's notes on Waller. It was fourscore thousand pounds." A sketch in chiaro oscuro, by Van Dyck, of the Procession of the Order was actually prepared, and approved of by the King; it included several portraits. That it was never worked up into a painting is greatly to be lamented: it was, however, preserved, and in Walpole's time was in the possession of Lord Chancellor Henley, at the Grange, in Hampshire. There is, one is glad to find, some doubt whether the extortionate demand of Van Dyck was ever made; subsequent events sufficiently accounted for the issue without ascribing it to the avarice of one who was apt rather to spend, than to accumulate. The sum specified was utterly out of keeping with Van Dyck's ordinary prices.

In 1641 Sir Anthony died. He was happily spared witnessing all the miseries and ravages of the civil war. He was also spared seeing the sale of all the royal collection during the Commonwealth.

Van Dyck was buried in Old St. Paul's:—a place of honour was allotted to his remains, which were interred near the tomb of John of Gaunt. By Lady Maria Ruthven he left one daughter, who married Mr. Stepney, a young cavalier, who rode in the Horse Guards when they were first established by Charles II. Lady Van Dyck married again; her second husband being Richard, son of Sir John Pryse, a Montgomeryshire Baronet.

To his illegitimate daughter, Maria Teresa, Van Dyck bequeathed the sum of four thousand pounds, making his sister Susannah, who had become a nun at Antwerp, trustee for that daughter. He provided also for his other two sisters; but to his wife Lady Maria, and to his infant daughter Justiniana Anna, he left his goods and effects, and all the money due to him from Charles I., from the English nobility, or from any other person. And these sums were to be equally divided between his wife and daughter. Lady Van Dyck was one of his executors; but the care of his child was given to another person, Katherine Cowley, with the sum of ten pounds yearly for her maintenance, till she should have attained her eighteenth year. He also left three pounds to the poor of St. Paul's, and the same sum to the poor of St. Anne's, Blackfriars.

These bequests, however, were void; for not until the year 1663 could the will be proved. The great rebellion had then swept away the possessions of many who owed Van Dyck money: the debts could not be collected, nor the accounts settled.

It must have been a sad assemblage, when, twenty-two years after he had passed away, a remnant of his friends met, to search, as it were, for the wrecks after a storm, and to see what they could pick up, separate, and assign to rightful owners, now that the whirlwind had passed, and calm weather had supervened.

One word about Van Dyck's tomb. Old St. Paul's, dating from 1083, was in a state of great dilapidation when Van Dyck lived in Blackfriars. It must have been originally a very fine structure, with its lady-chapel at the east end, its chapel in the north, dedicated to St. George; its chapel on the south, dedicated to St. Dunstan: then in the crypt below was the parish church of St. Faith, and at the south gate corner, towards the Thames, the parish church of St. Gregory. "St. Paul's," old Fuller says, "is indeed the Mother Church, having one babe (St. Faith) in her body, and another (St. Gregory) in her arms." But St. Paul's, when the bearers carried the coffin of Anthony Van Dyck to its honoured resting-place, was virtually roofless: the tower had been taken down, and it was roughly boarded over with wood and lead; Inigo Jones had begun the repairs, which like everything else were stopped by civil war. Meantime, a noble classic portico had been tacked on to this old edifice by "Iniquity" Jones.

On the north side of the choir John of Gaunt was buried; his "proper helmet and spear" hung over his stately monument, also his target covered with horn: here was the appointed place of sepulture for Anthony Van Dyck, a man born to immortalise his contemporaries. Here was to have been his monument; but his grave remains without any device or effigy to honour one, so honoured in his life. Anon, ere yet *his* monument could be erected, the old church was full of soldiers and their horses; the noble nave was made into a *manége* for Cromwell's troops; and sanctimonious profanity from those iron-hearted men might be heard echoing through the aisles near where Van Dyck's mouldering remains were deposited.

What Sir Kenelm Digby's feelings were upon the death of Van Dyck must be imagined, for no trace of them exists; but a man who had so warmly aided his friend in life, had not the sting of self-reproach to add to his sorrow for a bright and genial spirit gone from amongst those who prized it well. The more gifted of those friends did not fail to celebrate his praises. Sir Kenelm eulogised him in his discourses; Waller addressed a poem to him, and Cowley wrote an elegy on his death.

The amount of work done by Van Dyck was prodigious, when we consider how carefully it was done; although he died at the age of forty-two, he had painted as many pictures as Rubens. Nor was he, as we have seen, one of those masters who, as Charles I. said of David Beck, could "paint riding post." He took infinite pains with every detail; he was a fastidious conscientious painter, emulating, and with success, the perfections of Titian; he was as scrupulous in every detail, as his good mother had once been in painting her small flowers, or working in fine silk. Yet there were subjects in treating which he rose to the sublime; witness the noble figure of our Lord on the cross in the Antwerp Gallery; that single object, alone, abandoned,—the Son of God dying in agony,—a drear, sombre, yet not opaque background, showing forcibly that divine form, over which the shadow of the valley of death was passing;—the noble brow, the attitude, the limbs, the awful solitude—for solitude in suffering strikes the deepest awe,—all prove how grand were sometimes the thoughts of one whose works were limited too exclusively to portraits.

In those, indeed, Van Dyck was inimitable. He had the great advantage of living amongst those youths, statesmen, and fair ladies, whom he painted. We see him always in some festive scene or another:—he was the first painter, so says the historian Sanderson, "who ever put ladies' dress into a careless romance." He delighted — thus proving his good taste in minor matters—in blue and white satins: he gave to women dignity, delicacy. You could tell their rank by their portraits, even though no jewels, save his favourite string of large pearls,—no ornaments, except the tuft of flowers and feathers, or the pendant pearl hanging on the ivory forehead of Henrietta Maria, were depicted. Accused of not flattering the sex, he honoured them by assigning to them intellect and modesty. The coarse *embonpoint* of Rubens' female figures; the voluptuousness of those limned by Titian; the vulgar, staring, handsome women of Kneller; the insipid loveliness of Sir Peter Lely's beauties,—are far less calculated to charm a refined mind, than the thoughtful, easy, staid, high-born matron portrayed by Van Dyck's pencil. Shattered by a life of excitement, racked with the gout, dying at an age when most men have only begun to be eminent, Van Dyck's works prove that it is not length of days,— it is earnestness, it is work,—that effect great things. Men, it is true, in those times, began the pursuits of a profession early; now, perhaps, we begin them, as far as the arts are concerned, too late. The enthusiasm of youth has almost passed away before the man has had opportunity to show himself. Success only comes when the hair is grey, and when the energy is damped. Young men at our universities, also, went forth earlier into the world; they were not so crammed, so worn out before they actually began the battle of life as now. See Van Dyck on what Horace Walpole calls "his throne," at the Earl of Pembroke's at Wilton, where a great saloon is filled with his pictures; see the invaluable collection of his sketches in the Louvre, and at Chatsworth, and say whether in any but in the freshness of life's spring, such marvels could have been wrought.

To his friend Sir Kenelm, years of vicissitude remained. The pleasant days at Blackfriars, the delicious retirement of Eltham, the refined enjoyments of Whitehall, were over. Hitherto, with the exception of his wife's death, nothing but prosperity had marked his career. "His changing and rechanging his religion," to borrow the words of Lord Clarendon, "and some personal vices and licences in his life, which would have suppressed and sunk any other man, had never clouded or eclipsed him, from appearing in the best places, and the best company, and with the best estimation and satisfaction."

For some time previous to the year 1641, Sir Kenelm was in France, where his fame had preceded him. It was at an earlier period of his career that he wrote his "Discourse" on the sympathetic powders; professing it to comprise a cure consisting of the use of a certain mixture applied to anything which had received the blood of a wounded person, who, even if far away from the person who applied it, would receive relief. Observations on its use were registered by Lord Bacon, on this account, and on others: Sir Kenelm was the object of great attention to the *savants* of Paris, as well as to those of his own country.

Upon King Charles's preparing to make war upon the Scots, he called on his Protestant subjects to give him their assistance and contributions; whilst the Queen induced Sir Kenelm Digby and Mr. Walter Montague, to address a circular letter for the same purpose to the Catholics. A considerable sum was obtained, but Sir Kenelm was summoned before the bar of the House of Commons, and an address was presented to the King, praying him to remove all Roman Catholics from about his person, and specifying Sir Kenelm Digby and Mr. Walter Montague.

He was, therefore, obliged to leave England, and returned, in 1643, only to suffer imprisonment, being kept in close durance in Winchester House, until Marie de' Medici, who had been enamoured of him twenty years before, obtained his release.

And now comes the part of Digby's life to which even the partial Clarendon alludes with regret. One condition of his release was that he would promise, on the faith of a Christian and the word of a gentleman, not "to engage in any practice or design prejudicial to the Parliament." He took that oath, and thus, we agree with Mr. Lodge, proved himself to be more "prudent than honest;" but he was not one who could rather die as a martyr, than live as a saint. His retirement in prison had been spent in literary occupations; his return to the great world of Paris, where he now repaired, did not prevent the appearance of his greatest work, namely, "A Treatise of the Nature of Bodies, and a Treatise declaring the operations and nature of man's soul, out of which the immortality of reasonable souls is evinced."

Such faith as could sustain him with the hopes of a better world was essential, for he at this time lost his eldest son at the battle of St. Neot's. His estates were nearly involved in the general ruin, but were compounded for, and his sovereign, the beloved Charles I. of his youth, his master, companion, and friend, had perished on the scaffold.

Digby's inconsistencies must have given at once pain and amusement to his contemporaries. He visited Descartes, then in Holland,—*incognito*; but conversing on philosophical subjects betrayed himself.

"Ah!" said Descartes, "I doubt not but that you are the famous Sir Kenelm Digby."

"And if you, sir," answered Sir Kenelm, "were not the celebrated M. Descartes, I should not have come here on purpose to see you."

Their conversation consisted, according to the author of the "Life of St. Evremond," of a discussion on the possibility of lengthening out life to the ages of the patriarchs. Descartes assured Sir Kenelm that he had long been projecting a scheme for that purpose; many conferences on the same scheme took place between the two *savants* in Paris, but whilst Descartes was concocting plans for length of days, his own were ended, just before his speculations were ready for dessemination.

In 1648, efforts were made by an agent of Parliament in favour of Sir Kenelm; and from a document, headed "A true copie of a letter written by an Independent Agent for the Army from Paris in France, to an Independ[t] Member of the House of Coṁons, a great creature and Patriott of the Army," it appears that interest was made to procure him permission to return. The writer, "among other things," says, "he (Sir Kenelm) complains of the want of bosom friends, but has fallen into the acquaintance of 3 or 4 catholiques of very great ingenuity, and, in their way, of very much religion," &c., &c. "It seems," he adds, "my Lo[d] Say hath undertaken to procure a passe from the House for Sir Ken Digby to come over to England; he is not according to yo[r] rule a Denlinquent, but it seemes came over into France by the H. of Coṁons licence, acquitted from any crime; let me desire you when it comes to be moved in yo[r] House, give it the best promotion you can: one would thinke a busines soe reasonable should finde noe opposition (but to such a constitution as you are of, noe man can tell what is reasonable):—he never was in Armes and I beleeve can easily answer any thing that can be objected (save his Religion) why he should be under sequestration. Lett me entreate you to speake to as many of your acquaintance as you can, that when it comes to be moved, it cannot be refused," &c.*

After various wanderings, in his post as Chancellor to Queen Henrietta Maria, the vanity and inconsistency of Sir Kenelm broke out. He visited Rome, and treated Innocent X. with such haughtiness and freedom, that one day he gave the Pontiff the lie. The Pope returned the compliment by saying that Sir Kenelm was mad. Digby has been accused, too, of having made too free with the money subscribed by the Catholics. He reconciled himself to Cromwell, and, in 1655, was well received by the Protector in England; nevertheless, on the accession of Charles II., that monarch, who forgot all wrongs, and left all benefits unrewarded, welcomed Sir Kenelm to the court, and the following letter addressed by Digby to Sir Henry Benet, Principal Secretary of War, shows that he now joined heart and soul against those whom he termed the " fanatickes."

" Sir,

"You will receive this by Mr. Erington, who is the man that discovered the last fanatickes that were taken and executed. His doing that service hath occasioned him much persecution from severall of that party, both in assaulting and wounding him wth danger of his life, and in stirring y^t vexatious suits in law against him. His request to you is that you would be pleased to recomend him to my Lord Chief Justice (when there shall be one) to take notice of him, and do him right in a compendious way, that he may attend to follow his trade without such dayly interruptions and molestations as they give him. He had a pension from the Chest

---

* State Paper Office, Domestic, Chas. I. 1648, 28th Nov.

at Chatham, for the service he . . . . . d the wounds he received in the Warr . . . . . Hollanders wch Cromwell tooke a* . . . . . heard he was very affectionate to the King. Others, in the same ranke wth him, haue their pensions continued to them by the King's order. Now if he might haue his reuiued, the King might by this means gratify a poore man that hath deserued well of him, without being at any charge himselfe.

"I am, sir,
"Y^r most humble and most obedient servant,
"KENELME DIGBY.†

"19th Octob. 1663."

After the Restoration, we find Sir Kenelm living in his house at Covent Garden,—" The last fair house" westward, according to Aubrey:—surrounded by the great and the eminent in letters and science, and having in his own dwelling a laboratory for the prosecution of his experiments. Although the ministry were aware of the unworthy court paid by Sir Kenelm to Cromwell, the King appointed, him in the settlement of the Royal Society, to be one of the Council, by the title of " Sir Kenelm Digby, Knight, Chancellor to our dear mother Queen Mary."

That was an era when scientific pursuits were popular, and Charles II. himself was a *dilettante* in chemistry. Sir Kenelm, racked as he was with a cruel disease, attended the meetings of the society, and assisted at the discoveries then taking place. He assembled all the learned in his own house, and, after the manner of the French, had a sort of academy or literary assembly there. But disease brought him low; he was projecting a journey to France for medical advice, when death closed all the projects of his active life. He expired on his birthday, June 11th, 1665.

* The parts dotted are in a piece torn away from the letter at the bottom.
† Endorsed or directed, "For Sir Henry Benet, Principal Secretary of Ware," State Paper Office. Not calandered: but communicated by Mrs. Everet Green.

Wood, perhaps more wittily than justly, has said, that "such were Digby's natural and acquired advantages, so noble was his address, so graceful his elocution, that, had he dropped from the clouds on any part of the world, he would have made himself respected." "Yes," the Jesuits would say, "but then he ought not to stay there longer than six weeks." The inquiring mind of Digby little suited the bigoted religionists with whom he had allied himself. As a philosopher, an orator, a soldier, a courtier, his talents were wonderfully conspicuous; neither could the extent of his knowledge of theological subjects be disputed. Of no branch of human science was he ignorant; his profound intellect illustrated every subject to which he devoted his attention. His writings are full of eloquence: and whilst at the Royal Society, and in the meetings of the Philosophic Society, at Montpellier, his lucid method of proposing and refuting matters to the members was the theme of all praise.

In his personal demeanour, Sir Kenelm presented a model of the true English gentleman; a character which his ill-fated and erring father had borne before him. His noble form, stately, and always in splendid attire; his gracious manners, his facility in speaking six languages, would have rendered him an object of great attraction abroad, and done credit to his country, had not his vanity and versatility, his captiousness — which led him to fight several duels — and his eccentricity, induced many to call him mad. But it was the madness of a noble mind.

His personal character, his loves, his friendship, have chiefly been dilated on here; but in referring to his literary remains we cannot avoid mentioning the noble MS. which he collected, at the expense of a thousand pounds, from public histories, and from letters and records in the Tower, relating to the Digby family in all its branches. He knew the importance of family history, in which we are so lamentably deficient in this country. He had collected a very valuable library which, at the commencement of the civil war, was removed into France, and when he died, as he was no subject of the French king, it became, according to the *Droit d'Aubaine*, the property of his Gallic Majesty; but was purchased by the Earl of Bristol.

By Sir Kenelm the memory of Venetia was revered till his death. In his will, which was made about six months before his death, he ordered his body to be laid by her side in Christ Church, desiring that no inscription should be placed on the tomb. Sir Kenelm's estates were left to executors, to be sold in order to pay his debts.

John Digby, his second son, married the daughter of Sir John Conway, of Bodry, in Flintshire; and from her daughter Honora, who married Sir John Glynne, Sir Stephen Glynne is descended. He is, therefore, the representative of Sir Kenelm Digby, and, through the fair Venetia, of the great houses also of Stanley and Percy.

Sir Kenelm, although he desired not that his "follies should remain after him on record," left private memoirs of his own life, more especially of the passages relating to Venetia. This production, which was first published from the original manuscript in 1827, ends in a declaration that the narrative, written as it is in feigned names, was composed in order that he might look back upon his "past and sweet errors." The remembrance of Venetia pervades the whole. "For the present," he thus concludes, "I will say no more, but will continue my prayers to God for a fair wind to bring me once again to see that person whose memory begot this discourse."

END OF THE FIRST VOLUME.